P9-BAV-605

RED NOTICE

Georgina Public Library
Keswick Branch
90 Wexford Dr
Keswick, ON, L4P 3P7

www.transworldbooks.co.uk

RED NOTICE

Andy McNab

BANTAM PRESS

LONDON • TORONTO • SYDNEY • AUCKLAND • JOHANNESBURG

TRANSWORLD PUBLISHERS
61–63 Uxbridge Road, London W5 5SA
A Random House Group Company
www.transworldbooks.co.uk

First published in Great Britain
in 2012 by Bantam Press
an imprint of Transworld Publishers

A CIP catalogue record for this book
is available from the British Library.

ISBNs 9780593069486 (cased)
9780593069493 (tpb)

Addresses for Random House Group Ltd companies outside the UK
can be found at: www.randomhouse.co.uk
The Random House Group Ltd Reg. No. 954009

The Random House Group Limited supports the Forest Stewardship Council (FSC®), the
leading international forest-certification organization. Our books carrying the FSC label are
printed on FSC®-certified paper. FSC is the only forest-certification scheme endorsed by
the leading environmental organizations, including Greenpeace. Our paper procurement
policy can be found at www.randomhouse.co.uk/environment

Typeset in 11/14pt Palatino by
Falcon Oast Graphic Art Ltd.
Printed and bound in Great Britain by
CPI Group (UK) Ltd, Croydon, CR0 4YY

2 4 6 8 10 9 7 5 3 1

MIX
Paper from
responsible sources
FSC
www.fsc.org
FSC® C016897

Prologue

Borjomi, Georgia

25 September 1996
05.17 hrs

Dawn had begun to streak the eastern sky as the two mud-spattered trucks inched their way up the road in the faint glow from their sidelights. They jolted over rain-filled potholes and scree and came to a halt just short of the crest of the hill.

Their movements measured and cautious, a dozen armed men climbed down from the rear of each vehicle. Their breath billowed around them in the freezing air. Checking their safety catches, they stamped their feet to restore circulation and eased the stiffness from their legs. Some placed a last cigarette in the middle of their week-old beards and lit up.

They checked their equipment, ensuring pouches were still secure. If it had a button or a Velcro strip, it was there to be fastened. Two of the team struggled to hoist heavy weapons systems onto their shoulders.

Their commander stood a short distance apart from his men. Laszlo had an aversion to the smell of nicotine. He wore the same stained camouflage fatigues as his troops and had a similarly Slavic cast to his features, complete with coarse, almost black beard, but carried himself with an arrogance they didn't share. He was just short of six feet in height, but his sinuous limbs and slim frame made him look taller. His mouth was downturned and his eyes were the washed-out grey-blue of a winter sky; his skin was so pale he looked as if he'd lived his life in permanent shadow.

Another man exited the cab of the nearest truck. Laszlo's cool gaze missed nothing as he approached. The newcomer's civilian clothes were of a cut and quality that were neither cheap nor local. He wasn't a Slav, he was from the West. Europe? The USA? It was hard to tell. They all looked the same. His brown hair was starting to grow out from its short back and sides, and he, too, had a good week's growth on his chiselled jaw.

The man might not have been one of Laszlo's team, but the comfortable way he held his AK, the folding butt closed down in his hand as if it were a natural extension of his body, showed that he was no stranger to shot and shell. The weapon – all of his equipment – was also of Soviet origin. In Yeltsin's Russia, there was no shortage of underworld gangs willing to steal and trade such things, or of corrupt officers happy to empty their armouries in return for cold, hard cash.

The man had no fear of repercussion from what he was about to do. There would be nothing to suggest this had been anything but a purely local affair. He was sterile of ID and personal documentation. Like the rest of the team, it was as if he didn't exist. He had a name – Marcus – but Laszlo knew it wasn't his own. The team commander had taken steps to discover his companion's real identity. Information was a commodity to be traded, like drugs, weapons and women, and Laszlo always liked to bargain from a position of strength.

He stood for a couple more minutes, watching the new day creep across the landscape. To his right, a steep, boulder-strewn slope tumbled to a fast-flowing river. Water the colour of chocolate surged downstream. The force of the current had carved out the soil for a ten-metre stretch along the far bank, exposing a latticework of tree-roots that gleamed white against the mud, like the ribs of a putrefying corpse.

On the other side of the road, a dense pine forest cloaked the lower slopes of the mountains that filled the northern horizon. It seemed to float in a sea of mist. The treetops swayed each time there was a gust of wind. As he watched, the sun's first rays painted the snow-capped peaks with gold. In the west, just visible now in the strengthening light, a black gash as straight as a Roman road showed the course of the pipeline being driven through this remote valley. Directly in its path, just over the hill from where they now stood, a huddle of buildings lay surrounded by a patchwork of fields.

As soon as the man reached him, Laszlo turned. The wind whipped up a shower of pine needles as the two of them moved through the edge of the forest. As they neared the crest of the hill, they flattened themselves to the earth and wormed their way to a point from which they could study the approach to Borjomi.

On the slope below, the trees gave way to fields of yellowing grass, dusted with frost and punctuated by mounds of autumn hay secured beneath tarpaulins. Beyond them, houses were clustered around a dusty square. A rusting iron water pump and a long stone horse-trough stood at its centre, half shaded by a large, stag-headed oak tree.

The buildings at the heart of the village were of wood and stone, with sun-faded shutters and roofs of patched tiles or corrugated iron, steeply pitched to shed the winter snows. The gables of some had once been richly carved but were now so weathered, cracked and split with age that the embellishments were barely visible.

While those houses looked almost as ancient as the oak tree they faced, the buildings around them were drab, Soviet-era constructions, their crumbling concrete façades pockmarked by bullet holes. A huge barn, built of unmilled wood with gaps between the planks, boasted a roof of heavily patched corrugated-iron sheets.

The whole place was mired in mud and poverty. Tangles of

scrap metal and rotting timbers decorated the yards. A solitary motor vehicle, a battered Lada with rust-streaked bodywork, was parked next to a pair of horse-drawn farm carts. Apart from a handful of chickens scuttling about and a few cows mooching in the fields, the place seemed to be deserted.

At the side of the road just outside the village, an old door had been nailed to two fence posts driven into the ground. Daubed on it, in crude hand-lettering, was an inscription in Russian, Georgian and Ossetic: 'Protect our village.'

The two men worked their way back from the brow and conferred in low tones. Although his companion was now issuing orders to him, Laszlo's stance and attitude showed that he did not regard him as his superior in any way.

'Ready?' The man's Russian was halting but understandable. And now his accent gave him away.

Laszlo nodded. 'Ready, Englishman.' He signalled to his men and led them down the hill, moving tactically, one foot always on the ground. Half the team stayed where they were to cover the advance of the rest. Using the haystacks to mask their approach, they too went static and returned the favour.

A cock crowed inside a barn and wisps of grey smoke began to rise from a chimney as some unseen inhabitant coaxed his fire into life. Laszlo was wary. It wasn't always like this. An attack could be initiated at any moment. He'd taken incoming from sleepy backwaters like this and lost men. That was why he favoured a rolling start-line. If his team took fire as they approached they'd just roll into the attack and fight their way forward.

They reached the shadows of a tumbledown wall on the edge of the settlement and waited there, all eyes focused on the Englishman as he took one last look at the target to confirm that nothing had changed since he issued his last set of orders the day before.

He'd led them into a field for a run-through in slow time, letting the whole team see what each of the component groups would be doing during the attack. They'd rehearsed the what-ifs: what if the team had a man down? What if a group got separated from the main force? What if the team took heavy fire from an RPG?

Now that the Englishman had seen in real time what he'd told them to call the battle space, he knew there was nothing to add. His voice was calm as he spoke to Laszlo.

The South Ossetian checked that his men were in place and ready, raised his hand, paused a moment, and let it fall.

The team burst from cover. With the Englishman leading one group and Laszlo the other, they advanced along both sides of the main street. Dogs set up a chorus of barks and howls and a few villagers began stumbling from their houses, some clutching hunting rifles and shotguns, one or two with AKs, but the attacking force, better armed and better trained, cut them down before they fired a single round.

Laszlo led his men from house to house. The crump of HE grenades and the crash of splintering wood were interspersed with cries and screams. Half dressed and rubbing sleep from their eyes, the remaining occupants were dragged from their homes, herded into the open, kicked and punched face down into the mud, then immobilized with plastic zip-ties.

While the Englishman stayed with his group and controlled their captives, Laszlo led his team further along the line of buildings. He paused for a couple of seconds, dropped into cover and looked back towards the others. A young villager, perhaps no more than a teenager, was sprinting towards the forest.

Two of the insurgents fired at him and missed. The Englishman dropped to one knee, took careful aim and brought him down with a single shot into the centre of his body mass, then moved forward and finished him with a second to the head.

Laszlo smiled to himself and turned his attention back to the last of the houses. Once it, too, had been searched and cleared, and the occupants secured, the looting began. Food and alcohol were gathered up with as much enthusiasm as the modest treasures the villagers possessed.

Laszlo took a gulp of a fiery local spirit, then passed the

bottle among his men. One carried off a fading sepia photograph of a couple dressed for their wedding against a gaudily painted backdrop of a castle. Wanting the ornate frame but not the image it contained, he stamped down with his boot, smashing the glass and ripping the photograph to shreds. He picked out the last shards and propped the frame carefully against the trunk of the oak tree.

Another emerged from an outbuilding clutching a pair of live chickens in each hand. He wrung their necks with practised ease and added them to the growing pile of booty.

On Laszlo's order, the attackers began to separate their male captives from the women, who wailed and keened as husbands and sons were marched and kicked towards the barn at the far edge of the village. Those who resisted were shot where they stood. The rest were herded inside and watched helplessly as its double doors were shut and barred.

Laszlo listened for a moment to the terrified shouts and cries of those trapped within, then nodded to the two men carrying the heavier weapons systems.

They staggered forwards, smashed the windows and directed searing blasts of flame into the barn's interior. Laszlo had selected these weapons with purpose – for the physical pain endured by the dying, and the legacy of mental terror suffered by those unfortunate enough to survive.

In seconds, fuelled by the dry timbers, the hay and straw stored there, the barn was ablaze from end to end. His men stood watch as it burned, and when two villagers somehow succeeded in smashing their way through the disintegrating wall, Laszlo raised his weapon to his shoulder and dropped both targets instantly.

The terrible screams of the remaining victims were soon drowned by the roar of the flames and the crash of falling beams. As the barn collapsed in on itself, the massacre extended even to the villagers' hounds and livestock. The cattle were burned alive with their owners or mown down by gunfire; the dogs were dispatched with a knife thrust or 7.62mm short round.

The flamethrowers now moved among the houses, pausing at each to direct a jet of blazing fluid through the doorway or a shattered window. As they moved on to the next, the one behind them became an inferno. More cries from the women captives were brutally silenced by rifle butts. The attackers showed as little mercy as the Nazis had done in this part of the world just over half a century before.

The SS's *Flammenwerfer*, designed as an infantry weapon to clear out trenches and buildings, had become an instrument of terror when used against civilian populations. It held twelve litres of petrol mixed with tar to make it heavier and increase its range to twenty-five metres. The flaming oil was ignited by a hydrogen torch.

Flammenwerfer operators had been so hated that the trigger and muzzle section of their weapon soon had had to be disguised to look like a standard infantry rifle in an attempt to keep them from being singled out by enemy snipers. Whole villages had been annihilated in its path. Maybe the men here today had had relatives who'd perished in their flames and the pain and fear had been passed down the generations.

Sambor, the more imposing of the operators, was Laszlo's 'little' brother by just thirteen months. He had the same almost lifeless eyes and pallid complexion, but that was where the similarity ended. He had inherited the rest of his physique from his father's family. His massive hands were twice the size of Laszlo's, his fingers like sausages and his hulking frame topped by a riot of dark brown hair, greasy after weeks in the field, which fell to his shoulders.

A child who had somehow escaped detection stumbled out of a nearby building, coughing and choking, smoke streaming from his smouldering hair and clothes. Sambor swung the barrel of his flamethrower back towards the boy and turned him into a human torch. With an unearthly shriek, the blazing figure blundered into a wall before sliding to the ground.

As the dense black column of smoke rose high above the village, Laszlo and two of his men turned their attention to the makeshift sign. Using a piece of scrap iron as a crowbar, they prised the old door away from the posts and pitched it through the window of a blazing house. Within seconds the flames were licking at the painted inscription. The last trace of defiance had now been obliterated, and the centuries-old village erased from the map.

As the ashes swirled around them, the insurgents gathered in the village square, surrounding the captive women. The Englishman had taken as many lives as any, but his expression betrayed nothing of his current thoughts.

Laszlo turned to him. 'You should leave now. Unless . . .' He gestured to the women and gave him a questioning glance. One sat silent, rocking slowly backwards and forwards as her tears carved white streaks through the dirt on her cheeks; others sobbed or pleaded with their stone-faced captors, who were already loosening their belts.

The Englishman shook his head and walked back up the hill towards the waiting trucks. Behind him he could hear a fresh chorus of wavering cries, rising and falling like sirens as the fighters began to take their reward.

Laszlo wouldn't be taking part in what followed. It was a gift from him to his men. Or that was what he had told them. In truth, for Laszlo and the Englishman, this was the final flourish. Just as the flamethrowers spread fear among their potential victims, so did the prospect of rape; and fear, eventually, would bring compliance.

1

London
Friday, 9 September 2011
14.40 hrs

Pale sunshine bathed the Heath, lighting up the autumn colours of the trees. Nannies clustered on benches, gossiping about their employers while their charges dozed in nearby buggies. A pair of Labradors chased each other in the meadows, deaf to the pleas of their owners, and in the distance a handful of hardy swimmers could be glimpsed braving the bathing pond's frigid waters. Beyond the grand Victorian and Edwardian houses fringing the grassland, the sunlight glinted on the steel and glass towers of the City.

A young couple strolled along a path near the edge of the Heath, arms intertwined, oblivious to everything but each other. Without warning, four black-clad figures burst from the bushes and bundled them swiftly out of sight. Thrown headlong to the ground, the girl arched her back and tried to turn her head as a gloved hand was clamped over her mouth and her wrists were bound with zip-ties. Her eyes widened at the glimpse of matt-black weaponry and the respirator-covered faces of their captors.

The sergeant in command of the fully bombed-up assault team leaned in close. 'Sssh. Stop flapping, hen. You'll not be harmed.' Known as Jockey to his mates, because of his size, and Nasty Bastard to his enemies, he knew his heavy-duty Gorbals accent and the rasp of the respirator's filter were about as comforting as Darth Vader reading a bedtime story, so he tightened his grip and gave it to them straight. 'Both of you – just lie fucking still and keep quiet. Understand?'

They both gave a hesitant nod.

He knelt back on his haunches, hit his pressel switch and spoke quietly into his mic. 'Blue One. Third party secure.'

2

Half a mile away, near the centre of what the locals liked to call the Village, the door of one of Hampstead's more characterful pubs bore a sign announcing that it was 'Closed due to illness'. Anyone peering through the leaded windows, between the immaculately sculpted flower baskets, might therefore have been surprised to find that the chairs and high-backed settles in its panelled bar were packed with people.

The landlord was perched on a stool at one end, staring wistfully through the half-drawn curtains at the procession of potential customers moving down the street.

His paintings, horse brasses and *faux*-rustic ornaments had all been taken down and stacked in a corner. In their place were massed ranks of portable flat-screens displaying live CCTV and satellite feeds, local news reports and classified video-conferences. A series of grainy A4 prints was clamped to a magnetic whiteboard, which now held pride of place. Closer inspection would reveal that they were all at least a decade out of date, and of just one man, clean-shaven and with a mop of shoulder-length dark hair, against the backdrop of a busy Moscow street.

The landlord gave an ostentatious sigh. 'How much longer is this going to take?'

Clustered around laptops or hunched over communications equipment, his current clientele – some in street clothes, some in police uniform, others still in black Special Forces party gear – didn't reward him with a second glance.

'Come on, lads, I'm losing money hand over fist here.'

One of the soldiers finally raised his head. 'It'll take as long as it takes, mate. Maybe an hour, maybe all day. Perhaps even all fucking night. You'll be well compensated for loss of income, so do yourself a favour, will you? Stop bumping your gums and get us another brew. Oh, and a few sandwiches and biscuits wouldn't hurt either.'

At the table in the centre of the room, flanked by two lower-ranking officers, James Woolf of MI5 – or, as he always insisted it was called, the Security Service – sat like stone, listening to the mobile phone pressed to his ear.

Seated next to Major Ashton was a stocky West Country-born sergeant with a shock of wiry black hair. With eight years' service in the Regiment, Gavin Marks, the 3i/c, was the same age as the boss, but hadn't had the privilege of the same education. He'd started out as a Royal Marine, but soon seen the light. At least, that was what everyone who hadn't joined the Regiment from the Navy kept telling him.

He spoke into his throat mic. 'Blue One, roger that. When we get the "Go" the police will come and collect them.'

The 'team' consisted of two sub-teams, Red and Blue, each with an assault group and a sniper group, which meant that they could cover two incidents at once.

'All call-signs, this is Alpha. Radio check. Blue Two?'

The speakers crackled into life.

'Blue Two.'

'Blue Three?'

'Blue Three.'

'Blue Four?'

The response this time was a double click as Blue Four squelched his radio button. As he did so, the listeners could hear the faint background noise of yapping dogs and a jet on its final descent into Heathrow.

'Blue Five?'

Gavin glanced at the notepad in front of him. 'Blue Five. Confirm the sizes on those charges.'

'Blue Five. Two by one metres.'

3

Up on the Heath, the captive couple had hardly drawn breath, unable to tear their eyes away from the four-man SAS assault team and their welter of weapons and equipment.

Screened by the bushes, Blue One peered through their weapon optics at the target house. The Heath was lined with mansions like this. Wealthy Victorian industrialists had built them, not just to live in but to make the kind of statement about their position in the world that their current owners – the new aristocracy of film stars, footballers and foreign multi-millionaires – were happy to broadcast.

A nondescript Transit van was parked up on the higher ground at the edge of the Heath. Behind its darkened rear window, Keenan Marshall, a tanned Cornishman, whose newly disciplined hair did nothing to camouflage the surf-dude he used to be, trained the optic sight of his AWSM (Arctic Warfare Super Magnum) sniper rifle with suppressed barrel on the front elevation of the target house.

Keenan caught a flicker of movement from the upper floor and called in. 'Stand by, stand by. Sierra One has a possible X-ray [target] on white three-six. Green on blue.'

Green on blue signalled the colour of the potential hostile's clothing.

Gavin's response was immediate: 'Armed or unarmed?'

'Can't confirm. Wooden shutters obscuring.'

'Roger that. Give us what you've got.'

'Sash windows. Double-glazed. Wooden frames. Recommend medium ladders. Can't confirm downstairs windows.'

'Roger that. Blue One, acknowledge.'

The Scotsman came back. 'Blue One. Roger that. Possible X-ray now unsighted. Downstairs: no signs of life. No condensation. No shutters. White curtains. Front-door security gates are locked.' They might have been no more than seconds from launching the assault, but his voice betrayed less emotion than that of a Scandinavian newsreader.

A fresh voice broke in: 'Stand by. Stand by. Sierra Four has a possible Yankee [hostage]. Female, coming out of Green ... wait ... wait ...' Sierra Four was telling them he had more to say: everyone else should stay off the net. 'She looks pregnant.'

A woman who looked like she was in her twenties, with blonde hair and a maternity dress so short that it showed almost every inch of her endless legs, had appeared at the side of the house and was walking down the garden. One hand cradled her bump, the other held a plastic spray with which she was squirting the flowers as she strolled along.

Jockey sparked back into life: 'Blue One. Confirm she's pregnant.'

Gavin's voice, still controlled but now with a note of urgency: 'All stations, cancel gas. Do – not – use – gas. Out.'

The jury was out about chemicals affecting a foetus's development. But no one was here to kill or deform unborn children.

'Stand by, stand by. Blue One has Posh Lad in the cordon approaching the female.'

4

Tom 'Posh Lad' Buckingham adjusted his earpiece and stepped out from behind the tree he'd been using as cover. He saw the blonde's face register surprise as he began walking across the garden towards her. He reckoned she was in her early thirties, roughly his age, though the clothes he was wearing – tweed jacket, Viyella shirt and cavalry-twill trousers – made him look much older.

He'd chosen the sort of outfit some upper-crust Englishmen wear when they're trying – unsuccessfully – for a casual look, topped off on this occasion with an expensive leather satchel slung over the shoulder. Gavin had given it the serious thumbs-up as Tom had changed for the op that morning. 'To the manor born, mate. You look like Prince Charles getting ready to head down to Highgrove for a chat with his plants.'

'It's just a matter of having the right gear for the occasion, Gav, you know that. Like when you slip into the velvet hot pants, nipple clamps and Spandex thong combo for a big night out.'

As he approached the blonde now, he brushed an imaginary speck of fluff from the sleeve of his tweed jacket and called, 'Hello there!' in his best Etonian drawl. He gave her a disarming smile. 'You have *such* a lovely garden.'

The blonde smiled back. 'Thank you, but—'

'Did you design this yourself?' He half turned away from her to admire one of the flowerbeds.

She gave a hesitant nod.

'I thought so,' he said. 'And aren't these daffodils magnificent?' He gestured towards the display of red roses tumbling over the pergola beside her, still flowering in early autumn. 'Absolutely stunning.' He pulled out his iPhone and took a picture of them.

'Excuse . . . please . . .' The blonde looked nervous now. Her Eastern European accent was evident, and her hand pressed more tightly against her bump, as if shielding her unborn child from this stranger.

He continued talking, blithely failing to register her unease: 'I'm a volunteer for the Garden History Society. We list one new garden every year in our official register . . . and I'd say yours would be a really strong candidate. Would you mind if I put it forward for selection?'

'Is just hobby. Not for public . . .' She searched for the right word. 'Not for other people . . .'

Without a pause, he began speaking in Russian. 'Would it be easier if we spoke in your mother tongue? I wrote my thesis on the Aptekarsky Ogorod Botanical Garden in Moscow. Have you ever been there?'

'No.' She showed real concern now, her eyes darting from side to side, scanning the garden behind him.

'Where are you from?' he said, once more affecting not to notice her discomfort.

She gestured towards her bump. 'I'm sorry, you must . . . Excuse, please, I . . . I very tired. Perhaps one other day . . .'

He treated her to an even more disarming smile. 'How wonderful! Many congratulations! You know what? My wife's just given birth to our first – a little girl. Small world, eh? How many months pregnant are you?'

'Seven . . .'

'A boy or a girl?'

She hesitated. 'I . . . I do not know. They can't tell yet.'

The smile still lighting up his face, Tom shot out a hand, seized her wrist and twisted it back viciously, forcing her to the ground. She cursed and struggled as he whipped an autojet syringe from his satchel with his free hand and plunged the needle deep into her thigh. Screened from the house by the pergola, he kept his grip on her wrist as the sedative took effect.

'You fucked up, I'm afraid.' His tone was still calm and matter-of-fact. 'They can tell the sex of a baby at three months. Oh, and daffodils are spring flowers, and yellow, not red.'

She slumped, unconscious. He zip-tied her hands, then pulled up her maternity dress, exposing her stomach. The pregnancy bump was an 'empathy bulge' that a certain sort of man might wear in a pathetic attempt to share his wife's experience of pregnancy. Except that this one wasn't warm and fuzzy. A light green substance the consistency of Play-Doh was jammed into the pouch.

Tom could smell the distinctive linseed aroma of the eastern-manufactured, low-quality plastic explosive. The precise make didn't matter to him. He was more concerned about the thin steel detonator wires coming out of the PE and twisted around a red and blue two-flex. They disappeared into her clothing, *en route* to a battery pack. All she had to do was complete the circuit by pressing a button in her coat pocket. The killing area would extend about twenty metres. And Tom was smack in the middle of it.

Swiftly but carefully, he pulled the aluminium tube from the explosive and separated it from the two-flex, then twisted the two steel wires together to prevent an accidental detonation. Radio transmissions could arc across the two wires and complete the circuit. He pushed the tube down into the soft soil of the rose bed. He rolled the blonde on to her front, turning her head to keep her airway open.

Still crouching beside the pergola, he spoke into his lapel. 'That's the female contained.'

Gavin's response was instantaneous. 'And the baby?'

'No baby. Just a belly-rig full of PE. Looks like the gas is back on.'

As Gavin called it to the others – 'All stations, this is Alpha, the gas is back on. Out' – Tom took a respirator from his satchel, fitted it to his face, then pulled out a fat-barrelled ARWEN 37 launcher. 'Alpha. Come on.' His words echoed across the net. 'We're compromised. We've got to go. We've got to go *now*.'

From a distance, the ARWEN's bulbous 37mm barrel and revolving five-round cylinder had the look of a kid's Super Soaker – but delivered a whole lot more than a water jet. Its kinetic energy baton rounds were powerful enough to drop a small horse. Its 'value' impact rounds could not only drop the horse but envelop it in its own gas cloud. And its pure gas rounds – CN (chloroacetophenone) was the irritant of choice – could fuck up anyone's day. Finally, if required, the weapon could fire pure smoke to cover the movement of assault teams.

Tom had pre-loaded five Barricade Penetrating Irritant Rounds intended for use against car windscreens, interior doors and plywood up to 13mm thick.

A disc of CN within the round ruptured as it penetrated the barricade, whereupon its combination of rapid deceleration and rotational spin dispersed a cloud of fine powder inside the target area. The spec described it as 'non-lethal' or – as Tom preferred – 'compliance'. There was no CN 'gas' being used on this job, but everyone found it easier to call it that.

5

'Alpha. Wait out. Wait out. I do not have control. All stations wait out.' Gavin gave Woolf a quizzical look. He wanted to crack on as much as the rest of the team. 'Well?'

The MI5 man, still with his mobile phone glued to his ear, avoided his gaze. 'I've no decision from COBRA yet.'

Gavin gave a weary shake of his head and, not for the first time that day, exchanged a 'What the fuck?' look with Major Ashton. He shot a quick glance at the rolling news bulletin, hoping that the stock-market update wasn't about to give way to hysteria in Hampstead. Ever since the Iranian Embassy siege fiasco, when the world had watched the SAS assault teams storm the building on live TV, the media had been kept well out of the way of Regiment operations. Had any of the terrorists been watching the TV coverage during the build-up to the assault, the hostages might all have been killed before the troopers could reach them. And these days, when every Tom, Dick and Harry had a camera phone, it was only a matter of time before an operation got prematurely exposed or totally fucked up.

Ashton saw Woolf's free hand tug more vigorously at a strand of his thinning hair as he barked into his secure mobile. Old habits died hard under pressure. 'The situation is now *critical*. I need COBRA's authorization at once. Not in five minutes, but *now*.'

The Civil Contingencies Committee – incorrectly but universally known as 'COBRA' after the acronym for Cabinet Office Briefing Room 'A' in which it had once met – was tasked to deal with every emergency from fuel-transporter strikes to terrorist attacks. An excellent set-up in theory, as it brought together the supreme commanders and most highly qualified specialists to manage any crisis situation, but in practice, as he and Woolf already knew, and Gavin was discovering, the sheer weight of expertise often stood in the way of a speedy and coherent response.

Woolf was fuming, and with good reason. Ashton could picture the chaotic scenes that would be playing themselves out in the corridors beneath Whitehall.

6

The screens covering the end wall of the conference chamber carried the same CCTV and satellite feeds as the command centre in Hampstead. The room was windowless; the 'skylight' in its ceiling merely concealed a bank of SAD illumination units.

A huge rectangular table filled most of the available floor space, the leather seats surrounding it occupied by ministers and civil servants from the Home and Foreign Offices and the MoD, together with the DSF (director of UKSF, United Kingdom Special Forces), and an assistant commissioner of the Metropolitan Police, who was in constant telephone contact with Woolf.

Many of them had just walked to the fortified cellar beneath Whitehall. Sited between the Houses of Parliament and Trafalgar Square, COBRA was linked by corridor to Downing Street, the Foreign and Commonwealth Office and the Cabinet Office.

The murmur of conversation was barely audible above the hum of the air-conditioning as they waited for the home secretary, chairing the meeting as usual, to finish consulting with the senior civil servant at her elbow and call them back to order. Her grey hair testified to her long experience, but her porcelain features and impeccable diction still led some people to make the mistake of underrating her. They were the same people who also mistook her kindness for weakness. It was a serious error. She was as tough as an old squaddie's boot, with the language to match, and could be as ruthless with her subordinates as she was with her political adversaries. She was used to junior ministers jockeying for position and squabbling over their places at the table.

'Shall we stop pissing about, then?' she said at last, and though her voice was low, it cut through every other conversation and focused attention on her. 'Control will be handed over to the SAS for a hard arrest of Laszlo Antonov.'

There was a series of nods and murmurs of assent. But Edward Clements, a career FCO man in his mid-fifties, wearing the civil servant's uniform of pinstriped suit, crisp white shirt and tie – no hot colours or strong patterns, of course – raised his hand. 'Let's just take a deep breath here, shall we, Minister?' His voice was as smooth and mellow as the malt whisky he liked to drink in his London club. 'That suicide vest won't be the only weapon Antonov has procured.'

The home secretary gave him one of her steeliest glares. 'Do I take it, then, that the Foreign Office has specific intelligence on that front?'

Clements gave a brisk nod. 'Yes, Home Secretary.'

'So we should proceed with extreme caution.'

He shook his head. 'I couldn't disagree more. There's all the more reason to authorize immediate military action rather than a non-lethal arrest.'

'If you want to achieve a bloodbath, perhaps,' she said acidly. 'The military and the police always tell us, "We can do it" – but why wouldn't they? It's money on their budgets, and a poke in the eye for their rivals in the Security Service and the SIS. But we can – and should – be rather more objective and measured in our response.

'It's very easy to be an armchair warrior, but which of you . . .' she glanced around the room, making sure she still had everyone's full attention '. . . is prepared to take

27

responsibility for that decision? Which of you would be willing to shoulder the blame if it all goes pear-shaped?' She gave the DSF a look that left him in no doubt that she spoke his language. There would be no bullshit getting past *her*.

She glanced around the table once more. Most of the assembled officials and all of the politicians avoided her eye. 'Precisely,' she said. 'Nobody. I'll be the one in the firing line.'

Clements leaned forward. 'Be that as it may, Home Secretary . . .' He cleared his throat and waited until everyone was listening. 'Make no mistake. If he's cornered, Antonov has the commitment – and the full intention – to use his weapons.'

'Which is precisely why there's a Red Notice on this animal.' The home secretary gave him another glare. She had no time for civil-service theatrics.

Laszlo Antonov had been officially charged with war crimes at the International Criminal Court in The Hague, and a Red Notice had been issued by Interpol. Interpol did not have the authority to issue arrest warrants in the formal sense – that was the domain of the sovereign member states – but a Red Notice was the closest thing there was to an international arrest warrant.

Antonov was a South Ossetian, and had known war all his life. North Ossetia was part of Russia, but South Ossetia had always been the subject of dispute between Georgia and Russia. Most South Ossetians carried Russian passports and wanted to break away from Tbilisi. They had declared it a republic in 1990 and the Georgian government had sent in tanks. A series of conflicts followed.

Laszlo, by then a well-seasoned fighter and nationalist, had turned to the Russians for support. The Georgians were preparing to slaughter his people again, and he needed to defend himself. Happy to have a vicious and well-trained proxy, the Russians gave him the funding and the weaponry to raise a clandestine paramilitary unit from men he had fought with for years. Officially it was called the 22nd Black Bear Brigade, but the locals referred to them simply as the Black Bears. Laszlo was the unquestioned leader and his brother, Sambor, was second-in-command.

The Black Bears fought like a Special Forces unit: they lived covertly in the field for weeks, attacking Georgians in small numbers before fading into the night; destroying their line of supply and communication and killing as many high-ranking officers as they could until their army was incapable of making tactical decisions on the ground. Laszlo conducted his war with speed, aggression and surprise, in a way that even the SAS would have admired.

When Georgia launched an offensive in 2008 to retake the breakaway republic, about fourteen hundred locals had been slaughtered. In retaliation, Laszlo had led a massacre of more than six hundred innocent ethnic Georgian men, women and children in one night of carnage. He had then provided the Russians with vital information that helped Moscow make the decision to send troops and tanks over the border to 'protect Russia's citizens'.

The home secretary had been informed the moment the Security Service had discovered Laszlo was in the UK, and James Woolf, section chief, Branch G, had become the senior case officer.

'And this government will honour all its commitments and agreements with the ICC.'

Clements rolled his eyes. He never quite understood how the government decided on their cabinet appointments. This latest home secretary had come from the Department for Work and Pensions, where she'd been responsible for work rights and benefits for the disabled, not protecting a country. 'Spare us the synthetic moral outrage, Sarah.'

He ignored the horrified looks from those around the table. Even in these informal times, few civil servants, no matter how senior, would have been quite so forthright when speaking to one of their political masters. 'If we went round arresting every tyrant and warlord with blood on his hands, we'd have to build another fifty jails to house them all, and we'd lose so much export business that our economy would collapse even more quickly than it already is. The death of a few hundred civilians in South Ossetia now and then didn't even rouse the indignation of the *Guardian*'s bleeding-hearts brigade, let alone the rest of the press. I'll tell you how interested any of us was: the only imagery we have of him dates back to 2001.'

He paused long enough for that fact to sink in.

'Can you imagine the media storm that would break if even one British citizen out for a gentle stroll on Hampstead Heath is shot by a foreign gunman because the government insisted on a kid-gloves arrest rather than sending in the SAS to do what they do best? Do I really have to remind you about the Libyan Embassy and the shooting of WPC Yvonne Fletcher?'

'That's scarcely relevant in this case,' she said. 'Legally we have no choice but to arrest him or risk worldwide embarrassment. This isn't the backwoods of Afghanistan, Clements. This is the UK, and our security forces have to operate here in the full glare of media attention, and within the law.'

'You're right, of course, Home Secretary.' Clements's voice now dripped sarcasm. 'A firefight on Hampstead Heath would be so much easier to defend to the media if it resulted in the death of a ruthless and notorious terrorist during an operation to arrest him.' He glanced at the DSF. 'If that regrettable event were to occur, I am correct in assuming, am I not, that it would be revealed that Antonov was known to be armed and extremely dangerous?'

The UKSF commander's face immediately betrayed his dislike of Clements. 'You would be correct in assuming that my men would meet force with force, Mr Clements. But if you're implying—'

Clements held up his hand. 'I'm implying nothing,' he said. 'I'm merely trying to ensure that your men are free to take all necessary measures to halt this appalling terrorist and not be placed in jeopardy by needless restrictions on their freedom of action.'

COBRA meetings weren't minuted. The politicians could say what they liked: their words would never be available as evidence. The Thatcher government had offered the Regiment immunity from prosecution during its dark and dirty war against the IRA, but they had quite correctly turned the offer down. They had known that once the agreement was exposed it would be members of the SAS in the dock for breaking the law, not the politicos. They would simply say they had no recollection of any conversation or agreement that let the UKSF do such things in the UK.

'The welfare of my men is my principal concern, Mr Clements.' The DSF knew he had to be careful. 'But whatever the terms of their deployment, and whatever resistance Antonov puts up, I can assure you that there will be no fire-fight on Hampstead Heath. If there is collateral damage, it will be contained within the house itself.'

'Just the domestic staff, then, and they're probably all Russian,' Clements said. 'Brilliant. So in order to ensure that Antonov is arrested rather than eliminated, we're going to send in the SAS with one hand tied behind their backs, increasing the risk to their own lives, not to mention those of the cooks, maids and gardeners. A hundred and fifteen thousand pounds per head in compensation will be a small price to pay for such good press.'

'Thank you for being so constructive, as always, Edward.' The home secretary's sarcasm matched his own. She hit the table with both hands, hard. The walls were too thick for the sound to echo, but it got everyone's attention all the same. 'Right. If we've all finished?' Her expression defied anyone to disagree. 'Then let's get on with it, shall we? But I hope I've made it sufficiently clear that I expect this to be a non-lethal operation.'

Her gaze travelled from the DSF to the Met's assistant commissioner.

As Clements collected his papers and strode from the room, the commissioner picked up the mobile phone lying on the table in front of him and spoke into it.

7

Half a dozen miles away, still sitting at the table in the back bar, Woolf waited, listening to COBRA's muffled waffle. As the words in his ears began to sound as if they had been caught in a blender, he thought about his much younger third wife. Today was their first wedding anniversary. He stroked a hand over his thinning hair. When this was all over, maybe he'd make the appointment in Harley Street she'd been on about. As a present for them both.

Woolf held up a hand for silence and turned to Gavin. 'COBRA wants confirmation that this is an operation for the hard arrest of one Laszlo Antonov.'

'Confirmed,' Gavin said.

'Confirm that there will be no threat to his life or reason.'

'Confirmed.'

'Confirm that you will be using non-lethal weapons.'

'He just fucking said that.' Ashton was unable to control his impatience.

Gavin smiled to himself. For some reason, the F-word always sounded twice as obscene when delivered in Ashton's Home Counties accent.

'But we'll take on the threat as the operational situation

requires,' Ashton said. 'So, if the arse-covering session is finally over, we need control – now!'

Scowling, Woolf looked in vain for his notepad, then reached for a beer mat and scrawled a few words on the back. He signed his name, handed the mat to Ashton, with the reluctance of an atheist putting his last ten-pound-note into a church collection plate, and made the formal declaration: 'I hand over control pursuant to the provisions of the Military Aid to the Civil Power Act. J. Woolf.'

Ashton gave a theatrical sigh of relief, then nodded to Gavin, who immediately got on the net. 'All stations, this is Alpha. I have control. Stand by, stand by . . . Go!'

8

In a side street in West Hampstead, an area that had little more than its name in common with the upmarket Village it bordered, a woman was pressing shirts in the back room of a dingy dry-cleaner's, its windows so fogged with dirt and steam that they were almost opaque.

While she worked, her ten-year-old daughter sat on the floor at her feet, playing with a car-boot-sale Game Boy. Although she could not have been much older than thirty-five, the woman's hair was already streaked with grey and her face was lined and worn. She put down her iron as the phone began to ring.

She picked it up, reached for a notepad, listened in silence for a few moments, then hung up without a word. Was something wrong? Had she made a mistake? She'd been told to expect the call some time on Monday . . . 'Go and put your coat on,' she said, in Russian, to her daughter. 'Hurry!'

As the child disappeared, the woman pulled a folding wheelchair from behind the door. She manhandled it through the shop and onto the pavement outside. Keeping an anxious eye on it, she took a piece of battered cardboard from under the counter and wrote on it in awkward capital letters: 'BACK IN 20 MINUTES. SORRY IF PROBLEM.'

She taped the message to the window, hurried her daughter, still clutching her Game Boy, out of the shop, and locked the door behind them. The little girl ran alongside her, struggling to keep up, and pestered without success to be allowed to ride in the chair.

9

As Gavin gave the 'Go', Tom broke cover. Ignoring the prone figure of the blonde, he ran towards White, then dropped to one knee and aimed his ARWEN baton gun at the upper windows of the house.

He pumped two rounds into each of the unshuttered windows. As they smashed through the glass each circular disc ruptured and spun into the rooms, blinding anyone within range.

Tom reloaded and switched to the lower windows, but this time, though the glass panes disintegrated, the fine CN irritant billowed outside the building. He sprinted through the gas, flattened himself against the wall and whipped out a telescoping steel rod. As he cleared the remaining glass and peeled back the shredded curtains, instead of looking into a room, he found himself facing a concrete wall.

There was the thud of another detonation outside on Red as more charges blew apart the steel security gates set into the wall. Two black Range Rovers ploughed through the garden, churning up the immaculate lawns and passing on either side of the rose pergola where the Russian blonde still lay, immobilized and unconscious. Aluminium ladders were fixed to the roofs of the cars and Red Three and Four stood on the bumpers and running boards as they roared towards the house, eyes fixed on the windows Tom had already destroyed.

An X-ray appeared at one, threw up his AK-47 and kicked off a three-round burst. One of the Blue team dropped off the Range Rover and hit the grass, nursing a ragged hole in his leg.

Before the guard could fire again Keenan, still perched in the crook of the tree, filled his sight with the target's head, took up first pressure, aimed at the base of his nose, exhaled a long breath that was more like a sigh, and squeezed the trigger. Firing a subsonic round, his sniper rifle hardly made a sound.

'Sierra One,' Keenan said. 'I had to take the shot.'

Gavin had watched the 7.62mm round make contact on the monitor and knew it had been the right decision. 'Alpha, roger that.'

The Range Rovers slewed to a halt in front of the house as the two Blue team medics dragged the injured man into cover. A moment later the ladders clanged against the walls next to the shuttered windows and the assault teams clambered up them to make entry into the CN-filled rooms.

Tom and Blue Five were ahead of them, sweeping through the downstairs rooms. Domestic servants, many still incapacitated and in shock after the detonations on White and Red, were curled up on the floor in pain as the CN did its job.

Jockey and his team, Blue One, had made the second explosive entry. They met no resistance as they moved from room to room, but it was only when he opened a door that should have led to the hall that he found out why. The Scotsman's face registered neither surprise nor alarm: like the rest of the team he was now on auto-pilot. The reason the Regiment were so good at assaulting buildings was because they trained every single day. Jockey got on the net. 'More concrete, they've blocked us in sectors.'

10

Two dark shapes cradling AK-47s ran to intercept Tom and Blue Five as they burst into the hall and made for the stairs. The guards swung up their weapons; Tom dropped to one knee and fired two Value rounds, which struck them not with the soft thud of a projectile hitting flesh but with a hard, almost metallic sound that indicated they were wearing body armour.

The two men were driven backwards by the force of the impact but remained upright until the CN clouds started to take effect. Tom closed in and gave them another two rounds between their legs that took them down. He checked their faces. The imagery of Laszlo might be old, but there was one thing that time wouldn't change: the South Ossetian's washed-out grey-blue eyes.

Tom ran for the stairs. Bryce Rea, Blue Five commander, was right behind him with another of his team. The other two zip-tied the fallen guards while they were still fucked up by the CN.

The din of percussive bangs, thuds and shouts thundered from the upper floor as the Blue team cleared the house, fighting their way through yet more false doors and barricades. Tom's group found no further obstructions as they cleared the hall and raced up the sweeping staircase. He crossed the landing, the plan of the upper floors firmly imprinted on his mind.

He pushed open the master-bedroom door and dived through it, his gaze tracking the moving barrel of his rifle until it came to rest on a body-shaped hump on the emperor-sized bed. Tom pumped two rounds into it as the rest of the team made entry. He moved forward, ripped the duvet aside. The two pillows beneath it were dented by the hits, but were too soft a target to project their CN.

Blue Five cleared the bathroom and dressing room.

The half-full cup of coffee on the bedside table was still warm to the touch. 'He's here somewhere . . .' Tom's voice rasped through the respirator.

Bryce yelled, 'It could be the blonde's.'

'Could be.' Tom headed for the door. 'But in that case, whose is the one on the dressing-table?'

The net was heaving with assault teams telling Alpha that their areas were clear. Then Jockey chipped in: 'Stand by, stand by. Blue One has a possible escape route under the main hall stairs. Wait out.'

Tom's team peeled out of the room. They found the Scotsman fitting a framed charge down the hinged side of a steel-reinforced door. They flattened themselves against the wall. Jockey detonated the charge, then led the way into the basement. It was pitch black down there, but he left the light switch untouched in case it was booby-trapped. Hyperalert, he moved down the steps, his gaze tracking the beam of the Maglite fixed to the barrel of his MP5. His team followed, ready to fire their ARWENs the instant the torch beam illuminated a target.

They found themselves in a large, completely empty cellar. There were none of the usual rich man's embellishments, no swimming pool, no home cinema, no cavernous wine store, just bare, freshly skimmed concrete.

Tom headed for the doorway opposite.

He stood to the left of the frame, ARWEN in the shoulder, forefinger on the trigger, muzzle pointed to where the door would swing open towards the assault teams. Jockey joined him, Maglite at the ready. Blue Five gripped the handle, turned it and pulled.

11

Delphine sifted through the evening's bookings, then glanced at her watch for the twentieth time in as many minutes. The seventeen months she'd been working at the Green Dragon had gone in a flash, but this afternoon was crawling by.

A warren of low beams, bumpy walls and creaking floorboards, the old coaching inn felt as if it had been around as long as Hereford had. It was ye kind of olde place where the Rotary Club met every Friday, and Saga coach tours stopped for scones and tea after a trip to the nearby cathedral. It also had a grand Georgian frontage on Broad Street that often led visitors to expect a level of style and service that the hotel simply could not offer.

Delphine had a degree in hotel management from the University of Paris-Sud 11, and was working her way up through the ranks of the chain that owned the Green Dragon. She didn't find Hereford the most exciting of places. At first it had seemed like any other six-month posting, one to be endured before she moved on with barely a backward glance.

The youngest of three girls, she'd been brought up in a small guesthouse their parents ran just outside Nice, on the Monaco side of the city, overlooking the sea. Both her sisters were now married, with children, and lived in Paris. But

Delphine wasn't ready for that just yet. She wanted to see the world.

She worked in the office by day and on Reception at night, soaking up the hands-on experience. All being well, within a year she would be ready to manage one of the three compliance teams that travelled the world checking the chain's hotels, making sure the guests' 'high-comfort experience' was everything it should be.

The two previous years on the management course had gone according to plan. She had excelled in Dubai, Berlin and Vancouver. But then, in her first week in rain-lashed Hereford, she'd met Tom Buckingham.

Until then she had never heard of the SAS, but had known immediately that they were trouble. The group gathered around the bar were men who carried themselves . . . if not with a swagger, then with complete self-confidence, as if life held no surprises for them and presented no problems they couldn't solve. Their clothes were casual – blue jeans, T-shirts and tight leather jackets – but seemed almost like a uniform. As soon as they appeared, the local girls hovered around them, like bees.

Delphine had seen one reach into his jacket, heard the rasp of Velcro. She gave her flatmate a quizzical glance. 'Are buttons and zips too complicated for your British men?'

Moira, a bottle-blonde a couple of years ahead of her, had put a finger to her lips. 'It's not just their pockets. It's everything. Work and play. They like everything well fastened. You can ask them stuff, but you'll never get an answer.'

One of the group was in a wheelchair, another on crutches, with a shiny new steel leg that glinted beneath his trouser leg when he sat down. They were treated as part of the gang and subjected to the same relentless banter, but complex emotions could be read in their more unguarded looks. Delphine had wondered if the pleasure they took in being reunited with their friends was not outweighed by painful reminders of a life that had once been theirs and would never return.

'I think maybe these boys are a little bit sad . . .'

Moira took her to one side. 'Trust me, Delphine, they'll all be chasing you. Even the ones with no legs. You're a beautiful girl.'

Delphine felt her cheeks go pink and shook her head. She was tall and slim, with jet black hair cut into a bob and a fringe that brushed her dark brown eyes, but she never thought of herself as special.

Moira was in full advice mode. 'If you want my two-penny-worth, pick one of the townies, not these guys. The Men in Black are full of charm and chat, but everything's a competition – and that includes who'll be the first to screw the new girl.

'And don't ever make the mistake of falling in love. The Regiment isn't just a job, it's the whole of their lives. That doesn't leave much room for wives or girlfriends. No matter how hard you try, you're always going to be second best.' Her lips had tightened and there was a note in her voice that was both bitter and wistful. Her gaze shifted to the window and she stared, unseeing, out into the darkness.

'What is this "Regiment"?' Delphine said.

Moira had stared at her, astonished, then burst out laughing. 'My, you have got a lot to learn about Hereford, haven't you? It's the SAS. You know – the Iranian Embassy siege, the boys who cleared the caves in Afghanistan?'

Nothing was registering with Delphine.

'The fit-looking guys? They're soldiers – Special Forces.' Moira winked. 'But, trust me, they're not half as special as they think they are.'

As Moira had predicted, a succession of them tried their luck with Delphine that first evening, and over the following nights virtually all of them put the word on her at one time or another, but she brushed them off. They were young, fit and strong, and some were good-looking, but she had watched the succession of local girls coming and going, leaving with one or other of the men one night and ignored the next, and was determined that that was not going to happen to her.

The one they called Posh Lad hadn't spoken to her, but she

was aware of his eyes on her, and as she talked with Moira and her friends she found herself glancing surreptitiously at him in return. He seemed more thoughtful than his mates; she sensed there were depths to him that most of the others didn't share. She was captivated by the way that, when he was deep in thought, his fingers often strayed absently to the crinkled white scar etched across his temple, beneath his short, side-parted dark brown hair. He traced its contours like a blind man reading braille.

Gavin was the first to notice. He'd tried – and failed – to chat up Delphine once before, but then decided on a change of tack. When it became clear that the West Country magic still wasn't working, he took half a step back and said, 'But I'm wearing one of his shirts . . .'

She just looked puzzled.

'*And* his jeans.' He stuck out a denim-clad leg for her to admire. 'A new pair.'

Delphine frowned.

'I know I'm not up there with Posh Lad, but I thought you might fancy me a bit if I was wearing his clothes.'

Now she was embarrassed. 'Why do you call him that?'

Gavin smiled. He knew he was about to do Tom's ground-work, but so what? He was a mate. And if he scored, Gavin would take all the credit. 'One: rich family. Two: he always uses the right tense. Three: he owns a fountain pen. Four: he's got name-tapes in his socks. That's pretty posh to trogs like us.'

'Why do you make so much fun of him? He sounds a good man.'

'He is. A very good man. There's nothing grim – nobody thinks any the less of him because he's posh – it's just banter. Anyway, happy days. See you around.'

When Tom had asked her out about two weeks after they'd first set eyes on each other, she had turned him down. But she'd hesitated as she did so, and found herself blushing again.

He'd held her gaze for a moment. 'I'll only ask once more, and that's it.'

'That'll be a relief for us both.'

His look had darkened for an instant, and then he burst out laughing. 'You don't like us soldiers much, do you?'

'How can I tell? You're the first ones I've ever met and I don't know you all.'

'Then spend your time getting to know just me. It'll be easier than trying to learn so many new names.'

She smiled. 'Was that the "only once more" you were talking about?'

A grin had spread across his face. 'I'm not sure. It might be. Would your answer be the same?' He paused, trying to read her expression. When he spoke again, to her surprise it was in flawless, almost accentless French. 'Don't believe everything some people tell you,' he said, glancing towards Moira. 'We're not all heartless bastards.' There was another pause. 'So . . . now or never, what will it be?'

She had studied him in silence for a moment. 'Now,' she said, and surprised herself by doing so. 'And then perhaps never again.' She wrote her mobile number on a scrap of paper and handed it to him. 'Better go back to your friends now,' she said. 'And tell them you've won the bet.'

He laughed. 'Don't knock it! The winnings will pay for dinner tomorrow night.'

'I'm working,' she said, switching back to English.

'I'm sure Moira wouldn't mind covering for you, would you, Moira? Call her in sick?'

Moira had looked up from the paper she'd been pretending to read. '*Me* do *you* a favour, Tom Buckingham? Why on earth would I want to do that?'

'Because you'll be doing Delphine a favour, too.'

She'd smiled, despite herself. 'I'm not so sure about that.'

'Sorted, then.' He turned back to Delphine. 'I'll pick you up at eight. Where are you living?'

'She's renting the spare room at mine,' Moira said. 'You still remember the way there, don't you?'

Delphine's eyes narrowed, but Moira's expression gave nothing away.

*

As Tom had walked back to the bar, there was a burst of banter and barracking from his mates. 'Mate, better luck next time. Maybe she just wants a bit of rough.'

'Yeah, nice try, Posh Lad,' Jockey said. 'But not even your best parlay-voo could break down the ice maiden, eh?'

'I think she wants a real action man like me,' Keenan said. 'Not some limp-wristed, boater-wearing nancy-boy.'

'Yeah, you're probably right,' Tom had said, savouring the moment. 'I was a fool even to try. On the other hand . . .' He'd flashed the scrap of paper. 'I do seem to be the only one around here who's got her phone number. Your round is it, Jockey?'

12

The torch beam penetrated the strip of darkness widening behind it. Tom kept his ARWEN barrel over Jockey's right shoulder as they moved through the gap into an equally bare room. Its walls were broken only by a massive steel door beneath a small, wired-glass window.

They repeated the pattern and this time Bryce grabbed the handle. It didn't open. His team prepared their last charge as the net hummed with instructions for the loading of prisoners, their handover to the police and the corralling of the media.

As Maglites lit the darkness around the door so that the charge could be positioned, Tom glimpsed a flash of bare metal just beneath the window frame. 'Fuck! Bryce – bin it! Look at this.' He pointed to a minute length of copper wire that led from the wall to the bottom edge of the steel window frame. 'The window's wired to something. Which probably means the door is too. No prizes for guessing what.'

Bryce studied the window for a moment, then scraped away a little of the putty surrounding the wire. 'It feeds through to the other side,' he said. 'Break any of the wires set in that glass and I'm guessing it'd be time to put your head between your legs—'

'And kiss your arse goodbye.' Tom leaned his back against

the door, knees bent, creating a platform with his thighs. 'Jockey, get up there and have a look.'

Jockey climbed onto Tom's legs, put one Hi-Tec assault boot on his shoulder, then the other, and peered through the window. Five seconds later he was back down and on the net. 'Alpha, this is Blue One – we have an IED in the basement, blocking our advance. At least twenty kilos of PE. There's a tunnel beyond it. Has to be X-ray One's escape route.'

Bryce started to move his team back the way they had come. He knew what was about to happen.

Tom did too, and followed. The ATO (Ammunition Technical Officer) would take care of the IED, and the police would take back operational command of the incident. Military Aid to the Civil Power (MACP) was always a bit of a slap in the face for the Met. It meant armed assistance when the police were unable to cope – with riot, organized crime or terrorism. It was always a big deal for them to hand over control of a criminal situation to the military on UK soil, so they didn't waste a minute snatching it back.

Gavin's voice crackled in the Blue team's ears. 'Alpha, roger that. Blue One, stay with the IED until the ATO arrives. All other call-signs withdraw. Move back to the holding area. Out.'

13

'Laszlo's gone.' Gavin tried to rub the tiredness from his eyes. 'And he's left a bloody great IED as a farewell present. Days like this make me wish I was a Frog . . .'

Ashton nodded. 'Or a Russian.'

The Compagnies Républicaines de Sécurité (CRS) were specially trained to deal with riots and other circumstances that fell awkwardly between the maintenance of law and order and outright war. The Interior Ministry of the Russian Federation had its own armed troops to deal with major riots, terrorism and low-level insurrection.

'Fuck it.' Gavin brought his fist down on the table. 'We'd have had him if that lot –' he jerked his head in the vague direction of central London '– had got their shit together.'

'Some you win.' Ashton got to his feet and stretched his arms above his head. 'OK, wrap it up. We need to be out of here before the media circus hits town.'

Woolf continued to bark instructions into his phone. 'That's what I said, and that's what I want: a nationwide lockdown. Every airport, seaport and railway station. Get it done *now*.'

He broke the connection and met the 3i/c's stare.

'We waited too fucking long,' Gavin said.

'Bollocks. *You* messed up, pure and simple. And now we're going to have to go and find him all over again.'

Gavin gave a snort. 'Unless he grows wings, how hard can it be? It's a fucking island, isn't it?'

'It took three years to track him down the first time. He may be a mass-murdering psychopath to us, but he's the number-one poster boy in South Ossetia. You just saw how men – and even women, for heaven's sake – are prepared to die for him. Laszlo is like a god to them. If he goes underground again, the Russian network will make damn sure we don't get anywhere near him.'

'You'd better crack on before he does, then.'

'*Crack on?* Of course we're going to bloody crack on.' Woolf was close to blowing a fuse. 'Because while you Special Forces "blades" are diving for cover, we'll have every toe-rag reporter in our faces, every paper in the world printing pictures of Laszlo's victims and demanding to know why we – we, not you – failed them.' He grabbed his papers and stormed out of the room, but rather spoiled the effect when he realized he had left his mobile behind and had to retrace his steps, avoiding Gavin's eye, to collect it.

Gavin packed up his kit as sirens wailed and the beat of TV-network helicopters filled the air. He grinned at the landlord. 'Mate, you can have your pub back now. It's been a real pleasure. Next time, why don't you come over to ours?'

'And my pictures and ornaments? Who's going to put those back?'

'I'll give you a clue,' Gavin said. 'Three letters, starts with *y* and rhymes with "screw". Have a nice day now.'

14

The woman walked downhill, away from the Heath, towards the dry-cleaner's. Her daughter stuck close by her side. The police cars and helicopters were frightening her. And so was the man in the wheelchair.

He seemed hunched with age and pain and, shadowed by his hat, his face was as pale as a ghost's. A scarf was wrapped around his neck and a blanket covered him right up to his chin.

'Where are we going now?' the child said. 'Can we go home?'

The woman shook her head. 'Later, darling. First we have to go back to the shop.'

'But I want to go home, Mamochka.'

'Not now, little one. Later, I promise.'

The man in the wheelchair smiled at the child and held out a hand from under the blanket for her to grip. 'What is your name, little one?'

She didn't take the hand, moving still closer to her mother. 'Lilya.'

'Do you like living here, Lilya?'

'It's not like my real home.' Her tone was sullen. She missed her little friends and her uncles, who spoiled her with sweets.

'A lot of things here are not like home,' her mother said.

'Some are better, some are worse, but at least we are safe.'

They turned a corner, away from the police vans throwing out streams of officers to create an outer cordon around the incident on the Heath.

'And what can go wrong on such a beautiful day?' the man said. 'It's so warm you would scarcely believe it was autumn. Tell you what, Lilya, I have just one little job to do in that steamy, smelly dry-cleaner's, and then we can all go and get some ice-cream. Would you like that?'

She brightened at once and even took his hand as a couple of speeding police cars screamed past. A moment later, a van turned in towards them and pulled up with a screech of brakes. Two policemen jumped out and threw on their hi-vis jackets. The van drove past and stopped once more. More men streamed out and began erecting a barrier across the street.

The woman slowed her pace as the two officers approached them. Her daughter gave her an uncertain look.

'Don't worry, Lilya.' The man squeezed her hand. 'Policemen here are not like the ones at home. Give them a nice smile. Now, let's keep moving. We don't want to miss that ice-cream, do we?'

The policemen's instructions were to be on the alert for a solitary six-foot male of East European appearance, in his mid-thirties, of slim build with pale complexion and dark brown hair. A frail old man in a wheelchair, clutching his grand-daughter's hand, barely merited a second glance. He hardly looked strong enough to keep his thick, black-framed glasses perched on his aquiline nose.

They gave the anxious-looking woman a polite nod and carried on up the street, their gaze raking the gardens to either side. Rotors chopped the air above them as a police helicopter swooped overhead and began to hover over the edge of the Heath, dominating the sky to prevent the media getting any closer to the incident.

15

Jockey's crew were on their way. Tom and the rest of the Blue team filed back into the holding area – the school gym that had been commandeered for resting, feeding and rehearsal.

He pulled the respirator from his face, leaving an angry red weal where the sealing band had fitted tight against his skin. His hair and forehead were streaked with sweat.

The general hum was that the man down had been stabilized and was in hospital. The world didn't collapse because one of them got zapped. It was what sometimes happened; Davy, the man down, knew that as much as anyone. He'd been on a raid to capture insurgents just outside Baghdad when one of the team had taken a round that had carved a big chunk out of his stomach. The wound was big, wet and bloody, but Davy had thought he was looking too good as they flew back into the Green Zone. Tom had watched him give the boy a couple of kicks so the pain would show in the pictures he was taking for the squadron office. They now had pride of place dead centre of the photo board.

Tom unloaded his ARWEN and the Sig 9mm pistol on his belt and slid them, with their unspent rounds, into his ready-bag, alongside the party gear that made up his assault kit.

The others followed suit, changing into civvies for the drive back to Hereford. They compared notes on the operation and subjected each other to the usual merciless banter.

Tom peeled off his jacket and shirt and tore open his body armour. The rip of Velcro straps sounded like a chorus of jungle frogs.

'I dropped him.' Keenan stretched out his arm and drew an imaginary sight picture on a tree beyond the holding area. 'Sweet.'

'Yeah, yeah, tidy darts, mate.' Bryce was checking that the MOE (method of entry) kit had all been loaded onto the white Transit. 'But Tom gets tonight's star prize – for giving one to the Barbie.'

'Yeah . . .' Vatu, a huge Fijian with a flamboyant moustache, was inside the vehicle, stowing boxes. 'If she'd detonated that belly-rig, Tom would have been asking God for the name of his tailor, and the rest of us would have been picking her pubes out of our teeth for weeks.'

Jockey's team had just entered the holding area. 'A needle's the only thing Tom gets to stick into girls.' The trademark Glaswegian growl made even the most innocent remark sound like a threat. Especially when his red, sweat-covered face looked like it'd just spent a week in a sauna.

Tom laughed. 'You'd know all about needles, Jockey. Drugging them's the only way you get any.'

'Yes, and I won't give you the benefit of my expertise unless you sing it for me. Come on, you know you love it.'

Right on cue, Tom's mobile phone sparked up inside his ready-bag, its ringtone the chorus of 'The Eton Boating Song' that Jockey kept downloading onto it whenever he got the chance. Tom held it towards the Scotsman, conducting the ringtone choir expansively with his other hand. He checked the number and moved a little away from the others to take the call.

'Delphine . . . We're just wrapping up now. We've been on a job.'

'I know. I 'ave just seen the news.' Her French accent still blew him away. 'They said there was a massive gas explosion on the Heath, but I saw the Range Rovers. Are you still there?'

Eighteen months they'd been going out, and even hearing her on a mobile made him go weak at the knees. 'You know I can't answer that, don't you?'

'Not even that? How could that possibly be a secret? This drives me mad.' There was an echoing silence at the end of the line. 'I love you, Tom. But I hate you.'

'Fun, though, isn't it?'

'No, not any more,' she said wearily. 'It was once, but not any more. Are you not even allowed to tell me if you're OK? That's why I called. Or is that a state secret too?'

'No, I'm fine.'

'And will you be back soon?'

'Yeah. I'll drive to Hereford, sort the kit, quick debrief and shower. I should be ready by about eight.' He dropped his voice and switched to French. 'Delphine, you know I can't wait to see you. And I'll make it up to you, I promise.'

His mates nudged each other and inched towards him, trying to overhear what he was saying.

'We will see.' She paused before switching back to English. He heard her voice soften. 'I'll be with you in a minute.'

'What? I wish . . .'

'Not you.' Her voice was still smooth and welcoming. 'I was talking to a guest. I have to go now, but you will be here, won't you? You promise? I need to talk to you. It is important.'

'I promise.'

'I promise,' Jockey said, mincing around with his hand on his hip.

'Don't believe him, love,' Bryce shouted. 'He'll promise anything to get into your pants.'

'I have to go,' Delphine said. 'But we need to talk. I'll see you tonight.' There was a click as she broke the connection.

Tom glared at Jockey. 'Didn't your mummy tell you it was rude to eavesdrop on other people's conversations?'

'No,' Jockey said. 'She was far too busy pouring super-market vodka down her neck and ripping the heads off parking meters. But listening to you talking there showed me why I should've stayed in school.' He gave a sorrowful shake of his head. 'I really envy you, mate. I missed out big-time.'

Tom furrowed his brow, not sure if this was genuine or just another wind-up. 'No, you didn't, you mad Scotsman. You can still wear that skirt and pretend to be Monarch of the Glen.'

'I'm serious, mate. You've got the ability to punch well above your weight.' Jockey's face creased into a grin. 'Shit, the moment you fucking start with that parlay-voo business I'd fucking shag you myself. If I wasn't afraid of catching something.'

Tom deleted the ringtone for the hundredth time. 'Don't worry, Jockey, you can't catch intelligence.' He shoved his mobile into his jacket pocket.

'Cunt.' Jockey threw his respirator at Tom's head.

Tom swerved out of the way, like a boxer riding a punch, as Gavin walked into the holding area to see what stage of the pack-up-and-fuck-off routine the team had reached.

'Right, listen in!' He had to shout to get everyone's attention. 'We're not on island time so get a bloody move on. I want the Range Rovers out first, then the Transits, all at five-minute intervals. No speeding, no blue lights. Just get out of here ASAP before the ladies and gentlemen of the media find out who and where we are. They're sniffing around out there already.' He paused. 'And Posh Lad here needs to stop and buy the woman of his sticky little dreams a bunch of flowers from motorway services. It'll do her a power of good.'

Tom gave him a pitying look. 'And you wonder why your wife burned all your clothes?'

Tom and Gavin jumped into one of the black Range Rovers at the rear of the holding area and moved off, followed at intervals by the rest of the convoy.

As they cut through West Hampstead, heading towards the motorway, they drove past a dry-cleaner's. A handwritten sign in the window announced: 'BACK IN 20 MINUTES. SORRY IF PROBLEM.'

16

The woman leaned on the handles of the wheelchair to lift its front wheels clear of the step, then heaved and pushed it into the shop. She locked the door and knelt down behind the counter. 'I have what you wanted.'

She produced a bundle from a lower shelf, stripped away the polythene wrapping and held up a set of grimy, well-worn overalls.

He nodded. '*Exactly* what I wanted. Thank you.'

'If you want to try them on, you can use the room upstairs.'

He looked over his shoulder, checked that the street outside was empty, then threw aside the blanket.

He towered above the woman. She was in awe. The stories she had heard about him must be true.

'Will you be needing the wheelchair again?'

'I think it has served its purpose now. Thank you again for your help.'

'It's an honour to be of service to you, Mr Antonov.' She blushed as she spoke. 'May I call you Laszlo?'

He smiled, as if he was giving a polite child the OK to take a sweet from the tin.

'My friends will be so jealous when I tell them . . .'

The smile faded.

'I'm sorry, Laszlo.' Fear was the overriding emotion now. 'I didn't mean . . . Obviously I won't breathe a word to anyone . . . until I know that you are safely out of this country and back in our beloved homeland once more.'

'Of course,' Laszlo said. 'I understand. Don't alarm yourself.' The smile was back, but there was a coldness in his eyes.

She found herself reaching out a hand to her daughter and pulling her close.

Laszlo walked to the front window of the shop and looked up and down the deserted street. When he finally turned back to face them, he raised his arms invitingly. 'Lilya, are you ready for that ice-cream?' He smacked his lips. 'And what is your favourite flavour?'

'Chocolate!' She hesitated. 'But I thought you said you had a little job to do first . . .'

'Ah, yes, that little job. You're right, I should attend to that, shouldn't I? I'll do it now.' But he made no move, still staring at the two of them.

There was an unnatural stillness in the room, the only sound or movement a fly buzzing at a window pane.

Realization began to dawn in the woman's eyes. 'Darling,' she said, trying to keep the panic from her voice. 'Run upstairs and play with your Game Boy for a while. The gentleman needs to talk to me about something . . . something private. Quickly now.'

The child faltered, puzzled by her mother's sudden look of desperation. 'But—'

'Don't argue,' her mother said. 'Just go.'

There was a note in her voice that her daughter hadn't heard before. She looked from her to Laszlo, then turned, Game Boy clutched in her hand, and began to make her way towards the stairs.

There was a strange noise from behind her, almost like a closing door, followed by a dull thud. She turned back and her eyes widened. Her mother lay sprawled on the floor, her head surrounded by a spreading crimson corona. A neat hole had been punched above her eyebrow, but the exit wound at the rear of her skull was the size of a teacup.

The child swung to face Laszlo and saw through her tears that the snub nose of his silenced revolver was now pointing at her. The barrel kicked twice. The Game Boy flew from her hand as she fell beside her mother. She didn't hear it land.

His movements still slow and unhurried, Laszlo turned to the window and again checked the street. He made certain the shop door was locked then tore down the back-in-twenty note and turned the permanent sign to *Closed*. Taking hold of the woman by the ankles, he pulled her body along the floor to the back room, her hair smearing the floor with blood, like a mop. He dragged her daughter through as well, then ripped a freshly cleaned woollen coat from its hanger and used it to wipe away any blood that was visible from the pavement.

Laszlo climbed the stairs to the tiny room above the shop. He boiled the kettle and made himself some black tea. Rejecting the Mr Men yoghurts, he ate some bread and cheese from the fridge, then turned on the television and tuned it to a news channel. He settled on the cheap vinyl sofa, brushing aside the kapok stuffing that spilled from one of its seams.

The lead item on the bulletin focused on the mysterious explosions that had rocked a Victorian mansion at the edge of Hampstead Heath. A police spokesman, reading from his notes in the Robocop-speak that police media-training courses had apparently been unable to eliminate, said that there had been no terrorist incident: a gas leak was thought to have been the cause of the blasts. As a precaution, the neighbouring houses had been evacuated. But the media weren't buying it. Their aerial cameras showed the police cordon that had taken just minutes to get into position, and they broadcast eyewitness reports of men dressed, as one middle-aged woman put it, 'like those SAS chaps'.

A slow smile spread across Laszlo's face.

A succession of would-be customers tried the shop door and went away again. One particularly persistent one kept banging on the glass. The letterbox gave a metallic rattle. 'I know you're in there,' an irate male voice yelled. 'I can see the TV through the upstairs window. I've got an important event tonight and I need my dinner jacket.'

At first Laszlo ignored him. As the banging grew louder, he moved quietly to the head of the stairs and waited. There was more furious shouting and banging on the door but then he heard retreating footsteps, the slam of a car door and a squeal of tyres.

Laszlo walked back into the room and switched off the TV. He selected a SIM card from several he had in his jacket pocket, put it into his mobile phone and made a call. He spoke in Russian to his little brother. There was affection in his voice, something no one but Sambor had heard since the deaths of their mother and father. They exchanged pleasantries before getting down to business.

'I have been compromised.' Laszlo brushed aside Sambor's concern. 'It is not a problem, brother. I am OK. We have to move the plan forward. We start tomorrow morning.'

Laszlo listened as his brother confirmed that everyone was now in place, and fully prepared. Sambor thanked him for keeping his promise.

After breaking the connection Laszlo took out the SIM card, cut it into four pieces with the kitchen scissors and flushed it down the toilet. Then he swung his legs up on the sofa, closed his eyes and settled down to wait.

17

Delphine had put her hair in a loose ponytail and worn a tunic dress in jade green silk for her first date with Tom.

'You look absolutely stunning,' Moira had said, as she stood in front of the mirror, checking her own hair. 'But might you not be a little ... over-dressed? You don't know where he's taking you, do you?' They both heard the throaty sound of a motorbike engine outside. 'Or how you're going to get there ...'

Delphine went to answer the door, and found Tom wearing his usual jeans, T-shirt and leather jacket.

'You look fantastic,' he said, then sheepishly held out a motorcycle helmet to her. 'Er, did I forget to mention I'd be picking you up on my bike?'

'It's all right,' she said. 'I get motion sickness in cars.'

Tom wasn't sure if she was just trying to be nice. He drank up every detail of her happy, smiling face.

'And I used to ride a moped all the time in Nice.'

'Um ... I'm afraid Hereford isn't the South of France.'

She flashed him a dazzling smile. 'That's true in so many more ways than you can imagine.'

'You're not wrong,' he said. 'But right now I'm just worried about the temperature.'

'Shall I change?'

He shook his head. 'Wear my jacket over your dress. I'll be fine in my T-shirt – it's a warm night, by Hereford standards anyway.'

She slid onto the pillion seat of Tom's new BMW GS1200, leaned into his back and put her arms around him as he twisted the throttle, gunned the engine and pulled out of the car park. As he accelerated, weaving the bike through the sparse evening traffic, she clung tightly to him, feeling the hard muscle of his body against her arms and chest.

He took her to a gastro-pub in Fownhope, a village a few minutes outside town. The knowing look the waiter gave him as he showed them to a corner table suggested to Delphine that she wasn't the first girl he'd taken there.

She'd expected him to dominate the conversation, spinning yarns of countries he'd seen and battles he'd fought. After all, wasn't that what soldiers did? But she was wrong. As they talked over dinner, she was surprised to find that he was attentive and interested in her, asking her a string of questions about herself and her life before she'd come to Hereford.

After a while she began to wonder if it reflected genuine interest in her or was more a tactic to stop her asking him too much about his own life.

'You're not very forthcoming about yourself, are you, Tom?'

'I guess it's the way all of us are,' he said. 'Everything we do at work is on a need-to-know basis – if you don't need to know, then you don't get told.'

Delphine smiled. 'I wasn't planning to torture you and I don't want to know any state secrets. I'm just interested in you. But if you don't want to tell me, or you're too shy . . . though I'd find that hard to believe . . .'

Tom's discomfort was already showing. Delphine momentarily glimpsed the little boy hiding inside the man. 'I thought resistance to interrogation was something you had to learn for work, not for when you're out with a friend.'

He raised an eyebrow. 'Just a friend?'

'For the moment, yes. Later on, well . . . who knows? But

what's that English phrase? Let's not run before we can walk?'

She'd been determined not to sleep with him that first time. Not because of any old-fashioned morality – she wasn't saving herself for her wedding night – she just didn't want to be another notch on a regimental bedpost. But at the end of the evening it had seemed the most natural thing in the world to go back to his house with him. It wasn't even discussed: they both knew that was the way it was going to be.

That had been eighteen months ago and they'd been going out together ever since, though she was sometimes uncertain if she knew him any better now than she had on that first date.

After they'd been seeing each other for about four months, Tom had called her at work. 'I have to go to my parents' house at the weekend. It's their wedding anniversary. You can come too, if you like.'

'You don't sound very keen on either the idea of the anniversary or of me coming with you,' she'd said.

'No, I really want you to. If I sound uncertain, I guess it's just because I'm not sure how much you'll enjoy it.'

'Well,' she had said, with a smile in her voice, 'it will satisfy my curiosity at least.'

18

'Well, now you've met my parents, do you want to call the whole thing off?' Tom had joked, as they shared a pot of coffee in Delphine's flat the morning after they'd got back. It was almost the first chance they'd had to talk. A motorbike ride is never a good time to have a conversation, and by the time they'd reached Hereford it was two in the morning.

'They weren't so bad,' she said. 'Like all parents, I'm sure they just want the best for you.'

'Perhaps, but aren't I the best judge of what that is?'

'They do have a bit of a point. If you could have your pick of careers or live the life of a country gent, why be a soldier – even an SAS one?'

'How many times do I have to say this? I *like* it.'

She nodded over her mug and held out a hand. 'And if it costs you your life one day?'

'It'll still have been worth it. You know the old saying, "Better to live a day on your feet than a lifetime on your knees"?'

She inclined her head, realizing that she had a mistress to compete with. 'I've never heard you speak with such intensity about anything before.'

He gave a rueful smile. 'Maybe it's because you've never asked before.'

'Oh, I've asked,' she said. 'It's just that you've never heard me.'

'Don't get me wrong,' he said. 'I'm not planning to be Lawrence of Arabia for ever. I've seen too many grizzled old sweats droning on about how things were different – and better – back in the day, and how the youth of today doesn't know what soldiering is. The moment I stop enjoying it and start enduring it, I'll quit. There are plenty of other things I want to do with my life, but for now there's no place I'd rather be, and no job I'd rather be doing.'

'And if the price of that is that you wind up in a wheelchair, like some of your friends?'

He shrugged. 'I don't treat that risk lightly. But I know it can't be eliminated altogether. Shit happens, and I know that there's a chance it may happen to me. It's the price of admission, if you like, to what we do. But it's not going to stop me. I volunteered. No one forced me to do this job.'

'And what about the normal, everyday things in life – buying a home, raising a family, cooking the dinner, cutting the grass – where do they fit in?'

'At the moment they don't. But that will change one day,' he added hastily, as he saw her lips tighten and a bleak look in her eye. 'I want children, one day, lots of them but I want to be around for them. I've seen too many mates get married, have kids, then find themselves divorced a few years later because their wives got sick of trying to run a family on their own. I've even heard a few women say they prefer it when their men are away on ops because they're just a nuisance when they're at home, disrupting everyone's routine. Well, that's not going to happen to me.' He paused. 'Or my wife.'

'OK,' she said. 'I can accept that you're a soldier and you love your work, and that your mates are as close to you as your family, or maybe even closer, but does everything have to be quite so macho? This is the twenty-first century, not the Stone Age. Does any display of affection or tenderness, any interest in life outside the SAS really have to be taken as a sign of weakness? And would the world end if just once you said, "Sorry, I can't make it," when your friends or your precious Regiment asked you to do something?'

'You and the Regiment are the two most important things in my life, Delphine,' Tom said. 'You know I love you, really I do, and I hope that we'll have a life together long after I've left Hereford, but please don't ask me right now to choose between you and the work I do.'

'Because I wouldn't like the choice you'd make?'

'I didn't say that.'

'No,' Delphine said. 'You didn't have to.'

They sat in silence for a while. 'Anyway,' he said brightly, putting down his mug on the nearest pile of hotel trade mags, 'the trial by ordeal with my parents is over, and we don't have to go back there any time soon.'

'I wouldn't mind,' she said. 'I'd go if you wanted to.'

'Well,' he gave a sly smile, 'perhaps we will in a few months, if we're still together by then.'

'You're right,' she said. 'I could probably be doing a lot better for myself.'

He gave her a quizzical look, then broke into a broad grin.

At the end of her six-month posting at the Green Dragon, Delphine had applied for an extension, and done so again six months later, even though it was against the wishes and advice of her boss. He couldn't understand why she didn't want to move on, after all her hard work.

In the end he'd extracted a promise that this would be her last six months, which was now almost up. But tonight, when Tom arrived, there was a more pressing situation she was desperate to discuss. Her future with Tom or, rather, the lack of it. The mistress had won. So much so that, for the last few weeks, every time she had tried to do so, something had cropped up at the Lines: Tom had been called in for a briefing, for training, a deployment, an operation, but often, she suspected, just to go out yet again with the lads.

But that was all history. She'd seen the news on TV. The speculation that the SAS had been involved in the mysterious explosions in Hampstead earlier in the day was probably right. Tom was heading back to Hereford and should be with her soon – maybe. She'd booked a table for dinner at the pub in Fownhope. She'd asked for the same table as they'd had on the night of their first date, even asked for a bottle of the same wine to be on the table waiting for him.

19

Tom and Gavin had just turned off the M4 at Swindon. It would be another hour and a half before they got back to Hereford.

Gavin sighed, fidgeted some more, then took his feet down from the dash. 'Mate, do me a fucking favour. Let me bung some proper music on for a change. That racket's doin' me head in.' He reached across to switch the radio to a rock station.

'Racket?' Tom shook his head in mock disbelief. 'That's Lang Lang playing Stravinsky's *Rite of Spring*. I thought it was your favourite.'

'Never heard of them. Any relation to the Ting Tings?' Gavin gave a sly smile. 'I'm guessing they're French. You have romantic evenings by the fire listening to them, yeah?'

Tom grinned. 'Where do I begin? You're about a third to a half right, which is probably about as good as it ever gets with you, isn't it? Stravinsky was a Russian, though he did live in France for a long time, and Lang Lang is Chinese.'

'Yeah, yeah, yah, yah, yada fucking yada. Whoever they fucking are, and wherever they fucking come from, it all sounds the fucking same to me.'

'Gav, you'd give Philistines a bad name, you would. I even bought you the CD last year, remember?'

'Yeah, I know, and thank you. It makes a great beer mat. Barry White's all you need to knock the birds bandy.'

Tom reached across and switched the radio back to Stravinsky. 'Get used to it, mate. My roof, my rules. You're living with me now. And if you ever manage to find someone stupid enough to marry you again, I intend to make sure they'll be getting a cultured man.' He shot him a sideways glance. 'Trust me, she'll love you for it. Now relax, listen and learn.'

Tom leaned back in his seat, tapping out the rhythm on the steering-wheel. After another loud sigh, Gavin reclined his seat as far as it would go, closed his eyes and pretended to go to sleep.

They eventually rolled into the Lines, just outside Hereford, and the Blue team's hangar. The new Lines, an old RAF camp, had been officially opened in 2000 after the Regiment had moved from Stirling Lines on the edge of the city. The old Lines had looked more like a 1980s red-brick university and hadn't had the room needed for an ever-growing Special Forces contingent, or been able to accommodate larger aircraft like Chinooks. When the RAF had abandoned the base, it was a no-brainer.

'Why the Lines?' Delphine had asked him.

The term had been used in the British Army for hundreds of years, Tom had explained, and referred to the tent lines that solders inhabited in the field. 'The rows of tents had to be in perfect alignment – even the guy ropes and pegs had to be just so.'

Now Gavin sat up, yawned and stretched, then jumped out. 'We'd better motor,' he said. 'It's five o'clock already and we've got a big night ahead of us.'

'Always the optimist, aren't you?' Tom pulled his ready-bag out of the back of the wagon. 'I'm the one with the big night ahead. The most you've got to look forward to is a couple of pints with the lads, then falling asleep on the sofa watching *Hollyoaks* on catch-up.'

'Mate, you're wrong there.' Gavin shouldered his own ready-bag and headed for the door. 'In fact, I intend to have a very big night with all the money I'll be collecting later.'

20

The rest of Blue team arrived over the next forty minutes and spent a couple of hours cleaning their weapons and sorting out their kit. There was a quick debrief in the crew room with Major Ashton, though not the full post-mortem, which wouldn't take place until the next day.

Tom headed for the washroom. He'd towelled himself dry and was dressed before most of the rest were out of the showers. His Omega Planet Ocean told him it was fast approaching 20.00 hours. He weighed it for a moment in his hand. Lots of guys in the Regiment had one, but it never failed to give him a kick. The offer of a special edition watch had been made by the company a couple of years earlier, the sort of deal usually reserved for Formula One teams and Premiership clubs. It was a good marketing ploy, and the Regiment guys got a great watch at a discount.

The Regiment version looked like a regular Planet Ocean, until you turned it over. The engraved case-back had a winged dagger in the centre, '22 Special Air Service' around the circle, and the first two letters of the wearer's surname, followed by two digits indicating the year he'd passed Selection, then the last four digits of his army number. On the case side, between the shoulders, he could still read,

'ALWAYS A LITTLE FURTHER', taken from the SAS pilgrim poem.

He snapped it onto his wrist, grabbed his motorcycle helmet from his locker and was heading across the car park to his BMW when he heard a shout from behind him. He looked back and saw Ashton come out of the team office and hurry across the car park.

'You want me, Boss?' Tom started to put his helmet on. He was on a mission.

'Where are you going?'

'I promised to meet Delphine and –' he glanced at his watch again '– I'm already running late.'

'You've not forgotten it's Fight Night, have you?'

'Oh, shit.' The helmet started to lift away from his head. 'Yeah, I had, I'm afraid.'

'I haven't,' Ashton said. 'Not after what happened last year.'

Tom nodded. 'So you'll be looking for a bit of payback . . .'

'I'd hate to be the cause of a domestic. But I think you owe me that much.' Ashton adopted just the right note of sarcasm.

Tom bristled. 'The thing is, I haven't seen Delphine in weeks, what with that team job in Yemen and a few other things, and I had to stand her up again last night because of Hampstead.'

Ashton shrugged. 'But you're on the list, Tom. You can't back down now, can you? Besides, I've been training.'

Tom stared at him for a moment, weighing up his options. He came to the conclusion he had very few. 'You'd better go and get ready, then, hadn't you, Boss?'

Ashton gave a triumphant smile, then turned on his heel and headed back towards the office. He called over his shoulder, 'Stand by to be on your arse within a minute.'

Tom fumbled in his pocket for his phone.

It rang twice before she answered. 'Tom?'

'Yeah . . . I'm . . . er . . . back.'

'Perfect timing. I've just finished work and I've booked a—'

Tom had to cut in to minimize the disappointment. 'I'm going to be a while longer, I'm afraid. I've just been reminded it's Fight Night.'

'What? Again? I've booked a table and . . .' Her voice tailed away. He couldn't tell if she was angry or tears were welling.

'It's only once a year. I forgot about it . . . but I can't get out of it. I'm on the list. I said I'd fight. I'm really, really sorry, but I can't let the team down. It doesn't mean—'

'The mistress always wins,' she snapped. Her voice rose an octave as she tried to control herself. 'Tom, this is important to me . . . to us. I need to talk to you, tonight.'

'You will – I *will* be there. It's just that I have to do this first. I was looking forward to seeing you so much I forgot I'd committed to this. I'm so sorry . . .'

Delphine's tone stayed calm. 'There is no need to be sorry. I blame myself for being stupid enough to think that this time you actually would turn up when you said you would.'

'No, it's my fault, Delphine, and I will make it up to you later, I promise. But I really do have to go. It won't take long. I won't stay – I'll come straight over. I can get this done and dusted in less than an hour.'

'And just how will you manage to do that?'

'I'll throw the fight,' he said. 'I'll never hear the end of it from the lads, but I could be on my way out of the door again within an hour at the very most.'

Delphine's voice showed her surprise, despite herself. 'You would really do that for me?'

'Absolutely. Why don't you cancel the table, head home and chill out with a glass of wine and I'll come straight round to the flat?'

'You promise?' she said.

'I promise.'

Delphine thought about it for a moment. 'All right, then. I'll be waiting. But not for too long. Don't let me down again, Tom, please.'

21

Tom pressed the red button and headed for the sergeants' mess. The bar was packed. He pushed his way through and bought himself and Gavin a beer, then walked through to the next room. A giant pink and blue inflatable bouncy castle was set up in the middle of the floor, the kind normally used for kids' parties. A crowd of men had already gathered around it, claiming the best vantage-points, and there were cheers and a few jeers as Tom came in.

The draw for who fought whom had been made four days ago. There were two general teams: the officers' mess versus the sergeants' mess. Anyone could put their name down, and if there weren't enough takers the CO and the RSM would nominate volunteers. They had the right to choose because they also had to fight, along with each of the four Sabre Squadron commanders. Their job was to lead from the front.

Fight Nights were more than a social event: they were an important part of producing good soldiers. Of course the men had to be aggressive, and all of them were or they wouldn't have passed Selection. But there was more to it than that. They were bonding exercises between the two management groups of the Regiment.

The officers would normally serve a three-year tour before

returning to their parent unit and might go back for one more tour. The continuity of the Regiment lay with the sergeants and warrant officers. As with any infantry battalion, they held the experience of the unit.

Many things happened in an army that civilians like Delphine could not understand. On the face of it, Fight Nights looked dangerous or stupid and immature, but they had evolved over many years and always had a rationale. They built respect through shared physical pain and endurance. Maybe that was why Tom always put himself up for it, or maybe he just liked to fight. Maybe it was both. He could never work it out, but that didn't matter. The only thing that did was that he was stepping up to the plate, not letting anyone down, including himself. Even if, tonight, he was going into the ring to lose.

Almost every man had a stack of cans of beer near at hand, and the air was already heavy with alcohol fumes. A warrant officer was sitting at the table on the far side of the room, in front of a whiteboard with a marker dangling from it on a piece of string. Tom and Ashton, his squadron commander, were up first.

'Wouldn't have it any other way, Lenny,' Tom said, slapping his money on the table.

Bryce was right behind him. 'I won't be going home empty-handed.' He pulled his T-shirt over his head, flexed his pecs and pointed to the names of his six kids tattooed on his chest. 'My babies need new shoes.'

'You'd be better off spending your winnings on getting the snip, mate, and doing humanity a favour.' Keenan wasn't fighting. He never did, not wanting to lose his beach-bum good looks. 'And just think of the money you'd save on nappies.'

'And tattoos,' Jockey said, as he strolled over to join them.

Bryce was still shuddering at the thought of a vasectomy and had covered his groin with his hands. 'I'll never have the snip,' he said. 'Even if we have sixty kids. Every sperm is sacred to me – and the missus. And I don't mind admitting that there's one thing that scares me shitless. I tell you now, I'd rather play Russian roulette with a revolver with no empty chambers than let someone loose on my balls with a scalpel.'

'Haven't you heard, Bryce?' Keenan opened his arms wide and slapped his hands together. 'They do it with two bricks these days.'

'Yeah, yeah.' Bryce had heard it all before. 'I know. *Does it hurt?* Only if you get your thumbs trapped. Jesus, Keenan, I know Cornwall's fucking backward, but you'd think there'd be a few jokes going around there that were less than a hundred years old.' He glanced over to the doorway and broke into a broad smile. 'Look out, it's show time. Here come the Ruperts.'

Led by Ashton, a group of officers walked in as the sound-track from *Rocky* burst out of the wall speakers. The guests were greeted by a rousing chorus of boos. The NCOs pelted them with empty beer cans, but Ashton and the others ducked and dodged them as they headed for the bouncy castle. Last year Fight Night had been held in the officers' mess and their guests had had a similar reception. No one knew why it happened; it just always did.

The RSM jumped onto a chair. 'Gentlemen!'

The *Rocky* fanfare died and everyone shut up, as you did when the RSM wanted you to, no matter who you were.

'Before anything else, I want to give you a sit-rep on Davy. He's stable. He's lost some muscle mass on his left thigh, but he should be back with B Squadron by the end of the tour.'

There was a loud roar of approval and applause. The RSM let it run for a few seconds more. 'OK, listen in! We welcome the officers' mess for the evening and we welcome the chance once more to kick their arse!'

There were cheers and boos from the two groups before the RSM quietened them again. 'Remember, five minutes of hard, aggressive fighting but nothing between the legs or in the eyes. And no biting. Apart from that, the first man down and can't get up loses – or the first man to go down three times. Winners can elect to continue fighting the next fight if they wish. It means double points for their team. Who's first?' He turned to check the board. 'OK, Buckingham and Mr Ashton.'

Rocky kicked out from the speakers once more as Ashton headed for the castle, punching his gloves together like a pro. They were boxing-bag gloves, compact and hard. Until a few years ago they'd used martial arts gloves, but exposed fingers meant the fighters could grab each other. This wasn't as much fun to watch as punching, and the fights were over much quicker.

Ashton bounced into the castle arms to the roar of the officers' team.

Tom grinned. 'You won't catch me napping this time.'

Gavin slapped Tom on the back as he stepped towards the fight. 'Mate, get in there and get among it, but keep a bit back for a few more scraps later on. I've just bet Jockey a thousand quid you'll last at least five fights.'

Tom stopped in his tracks, drawing instant jeers from the officers. 'Giving up already?'

'You're joking, aren't you, Gav?'

'No, mate, deadly serious. Why not? Last year you saw off four before getting dropped. It's the easiest money I'll ever make.'

Jockey looked him over like a farmer at an auction mart assessing a steer. 'Hope you're not going to let yourself down, Posh Lad,' he said. 'You're not looking in such good shape. I'd say you've put on a few pounds.'

'Trouble is, Jockey,' Tom said, 'every time I shag your girl-friend, she gives me a biscuit.'

'Very funny, Posh Lad.' Jockey liked that one and looked forward to using it on someone else. 'Let's just see if you're still laughing after I've punched your lights out later on.' He started a headbanger's version of 'The Eton Boating Song' as Tom strode towards the bouncy castle to the cheers of the sergeants' mess. Jockey's shouts joined the barrage of support and advice.

'Sort out the fucking Rupert, Tom.'

'Deck the dickhead.'

'Make sure the only way he'll be able to clean his teeth is by sticking a toothbrush up his arse.'

Tom stepped onto the bouncy castle and faced Ashton, all business.

Ashton put on his most confident smile for his supporters, then turned back to face Tom and gave him his best stab at a thousand-yard stare. 'This year is going to be my year!' The officers roared their support.

Tom was barely aware that Ashton had spoken at all. Every ounce of him was focused on what he was about to do. He saw a bead of sweat trickle down Ashton's nose and a vein pulsing at his temple. By contrast, Tom's pulse was barely above normal and his breathing slow. His mind was clear of all distracting thoughts. All he felt was a cold, calculated, almost clinical desire to get on with the job. Ashton did not exist for him as an individual, merely as an opponent to be destroyed as quickly and ruthlessly as possible. Afterwards they would have a beer and talk about any rubbish that came into their heads.

The camp's Grenadian physical training instructor was the ref. He was suffering from advanced alopecia, and the clumps of tight curly hair he had left looked like the island group he came from. That was what he said, anyway. The PTI got them to touch gloves. Then they were fighting. Within the blink of an eye, while Ashton was still going into his fighting stance, Tom had leaped in, landed a heavy punch on the Boss's face, and followed it with three more, his fists beating a quick-fire tattoo.

People like Tom had the ability to keep totally in control and still think clearly when the adrenalin was pumping. It had nothing to do with bravery. It had to do with being in control of his heartbeat when it would be natural to flap big-time, and that only came from long hours of training.

Stress actually improved Tom's performance. It always had. Even at Eton, Tom had stood out on the rugby pitch when the pressure was on. Most people's heart rate rose with their adrenalin level – all good stuff when you needed flight-or-fight to get you out of trouble. However, there was an optimal state of arousal – when a heart rate was between 115 and 145 beats per minute. Anything above that and the body stopped being able to control what it was doing because the brain started to shut down.

Most people then became as enraged as an angry dog – which was why some wet and soiled themselves in a firefight. Their heartbeat was so fast – 175 or above – that the brain told itself that control of the bowels and bladder was no longer an essential activity: it had bigger problems. It needed to protect the body it was in so had to keep focused on the challenge. It made all its muscles go as hard as armour to limit bleeding if its body was zapped. But all that effort, which took less than a second to cut in, made it even more clumsy, stupid and help-less in a fight.

That was why people found it hard to call 999 with their heart rate at warp speed and their co-ordination in decline. The brain forgot the number, or the eyes couldn't see the digits on the phone, or the finger didn't connect before its owner was screaming into the mouthpiece and flapping even more when no one answered.

With barely a pause, he followed the action with two hooks to Ashton's body, then a savage uppercut.

There was a roar from the crowd as Ashton caught air, toppled backwards, bounced off the wall of the bouncy castle and rebounded once more onto the castle's rubber floor.

Tom ignored the noise from around the ring, still all busi-ness, his eyes fixed on his opponent as he stumbled to his feet. Ashton might have gone down once, but he had to go down twice more or be knocked out before his fight was over. Tom used Ashton's momentum against him, bluffing to throw a punch, then swaying to one side, like a matador, as Ashton rushed him, and swivelling to land four quick punches into his kidneys.

As Ashton swung round to face him again, Tom let go one final, brutal punch, delivered with all the force he could put behind it. It smashed into Ashton's nose, crunching bone and gristle, and sending a spray of blood and sweat arcing upwards. Tom turned his back and headed for the castle sides to rest, knowing that Ashton would not be getting up any time soon.

A roar from the crowd exploded in his ears. He was back in the real world.

Gavin shouted Tom's name and rubbed his thumb and fingers together in the 'money' gesture.

It took him no more than twenty seconds and a swift flurry of punches, to dispose of the next officer, a young captain, who had only been in the Regiment for a few weeks and was so fresh-faced he looked like he still had down on his cheeks – but Tom knew the competition would be much tougher as the evening wore on and he began to come up against the LEs. They liked to fight as much as Tom did.

22

Delphine put on the same green tunic dress she'd worn for their first date. She'd made supper, but an hour had passed, then two, and there was still no sign of him. She spooned out some food and reheated it in the microwave, but after pushing it around the plate for ten minutes she left most of it untouched and threw the rest into the bin. And then she went and changed into jeans.

She checked her watch yet again and, even though she knew she was being ridiculous, lifted the phone to make sure it was working. As soon as she heard the dialling tone, she put it back on the hook, afraid she might miss his call. When she heard the door rattle a few moments later she ran to answer it, then tried to conceal her disappointment when she saw it was Moira coming in from work.

'I finished early,' Moira said. 'I left the new guy to do the last couple of hours. The place is as dead as a doornail, only half a dozen guests and the boys are all somewhere else – apparently it's Fight Night.' She saw Delphine's expression. 'Ah, you know that already . . .'

Delphine nodded, not trusting herself to speak.

Moira opened a bottle of chardonnay and poured her a big glass. 'Here,' she said. 'You look like you need this even more than I do.'

'Not for me,' Delphine said. 'But don't let me stop you.'

Moira pulled the glass towards her. 'Wish I had your will-power.' She swallowed a mouthful of wine, then studied Delphine over the rim of the glass. 'So, what are you going to do?'

'What I should have done six months ago, and what I planned to do tomorrow.' Delphine stood up, full of intent. 'I'm going home. Tonight. I will not wait any more.' She felt a tear trickle down her cheek as she said it, and angrily brushed it away.

Moira put her glass down and hugged Delphine to her. 'Maybe it's for the best,' she said. 'He won't change. I told you that way back. None of them ever do. He'll say he will, of course, and he'll promise you the earth to get you to stay, but the next time the Regiment – or one of his mates – so much as whistles, he'll be straight off again.' She broke off, em-barrassed, and looked at her watch. 'There's still time to catch the last London train. You could be in Paris before the morning. Come on, I'll book a cab and help you pack.'

Delphine pointed to the bag standing beside the bedroom door. 'No need.'

Ten minutes later a horn sounded and a taxi pulled up outside. Delphine hesitated on the doorstep, looking up and down the street.

'Don't fool yourself. He's not coming.'

Delphine knew that Moira's anger was finally getting the better of her, but she found in it an echo of her own.

'He had his chance, Delphine, and he blew it. It'll be hard, I know, but you deserve better than this. A lot better.' She gave her a hug. 'I'll miss you, but I'll come and see you once you get settled.'

The cab driver sounded his horn again.

Looking back through the rear window as they drove off, Delphine could see Moira, a hand still raised in farewell, standing alone in the deserted street.

Delphine caught the train to Newport, where she could change for the London Paddington express – the last of the day – with five minutes to spare. She put her bag in the rack, then stood in the doorway of the carriage, looking back along the platform, half hoping that, even at this late stage, Tom might appear. But a few moments later the door slid shut and the train pulled away into the darkness.

23

Tom had won four fights so far. He downed a jug of water, most of it spilling over his chest and onto the bouncy-castle floor. The next bout would be the hardest.

'Satnav' – but not to his face – was an LE (late entry) officer. He'd risen to the rank of WO2 and had been G Squadron's sergeant major before being offered a commission. There were three types of LE: angry, chilled and careerist. Satnav was in the first category. He'd been angry since the army had confiscated a necklace he'd made for his sister while sailing back with the Task Force from the Falklands. He hadn't understood why it wasn't right for a young guardsman to cut off the ears of dead Argentinians to make a necklace, no matter who it was for.

He'd got his nickname after getting geographically embarrassed while driving one of the team's Range Rovers from Hereford to a meeting with the Greater Manchester Police. He'd taken a wrong turn around Birmingham and landed up in Sheffield. No one would have known about it had the Range Rover not been pulled in by the very force he was supposed to be visiting while he was doing 120 mph down the motorway to try to rectify his mistake. They'd let him off as soon as they saw his ID, but by then the damage was done.

The officers always kept Satnav as the trump card in their pack. They'd been holding him back tonight until Tom was exhausted, and now he was. But there was one more fight to go for Gavin to win his money. And if he did, maybe he'd start buying his own clothes.

For reasons that nobody except Gavin and Mrs Gavin fully understood, she'd piled up all his possessions in the garden one evening and set fire to them. Gavin had been left with the clothes he'd stood up in, and was too tight to go down town and buy some more. His solution was simple. He was Tom's size. What was the problem?

The problem was: that had been five months ago. And he still hadn't opened his wallet. He hadn't bought any food for the house either. Tom had let it go. Gavin still had to pay for a mortgage, two cars, and the three-thousand-pound vet bill that had arrived after Mrs G's two dogs had fallen off a mountain ledge in the Brecon Beacons. Gavin had taken them on a weekend tab. His story was that they were so excited to be out and about they hadn't been looking where they were going. Mrs G hadn't bought that story for a minute, and had started building the pyre.

Gavin had got home just in time to watch his life go up in smoke. His only possession to survive was his Stravinsky CD. And that was only because he'd taken it down to the ranges to rip it a new spin hole.

Satnav could still bench-press his own weight, and for a man of his size that was no small achievement. Tom knew that if the fight got to close quarters Satnav would crush the life out of him. His only chance was to use his speed of thought, foot and hand. If that didn't work, he'd just try to keep off the floor.

Gavin seemed to read his thoughts. He shot an anxious glance through the castle window as Tom poured more water down his neck. 'Mate, old Satnav, he's a strong fucker, but I reckon he's hitting the weights too much and not doing enough on the speed bag.' He took another swig of his beer. 'Mate, we've got a lot riding on this one. The sooner I get some cash together, the sooner I'll be buying my own gear and the sooner I'll be out of your house. What more can I tell you?'

'He might be hitting the weights, but he's still a street fighter, like me. I'll have to keep on my toes for this one.'

Gavin spluttered into his beer. 'Excuse me? You? A *street* fighter? What part of the Malvern 'hood did you work, bro?'

A chorus of cheers and groans greeted Satnav's progress towards the castle.

'Fuck me . . .' Gavin breathed, as he saw the size of him. 'I've got a grand riding on this . . .'

'No pressure, then.' Tom handed him the empty jug.

'Mate, Satnav thinks he's hard, but he's a big pussycat really.'

Satnav was now close enough to listen in. He bared his teeth in something like a smile. 'You just keep mouthing off, Gavvers. Soon as I've finished with His Lordship here I'll be loading up and putting another round into that leg of yours.'

For the first time that night, Tom didn't have a height and weight advantage over his opponent – and Satnav was as quick to the punch. As soon as they'd touched gloves he landed a brain-rattler on the side of Tom's head, then switched downstairs with a hook that thudded into his ribs. He blocked Tom's counter with his biceps, then moved in, grappling with him and narrowly missing with a head butt as Tom tried to wrestle his arms free. They fell together and lay for a moment, still trading punches. The PTI signalled them up.

Through his adrenalin ear-muffs, Tom heard Gavin shouting, 'Come on, Posh Lad . . .' For the first time all night, there was a note of anxiety in his voice.

As the two fighters clambered to their feet and the PTI wiped down the floor with bar mats, Jockey gave Tom two thumbs up. 'Keep going as you are, big man!'

As the two fighters touched gloves again, Tom dummied a left hook, and as Satnav shifted his weight, swaying away from the expected punch, Tom hit him with a round-arm right. Satnav saw it coming at the last moment and began to duck. The shot took him high on the temple but he still staggered at the impact and Tom was on him at once, raining in punches until another big right hand put his opponent down.

Satnav wasn't finished. He launched himself forward in a rugby tackle from his hands and knees, but Tom saw him coming. Stooping low, he threw a right hand that had every ounce of his strength behind it. It smashed into the corner of Satnav's eye and the combined force of the punch and his own momentum jerked the other man's head around as if he'd been hit by a brick.

Tom half turned away, heading for the side of the castle. But Satnav still wasn't done. His eye already swollen and closing, he had enough presence of mind to grab Tom's ankle and jerk his feet from under him. Even as he fell, Tom managed to land another short arm right to Satnav's face, then dropped on him with his knees, driving the air from his lungs.

Satnav struggled to recover, but it wasn't happening. Tom rose to his feet and the PTI closed down the fight. Tom's supporters bayed their approval, and those with losing bets booed and jeered as Tom held both hands down for Satnav to grip and pull himself up.

They hugged and Satnav held Tom's right hand up in the air in congratulation. They both exited the castle and Tom accepted the can of beer that someone pushed into his hand and slapped Gavin on the back. 'I've got to go.'

He pulled his T-shirt over his head, grabbed his jacket and ran for the exit. His Omega told him it was just before 02.00 hours.

'Shit.'

By the time the door had slammed behind him, he was halfway across the car park. The Beamer was resting on its kick-stand. As he jumped onto the bike, Tom reflected, not for the first time, that the Lines was the only place in Hereford – probably the only place in Britain – where you could leave a fourteen-thousand-pound motorbike with the keys in the ignition and still find it there when you got back. He fired up the engine and rocketed off into the night.

24

It was nine miles to Delphine's place and Tom made it in seven minutes. The place was in darkness but he rang the bell and banged on the door. After a moment a light went on and he heard footsteps on the stairs. Moira opened the door, her hair mussed and her eyes gluey with sleep. She looked Tom over, taking in his cut and bruised face, his hair plastered to his scalp with sweat.

She made no move to stand aside and let him in. 'You do know what time it is, don't you?' she said. 'I'm on early shift tomorrow.'

'Yeah, I know, I know, sorry,' he said. 'So ... where's Delphine?'

'She's gone.' Moira couldn't keep the satisfaction from her voice.

'What do you mean? Gone where?'

'Gone home.'

'Home to France?'

'No, home to the Outer fucking Hebrides. Of course home to France. That's where she comes from, isn't it?' Moira was enjoying every moment. 'And if you'd ever turned up on time or spent more than ten seconds talking to her before you started shagging her, you might have known what was going on.'

'Why . . . what is going on? You mean she's seeing someone else?'

'Don't be even dumber than you look, Tom. Of course she's not.'

'So what the fuck is going on, then?'

'You'll have to ask her that, won't you?' Moira said. 'It's for her to tell you, not me. My guess is she's had enough of hanging around waiting for you to turn up.'

'When's she coming back?'

'Don't you get it? Have all those punches to the head scrambled the few brain cells you've got left? Not ever. She's bought a one-way ticket on the Eurostar, Tom. That's it. It's over.'

'Fuck me,' Tom said.

Moira leaned against the doorframe and looked him over again. 'I could do, I suppose . . .'

25

London
Saturday, 10 September
05.37 hrs

Laszlo put on the grey overalls over his other clothes while the sky was still dark. With a battered peaked cap pulled down low over his glasses, he took a careful look up and down the street. Satisfied, he closed and locked the shop door and walked away, his pace unhurried.

He stopped at the newspaper stand outside the corner shop. Every paper carried its own spin on what had happened the day before.

An al-Qaeda attack.

An al-Qaeda cell rounded up as they prepared bombs for the Olympic opening ceremony.

Drug-dealers.

Iranian sleeper cells preparing bombs to activate if we went to war over their nuclear programme.

The one thing all the stories had in common was that Laszlo wasn't mentioned – and the SAS were.

Manual workers on early shifts were pouring down the steps to catch their trains into the city but, seeing the CCTV cameras monitoring the station entrances and platforms, Laszlo did not follow them. Hands in pockets, he kept walking, just another drab, anonymous figure in the grey early-morning light.

Keeping to the side streets, he made his way slowly east, past Chalk Farm and Camden Town, then turned down a street flanking a new industrial estate. Until a few years earlier this area had been a warren of crumbling, almost Dickensian lanes and warehouses, bounded on all sides by railway tracks, but it was now in the throes of redevelopment. The old buildings had been torn down and glass-and-steel mini skyscrapers were rising out of the rubble beside towering cranes.

At the far end of the industrial estate the road crossed over the Regent's Canal. Laszlo's pace slowed and he glanced behind him, then stopped and rested his arms on the parapet of the bridge. He reached inside his overalls and slipped out his revolver. He regretted having to give it up. He always felt uneasy without a weapon of some kind. It sank at once. He knew it would be in good company. The police called London's waterways the biggest armoury in Britain.

He walked on, squinting into the low light of the rising sun.

26

Twenty miles to the west, Tom was burning his way through the motorway traffic and trying to make himself heard above the throaty rasp of the German engine as he talked to Gavin via the Bluetooth connection in his helmet.

'Of course I've tried her mobile. It's just going straight to voicemail.'

'Keep trying,' Gavin said. 'I'm sure she'll pick up.'

'I don't think so, mate. She's closed down comms so I can't try and persuade her to change her mind.'

'What are you going to do?'

'Try and persuade her to change her mind, of course. So, have you got the manifest? Which train is she on?'

'I hope you know I could get binned for this.' Gavin was in the office, tapping away on the team's secure PC. It was normally used for checking women's number-plates to find out if they'd been bullshitting during the chat-up phase.

'You did it for Jockey last year and you didn't get binned then.'

'True enough. But no one found out about that and, anyway, Jockey wasn't on thirty-minute standby at the time.'

The Blue team was on thirty-minute standby for the next month. None of the team members was allowed to leave

Hereford: they had to be back in the Lines within half an hour if COBRA pressed the button. If your call-out alarm went off on your belt or bedside cabinet and you didn't get there on time, you were in the binning zone.

'Relax,' Tom said. 'I'll be back in H before Ashton's finished having his cuts and bruises treated. He won't even know I've been away. And you owe me big-time after the wad I put in your pocket last night.'

'Bastard.'

There was a pause as Gavin worked his way through the Eurostar passenger listings. Like airline passenger manifests, they were routinely circulated to all anti-terrorist forces. 'Got it,' he said. 'You're going to have to motor some to get there in time. She's on the eight twenty-six. Coach Eight, seat thirty-two.'

'Sort a ticket for me, will you? I don't want just to wave at her from the champagne bar.'

'Sure.' Gavin took a deep breath. 'But, mate, for fuck's sake, don't be stuck on that train when the doors close or that'll be both of us packed up, kicked out and down the road, looking for a new job.'

'No drama. I'll be back. Have I ever let you down before?'

'You want the list?'

Tom had already broken the connection. The engine note rose to a howl as he twisted the throttle to the stops. A Jag was hogging the fast lane, so he swerved left and right to overtake it on the inside.

27

A hundred metres ahead, between the red-brick bunker of the British Library and the Gothic pinnacles of the Renaissance Hotel, Laszlo could see the rush-hour traffic building up along Euston Road. Closer to him, a line of black taxis waited for trade, their idling diesel engines adding to the smog hanging in the still, cool air. Laszlo hung on his heels for a moment, eyeing the CCTV cameras over the station entrance. Then he stepped back into the shadow of a doorway.

He took out his mobile phone, inserted a fresh SIM card and sent a brief text. No more than a minute later he heard the ping of a response. He glanced down at the incoming message:

Clear sailing – will let you know if you get compromised.

Only now would he walk towards the great arched and glazed roof of St Pancras, knowing that if he was spotted and flagged up to all departments of security this country had to bear down on him, someone was covering his back and would warn him, just as they had done in Hampstead the day before.

Keeping his pace measured, he entered the Victorian brick and twenty-first-century glass monolith through the northern entrance and walked straight through the concourse, past the domestic platforms, the shops and cafés, following the signs to the toilets.

A cleaner, in almost identical grey overalls to the ones Laszlo was wearing, was mopping the floor beside the urinals. The grey plastic cart holding his materials stood at the end of the row of washbasins, and the yellow 'Male Cleaner in Washroom' cone stood proudly in the middle of the walkway. Laszlo moved to the far basin and watched the cleaner's reflection as he pushed open the end cubicle and began mopping inside it.

Whatever he was singing to himself, it was in Polish. But the cleaner obviously liked his job. Eventually he emerged and returned to his trolley.

Laszlo approached him with a smile to match the song. 'Excuse me – the disabled toilet, it's a terrible mess. Can you come?'

He led the obliging Pole towards the larger, radar-controlled disabled doors and stopped by the nearest. The Pole mumbled to himself and reached for the key fob beside the ID card that hung from a red nylon lanyard around his neck. The fluorescent light glinted off a very shiny wedding ring on his left hand. The door clicked open. Laszlo stood aside to let him in, then followed.

Laszlo gave the man no time to ask, 'What mess?' He closed the door behind him, locked it and, with the full force of his hurtling body, grabbed the cleaner's head and rammed it against the wall.

There was a dull thud as his skull made contact with the brickwork. He staggered, his hands scrabbling to protect himself. Laszlo grabbed the hair at the nape of his neck, pounded the man's forehead on the edge of the washbasin, then lowered him to the ground, knelt astride him and wrung out what was left of the newlywed's life.

He unclipped his victim's lanyard, rinsed two spots of blood off his overalls, then exited the toilet. Locking the door from the outside with an Allen key, he fished an 'Out of Order' sign from the cleaning cart and hung it on the handle.

Laszlo tossed his glasses into the rubbish in the cart as he pushed it back into the concourse.

He headed for the Eurostar terminal. Armed police and extra security personnel were on patrol wherever he looked, but he steered a careful course as far from them and the CCTV cameras as possible. With his baseball cap pulled low over his eyes, his head down and his gaze fixed on the cleaning cart, he avoided eye contact with the passengers scurrying around him.

As he moved towards International Departures, he brushed past a strikingly beautiful, dark-haired girl talking French into a mobile, who had collected her ticket from the self-service machine, stopped to buy gifts from a clothes shop, and was now wheeling her bag towards the security gates, a Starbucks coffee in her free hand.

Laszlo stopped his rubbish cart next to the bins, just short of Security and beneath a sign listing the items forbidden on Eurostar trains –

explosives, replica or toy guns, ice axes, butane gas, lighter fuel, fireworks, knives, scissors, household cutlery and hypodermic syringes.

Under the pretext of emptying the bin, Laszlo sorted swiftly through its contents. He picked up a discarded grooming kit, containing a razor, hairbrush and comb. The razor held only a small fixed blade, but it would have to do. Then he saw the corner of a box protruding from a Harrods bag: a set of kitchen knives, discarded before passing through Security by a passenger who was evidently too dumb to realize they would not be allowed on the train and too rich to worry about throwing them away. Laszlo flipped open the box and tested the edge of one of the blades with his thumb. It was razor sharp.

He dropped the box back into his cart and moved on. He felt more at ease now that he had a weapon. A blade wouldn't save him if he were compromised, but it would allow him to go down fighting. He'd take as many with him as he could.

Laszlo didn't worry about dying. He never had. Death was

the only certainty in life. The only questions were where, when and how. Infirm and in prison wasn't the way to end things: he'd be defiant to the last.

He pushed his cart towards the security screens reserved for Eurostar personnel and utility workers. The lens of a CCTV camera glinted high on the wall ahead. He kicked a piece of crumpled paper ahead of him, then stooped to pick it up. Keeping his head down and his face obscured, he appeared to scan the floor for other debris, his gaze also taking in the harassed security guards beside the X-ray machines and the streams of passengers shuffling through the security gates in their stockinged feet.

Laszlo chose his moment. He pushed his cart through, holding up his ID for inspection. No one paid him the slightest attention. The more menial the employee, the more invisible he became. Laszlo glanced at the departures board and headed towards the lift to the platforms. The pretty French girl pulled her case towards the escalators.

As the lift ascended, Laszlo opened the box of kitchen knives, palmed the longest and slipped it inside his sleeve. The doors opened and he squeezed past a group of Japanese tourists posing for photographs in front of the bronze sculpture of an embracing couple. The wheels of the cart rattled along the platform towards the Paris train.

He walked past the guard standing at the entrance to Coach Eight – the man was too busy running an appreciative eye over the French girl as she boarded to acknowledge his presence. Laszlo parked the cart in the centre of the platform and made for Coach Seven instead. A Eurostar attendant stepped down to intercept him. 'You're too late, mate. We're boarding. All cleaning personnel should be off the train by now.'

Laszlo shrugged apologetically. 'I've left my supplies in the toilet. If I don't get them back I'll be sacked. I'll only be a moment.'

The attendant hesitated. 'Oh, all right – but be quick about it, for heaven's sake. We're due to depart in five minutes.'

Laszlo gave him a grateful smile and stepped up into the

carriage. He went straight to the Disabled toilet and locked the door behind him. He took off his cap, stripped off his overalls and dumped them in the rubbish bin. He washed his face and hands and checked his reflection in the mirror. Satisfied, he nodded to himself. The man staring back at him looked like just another anonymous business executive on his way to Paris.

28

The Eurostar attendant had remained on the platform by the entrance to the carriage, but was growing increasingly anxious as the minutes ticked by. He glanced towards the rear of the train, where the dispatcher was chatting to the guard and chivvying the last few passengers as they hurried along the platform.

The attendant hesitated for a few more moments, then boarded the train. There was no sign of the cleaner, but the toilet was occupied. He knocked, waited, then knocked again. There was no response from within.

On the other side of the door, Laszlo stood motionless, the kitchen knife in his hand. He heard a rattle of keys and then a faint metallic click. 'What the hell do you think—'

The man never completed his sentence. Laszlo seized his hair, dragged him inside and kicked the door shut. Tightening his grip, he forced the man's chin down towards his chest and drew the blade across his throat. He dropped the knife to the floor and clamped his fingers around the man's jugular, stopping the blood spurting and covering their clothes. 'Stay calm. Don't struggle,' he murmured. 'It's too late . . . You have lost. Accept . . . just accept it. Think of your family. Think pleasant thoughts . . .'

The attendant's eyes bulged, but whether he was soothed by his killer's voice or too terrified to risk moving, he stopped struggling. Laszlo turned him around so that he was facing the toilet. Clamping his other hand on the back of the attendant's neck, he forced his face down, then released his grip on the jugular. At once, blood began pulsing into the bowl.

Laszlo felt the man's life ebbing from him. His head would soon begin to spin as his brain started to suffer from the lack of oxygen that his blood would normally provide.

Maintaining an iron grip, Laszlo held him there until the crimson stream faltered and stopped, then lowered his body to the floor. He went to the basin, rinsed the blood from his right hand with cold water, then stripped the man of his uniform.

29

Delphine walked down the aisle, looking for her seat. She put the presents for her niece and nephew into the luggage rack and was about to sit down when she saw a frail, white-haired man a few rows ahead of her struggling to lift his bag. 'Let me help you with that,' she said, taking it from him.

'Thank you. Just one of the joys of getting old, I'm afraid. I used to be as strong as a bull when I was young, but now I can barely turn the pages of my newspaper.' He gave her a wintry smile. 'The clockwork's running down, I suppose. And yet, do you know, the strange thing is I don't feel any different inside? In my mind I'm still the young buck I was all those years ago, but then I open my eyes and . . .' He paused. 'I'm sorry – as my daughter keeps telling me, I do have a tendency to ramble on . . .'

'You mustn't apologize,' Delphine said. 'I bet your daughter will miss you terribly while you're away. Are you staying in Paris or travelling on?'

'Staying in Paris,' he said. 'The first time I've been there in years.' He leaned towards her, a sparkle in his eye. He pointed to the bouquet of red roses, wrapped in cellophane, which he'd placed on the table in front of them. 'Don't laugh, but I'm on my way to meet a woman I haven't seen in forty years. I met her in Paris in 1967 – the Summer of Love.' He pointed to his bald head and gave a rueful smile. 'Not much of a long-haired hippie, these days, am I? Anyway, I fell in love with a Parisian girl. Giselle . . .'

'So beautiful!' Delphine sighed. 'Like the ballet . . .'

'We were . . .' he hesitated, searching for the right word '. . . very close. We lived together that winter in a commune on the Left Bank, but then all that peace and love went up in flames. You weren't even born in 1968, of course, but I'm sure you've heard of *les événements*. There was a real sense of revolution in the air. There were strikes, riots, running battles with the police – the smell of tear gas hung over the city for weeks. We argued a lot about politics – Giselle was a real firebrand, far more left-wing than me.' A look of sadness came into his eyes. 'After one big row, I'm sorry to say I ran away. I didn't have any money, or anywhere to go, but when I swallowed my stubborn pride and went back, Giselle had moved and no one knew where she had gone. I tried to find her, of course, but without success. In the end, after drifting around Paris for a few more weeks, I went back to England, cut my hair, got a job and began to settle down. In time I met another woman. We got married and had children and were happy together. Yet I never forgot Giselle . . .

'My wife died a few years ago, and strangely enough it was my daughter who persuaded me to go looking for her. In fact she tracked her down, through Facebook of all things. Giselle's widowed too, now, and I'm meeting her for lunch in Paris today. After that, who knows?'

He was lost in his thoughts for a while. Then he went on, 'You must think me a terrible old fool, pouring all this out to a complete stranger. I know it could so easily end in disappoint-ment and I'm trying not to get too excited about it . . .' he smiled '. . . but not very successfully, as you can see.'

Across the aisle from them a middle-aged businessman in a pinstriped suit breathed out heavily through his nose and refolded his newspaper in a way that managed to convey both irritation and impatience. The old man glanced at him, then looked back at Delphine. 'I'm sorry,' he said.

'I've taken up more than enough of your time already.'

She put a hand on his arm. 'Don't be sorry,' she said. 'I'm glad to have met you. It's a lovely story, and I really hope it has a happy ending for you.' She kissed him on the cheek and walked back down the carriage.

She settled herself in the seat by the window and sat listlessly turning the pages of a magazine. In the row in front of her, a mother with two young children was stowing her bags and answering a string of questions from her hyper-excited cherubic little boy. His chubby face and body suggested to Delphine that Disneyland came a close second to a diet of Happy Meals.

His sister was older, perhaps ten, and more curious about the world around her. While her mother was busy plugging in the Bluetooth attachment to the bottom of a new iPod to download *Toy Story 3* from her laptop, she knelt on her seat and pulled herself up so that she could look into the row behind her.

Delphine smiled as the child's face appeared above the back of the seat. 'Hello.'

'I'm going to Disneyland Paris,' she said, her expression serious.

'How wonderful,' Delphine said. 'You must be really looking forward to it.'

The little girl's face broke into a huge smile. 'We're going to stay in a hotel like a magic castle,' she said breathlessly, 'and see Woody and Buzz Lightyear and —'

'Come and sit down now, Rose,' her mother snapped, 'and drink your juice.' She turned to Delphine. 'I'm sorry,' she said. 'I hope she's not bothering you.'

'Not at all,' Delphine said. 'To be honest, I'm glad of the distraction. You look like you're going to have a busy few days. You'll probably need a holiday yourself by the time you've finished.'

'I know. My husband was supposed to be coming with us, but something cropped up at work, so now it's just the three of us. But we're getting used to that, aren't we, kids?'

She looked so forlorn as she said it that Delphine had to suppress the urge to give her a hug. 'Well,' she said, 'your children are lovely, a real credit to you. And if you want a bit of time to yourself, I'd be happy to babysit them for you. It would be no trouble – I need to get some practice in.' She stood up and held out her hand. 'I'm Delphine.'

'That's very kind of you,' she said. 'I'm Grace. You've already met Rose. And my son is called Daniel.'

He looked up at the mention of his name, gave Delphine a shy grin and went back to his colouring book. Grace studied Delphine for a moment, her gaze missing nothing, then gave her a sympathetic smile. 'And, Delphine, I hope everything works out well for you.'

'Is it that obvious?' Delphine found herself blushing. 'Thank you anyway.'

They were interrupted by an announcement from the guard. 'This is the eight twenty-six to Paris Gare du Nord International, calling at Ebbsfleet International and Paris. This train is now ready to depart.'

She flipped over a few more pages of her magazine as he repeated the announcement in French, then went back to staring out of the window, taking in her last sight of London for who knew how long? Hereford and Tom already felt a long way behind her. At least, that was what she told herself.

Tom loved her, she was sure of that, but Delphine had at last come to understand that, for all her obvious bitterness, Moira had been speaking no less than the truth when she had talked about the priorities of SAS men.

Tom was fiercely loyal to his mates, and Gavin in particular. He was like a brother to him. As Delphine had said to him one night, only half joking, 'If Gavin and I were both trapped in a burning building, you'd be carrying him out before you got round to rescuing me.'

Tom had laughed. 'What makes you think I'd come back for you at all?'

She'd asked Tom about his bond with Gavin a few times, but

he just said, 'We've been through a few tough times together and that makes you close,' then changed the subject.

She'd asked Gavin, too, one quiet night in the bar when Tom was away on an op. 'We've been mates a long time,' Gavin said. 'I'd trust Tom with my life. I know I can, because he's saved it for me in the past.'

'Can you tell me about it?' Delphine said, then saw his hesitation. 'No, forget it. I'm sorry I asked.'

'No, it's all right. It was a long time ago. There's still stuff I can't tell you, but I can give you some of it. We were in Afghanistan.'

'What's it like?' Delphine said.

'The country? Well, for a start it's quite beautiful—' He broke off, studied her expression, then burst out laughing. 'No, sorry, you thought I was getting all emotional? The mountains do look beautiful but the whole country's in complete shit state.' He shook his head at the memory. 'It's the boys from the Green Army – that's what we call the battalions – I feel really sorry for. They're supposed to be training the Afghans to take over security from them, but you can trust most of them as far as you can spit into the wind. When the boys go out on patrol, they have to have eyes front and side, watching for hostiles, and in the back of their heads as well in case one of the friendly forces decides to earn himself a bonus from the Taliban by slotting a couple of Brits.'

Delphine's expression made it immediately clear that she wasn't the slightest bit interested in the Green Army.

'Yeah, sorry, Delphine, I might have got carried away there for a moment . . .'

She'd thought it was more to do with avoidance than anything else, and had kept quiet so he'd finally had to fill the silence.

'There were four of us on a job in a border area, up near Pakistan. We were based with a US unit, and some of the Afghan National Army. It turned out a couple of them were Taliban infiltrators. They took their chance late one night when a lot of the guys were asleep. They threw grenades into a couple of containers, then went round with automatic weapons, shooting anyone they could find. They killed two of us, and nine regular army guys, before we killed them. I took a round.'

Gavin pointed at his leg.

'I was hit in the thigh. The round partially severed my femoral artery. There was blood spurting everywhere like a fountain. I was sure I was going to die. It doesn't take long when you have a gusher.

'Tom didn't have time for morphine so, while I screamed the place down, he just dug around in the wound with his fingers, found the artery, pinched it off to stop the bleeding and put a tourniquet on it until a Green medic turned up with clamps.

'I'd lost so much blood I was out of it, but he put me on his back and carried me to the landing zone under fire. It was raining rounds. I was flown out of there and the medics saved my leg, but it was Tom who saved my life.' He'd been staring at his hands as he spoke, barely aware of her presence, and he gave an embarrassed smile as he looked up and met her gaze. 'So . . . yeah . . .' he said. 'We're pretty close.'

'So am I going to have to save his life to get that close?' Delphine had asked.

He had smiled. 'No, I'd say you were pretty close already, wouldn't you?'

Now Delphine pushed the memory away and gave a weary shake of her head. Gavin had been wrong. Whatever Delphine might have felt for Tom, he had never seemed that close to her. Not close enough, anyway.

30

A black and grey BMW motorbike swung off the Euston Road to the accompaniment of squealing tyres and irate car horns, and roared up to the entrance of the Renaissance Hotel. Tom screeched to a halt and jumped off. Propping the bike on its kick-stand, he threw the keys and his helmet to the valet parking attendant. 'Tuck that away somewhere, would you, mate?' he said, pulling a twenty-pound note from his pocket and slapping it into the young man's palm.

'You *are* staying at the hotel, sir?'

'Sure,' Tom said, over his shoulder as he made for the door. 'I'm just checking in now. I'll let you know the room number in a couple of minutes.'

'But, sir, no one can ride a bike. Maybe you could . . .'

Tom wasn't listening. He disappeared into the hotel lobby. Once inside, he turned immediately right, ran through the bar and out on to the station concourse. The giant clock on the end wall was showing 8:17. He took the steps to the lower level two at a time, picked up his ticket from the self-service machine with the reference number Gavin had texted, almost tearing his hair out at the time it took, then sprinted through the crowd and up to the security barriers.

The security officer gave Tom a suspicious look. 'No luggage, sir?' he said.

'No, just me.' Tom treated him to his most engaging smile. 'And I'm running very late for my train, as usual . . .'

The security officer did not return it. He eyed Tom's rumpled hair, the sweat on his brow and his bruised and battered face. 'What happened?' he said.

'Training.' Tom pulled out his MoD ID card. 'Look, I've really got to catch the eight twenty-six.'

'Sorry,' the security officer said. 'That ID won't get you any favours today. We've got an alert on. So . . . shoes, belt and wallet in the tray . . . if you'd be so kind.'

Tom shot an agonized glance at the clock: 8:20. He whipped off his shoes and belt, threw them onto the conveyor-belt with his wallet, and walked through the security gate. He stuffed his wallet back into his pocket but kept his belt and shoes in his hand as he passed through French immigration, then sprinted to the escalator in his socks, and ran up it, elbowing a tourist aside.

'Hey, buddy, what makes you so goddamn important that you can't take your turn like the rest of us?'

Tom heard the dispatcher give a final blast on his whistle. Ignoring a warning shout, he lunged for the carriage as the door started to close, squeezed through the gap and stood in the lobby, chest heaving. The sweat dripped from his face onto the carpet as the door clunked shut behind him.

A few moments later, the Eurostar began to move. When he'd got his breath back and his kit on, Tom straightened up and scanned the length of the carriage. He spotted Delphine at once, sitting with her back to him and staring out of the window as they emerged from under the great glass roof into the morning sun. Her iPhone lay on the table in front of her. Tom pulled out his mobile and dialled her number as he walked quietly down the aisle.

31

As her phone began buzzing, Delphine leaned forward to check the caller ID. When she saw Tom's name, she gave a slow shake of her head, rejected the call and then switched off the phone.

'Do you really hate me that much?' Tom whispered in her ear. He winked at Rose and Daniel, then sat down facing her.

'What do you think?' she said. She knew where the marks on Tom's face had come from, the very thing that had kept him from her, but she still wanted to comfort him. It took all of her determination not to show any concern. 'I gave you one last chance to keep your word to me. And as usual the mistress won.'

'Please don't say that . . . Look, I'm sorry. And I'm here now to make it up to you.'

She shook her head. 'It's too late.' Her face sank into shadow as the train began its seven-mile run underground to Stratford.

'It's not too late. The train stops at Ebbsfleet. We can get off there and catch one straight back again.'

She shook her head. 'I'm not coming back.'

'Then at least let's get off at Ebbsfleet, have a coffee and talk things over. Just let me explain things and tell you how I feel. If you're still determined to go home when you've heard me out, you can just catch the next train.' He tried to read her expression, but she showed no sign of softening. 'Come on, Delphine, you can't end it this way. Come home with me now and we'll sort this out.'

'You don't get it, do you, Tom? I am going home. You could have saved yourself the journey. That's what I was going to tell you last night – if you'd bothered to turn up.'

'I came as soon as I could. Gavin had a problem and I had to help him out.'

'And that just proves the point. I – *we* – have a problem, too, but, as always, the Regiment and your mates took priority.' She paused. 'Anyway, none of that matters now. I'm going back to France.'

'And when did you decide this? You've never breathed a word about it until now.'

'You knew my contract was almost up,' she said.

'You've renewed it before. Why not again?'

'Because my career was just like us – not going anywhere fast.' She studied him for a moment. 'I was going to tell you last night, but when you didn't turn up, I just thought this way would be easier – for both of us.' She stared at him in silence. 'So I'm afraid you had a wasted journey, because my mind is made up. And what are you doing here anyway? You're supposed to be on thirty-minute standby, aren't you?'

He took her hand in his. 'I'd get binned if things kick off, but that's a risk I'll have to take. You're worth taking a few risks for.'

She looked at him, then gently disengaged her hand from his. 'It's a pity you didn't realize that earlier – but I'm sorry, Tom, it really is too late. It's a lovely gesture, but in the end, that's all it is.' She stared out of the window into the darkness of the tunnel, not even wanting to meet his gaze.

'This can't be the end of us, Delphine, it mustn't be. For God's sake, please – what do you want from me?'

'No, Tom, what do *you* want from *me*?'

It was the million-pound question, and he didn't have the answer.

Her eyes burned into him. 'You're on thirty-minute standby? Well, I know what it's like. I feel permanently on standby. If your mates and your Regiment give you a night off, you might get around to spending a few hours with me, but the rest of the time, I might as well not exist. And meanwhile, I'm putting my life on hold, in the vain hope that some day you might eventually get around to making me part of yours.'

'That's just not true.'

'I'm sorry, Tom. It is true. And unlike the Hereford girls, who'd do anything for a Man in Black, I don't need you or your precious Regiment.'

'Well, I need you.' He took a breath, really not wanting to know the answer to the question he was about to ask. 'Is there someone else?'

She looked back at him, then caught sight of Rose, watching her, wide-eyed, from the seat in front. 'I'll talk to you in a little while, *ma chérie* . . .' Delphine forced a smile, not wanting to worry her '. . . but first I just need to have a talk with my big ugly friend here. *Ça va?*'

Rose hesitated, then abruptly disappeared from view as her mother pulled her back down onto her seat with another muttered apology.

Delphine shook her head. 'This is ridiculous. We are not going to have this conversation here.'

'OK,' Tom said. 'So, like I said, let's get off at Ebbsfleet, have a brew and talk there. And if you're not happy at the end of it, you can catch the next train.'

The Eurostar roared into another tunnel, and the change in pressure made their ears pop. Tom opened his mouth and yawned, but Delphine couldn't clear her ears. As Tom looked at her, he realized that she was chalk white and her brow was clammy with sweat. 'Are you all right?'

She shook her head. 'No, I'm not. I'm not at all right. In fact, I think I'm going to be sick.'

'Come on, then . . .'

He helped her to her feet and she leaned against him as he steered her down the aisle. The lavatory at the end of the carriage was occupied and, after a quick glance at Delphine, Tom hurried her through towards the Disabled toilet at the far end of the next coach.

32

Laszlo crouched over the body.

The trousers of the grey suit were a little short, particularly when his knees were bent, but that didn't bother him. The uniform suited his purpose. He slipped the attendant's keys into his pocket, then straightened up.

He stepped over to the mirror and examined himself and his new disguise. Satisfied, he listened at the door for a few moments, then opened it and stepped outside.

As he looked up, he saw a couple hurrying towards him. Their urgency, the deathly pallor of the woman's face and the fact that she was totally unaware of anything but her own discomfort left him in no doubt about where she was heading.

He stepped in front of them. 'Sorry,' he said, with an ingratiating smile. 'This toilet is flooded. Please use the one in the next coach.' He turned his back on them, fumbled with the keys and locked the door.

As the attendant turned back, Tom held his gaze.

Delphine shuddered, covering her mouth with her hand, and walked on. Tom stared at him for a few more moments, frowning, then hurried after her. When he got there, the toilet door at the far end of the aisle was already locked.

'Are you all right?'

He was answered by a groan, the sound of retching and vomiting and, finally, the flushing of the toilet.

The train swept into Ebbsfleet station. The doors opened, a handful of passengers got off and many more boarded. Tom rapped on the toilet door. 'Delphine? If we hurry we can get off here.'

Even as he said it, he heard the beeps signalling that the doors were about to close. By the time Delphine emerged, dabbing at the corners of her mouth with a tissue, they were already picking up speed.

'Looks like I'm going to Paris after all.' Tom helped her clean herself up.

But by then it wasn't Delphine who had kept him on the train.

33

Delphine was still as pale as a ghost as Tom steered her back through the carriages. 'Just wait here,' he said, as he helped her into her seat. 'There's something I need to check. I'll be right back.'

'Why? What is it? Where are you going? What are you doing?'

'You're not going to like this.' He bent down to kiss her cheek. 'But something just came up.'

She stared at him, anger flaring in her eyes. 'So the great romantic gesture of pursuing me to London, and to Paris if necessary, was just a sham, was it? And to think for a moment I almost believed you.'

He didn't hear any of it. He was already moving away from her, back along the carriage.

He hurried to the Disabled toilet. Too many people disregarded things they thought weren't right because it wasn't worth the embarrassment to check them out. Thieves and terrorists melted away because passers-by, particularly of the British variety, were too heads-down, not wanting to make a fuss. But Tom wasn't one of those people. He'd check things out. It didn't matter that he was out of Hereford when he shouldn't be; it didn't matter if Delphine thought even less of him. It was the right thing to do.

Even if he got binned for calling in a possible on a train he shouldn't be on, so what? It would just bring on the next stage of his life more quickly than he'd planned. That was nothing compared to the nightmare of not taking action and discovering later that he'd let Laszlo slip through his fingers.

And there was another, even more important, reason why he needed to check out the possible: Delphine's life, and the lives of hundreds of other innocents on the train. The smell of death followed Laszlo wherever he went, and Tom didn't want it anywhere near the woman he loved.

The red 'Occupied' sign was still illuminated, but Tom ignored it and banged on the door. There was no response from inside. He banged again, harder, then took a pace back and booted the door just below the lock. He heard a shout and the head steward, anger written across his face, surged up to him. How dare someone try to damage his train? 'What on earth do you think you're doing? Can't you see it's occupied? Stop it now, or I'm going to have to call the police. I'll have you arrested and removed from the train.'

Tom ignored him, shrugged off his restraining hand and booted the door once more. There was a splintering sound and, after another vicious kick, it was dangling uselessly from its frame. There was an obstacle behind it, but Tom forced his way through the gap.

The toilet bowl was splattered with blood. On the floor next to it lay the body, stripped to its underwear. Tom didn't have to check the man's pulse to know that he was dead. The colour of the flesh around the neck wound had already told him that. As he stared at the body, his mind racing, Tom heard a gasp.

'Derek!' The head steward was peering round the door, staring wide-eyed.

'You know him?' Tom had to repeat the question before the man could stammer out a reply.

'He's one of our attendants.' His knees gave way beneath him.

Tom caught him before he fell and manoeuvred him into the

cubicle. 'There's nothing you can do for him now. Just get a grip on yourself. Calm down. Come on, deep breaths . . .'

The head steward was trying to do as he was told. But Tom knew it wasn't only shock that had got to him. It was fear.

'Deep breaths, don't look down, just look at me. That's it. No one's going to hurt you.'

Tom flashed his MoD ID card. The head steward barely registered it. Shaking with fright, he was unable to tear his eyes away from the dead man. Tom took his arm and turned him around, so that he was facing the small wall mirror above the sink. 'Don't look down. Come on, just watch me.'

Tom peered over the head steward's shoulder, trying to make eye contact. The steward's eyeballs were rotating faster than the display on a one-armed bandit. It was if he was being tasered.

'Listen . . .' Tom checked the man's name badge. 'Listen, Colin. The man who murdered Derek . . . Did you see the TV news last night? You know those explosions in Hampstead? It wasn't a gas leak. It was an attempt to arrest the man who's just killed your mate. He's a wanted war criminal. He's killed over six hundred civilians – innocent people. And, trust me, he won't hesitate to do it again. I need your help. Are you going to help me, Colin?'

'Should . . . should we stop the train?'

'No. He's smart. If you do that, he'll know he's been spotted. Then we'll have a real drama on our hands. All I need you to do for the moment is to stand outside this toilet and keep the passengers away from here, OK? Just tell them it's out of order and they'll have to use the one in the next coach – and keep this quiet. All of our lives depend on that. I need your help, mate, do you understand?'

The head steward nodded again.

'Say it,' Tom said, waiting until he got an answer before releasing the man's arms.

'I understand,' the head steward said at last.

'Good. I'll be back soon.'

Tom looked round as someone outside tried to push the door

open. Delphine had followed him down the carriage and was now staring, horror-struck, at the body. She opened her mouth to scream but Tom grabbed her, covered her lips with his hand, and brought her into the toilet as well. He hugged her to him. 'Sssh . . . It's all right, Delphine, it's all right.' He stroked her hair. 'Everything's OK . . . I'm here . . .' He waited a moment for her sobbing to subside, then carefully released her and wiped away her tears. He steered her away, with her back to the scene she had just witnessed. 'I have to call this in.'

He glanced up and down the carriage, took out his iPhone and speed-dialled.

Gavin answered on the first ring. The caller ID might be in the Lines but Tom still wasn't. 'Mate, the boss is about ten metres away from me at the moment, and it's only a matter of time before he asks me where the fuck you are. So, with or without Delphine – and don't get me wrong, I hope it's with – I need you back here soon as.'

'I'm afraid there may be a bit of a delay.' Tom turned to check on Delphine and Colin. He stopped talking long enough for Gavin to hear what he'd been dreading.

'Shit, I *told* you not to get stuck on the train . . .' Another thought hit him. 'Mate? You're still in the UK, aren't you?'

'Sorry, I couldn't get off at Ebbsfleet. Next stop's Paris.'

'What? You gone fucking mad? It's not just you that's going to be in the shit. My arse is one hundred per cent grass if you get caught. It's worse than—'

'Shut up and listen.' Tom cut through his complaints. 'I've just pinged X-ray One. Beard, short hair, almost a number-three cut, thinning on top. He's dressed in a grey Eurostar uniform.'

'You taking the piss? Trying to play hero won't get us out of the shit, mate. I know bullshit baffles brains but you shouldn't be on the fucking train in the first place, remember?'

Tom's voice was suddenly cold, clear and slow. 'This is no bullshit. I've also got a dead Eurostar attendant with no uniform. That makes it definitely X-ray One, don't you think? You need to call it in. You know the train number. We'll be in

Paris in about two hours. Call it in, Gav, for fuck's sake. We've got to tell the French. Don't let them stop this thing or we'll have a nightmare. I'll call with a sit-rep the other side of the tunnel.'

Gavin had got the message loud and clear. 'Roger that. Mate, keep both of you safe.'

The last thing Tom heard before he cut the call was Gavin turning towards the team office where Ashton must have been at his desk. 'Boss! We got shit on!'

34

Tom took Delphine's hand. 'Colin, remember, I need you to stay right where you are, mate.'

'Wait! Wh-where are you going?' The chief steward's voice was a strangulated whisper.

'Don't worry, I won't be long. You'll be fine here. Just do what I asked you, OK?'

Tom led Delphine towards the back of the train. Though his expression and body language showed no outward sign of tension, his gaze was never still, scanning the faces of the passengers they passed, alert for any sign of threat.

'Do you think he knows you know?' Delphine's nausea had been overridden by the adrenalin rush of fear.

Tom raised his hand. 'No.'

His voice was low. Delphine had never heard it like that. Tom was in work mode, and this was her worst nightmare, but she suddenly knew with absolute certainty that he would die rather than see her harmed. And that dying was not part of his plan.

'OK.' She fell silent, but couldn't stop her eyes straying to the other passengers as she passed them. With her imagination in overdrive, she saw potential enemies wherever she looked. She hesitated as she reached the seats where Grace, Rose and

Daniel were sitting, then hurried by without speaking or catching their eye.

Tom led her to an empty window seat, right at the back of the end coach. 'Sit there. And don't move unless I come for you.'

Without waiting for a reply, he walked back to where she'd been sitting and collected her bags. When he returned, instead of putting them in the rack, he put them on the table in front of her.

She gave him a puzzled look. 'Won't this seem a little odd?'

'No, it'll just look like you're paranoid about losing sight of your luggage. And if things go to rat shit, it'll act as a barricade. Keep low behind the luggage. It'll give you some protection.'

'Rat shit?' she said, unable to keep the fear from her voice.

He gave her a reassuring smile. 'It's just a precaution,' he said. 'Don't worry. I'll make sure everything's OK.'

'Tom.' She held out an arm. 'It's not me I'm worried about.'

'This is what I do, remember.' Tom gripped her hand within both of his and kissed it gently before letting it drop onto her lap. 'I'll be fine.'

He headed back the way they'd come. If he was right, Laszlo would now keep his head down until he reached Paris. Or maybe he'd stop the train somehow and make a jump for it once they were on the other side of the tunnel.

That didn't matter for now. What did was that if Laszlo passed the toilet and saw the damage, he would know immediately that he was compromised.

And if that happened, Tom would have to take him on there and then, and hold him until the Brits, French – anyone – came and helped him.

35

Ashton had sent the call about Laszlo Antonov up the chain of command, and within fifteen minutes Woolf had been briefed. The home secretary was alerted and she, in turn, alerted her French counterpart. Woolf was given permission by the rapidly assembling COBRA to put the counter-terrorist team on standby. They needed a contingency plan this side of the tunnel.

Within a few minutes of their beepers going off, the first members of Blue team were arriving in the Lines. Inside twenty-five the full crew had assembled and were busy moaning about being called away from much more important business.

'I had a fucking full house, kings on sevens.' Jockey was the unofficial president of the poker club, the horseracing club and the snooker club. He had it as bad as a Premiership player. He'd bet on where a fly would land, or which drop of rain running down a window would be first to the sill. 'The only decent hand I've had and I had to fucking fold it.'

'You think you've got problems?' Keenan was busy texting his disappointment. 'I got numbers off a couple of the cutest joggers you've ever seen in your life while I was out running this morning. Well, the daughter, anyway. They were both coming round to my place later on. I tell you, I was a racing certainty for a threesome.'

'Never mind.' Bryce seemed to be the only happy member of the team this morning. 'I'll give my mate in A Squadron a call – he can pop round and fill in for you.'

'Just try it,' Keenan growled, 'and you'll be the one getting filled in.'

Bryce laughed. 'I don't know what you're all moaning about. I for one am fucking delighted we got called in. The missus dragged me around a furniture shop last night. Today was going to be one long nightmare session with a hammer, a screwdriver, an Allen key and a shedload of flat-pack cupboards that won't fit together. Now she's going to have to do it all on her jack. The longer this job lasts the better.' He gave a broad smile and let rip a huge fart for emphasis.

'Right.' Gavin entered the crew room and the team fell silent. 'Let's brief and get the show on the road. Posh Lad is on Eurostar to Paris and X-ray One is on the same train.'

There was a general murmur as the team looked about and realized Tom wasn't with them.

'Why the stupid fucking idiot is on the train will be explained after the job. The fact is they should be in the tunnel by now. The French will hit it in Paris, or maybe before it reaches the city. I don't know and don't care. That's their problem.

'However, we've got to have a contingency plan in place at Folkestone just in case things go tits up. As far as we know, X-ray One is not aware that he's been pinged, but he's already left one body on the train and he won't hesitate to add a few more to his tally if he thinks he's cornered. Tom is sending a sit-rep once he's out of the tunnel, so we might know more then.'

'Fuck me.' Jockey looked about him, making sure he had an audience. 'How did Posh Lad know Laszlo was on the train? Do they teach psychic powers at Eton as well as how to use a fish knife and be prime minister?'

Jockey got the laughs he was after. Even Gavin gave it a couple of seconds before he reasserted control. 'OK, listen in.

I'm leaving in the heli now, with the advance party for the holding area. The whole team is to fast-drive to the Folkestone hangar. The grid reference and satnav co-ordinates are on the office board.'

All key locations were regularly recced by the Regiment in case of an incident. The past twenty years' construction of new locations – airports, ferry ports, important government buildings – had all included a holding area for the Regiment, or what was known in the real world as UKSF. In other locations, holding areas had been identified for use when needed.

'OK, Blue team, any questions?' There shouldn't have been. Call-outs were continually rehearsed. All kit would have been packed in the vehicles and the men ready to move. If not, they shouldn't have been in the Regiment.

Gavin waited two seconds before continuing. 'If all goes well on the train, and Tom hasn't fucked up by the time you get to Folkestone, the French will have lifted Laszlo. Remember to make your blues visible and drive safely. I don't give a shit about you lot, but I want those wagons back in one piece. I signed for them.'

They ran out of the crew room and towards their vehicles. Gavin and the three signallers who were attached to the team threw their ready-bags and comms kit onto a Transit that would take them to the helipad where a Dauphin was waiting with its rotors turning.

Also on his way from Regimental HQ to the heli pad was a member of 'the Slime'. Intelligence Corps personnel were referred to as Green Slime because of the unfortunate colour of their berets. The Slime set-up in Hereford was an integral part of any operation.

The Prince's Gate siege in 1980 had demonstrated the value of good and accurate intelligence. During the lead-up to the actual assault, specialists from MI5 had been tasked with drilling holes in the walls and inserting tiny microphones and cameras to gain a detailed picture of who was where inside the building. But the information about the construction of the place was piss-poor, and the walls turned out to be too thick for the probes to penetrate. The result was that, although the team had a model of the construction of the building, they did not know exactly where the X-rays or Yankees were located.

Since then, the Regiment had collated a massive database that included such essential information as the thickness of walls and doors in every building that was a possible terrorist target, and the designs of all military and civilian aircraft and shipping. The database was portable, so wherever an incident occurred they could take it with them and access the information. If they called up a certain hotel, for example, the Slime were able to pull up 3D images of the interior on screen, or do 360-degree pans from any given point.

Intelligence gathered on the numbers and locations of people inside the building could be added as it came to hand. Possible methods of entry could be suggested to the computer, which would then plot the best method of moving through the building from that point.

If the design of the building was not on the database, the teams could punch in details such as the construction of the outside walls, the number of windows and the location of particular rooms. The computer would then 'design' the interior and provide a probability factor for accuracy, altering both as more information was added. It seemed the Slime had every map, drawing and picture of every ship, aircraft and building in existence. There would be a second wave of Slime with their box of tricks, accompanied by a team of signallers, in the road party.

8 Flight AAC (Army Air Corps) had a fleet of four Dauphins and two Gazelles, and their sole job was to support the Regiment. Painted in civilian colours, the AS365 N3 Dauphins blended in with normal civilian air traffic and could transport the SAS covertly around the UK. They could also be used during counter-terrorism operations to get assault groups on top of buildings or when the holding area was so far away the attack had to be airborne. Up until 2008 the Regiment had used Agusta 109s. Two of them had been 'liberated' from the

125

Argentinians during the 1982 Falklands conflict. The 109s could carry a maximum of seven assaulters; the Dauphins could take nine at a squeeze.

Gavin's job as the 3i/c was to get to the incident ahead of the team. He'd start liaising with the police, who'd be ready to close down the tunnel entrance and contain whatever was happening in there if things went badly and the train stopped before it reached France.

Once the team arrived and moved into their holding area, they had to have fully functioning comms up and running within thirty minutes of the first wagon's arrival. Gavin had to give a set of orders covering all eventualities. Using whatever information he had gathered from the police, his next task would be to work out the Emergency Response. The ER wouldn't be much, but it was a plan. It would then be built on as more information was gathered for the Deliberate Options, plans of attack to cover any situation that might develop.

Gavin helped the sigs guys lug their comms kit into the back of the aircraft and was about to board when Ashton beckoned him out of the rotor wash. He had to shout over the noise of the turbines: 'What the fuck is Buckingham doing on that train?' When Gavin had originally given him the news, he hadn't asked for the details. There had been more important things to do.

Gavin had to lean in towards Ashton to be heard. He wasn't going to shout. He knew he was in trouble. 'Boss, Delphine's leaving him. She was heading for Paris and Tom went to talk her round and bring her back.

'I fucked up, simple as that. I let him go. But we caught a break as a result – Laszlo getting lifted, even if it is by the French. Happy days on that one.'

'Maybe so,' Ashton said. 'But when this is all over, you, me and Buckingham are going to be having a little chat.'

'Would that be with or without the coffee and biscuits?' Gavin said.

'Most assuredly without,' Ashton replied. 'Now get your arse to Folkestone.'

36

The rest of Blue team scrambled to load the last of their kit into the black Range Rovers. The vehicles had plates that identified them to traffic police, and always stood gassed up and ready.

They roared out of the Lines a couple of minutes later and sped down the road with magnetic blue-light units flashing on their roofs and behind their radiator grilles.

Police outriders on motorbikes were already moving ahead of them with lights flashing and sirens blaring, a rolling road-block to seal junctions and roundabouts, clearing traffic for the SAS convoy travelling behind them at speeds in excess of 100 miles an hour.

Red team, on three hours' standby, were already racing into the Lines. They'd stand by in their crew room in case they were needed for this incident, or any other. But, as Gavin had said, X-ray One should be in the hands of the French by the time he landed.

37

It wasn't just the SAS that had had their Saturday disrupted. The Chief Constable of Kent Constabulary, Michael Alderson, had been in the drive of his Maidstone home, loading his golf clubs into the boot of his Jag, when his wife had come running down the steps holding the phone. He waved her away. 'Take a message, Jane,' he said. 'I'm already running late.'

'I can't.' She thrust the instrument towards him. 'It's the office.'

'*Again?*' Alderson seemed to spend more of his life in fiscal control committees than actually doing his job. This was the third call about Monday's pre-meeting to discuss the car-fleet budget-control session on Tuesday. He'd waited more than a year to wangle an invitation to play Royal St George's, and finally had a day free to use it.

With a face like thunder, he barked into the mouthpiece, 'Yes, what is it now?'

He listened, then turned and started pulling his clubs out of the boot. 'Right, but if this turns out to be a false alarm . . .' He broke the connection, got into the car and slammed the door.

His wife was left holding phone and golf bag.

'Still Sandwich, sir?' His driver knew very well it wasn't, but liked to rub it in.

'No, London – and blue-light it.' With the scowl still on his face, he settled back in his seat and reached for his mobile. 'I finally get the chance for a round, and what happens? I get to spend a day playing soldiers with Margaret Thatcher's favourite fucking storm troopers instead.'

It wasn't just the loss of a day at Royal St George's that infuriated him. Alderson couldn't understand why the system operated like this. Every time there was a COBRA-scale incident, heads of department scrambled their people – emergency services, intelligence agencies, government departments – and set about dealing with the situation. But then those department heads were pulled off the job and summoned to COBRA. Now he was one of them – instead of staying put and commanding the situation on the ground.

The UK emergency committee always seemed to make a drama out of a crisis. It had been set up to help co-ordinate emergency responses, but in practice it slowed everyone down. In Alderson's view, it dragged people like him away from the sharp end in order to watch a bunch of politicians and civil servants elbowing each other out of the way as they rushed headlong towards the limelight.

Alderson took the view that it was high time to form a committee in which *real* experience was the criterion for membership – rather than the coincidence of the popular vote. But even though he hated what he knew would be happening, he wanted to be there. Someone needed to give them all a kick up the backside.

He wondered, not for the first time, if politicians should ever be allowed to make key decisions on tactical situations. If you had a broken leg, who would you want to operate on you? The Secretary of State for Health or an orthopaedic surgeon? He stuck his mobile to his ear and started directing his own people. At least they knew what they had to do, and how to do it.

He caught his driver grinning into the rear-view. 'Yes, very funny. It's all right for you, Mr Bloody Time-and-a-half. But what about St George's?'

The driver hit the grille blues on the chief constable's 5 series BMW and gunned it towards the motorway.

38

Her stomach still churning and bile threatening to melt the back of her throat, Delphine leaned back behind her makeshift barricade and did her best to take refuge in happier times.

The Georgian mansion at the edge of the Malvern Hills had been so grand and beautiful it had taken her breath away. A long drive, shaded by lime trees, had led through rolling wheat fields and past a paddock where four horses were grazing. As they'd pulled up at the entrance that first time, two fat and ageing chocolate Labradors had bounded out to greet them and slobbered over Tom.

Delphine had looked up at the immaculate white stucco façade, fluted pillars framing the panelled oak door and the date stone set into the pediment above it. She gave a low whistle that contained more than a trace of mockery. 'Seventeen twenty-five,' she said, with a smile. 'You didn't tell me you were a proper old-fashioned English country gentleman.'

'My father is,' he said. 'I'm just an ordinary soldier.'

'The Regiment doesn't do ordinary, does it? But even your mates in the troop are more the two-up-two-down terraced-house type.'

He laughed. 'Yeah, maybe. And perhaps even that would

seem like luxury to a lot of them. Jockey grew up in a rat-infested tenement with no father and an alcoholic mother. Bryce's dad was a miner – they were three to a room in a tiny pit cottage, in the pre-Thatcher days, when there were such things – and Keenan was shacked up with his mum in a council flat on a dog-rough estate in Plymouth. When she kicked him out, he lived in his van for a couple of years. And Vatu, he really did have a mud hut on a beach.'

Before Delphine could reply, his parents came out to welcome them. Without having met her, but having seen the house and grounds, Delphine had already guessed at what Tom's mother would be wearing. Her wool skirt and cashmere pullover, complete with single string of pearls, were no disappointment. She even had a trug – with gardening gloves, a pair of secateurs and some cut roses spilling out of it – on her arm. Her blonde hair was flecked with grey, but her classic English complexion made her look much younger than her mid-fifties.

Tom's father, florid-faced and sandy-haired, with a paunch straining against his tweed waistcoat, welcomed her over the threshold. He led the way to the library and poured Delphine the strongest gin and tonic she had ever tasted. 'Can't abide a weak gin,' he said, rather superfluously. 'When I have a martini, I like it so bone dry that I do no more than show the bottle of vermouth to the gin, then put it away again without opening it. I'm a bit like Winston Churchill, in that respect if nothing else. When he made one, instead of adding vermouth to the gin, he just used to bow in the direction of France.'

Delphine laughed. 'Not so different from Dean Martin, then. He just had the barman mention vermouth as he was pouring the gin. And Buñuel, the filmmaker, he talked about the perfect martini being created when a ray of light passed through a bottle of Noilly Prat and touched the pure spirit in the bottom of the glass.'

Tom's father looked across to his son. 'I think you've found a diamond this time, dear boy. This is a woman after my own heart. Make sure you hang on to her.'

After they'd chatted for a while, and his mother had shown Delphine around the house, Tom took her outside and gave her a tour of the estate. 'How's it going so far?' he said, as soon as they were out of earshot. 'Bearing up under the strain?'

'It's fine. I like them.' She saw his doubtful expression. 'No, really!'

Tom led her through the garden, down a winding path across the fields and past a small lake, where swallows skimmed the surface and moorhens shepherded their broods among the bulrushes at the water's edge.

'So, do your parents own all this?' Delphine said, looking around her.

He nodded. 'As far as the eye can see and then a little bit more. It was my mother's childhood home. She's "old money", as we say, like *l'ancien régime* in France – before they all got their heads sliced off in the Revolution.

'My dad's "new money", though. He made his in the City, but he took over the running of the estate when my grandfather died. My parents wanted me to go to college at Cirencester and learn estate management, ready to take over this place when the old man retires, but that was never going to happen. It's full of Sloanes and Hooray Henrys. I'd either have run amok with a shotgun and bagged a few of them, or I'd have gone out of my mind with boredom. Besides, I wanted to be a soldier.'

'But it's so beautiful here . . .'

Tom shrugged. 'Beautiful. And dull. It's not so bad in summer when there are a few visitors around, but in winter I could take you down to the village pub and tell you who would be in, where they'd be sitting, what they'd be wearing and what they'd be talking about before I even opened the door. There's one old bloke who plays darts there every single night of the year, Christmas included. I swear that sometimes I've walked out of the pub as he was throwing a dart, gone away for a few months, and got back in time to see it hit the board.'

'Isn't it just the same in Hereford?'

'In the sergeants' mess, maybe. But there are other attractions in one of the hotel bars.' He slipped his arm around her waist as they walked on down the fields.

There was a cottage and a cluster of outbuildings at the bottom of the hill, sheltered by an oak wood. 'I need to call in here and say hello,' Tom said. 'It won't take long.'

A middle-aged man answered the door. He was wearing muddy boots and a worn tweed jacket with a belt of orange baler twine. He broke into a huge grin at the sight of Tom and clasped him in a bear hug. 'Tommy Boy,' he said. 'Now you're a sight for sore eyes, I must say. Where have you been hiding?'

'Not hiding, Jack, just busy, but it's great to see you. This is Delphine.'

They shook hands, Delphine's dwarfed by Jack's huge paw, rough and reddened from outdoor work. 'Very pleased to meet you,' he said. He gave her the ghost of a wink. 'I keep telling him it's about time he found a good woman to settle down with.'

He came with them as they walked on around the estate, showing them the pheasant pens and the new trees he'd put in. He pointed to a cedar of Lebanon sapling, planted a few yards from the stump of a felled giant. 'It broke my heart to take that old tree down,' he said. 'It was a beautiful specimen and had been growing there for more than two centuries, almost as long as the house has stood there. They say the man who planted it brought the sapling back from the Holy Land in his hat and shared his water ration with it on the long sea voyage home.' He gave a self-deprecating smile. 'I didn't have to work quite so hard to get that one. I just bought it from a nursery. Still, it's nice to think that a tree I've planted will still be there long after I've passed on.'

He looked around him. 'So, we've made a few changes since you were last here, Tom, but some things haven't changed at all. Your dad's still too tight to invest in new machinery, so I'm having to drive the same knackered old thing every harvest.'

He gestured towards the corner of the field where an old combine was parked, its red paint sun-faded and streaked with rust. 'I taught Tom to drive this when he was a boy. It was the worst harvest we ever had. Well, in truth, he wasn't bad at it, though he did tend to go a bit off-line whenever a pretty girl walked down the lane.' He laughed and ducked under the mock-punch that Tom threw at him.

'He was always down here helping me when he was a boy. I couldn't shake him off! He wasn't much of a one for book-learning but he was a smart kid, just the same. And he could fix pretty much anything. I'd only have to show him something once and he'd never forget it.

'He was quite a scrapper, too, weren't you, Tom? Remember the time when Parnaby's boys set about you – real tough lads they were, farmhands from the next estate. Well, I reckon they thought he'd be a soft touch, with his private education and his posh accent, but Tom took them apart, didn't you? Flattened both of them and then saw off their elder brother when he came looking for revenge. I was squaring up to him myself, trying to protect Tom, though to be honest, I wasn't fancying my own chances that much, because that brother of theirs was a real big sod. Then Tom pushed past me and took him on himself.

'He was giving him a few inches in height and more than a few pounds in weight, but he cleaned him up good and proper. He ducked under a big right hook, doubled him up with a couple of punches right into the guts and then threw a right-hander that broke his nose. We didn't have any more trouble from those boys after that, did we, Tom?'

He broke off and gave an apologetic smile. 'Sorry, Delphine, I do tend to run off at the mouth sometimes. It must be living alone. Whenever I'm out in company, I suppose I must be trying to make up for the silence at home.'

She put a hand on his arm. 'It's fine,' she said. 'I'm learning all sorts of things about this misfit I didn't know.'

'Well, you could tell he was a proper fighter, even then. He had fantastic hand-speed, but above all he had a real fighter's brain, and a fighter's instincts. For most people in a punch-up, the red mist comes down and they rush in, throwing punches like they're going out of fashion. They often get decked as a result.' He paused. 'Tom was never like that. He was always ice cool, watching the other guy, reading and anticipating his moves, then putting him away like a slaughterman stunning a bullock. And do you remember that time when—'

'Yeah, Jack, I remember,' Tom said, hastily cutting him off before he could start another tale. 'But, look, we've got to get back now. Dad'll have us horse-whipped if we're late for dinner. Great to see you, though. Take care, huh?'

Jack took Delphine's hand in his. 'A real pleasure to meet you.' He turned to Tom. 'Look after this one. She's a real keeper, if you ask me.'

As they walked back up the fields, Delphine turned to wave goodbye, but Jack was already making his slow, solitary way back towards his house in the shadow of the wood.

Tom fell silent, perhaps embarrassed that so much of him had been revealed, or worrying that Delphine wouldn't want to be with someone like that – not just in the SAS but enjoying fighting.

To his surprise, Delphine slipped her hand into his, leaned into him and kissed him.

As they walked through the garden towards the house, they could hear a gong being struck. 'Oh, please,' Delphine said. 'What is this? *Downton Abbey*? I should be in a tiara and an evening gown, and you should be wearing a white tie and tails.'

'Just one of my mother's little foibles,' Tom said. 'As you may have noticed, she's very old school.'

39

'Tom must have taken quite a shine to you, my dear,' his mother had said to Delphine, as she passed the vegetables that evening. 'He has never brought any of his girlfriends home before. You must be a good influence on him. We're still hoping he'll come to his senses one day, settle down and take over the estate, or at least find a more suitable job. With his father's contacts in the City—' She broke off as she became aware of Tom glowering at her. 'Yes, I'm talking about you, darling,' she said. 'I was just saying that you could have had your pick of jobs and professions.'

'This is ancient history, Mother.' Tom gave Delphine a look that said he'd known bringing her was a mistake. 'Do we really have to cover this ground every time I visit? I'm a soldier, and I do it not because I'm forced to or because my parents want me to –' his wide eyes challenged her '– but because *I* want to. I like to fight. Why don't people understand? It's just as valid a profession as medicine or the law. I'm afraid you need to get used to it.'

'Profession?' She focused on Tom so completely it was as if no one else was in the room. 'It's not a profession.' She changed her tone to one of concern. 'Tom, you kill people.'

'When it's necessary. But, Mother, I'm not a psychopath.

136

I don't kill people for kicks. Surely you understand that.'

She shrugged as if she did, but that it was beside the point. Her tone went back to disappointed. 'If you really needed to join the army, you could have taken a commission. But look at you, you're not even an officer.' She gave a brittle smile, as if it had been meant as a joke, but Delphine had heard the edge in her voice.

'I'm not an officer because I don't want to be an officer. I'm happy where I am.'

Tom had been a disappointment to his parents; Delphine understood that now. They'd placed a silver spoon in his mouth when he was born, he'd told her. The spoon the family's great-great-great-grandfather had taken from the Duke of Wellington's field dining-table the night after his victory at Waterloo. The spoon all Buckinghams had sucked ever since. Tom had been the first to spit it out.

She discovered that Tom's two younger brothers had kept firmly on the family's pre-ordained trajectory. One was still at Eton, the other up at Oxford. Both had stunning futures ahead of them; that was the way their parents had mapped things out. Tom knew that they wouldn't have much choice in the matter.

'Mother, I keep explaining to you that I like my life as it is. Why can't you understand that, and be happy?'

She had no words to give back because she wasn't happy. It was as if Tom had deliberately joined the army as a squaddie to spite her.

He looked like he knew where this was going so just moved onto the next part of the drama that they played out every time he came home. No wonder he never brought any women back.

Tom's father studied his glass of claret as if he was looking for the ray of light that touched the spirit in the bottom. He obviously knew it was time to keep quiet and his head down.

Not only had Tom disappointed his parents by joining the army as a squaddie, he'd told Delphine in the pub one night, he'd joined the Rifles, an *infantry* regiment. He was consigning himself, in his father's view, to a lifetime of wet, cold and hunger. His parents couldn't even hide their regret at his passing-out parade. When mothers from housing estates in Leeds, Manchester, London and Glasgow had cried as they'd watched their little boys turn into young men, Tom's mother had joined in. But hers, he had told Delphine, were tears of sorrow. Where had she gone so wrong? Tom had had everything. Why settle for less than the best he could be? Why waste his life playing soldiers?

He sat there as his mother continued to look as if she was sucking a particularly sour lemon. Delphine read Tom's expression. Should he try to explain to her yet again, it said, and to his father, who shared the same disappointment but let his wife do the talking? He'd told Delphine he'd been saying exactly the same thing for the past twelve years. Even when he'd passed Selection there had been no message of congratulation. They still couldn't understand his lack of ambition. Why waste his time in the trenches? People with his privileged upbringing had much better things to do.

'Mother, everyone I know in Hereford is there on merit, not because their father was something in the City or their mother owns half of Worcestershire. I like that.'

His mother leaned over the table towards him, her face full of compassion. 'But, darling, we worry about you keeping safe. We were worried sick at the state of you.' She reached out and gently touched his scar.

'Mother, I got that at a Fight Night in Hereford. Nothing to do with my work.'

She took a breath, frustration perhaps getting the better of her as she tried to find the words that would show Delphine she was a good mother. But Tom was too quick for her. 'Mother, everything is fine. Sometimes, when the adrenalin's pumping, you don't really notice it. It's OK, really it is. People tend to be more frightened of the idea of fighting, in Afghanistan or on a Fight Night, than of the reality. It's just that you don't know about things like that, and there's no reason why you should.

'In a few years I might start doing something even you can

138

approve of, but this is my life for now, and though I don't expect you to like or understand it, I do expect you to respect my decision.'

There was a long silence while Tom's mother stared at him, as if she were trying to understand why her son had become such a stranger to her.

Delphine broke the silence. 'I understand.'

Tom let that sink in before his hand reached out to hers. 'Thank you.'

What she didn't say was that to her the conversation could just as easily have been about Tom having an undesirable lover. She was French, after all, not British all the way back to Alfred the Great like his mother had probably always planned. She now understood Tom better than ever. She loved him; probably had from the first week they had met. She also respected him, but she now knew more than ever that he had a powerful and seductive mistress with whom, if this relationship ever came to anything, she would be competing.

Tom's mother turned back to Delphine, trying hard to hide her anger and sadness. Her expression said that she had lost her son; she'd known it would happen one day, but wished it had been to an English rose of her choosing.

'I'm sorry, my dear.' She made an effort to widen her smile. 'How rude we are, monopolizing the conversation with domestic chit-chat when we have a guest at our table. Now, do tell me all about yourself. You come from Nice, I believe? Such a beautiful city. We were there ourselves just a couple of months ago, staying at the Negresco. My grandmother used to winter there.'

As Delphine started to talk about her home and her family, she tried to ignore Tom, who was visible over his mother's shoulder. He was miming being hanged, with his head on one side and his tongue lolling out of his mouth.

His father, meanwhile, had been tasting the wine, pouring a little into his glass, sniffing its bouquet, then sipping it and rolling it appreciatively around his mouth. As he looked up, he followed Delphine's gaze and rapped the base of his glass on the table. 'Tom, for God's sake, stop playing the fool. If you want something useful to do, you can pour Delphine a glass of this wine.

'It's a burgundy,' he said to Delphine, as Tom filled her glass and she sipped. 'As I always say, France for the wine, Italy for the coffee—'

'Ukraine for the prostitutes?' Tom interrupted.

His father almost choked on his wine.

'What?'

'Sorry, Mother.' Tom had a mischievous gleam in his eye that had probably always spelled trouble. 'If I were an officer I wouldn't be making jokes like that, now would I?'

Delphine spluttered into her glass as Tom's father turned an even more impressive shade of puce.

'No, you would not!'

'I mean, if I were an officer, I would have said Mayfair.'

40

Clements was out of his civil-service power suit and in his weekend casuals: beige slacks and a blue V-neck. He'd been standing in the queue in the Pimlico branch of Marks & Spencer, the same place he'd bought his off-duty uniform, when he got the call.

He hadn't liked the way the cashier had looked at him as she rang up his items: a pasta meal for one, a small salad, an individual chocolate pudding, and a bottle of passable claret. The look she gave him, hovering somewhere between sympathy and downright pity, made him feel as if he was wearing a badge on his chest reading: 'Sad loser who lives alone. No wife, no friends.' How was it, he asked himself, for the thousandth time in his life, that he could be so confident, so decisive, so abrasive, even around the most powerful politicians and civil-service mandarins, yet became so flustered and self-conscious when confronted by any mildly attractive woman, even a check-out operator in a supermarket?

He kept his eyes on the card-reader as he paid the bill, anxious to avoid eye contact, and it was almost a relief when his phone buzzed and he stepped away from the till to answer it.

'Where? . . . How long ago? . . . All right, I'm on my way.' He snatched his carrier bag, his confidence returned now. He took a cab home instead of doing the ten-minute walk. He needed to put a suit back on and dress the way he was born to.

Clements was almost excited at the thought of confronting the home secretary. Laszlo should have been killed in Hampstead, and for reasons she didn't need to know. While she had been at her red-brick university, probably studying philosophy and dreaming of a Brave New World, Clements had been trying to keep the present one from collapsing.

He felt pretty damned superior right now; even more so than usual. He gave the taxi driver a three-pound tip after he'd been dropped at his modest Westminster flat near Horseferry Magistrates' Court. Clements and his kind remained the backbone of this country, and this Laszlo débâcle was yet another example of why the home secretary should have listened to his advice without him having to give her all the ins and outs.

If she stopped deluding herself that she ran the Home Office, Laszlo would now be dead – and dead people couldn't talk. By now the French might very well have captured him, and if so he would appear before the ICC – and then this government of bright new things would be begging for Clements's help. Which, of course, as a public servant, he would give freely.

As he placed his key in the Yale lock, he couldn't help smiling in anticipation of the meeting ahead.

41

Using the stolen master-key, Laszlo had moved directly from the toilet and let himself into the employees' break room at the end of Coach Eight. Out of sight, he had helped himself to a cup of coffee and a couple of biscuits while he waited for the train to enter the tunnel. His mobile beeped with a text. He put down his cup.

they know you are on the train. exit now

Even without looking out of the window, Laszlo knew from the angle of the floor and the whoosh as they ran through a deep cutting that the Eurostar had reached the outskirts of Folkestone and was about to plunge beneath the Channel. His fingers flew across the keypad as he texted a reply.

Impossible

He waited a few seconds for the confirmation that the message had been sent, then switched to a new SIM card. He rebooted his phone, made a call and reverted to Russian. 'I've been flagged.'

There was a momentary pause while Sambor digested the information. 'OK. Where are you now?'

'About to enter the tunnel.'

'Keep safe, brother. We're on our way.'

42

Sambor put his van into gear and signalled to pull out into the queue of traffic waiting to drive onto the UK-bound HGV Shuttle.

Two identical white vans pulled out behind him. On the far side of the tracks beyond the steel chain-link fence that divided the north- and southbound lines, he could see the sign greeting arrivals: 'Bienvenue à Coquelles, Pas-de-Calais'. As he approached the Eurotunnel barriers, a British Customs officer stepped in front of the van and signalled to him to pull out of the queue into an inspection area. As he did so, the two white vans behind him followed suit.

Sambor cut the engine and got out. He still had hair and lots of it, dark brown and thick. His chest and shoulders were covered with a tatty black leather jacket. Over one shoulder he wore a battered nylon 'desert tan' Blackhawk Special Forces-issue grab bag. They were essentially padded laptop bags, but after some great marketing they were now an essential part of any soldier's kit. They'd become all the rage with the military since the Afghan war.

There was something damaged about Sambor, and it ran deeper than a face that wasn't as good-looking, after years of conflict, as it had once been. A nose broken in some long-ago brawl and never reset gave him an even more intimidating air than he'd had when he was younger. Even now, without a beard, he was still a monster – which was why he was always picked out in any security check. Normally he had to be hidden from the real world, but today exposure was needed.

The Customs officer walked to the back of the van and gestured to the doors. 'Open up, please.'

Stone-faced, Sambor strolled after him and unlocked the doors. As he swung one of them open, he seized the collar of the Customs officer's jacket, lifted and hurled him into the back. The unfortunate man crash-landed on the floor, and the colour drained from his face as he looked up at a dozen heavily armed men lining the benches on each side of him.

They all wore the same look of morbid curiosity as one of their number looped a wire garrotte over his head and jerked it tight. Fingers scrabbling in vain at his throat, thrashing and struggling, as his heels drummed a tattoo on the ridged metal beneath him, he was dead in less than a minute.

As he breathed his last, another of the insurgents rifled his pockets and stole his security card. He handed it to Sambor, who calmly closed the rear doors again and, with a nod to the two drivers behind him, got back into the cab and drove off.

The other Customs officers continued to work around them; none had noticed the disappearance of their colleague, and no one moved to halt the small convoy as it drove out of the inspection area.

So what if they had? Sambor thought. This was a rolling start-line: the fight had begun the moment they had got into the back of the wagons. These men had fought alongside Laszlo and Sambor for many, many years. To them, Laszlo was not a war criminal: he was an honourable man, a hero, a leader to whom they wanted to demonstrate their loyalty as payback for the guilt they could never escape. The only thing that was going to stop them was a round through the head.

Sambor stopped again at an automatic barrier at the far side of the security zone and used the dead officer's card to access the service road that led to the tracks on the southbound side.

The three vans climbed the ramp and came to a halt on the bridge above the track.

Each van was packed with at least a dozen men, armed with a mixture of automatic rifles and light machine-guns for when the situation went noisy; suppressed sub-machine-guns until it did; grenades and a variety of ropes, NVGs (night vision goggles) and fire-fighters' oxygen sets attached by bungee cords to 50cm-wide, old-school, plain wooden skateboards with plastic wheels and braces.

They were prepared physically and mentally for war. They'd all had at least nine lives, and had the burns, the dents, the bullet holes and the knife wounds to prove it. They waited, not caring about the gathering police presence. If you didn't fear dying, you didn't fear anything or anyone.

An HGV Shuttle approached on the tracks below them, beginning to accelerate as it pulled away from the platforms. One by one the insurgents climbed onto the parapet and, keeping clear of the power cables, they jumped. Each landed with a thud on the roof of the container cage and rolled to break his fall. A few seconds after the last was safely in position, the Shuttle, still accelerating, careered into the mouth of the tunnel.

The abrupt transition from cold, autumnal air to the warm, humid atmosphere in the tunnel caused a layer of condensation to form immediately on the skin of the wagons. Blown back by the rush of air from the slipstream, the spray lashed Sambor and his men, stinging their eyes.

Temporarily blinded, one rubbed at his face, and in doing so moved his arm and the weapon he carried too close to the power lines. There was a blinding blue flash and a whiff of ozone as the high-voltage current arced across the gap and fried him in an instant. His smouldering body tumbled from the roof of his container, smashed against the concrete wall and rebounded into the side of the cage before dropping to the ground alongside the tracks.

The train was now building up speed. Though he and his men were still hanging onto the top of the cages, Sambor showed no emotion as he counted down the seconds on his watch, then shouted back at his team.

At once, two men extracted cans of kerosene from their backpacks and began pouring it through the thick metal latticework onto the cab of the truck it housed. One popped a distress flare and dropped it into the spreading kerosene. It ignited at once. Thick grey smoke began belching through the bars and was whipped away by the slipstream.

Within seconds sensors in the Shuttle and the tunnel wall detected the heat and smoke. Warning signals flashed to the Eurostar control centre, lighting up the digital control board and deafening the staff with the clamour of alarms as the sprinkler system kicked in.

The *chef de trains* took no more than a moment to reach the decision to stop all traffic, close both lines and dispatch the fire trucks at the Calais emergency response depot into the service tunnel that ran between the north- and southbound tracks. The fire that had shut down the complex for weeks had been four years ago now, but its memory was still fresh. If this proved to be a false alarm or a fault in the sensors, a few hundred passengers would suffer no worse inconvenience than a short delay. If it was a genuine blaze, every passing second of inactivity only increased the risk of a catastrophe.

In less than a minute the fire-fighters, roused from their chairs and bunks by the howling siren, jumped aboard their custom-built truck and roared across the compound.

Deep in the tunnel, the HGV Shuttle was losing power and speed. Smoke and flames still belched from the steel latticework at its rear, despite the automated rainstorm doing its best to dampen them down.

Sambor and his men began clambering down from the roofs of their containers, using the lattice bars like the rungs of a ladder. Sprinkler water ran down their hair and faces.

The narrowness of the gap between the train and the tunnel wall forced them to assemble in single file beside the track.

Sambor did a cursory head count, and led the way towards the front of the train.

Although his control panel was lit up like a Christmas tree, the driver had not panicked. He was reaching for the brake lever to bring the train to a controlled halt when Sambor blew the lock to the rear entrance of the cabin.

He kicked the door open, stepped into the cab, brought up his weapon and shot the man dead with a double tap to the head. His ceramic rounds were designed for fighting at close quarters on ships and planes, where there was a danger of ricochet. They fragmented on impact with the man's skull and pulverized his brain without exiting his head. The only thing to hit the windscreen was a fine mist of blood.

The driver slumped over the controls. Even without power, the train's momentum kept it moving forward, still trailing smoke, until his lifeless body slid to the floor and the dead man's handle braking system brought the train to a juddering halt.

43

Delphine had recovered from what she'd thought might be another bout of sickness as she felt the Eurostar begin to slow.

Tom appeared at her side and she reached for his hand, enclosing it in hers. 'What's happening?' she breathed. 'Surely the French can't be stopping the train. You said that they need—'

'No,' Tom said. 'They'd never stop the train in the tunnel. Something else is going on.'

He leaned out into the aisle and peered up the carriage. The lights flickered and died, then came back on in dimmed emergency mode. The train was still moving, but painfully slowly. Finally, with a squeal of brakes, it came to a complete stop. There were moans and groans from the passengers, frustration and a hint of anger rather than fear. There had been so many breakdowns over the years, stories of passengers being delayed for hours . . .

Delphine tightened her grip on Tom's fingers because she knew differently. He knelt closer to her and brushed her cheek with his lips, then eased his hand gently from her grip and locked his gaze on hers. 'I'll have to leave you here a while longer.' His voice was little more than a murmur. He placed her hands on her lap. 'I want you to do as I say now, and stay here. No matter how noisy it gets, you stay put.'

'Noisy?' Delphine said.

'There may be some shooting, but even if you hear gunfire or an explosion, do not get off the train. Just take cover behind your bags, keep low and stay exactly where you are now. It's the safest place, and I'll know where to find you.'

'If there is danger here, wouldn't it be better to get off and run back along the tunnel?'

'No,' Tom said. 'I don't know what's out there. In here, you're safe for now. Keep anything valuable with you, in your jeans. We may have to move fast.'

Her skin tingled as he reached out and touched her cheek. 'Give me your mobile,' he said.

Delphine handed it to him. 'But it won't work in the tunnel. I don't have any reception . . .'

Tom didn't glance up as he tapped the keys. 'Bluetooth still works. I'm pairing it with mine.' He handed the phone back and got to his feet.

'Do you have to go?' Delphine looked up at him as he leaned down once more.

'I need to make sure that whatever is happening out there doesn't happen in here, to you.'

Their lips touched. Despite herself, Delphine liked how it felt.

44

Laszlo was a couple of coaches ahead of him, working his way towards the front of the train, when an Englishman in a pinstriped business suit caught sight of his Eurostar uniform and stood up, blocking the aisle.

'Why have we stopped?' he demanded. 'Why has there been no announcement? Don't you people know anything about customer care?'

'An announcement will be made shortly.' Laszlo's smile was as polished as any Eurostar smile-trained employee's. But his eyes betrayed the fact that he couldn't care less. 'Meanwhile, please remain in your seat.'

He tried to move past the irate passenger but the man grabbed his arm and held him back. 'This is simply not good enough,' he said. 'I have an important business meeting. I deserve an explanation.'

'Then I shall give you one.'

Laszlo drove his knee into the immaculately tailored groin. As the passenger doubled up, Laszlo grabbed a handful of his hair and smashed his nose on the edge of the table. When he released his grip, the man sank to his knees, his face a mask of blood.

'Thank you for choosing to travel with Eurostar today,' Laszlo muttered.

The shouts and screams of the other passengers pursued him as he moved on along the train.

Tom heard the screams ahead of him and, abandoning caution, began to run through the carriages. A dazed businessman, blood pouring from his nose, was being helped to his feet by another passenger.

'An attendant . . . assaulted me.' The pinstriped suit was as blood-stained and rumpled as its owner, who was now radiating more embarrassment than pain. 'He hasn't heard the last of this. I'll make sure he never—'

'Tall guy, with a beard?'

He nodded, spilling a fresh gobbet of blood-stained mucus on his lapel.

Tom checked the toilet signs at both ends of the carriage. 'Where did he go?'

'I don't know . . .' the injured passenger said, from behind his hands. 'I was on the fucking floor. I'd just been assaulted!'

Tom turned to the other passengers. 'Where did he go?'

A group of four lads-on-the-piss sat at a table piled high with Stella cans, not bothering to hide the fact that they'd quite enjoyed the show. The logo on their sweatshirts told him they worked for London Underground and their expressions made it clear that they knew how it felt to be accosted, abused, poked in the chest and treated like dirt in the course of a working day.

The only one without a baseball cap pointed towards the front of the train and Tom took off at a run.

45

Sambor and his men jumped off the Shuttle, as it ground to a halt near the midpoint of the tunnel, and prepared for phase two of their operation. So far everything was going to plan. They had been trained well, and years of experience had honed their skills. Fighting, killing and dying was the only life they knew.

Sambor located the nearest CCTV security camera and, hugging the wall, used the curvature of the tunnel and the pall of smoke to conceal his approach to it. Reaching up, he hacked into the cable feed with his knife. One of his team swung a backpack off his shoulder, fished out a steel probe and pushed it against the wire core. A torrent of sparks burst from the camera housing above their head, and from all the others, the entire length of the tunnel. He'd sent an electromagnetic pulse surging through the system.

Sambor shouted for his men, motioning them across the track in front of the train to a green metal door set in the concrete wall that connected the UK-bound tunnel with the service tunnel. He opened it and signalled to his men to follow him out of reach of the sprinkler system.

One hundred metres away, separated from his brother by the thickness of the tunnel wall, Laszlo clambered down from the motionless Eurostar and crept back along its flank, using the dim glow of the emergency lights from the carriage windows a metre above him to find his way through the darkness.

He soon saw a green metal door in the wall ahead. He ran to it and slipped into the service tunnel where Sambor and his men were waiting in the gloom. Sambor grasped him in a bear hug and planted a kiss on both his cheeks. Laszlo was just as pleased to see him. It wasn't only because of the plan they had made: the siblings were close; they trusted each other with their lives – and had done so many times.

'Little brother!' Laszlo returned the affection, happy to be talking in his mother tongue once more. It was always a relief. During their youth as ethnic Slavs living in South Ossetia, they had been constantly pressured by the dictatorship to refer to themselves as Georgians, and to speak Georgian. Georgia controlled their country, but they never forgot they were Ossetians, that Russia was their motherland, and Russian the language of their ancestors.

Laszlo and Sambor had been raised in a lawless nation that had descended into a constant state of conflict after the South Ossetians had declared their independence from Georgia in 1990. Their parents had tried to protect their sons by keeping their heads down and muddling through as best they could. Just finding enough food was a constant battle.

It had been clear from an early age that Laszlo was a gifted student, and his parents had known that the only place for him to further his education and be clear of the violence was with their fellow Slavs in Russia.

Sambor had had to stay at home: he wasn't bright enough to follow in Laszlo's footsteps, and they couldn't afford to send both boys. But there was no bad feeling between the two. Laszlo was the leader; he was mentally strong, just like their mother, the one who would lead the family out of poverty. Until then, they would carry on keeping their heads below the parapet and trying to survive.

Laszlo had not let his family down. He had achieved a PhD in physics, with a dissertation on gas-pipeline engineering; he had emerged from Russia a fervent nationalist. Given the poverty and death that he'd witnessed in South Ossetia under Georgian control, his fervour had its roots in genuine concerns.

Upon his return home, he had been unable to find work despite his skills. The few jobs available went to the ethnic Georgian minority. It was then that Laszlo had decided to follow a different path from the one his parents had planned. He had taken Sambor with him. They would keep their heads below the parapet no more.

'You kept your promise.'

'Of course.' Sambor held his brother at arms' length, but only so he could admire Laszlo's new facial hair. He hadn't seen him like this since the old days. 'Did you ever doubt it?'

'Not for a moment.'

'Are you ready to greet some of our old friends?' Sambor gestured towards the two men closest to them, both carrying belt-fed machine-guns. They stiffened proudly as Laszlo cast an eye over them and the rest of the warriors he had commanded when they were all Black Bears.

Sambor presented the grab bag to his brother, as if it were a coveted award.

Laszlo checked that its contents were still intact, then put the strap over his shoulder. 'Thank you, brother.' From this moment, it would not leave his side until the triumphant conclusion of their operation.

46

Tom was still making his way towards the front of the Eurostar, moving fast but scanning every passenger's face and checking each toilet as he came to it. Most of the passengers he passed had yet to feel there was any cause for concern: they sat with bored, indifferent or mildly irritated expressions as they waited for the train to start moving again.

The public-address system burst into life. 'This is the head steward speaking. We apologize for the delay. We hope to be moving again shortly. Meanwhile, please remain in your seats. The carriage doors will remain fastened for your safety. Thank you for your patience.'

The announcement created hardly a ripple of complaint among the passengers: Colin had done an excellent job, keeping everyone in 'fucking typical' mode.

As Tom entered the last carriage, he saw a red light blink above one of the carriage exits. A well-worn and seriously badged-up rucksack was preventing the door locking. Tom climbed down onto the concrete track bed and crouched, more out of instinct than anything else, his gaze sweeping in every direction.

The track was empty.

He scanned both sides of the train, checked the roof, then crouched low to peer beneath it. As he straightened again, he heard the smallest of noises, a barely audible mechanical hum behind the green metal door.

He began to move towards it.

47

Laszlo and his cadre in the service tunnel also heard the noise. But for them it was louder, and they knew what it was: they had been waiting for it. He smiled as the noise turned into a clearly identifiable engine note and they saw the glow of lights approaching. 'Right on time.'

His brother was in command of the fighting men and Laszlo would never usurp him. He stood to one side. At Sambor's instruction, they all faded into the shadows, fanning out along one wall of the tunnel.

Sambor himself remained at its centre, facing the approaching French fire truck. Caught in the glare of their headlights, he raised his hands, miming the appropriate degree of panic-stricken gratitude. The leading appliance screeched to a halt and the two behind soon followed suit.

Sambor headed for the front wagon, babbling in Russian, trying to explain what had happened. The brigade commander could only reply in French. 'Where is the fire? What has happened?'

The rest of the crews clambered out and began to unload their equipment.

Sambor got within two paces of the commander, stopped, legs apart to ensure stability as he pulled aside his leather jacket with his left hand, exposing the suppressed pistol tucked into his belt. He drew the weapon down with his right hand. There was a faint thud as the round left the barrel. It made contact with the skin immediately beneath the fireman's nostrils and took out his brain stem a fraction of a second before it emerged from the back of his skull, taking fragments of yellow helmet with it, and shattered against the appliance's bodywork.

There was a faint movement in the shadows and more South Ossetians stepped into view. Their weapons made barely a sound as the working parts moved to eject the empty case, reload a fresh round, and propel it from the barrel. They mowed the firemen down, one by one, with double taps into the centre of their body mass. Tufts of fibre from their uniforms puffed outwards like thistledown as they crashed to the ground.

48

Tom reached the green metal door and moved into the service tunnel. Laszlo, Sambor and their cohorts had their backs to him as they completed the slaughter of the unarmed French firemen.

One of the insurgents stopped firing and clipped a fresh mag into his weapon. Tom sprinted forward, keeping low. His target didn't even have time to turn his head as Tom grabbed the working-parts cover of the sub-machine-gun and, using his momentum, pushed down.

Partly through shock and partly as a result of the strength of the attack, the weapon fell from the assassin's hands. Turning it quickly and reaching for the pistol grip, Tom fired. The safety catch was on single shot, so Tom put another round into him as he fell, then dropped onto the concrete and used the body as cover.

He dropped two more of them before the rest realized that something was wrong. Laszlo, Sambor and those closest spun round, momentarily confused.

Only one fireman remained standing, bleeding profusely from his wounds. He took advantage of the distraction to dive for the wall and smash a dimly illuminated glass panel. Another volley tore into him, but as he fell, his hand hooked around the lever beneath, triggering one of the series of giant steel fire screens to crash down on the French side of the service tunnel.

Tom spotted the dim glow of another glass panel on the UK side, just before the green door. In the darkness, he couldn't spot the precise location of the next safety barrier. Would he seal himself in with Laszlo? He was about to find out. He made a run for it, firing in bursts to keep the enemy's heads down.

As his rounds slammed into the concrete around them, Laszlo's crew finally identified the threat. Braving the ceramic hailstorm that was now aimed in his direction, Tom dived for the panel. Smashing the glass with his fist, he forgot about the incoming, focused completely on pulling down the lever.

A second fire screen began to descend, threatening to cut him off from his escape route.

He sprayed the rest of his magazine at his pursuers then rolled under the rapidly descending barrier. As it fell to the ground, he lay for a second or two, listening to the staccato drumbeat of enemy rounds on the other side of the steel barricade, then the rattle and bang of their vain attempts to force it open.

49

Tom heard a muffled shout. Pressing his ear to the metal, he could make out Sambor's yell in Russian: 'Who the fuck was that?'

And Laszlo's growled response: 'What does it matter? We continue.'

The sound of heavy magnets being clamped onto the barrier a few seconds later echoed down the tunnel. Tom turned and hobbled towards the safety door, keeping close to the wall, away from the centre of the pressure wave and high-velocity secondary missiles that the imminent detonation would catapult his way.

Moments later, the area behind him erupted. The copper liner charge cut a rectangular hole through the steel as easily as if it were wet paper. The pressure wave jolted Tom's body and hurled him – his internal organs shuddering, the fillings in his teeth vibrating – through the doorway into the Paris-bound tunnel. Debris rained down, burying him beneath a pile of dust and rubble.

As the ringing in his ears subsided, he began to hear the screams and shouts of the Eurostar passengers. He could also hear Laszlo, Sambor and their men advancing towards the breach in the fire screen, picking their way through the cloud of noxious smoke billowing from the site of the explosion.

Tom was lying in their path. He had to move, and now. One round would be all it took to put an end to his chances of sorting out this nightmare.

He wrenched himself onto his hands and knees and tried to crawl. His legs wouldn't function. He dug his elbows into the rubble and hauled himself forward. The cover of the nearest carriage seemed to be a lifetime away. But he managed to slide beneath it as a dozen sets of boots pounded past him.

Cutting charges were set on the carriage doors at intervals along the train. Sixty seconds later they, too, detonated. The succession of pressure waves rippled along the tunnels to England and France. They didn't have anywhere else to go. As Tom struggled to recover, he knew that no one on either side would be in any doubt now that there was more than a fire going on down here.

He watched the insurgents swarm onto the train. The operation was as slick as anything the Blue team could have achieved. The charges guaranteed entry; they also subdued the occupants.

Tom thought only of Delphine. If one of the smouldering doors was hers, she'd be OK. Toilets and luggage racks separated the access points from the passenger seating. She'd be scared, but alive.

Laszlo's men burst into the carriages, brandishing their suppressed weapons. Panic spread like wildfire.

'*Shut up!*' Laszlo's voice cut through the bedlam in the forward section. 'Everyone! Hands on your heads, then heads down. Do it now!'

A man in his thirties, alone in a corner seat, suddenly leaped to his feet and started running down the aisle, away from the guns. The first shots went wide, but well-aimed rounds from Laszlo and Sambor cut him down.

Sambor moved quickly after him and finished him with a single shot to the head. Laszlo paused alongside him as the other passengers tried to process what had just happened. He knew it would be hard for them: no gunfire; no pre-game warm-up; just instant death. It wasn't the way they'd seen it in the movies.

'Could he be the one?'

Sambor kicked over the body so that they could have a closer look at his face.

Laszlo looked down. 'No. No dust residue on him from the detonation. Just another nonentity with no self-control.'

He showed no reaction to the howls around him, but he was pleased. They were getting the message. Fear really did bring compliance.

'So, you think our hero is still out there?'

'Perhaps.'

The only thing that mattered to Laszlo was the mission. Once a clear set of objectives had been decided upon, he knew he must never deviate from them, no matter what was thrown at him. Fighting and killing were easy; his mind had processed the why, the when and the how. Laszlo was an intellectual; a professor of the art of conflict. His heart provided the fire; his body was the finely honed instrument with which he forged his vision.

He scanned the carriage. Some of the passengers had obeyed his orders: they kept their heads low. Others, trembling with fright, were still too stunned to react. Speed and aggression were the key. They needed to be gripped instantly. He nodded to his men, and out came the Mace cans. Ten seconds later, the offenders were doubled up, coughing and retching, tears and green mucus decorating their faces.

He was glad they'd dropped the runner. These people needed to know what would happen if they didn't do exactly what they were told.

The next phase could now begin: herding the passengers towards the front half of the train. They had about four hundred people to control, and they needed to confine them.

50

Delphine had done exactly as Tom had instructed when the explosions started. She'd crouched behind her bags and stayed where she was as the pressure wave rocked the carriage. Her ears felt as if they were bursting.

The pinstriped businessman had been less prudent. Panicked, he had dived out of his seat, run towards the nearest detonation site and leaped into the darkness. Hyperventilating with fear, not knowing which way to run, he hadn't seen the heavily armed men emerge from the smoke. He hadn't had time to take a single step before he'd felt something pushed into the side of his head, just below the earlobe.

His killers stepped back from the side of the train and fired a burst at one of the windows. The suppressed weapons continued to make no sound, so the blizzard of incoming safety glass was the first sign of further attack. Safe behind her makeshift barricade, Delphine remained untouched, although the faces of two or three others were cut. But she wasn't unharmed. For the first time in as long as she could remember, she curled up like a small child and wept. It wasn't long before she realized she was weeping for Tom.

As the insurgents stormed the carriage, Delphine wriggled further down in her seat, dragging her bags on top of her. But she was spotted at once. A man mountain with wild hair and a glistening beard seized her arm, dragged her out from behind her protective barricade, and herded her towards the rest of the panic-stricken crowd of survivors.

She saw Grace, tears streaming down her face, clutching her children and trying to quieten their terrified cries. Delphine worked her way towards them through the heaving mob. 'It'll be all right,' she whispered, squeezing her arm. 'It's OK, children. Just stay quiet and keep still. The bad men will go soon.'

51

While their men secured the passengers and herded them through the train, Laszlo and Sambor stormed the driver's compartment. Laszlo issued his commands in a brisk monotone. 'Get on the floor. Put your hands behind your backs. And now stay absolutely still or we will kill you.' He knew that people generally couldn't control their fear: they needed his control because they had lost all sense of their own.

The driver proved not to be as stupid as Laszlo had assumed. He slid out of his driving seat like oil and lay flat on the floor, face down. He didn't move a muscle. Sambor zip-tied his wrists and ankles while Laszlo picked up his radio mic. He knew that Folkestone control centre would be standing by, desperate to know what was happening in the tunnel.

To begin with, he just heard breathing.

When he spoke, it was slowly and deliberately, in perfect, slightly accented English. 'My name is Laszlo Antonov. And I have complete control of this train and all its passengers. What happens to them next depends on the nature of your response. Now, put me in contact with whoever is in command of incident control.'

It was pointless dealing with anyone else. He knew how the system worked.

'Sorry . . .' The voice at the other end of the line was barely more than a squeak. 'You said Laszlo Anton—'

'Listen to me, young man. I want to talk to whoever will be liaising with COBRA. They know who I am. They know I am on this train. Just do what I say, and do it now. If *you* don't know what COBRA is, go and find someone who does.'

He listened in silence to the panic-stricken rambling of the Eurostar employee.

COBRA?

He knew nothing about the police arriving to seal off the tunnel.

He knew nothing about the SAS taking over their holding area.

But why would he? Everything had happened in less than an hour.

The idiot knew nothing, apart from the fact that the fire alarms had been triggered and the French were dealing with it. And that they were holding all movement on the UK side. The tunnel's entire CCTV system was down, and now the Eurostar crew were reporting explosions – explosions *on the train*. He'd thought he was dealing with a small fire, not a hijack and hostage emergency . . .

Out of his depth and thrust suddenly into a situation that was well beyond his pay grade, he began to stumble through a response, in a strange, robotic tone that suggested he was reading from a handbook or a *What to do when the shit hits the fan* instruction sheet. 'I . . . er . . . I need to establish the . . . er . . . circumstances . . . of this incident . . . before I can make a judgement on the . . . correct response . . .'

Laszlo remained the personification of cool. He'd been expecting something like this. Most organizations carried out paper exercises to deal with a crisis. But, as the 7/7 bombings had demonstrated, when it came to the real thing, people reacted very differently. For Laszlo, this was a good thing. It provided an opportunity to take command of the situation, and to demonstrate that whatever threats he made, he *would* carry them out. 'Then you, young man, have just killed the first hostage.'

He looked back along the carriage and pointed to a harassed blonde doing her best to comfort her two young children. The pretty French girl he'd seen at St Pancras reached out to protect the woman, but Sambor swept her aside. He grabbed the blonde's arm and dragged her away. As he began to shove her up the aisle, the kids burst into tears.

'Please,' the woman begged. 'My children . . .'

Laszlo inclined his head. 'Sure, why not? Bring them too.' There was no warmth in his smile.

Sambor gathered up the three of them. Laszlo held out the open radio mic with one hand, and rested the barrel of his sub-machine-gun across his forearm, pointing at the two children.

He turned his ice-cold stare back to the mother. 'Choose,' he said. His eyes darted between them. 'Which one?'

She stared at him uncomprehendingly. It was a moment before she realized his meaning. Then her legs buckled beneath her and she sank to the floor. 'Please, I beg you.' She clasped her hands together, pleading. 'They're only . . . babies . . . Please, please . . . take me instead . . .'

Laszlo held the microphone by her face and looked down at her in silence.

She sobbed and implored as the seconds ticked by.

'Very well.' He swung his barrel towards her.

She turned to her children and her hair caught in the muzzle, as if trying to reach out and stop what was about to happen. 'I love you both so very—'

Laszlo pulled the trigger. The bullet struck her in the top of the head. Her body slumped, leaving a few strands of hair wrapped around the weapon's foresight. As he swung the sub-machine-gun away they fluttered gently to the floor.

The carriage was completely silent. The little boy's eyes widened in disbelief. Then his sister gave a heartrending cry. She sank to her knees alongside their mother, trying to cradle her in her arms.

The boy remained as still as a statue, struck dumb with shock, staring at the muzzle of the gun that had killed his mother.

Laszlo brought the microphone back to his mouth. 'If I do not hear from someone authorized by COBRA within fifteen minutes, her children will be the next to die.'

In his earpiece, he could just hear sobbing.

Laszlo had always found weakness revolting. His reaction to it was visceral. 'Get a grip on yourself,' he barked. 'This woman at my feet showed great love, great strength and great dignity in death. But you? You disgust me. *Now, do what I say.*'

52

There was a faint movement in the darkness beneath the train. Tom ran his fingers, as grey as the dust around them, across his forehead and down his cheek. He gave himself a moment to take stock. His head was pounding; he was covered with cuts and bruises; his nose and mouth were filled with grit; but he had no serious wounds or injuries. Not that it mattered much: he still had to crack on, no matter what condition he was in.

He slid out and hauled himself upright. Hugging the tunnel wall, he moved forward in a crouch to avoid the lozenges of light cast from the carriage windows. The contrast between the glow of the emergency lamps and the darkness of the tunnel allowed him to stand in the strips of shadow and see inside the train without being seen himself.

A line of passengers stood facing him, hands on heads and faces pressed against the glass. The ones that hadn't been herded to the side were clustered on the seats, heads down. People were crying, begging, praying, comforting children; some just stared, accepting that their life would now come to an end.

Through the gaps between these visions of human despair and remorse, the muttered promises that if they ever got out of this they would change for the better, Tom spotted several of Laszlo's sidekicks. He eased himself closer, disabled the flash function on his phone camera and held it up, zooming in on each face in turn.

He kept going, hoping against hope that he'd spot Delphine. He eventually caught sight of her being comforted by a group of other hostages.

Relieved and elated, he risked inching his way into the pool of light spilling from an empty window close by, and stood stock still, willing her to glance in his direction.

As he watched, Delphine's look of desolation was suddenly replaced by a beaming smile. Tom put a finger to his lips. She gave a faint, almost imperceptible nod, then signalled to the right with her eyes. Laszlo and Sambor were issuing a string of orders to their men further up the carriage.

Laszlo froze, antennae on full alert. He cast a suspicious glare along the carriage, but Delphine had already re-positioned herself, her nose against the window and her eyes staring out into the darkness.

Tom edged further along the train and photographed the brothers. The lighting wasn't strong enough to obtain good imagery of anything inside, but that didn't matter. The team would need up-to-date shots of the X-rays and the computer geeks could sort out the pixels later. The quicker he got Delphine out of the train, the quicker Gavin would have the pictures and the quicker Tom could add some int to what the Slime had already gathered.

Sambor and Laszlo began to walk towards the driver's compartment. Tom tracked their progress by monitoring their shifting weight as it depressed the train's shock absorbers between the carriages, and kept in step with them. But when they reached the front of the train, he couldn't see through its small side windows or the sharply angled windscreen.

Using his iPhone display to light his way, he lowered himself to the concrete track bed, wriggled between the wheels and beneath the greasy tangle of wires and cables of the undercarriage.

53

Having parked the two recently orphaned children outside the cabin, Laszlo turned his back on them and sank into the driver's seat almost directly above where Tom lay. He reached for the radio mic.

'Time's up. Who is there to talk to me?'

Laszlo was well aware of the sequence of events that would have followed his discovery on the train. He knew, even if Eurostar didn't, that the chief constable of whichever constabulary covered the location of the incident would be first to take command. But how had he been flagged? He was more intrigued than angry. The man helping the pretty French girl to the toilet? Very possibly. He hadn't seen him since . . .

'This is Chief Constable Michael Alderson of Kent Constabulary. Who am I speaking to?'

Alderson had decided to keep his tone uncompromising but courteous. He'd come by all he knew about Laszlo from the five minutes he'd spent reading the file sent to his BlackBerry while juggling a flurry of calls to and from his commanders.

He'd had to secure the area, co-ordinate the emergency services and keep a grip on proceedings from the back of a speeding, London-bound BMW. But now he was static on the hard shoulder of the A2 – he'd asked the driver to pull in as soon as he'd got a full signal.

Alderson stuck a digit into his free ear to cut out the traffic noise and the clicking of the four-ways. The driver sat motionless, not even moving his head to check the fast-approaching traffic in the wing mirror.

Laszlo smiled to himself. 'You know very well who I am. Laszlo Antonov.' He paused, giving the policeman time for his name, and what it meant, to sink in. Maybe this Alderson would take the trouble to look more closely at the briefing notes he no doubt had in front of him.

'I want to begin by congratulating you, Chief Constable. You've just saved some lives. One moment, please . . .'

He covered the microphone with his hand and turned to Sambor, then wrinkled his nose in disgust. The children were now huddled on the floor behind him. The sight of their mother's murderer was enough to start them both shaking and whimpering all over again. And the brown patch spreading across the boy's new holiday trousers was painfully obvious.

'He's shat himself . . .'

Sambor gave a crooked smile. 'You seem to have that effect on people, my brother.'

'It's one of the secrets of my success.' Laszlo's smile faded. 'Get them out of here.'

'You want me to get rid of them?'

'Clean him up or kill them, I don't care which. Their lives are ruined now anyway.'

Sambor hustled the children out, and Laszlo turned back to the radio mic. 'Chief Constable Alderson, my apologies. How kind of you to take my call.'

'Mr Antonov, what is it you want?'

'To live a nice quiet life in Hampstead. As indeed I was – until the SAS came knocking on my door.' Laszlo leaned back in the chair, resting his feet on the head of the terrified train driver, who still lay face down on the floor with his hands and feet zip-tied. 'However, as you know, I've taken up a new, but purely temporary, residence near Folkestone.

'It's a little cramped for my taste, and there are far too many noisy neighbours but, as you may know, there are fewer of them than there were a little while ago.' He paused again, to let the message sink in. 'And there will be fewer still a few minutes from now, if our discussions do not prove fruitful.

'First, do not even *think* about putting power back online. It does not serve me at all, only you. The back-up system will suffice for now. Second, I should imagine the gentlemen from Hereford will be attempting to pay me a call – in about . . . let's see . . .' He checked his watch. 'Say three hours from now – that is, if you hand over control. Which you have to, of course, because the situation is already well beyond your very limited control. No doubt the home secretary will be ordering you to do so very soon, once COBRA is in session and the gravity of the situation is clear to all.

'So I'd obviously like us to have completed arrangements for the release of these poor people, in exchange for a safe passage for myself and my associates. Do you think you might be able to manage that, Chief Constable?'

'Mr Antonov, you ask a lot that I alone am in no position to guarantee. A demonstration of your good intentions might improve your situation, though. Perhaps the traditional release of the old, the infirm, the women and the children?'

'Demonstration of *good intentions*?' Laszlo kept his voice dangerously even. 'You seem to be under the illusion that this is a negotiation, Chief Constable. Let me assure you that it is not.'

'Quite so.' Alderson knew he wasn't going to get anywhere with that ploy. 'After all, it is the stated policy of Her Majesty's government never to negotiate with terrorists.'

'But I am not a terrorist. The ICC have decided that I am a war criminal. There is a difference, which I would ask you to respect. Some call me a freedom fighter, but the truth is, Chief Constable, I'm just a soldier, who carried out his duty, fighting for his country. If necessary, however, I'm quite prepared to kill every man, woman and child on this train.'

'Mr Antonov ... My name is Michael. May I call you Laszlo?'

'Of course you may, Michael.'

Laszlo liked the tone of this man. He knew that their time together would be short, however. Even before control was handed over, the chief constable would be out of the picture. The Security Service would install their own case officer; someone who did not need any notes or files. That was a shame – but it might mean he got to encounter the man who'd been tracking him for so long.

'Perhaps so. Perhaps you are a soldier. But that is for others to decide. What concerns me are the hundreds of lives you are putting at risk. I want to make sure that you get what you need so *they* stay alive.'

Laszlo was pleased with what Alderson had said. 'Thank you, Michael. And I, of course, will help you – if you provide me with the safe passage I require to a country with no extradition treaties in place with Great Britain.'

'No doubt you already have somewhere in mind.'

'Indeed I do,' Laszlo said. 'I've spent a pleasant few years in London, but now I think somewhere warmer, with less stringent banking regulations, would be much more suitable. I'll need to be sure of that before I deposit the hundred and fifty kilograms of gold that you're going to pay me.'

'Gold?'

'Correct. And I will require a Chinook helicopter. Both main fuel tanks full, and a full cabin fuel bladder to feed the main tanks.'

The chief constable couldn't square what he had read about this man with what he was saying. It was as if Laszlo had taken his plan of action from a 1970s B movie.

'More details will follow, Michael. Now you have thirty minutes to—'

The line went dead.

'Hello ... Hello?' He jiggled the switch a few times, then swore and banged down the radio mic.

*

Alderson checked the signal on his mobile. 'Hello? Laszlo?'

He checked the screen again before throwing it onto the seat.

The driver cut the four-ways and started to check for a break in the traffic. He had been with the chief constable long enough to know it was time to get his foot down even before his employer did.

'Right, fuck it, get moving.'

Laszlo kicked the driver. 'Where is the radio control? Where do we check?'

'Under us.' He didn't even give Laszlo time to take a breath. He just wanted to do what he was told, when he was told, and live to tell the tale. 'The control box is marked "TTR".'

54

Crouched on the track now, but still under the train, Tom drew back into the shadows, hidden behind one of the giant wheels of the locomotive. A few moments later, he heard a scuffling sound and saw a man clamber down and begin to inch his way along the darkened track towards the front of the engine.

The man knelt down, lit his torch and leaned forward, squinting at the undercarriage in the bluish light of its beam. He spotted something – a glint of metal, perhaps – at the end of a dangling cable. He reached towards it.

Tom seized the outstretched arm and wrenched it so vigorously that the South Ossetian's forehead cracked against the steel box housing the radio gear. Tom grabbed his neck before he had time to recover and pounded his skull into the steel railway line.

Now crouched above him, Tom straightened his arms to maximize the pressure around his opponent's throat and squeezed. He felt no emotion. The equation was simple: 'Him or me.' The quicker Tom killed him, the quicker the threat would be removed.

The man died without making a sound.

Tom took hold of the body and dragged it towards him until it was completely hidden beneath the train. He'd just finished when he heard more footsteps – and the unmistakable clink of belt-linked ammunition dangling from the top cover of a machine-gun.

The bodies split into two groups. One headed to the rear of the train, towards the UK, the other towards France, and Tom.

He had no choice but to stay as still as the dead man beside him. He held his breath and tensed every muscle in his body as the two sets of legs made their way up the side of the train towards him.

The link continued to swing back and forth against the Russian-made PKM general-purpose machine-gun as the legs drew level. His eyes swivelled as they passed where he lay and moved on towards the front of the train. That link wasn't 9mm ceramic, designed to minimize the ricochet risk. It was heavy 7.62mm ball ammo: lumps of lead encased in brass, designed to rip humans apart in vast numbers, as well as any vehicles or cover they might be trying to hide behind.

Tom inched forward, flattening himself against the track bed, and peered out from under the engine. The two insurgents were now in the gloom and out of sight, but he could hear what they were doing. The faint metallic sound of ammunition boxes being opened and link being laid out ready to load told him everything he needed to know.

They were setting up the gun position to cover approach routes to the train from this end of the southbound track and the entrance to the service tunnel. They'd hold up any attack, and give Laszlo enough warning and opportunity to kill a serious number of the assault team before they reached the train. If Tom had been in Laszlo's shoes, he'd have done the same. Except that Tom wasn't in the martyrdom game, and he had a feeling that Laszlo might almost be welcoming it. Which made him a very dangerous enemy indeed.

He was about to move back when he heard the side window of the driver's cabin slide open above him, then voices speaking Russian.

'This place still stinks . . .'

He edged towards the sound and flattened himself against

the side of the train, straining to hear what was being said.

'Both guns are now operational.'

'Good. Get the engineers to work.'

He heard a flurry of movement, then silence, followed by a shout: 'And what's happening with the radio?'

Shit. Tom quickly retreated to where the dead man lay and took his suppressed sub-machine-gun. As he started towards the rear of the train, two figures with heavy packs on their backs clambered down the steps and moved towards the door to the service tunnel.

55

'How much time before they take action?' Sambor asked. Laszlo had followed him down the aisle.

'Maybe an hour, once the radio is working. When we kill another of these sheep, they will have no choice but to send in our friends.'

'You never give me enough time . . .'

'There is not enough time in this life for you, little brother, whatever the task. You would spend all day deciding what to have for breakfast if I let you.'

Sambor laughed. 'And why not? Breakfast is the most important meal of the day.'

Laszlo sniffed the air again and directed a ferocious glare towards the two children huddled together in the corner of the carriage. They watched him with terrified eyes.

'What's the matter with you, brother? Are you going soft on me? Those brats still smell worse than a Georgian.' Laszlo addressed the nearest cluster of passengers. 'I want someone to clean them up and find them fresh clothes.'

Nobody moved.

'Who knows where they were sitting? Where their luggage is?'

Still nothing.

'I'll make this easier for you,' Laszlo growled. 'If there are no volunteers, the kids will be killed and thrown off the train.'

He looked slowly around the carriage. Their eyes were cast down, but he saw fear etched on every face. His lip curled with disdain.

'It is as I thought. The lives of these children are in your hands, but you do *nothing*. If you survive, I hope you will remember this moment of shame. You people disgust me.'

Tom had tracked the progress of the two men from the safety of the shadows.

Shielded momentarily from Laszlo and his huge sidekick by a bulkhead, he stepped forward into the light from the window closest to Delphine.

Attuned now to his presence, she caught sight of him almost immediately out of the corner of her eye, and turned her head slowly towards him.

Tom gestured at her, but she had no idea what he meant.

'I'll do it.' Delphine stood and raised her hand. 'I have some clothes that I think might fit them.'

Laszlo turned on his heel. 'Clothes? Where are these clothes?'

'They're in a shopping bag in Coach Eight.'

His eyes narrowed. 'So tell me, why are you so eager to volunteer?'

'Because they're only children. Because they've just lost their mother, they're very frightened, and I don't want any harm to come to them.'

'And are you a mother?' Laszlo's expression was still sceptical.

Delphine felt her mouth go dry. She shook her head.

Laszlo continued the interrogation as Sambor grabbed her arm. 'Then why do you travel with children's clothes?'

'Because I am—' She corrected herself. 'Because I *was* going to Paris to see my sister. They are gifts for my niece and nephew.'

He continued to study her face. A vein began to throb in her temple.

He took an agonizingly long time to reply. 'Very well, then. You have more courage than the rest of these cattle.' He gestured at the people around her.

Sambor's hand tightened on her elbow as he pushed her towards one of the armed guards stationed at the end of the carriage. 'Go with her.' His breath smelt of overcooked cabbage. 'And don't let her out of your sight.'

As she passed the next window, Delphine risked another glance outside, but Tom had already disappeared back into the darkness.

56

As the Dauphin swept him, the Slime and the signals group in towards Folkestone, Gavin could see that the slow lane of the M20 had already turned into a car park. The line of static trucks and artics stretched back towards Ashford.

Operation Stack had been initiated, closing a fourteen-mile coast-bound section of the Kent motorway between junctions eight and nine. Gavin imagined the HGV drivers, seasoned campaigners in the field, switching off their engines, making themselves a brew and settling down to watch sport or porn movies on the TVs in their cabs, or stretching out in their bunks for a few hours' kip.

The other lanes were jammed with cars, the moon faces of some drivers visible through their windscreens, staring up as the heli flashed overhead, maybe praying for divine intervention. 'Poor bastards,' Gavin muttered, into his headset mic. 'They're probably thinking they'll be on the move again any minute, in France by this afternoon.'

Private motorists with Eurotunnel tickets would eventually be given ferry vouchers. Gavin always found himself grinning at that. It was a bit like being handed a ticket to Fight Night and spending the evening in the ring.

The moment they'd closed the tunnel, the propaganda

machine had swung into action. The powers-that-be wanted to keep the situation as covert as possible for as long as possible. The news channels were saying that the whole complex had been paralysed by yet another power failure. Daytime TV producers were hoping to discover a Hollywood star aboard or a woman in premature labour; if they could tick both boxes at once, so much the better.

The French and UK governments couldn't have cared less, as long as they steered clear of the truth: they both knew that the public loved a bad news story; the media on each side of the Channel could have a field day pointing the finger at the old enemy.

The Dauphin circled over the intricate pattern of bridges, access roads, loading ramps and platforms. Hard over to his right, Gavin could see the point where the gleaming tracks converged and then disappeared into the twin black holes set into the chalk cliff face. Figures in hi-vis vests scurried this way and that between police vans, ambulances and fire appliances.

They skimmed the rooftops of the administration buildings and went into a hover as the pilot made his approach to the helipad in the emergency staging area.

Gavin could see Woolf staring back up at them, hands on hips and a sour expression on his face, wanting to get on with the job.

57

Thickets of steel crowd barriers had taken root outside the entrance to the terminal. Police in riot gear held back a mob of reporters and photographers, crowds of angry motorists and foot passengers, and a few spectators unable to resist the attraction of crowds and commotion.

The heli landed out of their sight, and Gavin and his signallers gathered their equipment. As Woolf strode over, Gavin wasted no time on preliminaries. 'You got comms with COBRA yet?'

Woolf shrugged. 'Only on mobile. And there are still none with the train. COBRA's tatting about. I got here from London quicker than they can get their bloody act together in Westminster. The French are already set up and, as far as I know, the situation hasn't moved on from bi-national status.'

Gavin nodded. Each would be doing what they could to sort things out from their end of the tunnel, but at some stage, the earlier the better, one of them would have to grip the situation. Which was where the whole process got complicated. As far as Gavin was concerned, the problem wasn't just too many chiefs and not enough Indians: it was the chiefs spending too much time admiring their headdresses and not enough leading the braves into battle.

As the rotors closed down and the signallers and Slime unloaded, the two men headed for the steel-shuttered entrance to the hangar.

The holding area was completely self-contained. One of the rectangular, green-powder-coated low-level buildings that dotted the site, it provided the Blue and Red teams and their vehicles with the perfect location – beyond prying eyes – for preparation and rehearsal.

Apart from a washroom block and enough power points to fire up the Blackpool illuminations, the interior was bare. Three men in hi-vis jackets stood beside a lot of trestle tables and cheap fold-up chairs stacked along one wall. Arms laden with ring binders and long cardboard tubes, they looked as nervous as schoolboys.

For some reason that Gavin never understood, people got star-struck when the Regiment turned up. He always did his best to put them immediately at their ease. Apart from anything else, he could get more information out of them that way.

'All right, lads?' He dumped his ready-bag by his feet. 'Why don't you get some of those tables out and we can have a look at what we've got, yeah?'

The signallers began to wire their satellite comms into the roof dishes, to hang flat-screens on the wall and network a series of laptop computers. The hi-vis lads fished the plans out of the tubes and laid them out while the Slime anchored their corners with whatever they could find. Gavin settled himself in a chair and glanced across at Woolf, who was continuing his mobile love affair with the Cabinet Office Briefing Room.

58

Clements was in his usual seat, behind and just to the right of the home secretary. His job was to keep her supplied with files and briefing notes, to restrain her if she embarked upon any flights of rhetoric, and to intervene if her eagerness to do the right thing looked likely to result in promises his underlings could not fulfil.

Most of the committee was now present, and there were more bodies than yesterday. There was even a junior minister from the Department of Transport, attending his first COBRA meeting. Judging by the look on his face, he was excited and worried in equal measure. What if he had to make a decision?

Clements had got there well before anyone else, and felt even more superior when each new arrival came in not wearing a suit. The rest were in their weekend clothes: jeans, cords or, in Alderson's case, a blue Pringle sweater and the kind of patterned trousers golfers used to wear in 1970. Clements never really thought these people might have normal lives. He simply didn't care. Politicians, like hamburger flippers, were transient; he amused himself by calling them shits who passed in the night. They would move on; he would still be here looking after the country.

There was a commotion outside as Sarah Garvey arrived,

accompanied by her staff and Home Office advisers. The committee rose. She had been at home when she'd got the call and immediately changed into work clothes, a blue suit – skirt and jacket. Like Clements, she understood the meaning of right dress, right time.

Peter Brookdale, a member of the prime minister's advisory team, was among her retinue. The former tabloid hack, now head of communications, held the home secretary back as she was about to enter the room and muttered urgently into her ear.

The committee remained in stand-up-and-wait-for-her-to-enter-or-sit-down-and-do-it-again mode. Clements watched Sarah and Brookdale. The spin doctor was in jeans and green sweatshirt, and anyone unaware of their respective roles would have had difficulty in deciding from their body language which was the minister and which the paid employee.

The home secretary read from a briefing sheet as she listened. Whatever was being said clearly didn't sit well with her. She jabbed her index finger at him to underline her reply, then turned back towards the committee room and entered.

'Gentlemen, please sit.'

Clements knew exactly what had been said. He'd seen and heard it all before. The PM was worried about how he would come out of this incident. If things went wrong, Brookdale would make sure the media knew it was all Sarah's fault. If they didn't, then his job was to make sure the PM got all the credit.

Clements greeted her with his best civil-service smile. 'Good morning, Home Secretary.'

She gave him a nod as everyone took their seats, then looked around the table. 'Good morning, everyone. Now, as I understand it, we've got an HGV Shuttle on fire in the UK-bound section and Antonov holding a trainload of passengers hostage in the French-bound tunnel. How many dead so far?'

'One confirmed, Home Secretary,' Alderson said. 'But we

have no idea what casualties have resulted from the explosions. And now I'm afraid we've lost contact.'

'It's hard to see how things could be much worse.'

Clements cleared his throat vigorously enough for everyone to know that he was taking control of the conversation. 'We believe the two incidents are connected, Home Secretary.'

Sarah Garvey turned a baleful eye on him, aware that Clements might be enjoying the moment. 'I stand corrected. Things *are* worse.'

'Yes, Home Secretary, much worse. If we had been successful in Hampstead we would not be sitting here this morning. And I'm sure that the electorate will bear that distinction in mind when they come to cast their votes in the by-election there next week.' He exchanged a give-me-strength look with the dark side, as Clements liked to call passing shits like Brookdale. The communications chief looked as unimpressed as the minister by Clements's opening statement.

Sarah Garvey was having none of his shenanigans today. There was work to be done. This was only her second chairing of COBRA and she needed help from people who could provide it. 'Mr Clements, unless you can come up with something rather more intelligent or useful – and, honestly, either will do – I'd recommend a period of quiet reflection. As Abraham Lincoln used to say, "Better to keep silent and be thought a fool, than to open your mouth and remove all doubt."'

Clements glanced at the other politicians around the table, noting their hastily suppressed smiles at his humiliation. What a pack of rats, he thought, always jockeying for position and favour, all smiles to your face, but racing to be the first to trample you underfoot if you fall foul of the party or the press.

Clements knew that ultimately, should he need to play it, he held the trump card when it came to any situation involving Laszlo. But now was not the time. 'We have had *some* good news, Home Secretary.'

'At last.' Her voice was heavy with sarcasm. 'And what would that be, pray?'

Clements held up a sheet of paper. 'The bi-national status has been suspended. The UK now has control. It was Antonov who initiated the suspension, by making contact with us rather than the French.'

'And that's supposed to be good news, is it? I should imagine the French are pissing themselves with laughter right now . . .' She was momentarily distracted as Brookdale stood up, BlackBerry in hand, and scuttled out of the room to give his master the news.

Clements shifted in his seat. 'Under international law we are empowered to take unilateral action to resolve the matter and, forgive me for sounding like a scratched record, but given the unfortunate events in Hampstead yesterday . . .' he paused to ensure he had her complete attention, and received a look of pure venom in return '. . . a firm and decisive intervention, ending the crisis and eliminating Antonov, would win the government a lot of kudos and some respite in the opinion polls.'

Brookdale returned to the room. He might not have caught everything that had been said, but the last part was all he was interested in. 'That would certainly be true,' he blurted, 'if the intervention were successful. But if it failed . . .' He left the sentence unfinished.

Clements didn't acknowledge him. 'Fortune favours the bold, Home Secretary. The SAS are already deploying, and they will not fail us. The chief constable here has the situation under control in the meantime.'

'The SAS were deployed in Hampstead too.' Sarah Garvey's tone was even more waspish.

'Yes,' Clements replied smoothly. He had her where he wanted her. 'And had it not been for the prevarication from this committee room, they would have apprehended Antonov before he could make his escape.'

Alderson looked at a sea of blank faces. He had never set eyes on most of the committee before now, and suspected that if he were to attend another incident in a few months' time most of this lot would have moved on. Yet again COBRA appeared to be little more than a photo-opportunity: its members seemed to believe that if they could be seen walking into the meeting, they'd appear to be achieving something.

He sparked up. Somebody had to. 'Home Secretary, the SAS have a man on the train. He may be able to help us.'

This was news to her. She swivelled to confront the DSF, the director of UKSF. 'Well?'

59

Delphine led Rose and Daniel through the deserted carriages, their slow progress lit only by the glow of the emergency lights. The guard at her shoulder made his impatience clear, but she resolutely adjusted her pace to that of the children. Daniel was struggling to walk in his soiled trousers. She tried to give him a reassuring smile. 'Not much further now, *mon chéri*. Just one more coach and we're there.'

Both kids reached out, held the hand that was offered them, and followed her like zombies. Towards the end of the next aisle, Delphine brought them to a halt. Unless the corpse had been moved, Grace would still be lying directly in their path. Even in the low light, the children . . . She shuddered. It didn't bear thinking about. They'd been through too much already.

'Rose . . . Daniel . . . We're going to play a little game . . .'

Tom had already reached Coach Eight. The sprinklers had stopped, and all he could hear was the sound of water dripping off the skin of the train and into the puddles that had gathered on the concrete below.

Heading for the frosted glass of the toilet window, he ducked down, crawled beneath the train and, rolling onto his back, worked his way across the track until he reached the septic tank. The thick plastic containers were removed once a day and replaced with empty ones. Checking out the noise level and staying aware of the gun position further along the track, he unscrewed the butterfly nuts securing the steel clips that kept it in place, then slid it smoothly out from under the toilet seat on its runners, like a kitchen drawer.

Delphine staggered a little with the weight of a child on each hip.

To keep to the rules, they had their eyes closed, and each time she took a step they counted off a number. Rose said it into her left ear, Daniel into her right. Delphine then translated the number into French and they had to say it back to her.

'And the next number is . . .'

'Four!'

'That's *quatre*.'

'*Quatre!*'

'Very good!'

Delphine reached her seat. She nodded in the direction of the carrier bag. The guard shoved her forward, picked it up and examined the contents in the gloom. After a moment he gave a grudging nod.

'And the next number is . . .'

'Five!'

'That's *cinq*,' Rose said proudly.

'Well done, Rose. Daniel?'

'*Cinq!*'

'Fantastic! Let's keep going!'

There was a dark shape on the floor immediately ahead of them. If she hadn't known better, she might have thought a couple of rucksacks or a loosely rolled rug had fallen from the rack.

'And the next number is . . .' She edged around Grace's body, grunting with the effort.

'*Six*,' Rose said. 'That's a really easy one.'

'Daniel?'

'*Six!*'

'Brilliant.'

There was a sniffle in her right ear. She felt the little boy's face wet against her cheek. 'My mummy is dead, isn't she?'

Delphine hesitated, uncertain how to reply. She didn't want to lie to them. 'We can't think about that now, *chéri*. Now what's the next number? It's eight, isn't it?'

Rose said, 'No, it's not, Delphine! It's seven.'

'Of course! And that is . . . ?'

'*Sept*,' Rose said.

Daniel stifled a sob.

She speeded up her pace, bouncing the children on her hips as she went. '*Huit, neuf, dix, onze, douze, treize* . . .'

Rose giggled and clung to her more tightly.

They reached the end of the carriage.

Once through the door she slid them down to the floor and squatted at Daniel's level, then took his and Rose's hand in hers and gave them a reassuring squeeze. She hesitated for a moment longer, trying to think of what she would say to her niece and nephew if her sister were now lying in a pool of blood behind them. 'I know it's very, very hard for you both, but we all need to help each other. I want you to do exactly as I tell you, even if it sounds strange.' She gave them her most radiant smile and hugged both children to her.

The guard jabbed her in the back with the barrel of his machine-gun. She stood up, gave him a withering glare, and snatched the bag from his hand. She tipped out the clothes and held up a dress for Rose and a pair of jeans and a sweat-shirt for Daniel. 'What do you think?' She placed them against their trembling bodies. 'Not too bad, are they? And I think the sizes will be close enough. Now come on, *mes petits*, let's get you cleaned up.'

She opened the toilet door and ushered them inside. As she tried to close it behind them, the guard wedged his boot across the frame. He hadn't said a single word since they'd been together, and he didn't start now. But his bestial grunt and the look of primal aggression on his face made his message clear.

'Oh, come on.' She waved an arm around the cubicle. 'We're

not going anywhere, are we? They're only little children, and you're a very big, scary man. Please, just let them be for a moment.'

The man just stared at her, unblinking and unmoved. After a moment she turned away from him, ran some water into the basin and pulled a handful of paper towels from the dispenser. She dropped to her knees, undid Daniel's new Buzz Lightyear belt and loosened his off-to-Disneyland jeans. Then she paused and looked up. 'Are you really sure you want to be downwind of this?'

Delphine removed Daniel's soiled trousers and pants and held out the stinking bundle. 'Since you're here,' she said, 'you might as well make yourself useful.' The guard recoiled, gagging, and allowed the door to slide shut.

Almost immediately, Delphine felt her mobile phone vibrate in her jeans. She pulled it out and read the text message on the Bluetooth display:

Lock door. Lift toilet seat.

Delphine quietly turned the lock, then washed and dried Daniel and helped him into the clean clothes. The trousers were a little large, but she tightened the belt another notch and rolled up the legs a couple of times. Then she helped Rose into the new dress, making sure she had something to comfort her. For Delphine in her childhood it had been a toy rabbit; for Rose it was an iPod in a bright pink sock.

She tiptoed to the door, listened for a second, then stepped back and flipped the seat. Tom, framed by the toilet bowl, his face crusted with oil and dirt, lay on his back beneath them.

Rose leaned forward too, and peered into the bowl. She opened her mouth to scream, but Delphine clamped a hand over her lips and said in an urgent whisper, 'It's OK, don't be frightened. He's going to help us. He's not a pretty sight, but he's our friend.'

Tom reached up and started to remove the square of flooring that provided the base of the toilet bowl. There was a slight scraping sound as he worked it free and lowered it to the ground. 'Right,' he murmured. 'The girl first.'

'Her name is Rose.' Delphine slipped her hands under Rose's armpits, lifted her up and lowered her through the hole in the floor. Tom grabbed her and helped her to the ground. He squeezed her hand, smiled encouragingly and held a finger to his lips. Then he reached up to take her brother.

'And this is Daniel. He's a very brave little boy.' Daniel was a foot shorter than Rose, but a good few Happy Meals plumper. As Delphine lowered him into the hole, he felt the rough edges of the surround scraping at his puppy fat and began to panic.

Tom grabbed his legs and tried to pull him through. Frightened and more than a little ashamed, Daniel started to cry.

'Sssh . . . sssh . . . it's OK, *chéri*. Just suck in your tummy – it'll be OK . . .'

Delphine cast an anxious glance at the door.

Tom looked along the track in both directions, then checked his watch. Laszlo wasn't going to wait for ever to find out why the radio hadn't been put back online, and what had happened to the man sent to repair it.

Delphine gripped Daniel more firmly under his armpits now that his legs were dangling under the carriage. She tried to calm him. 'It's all right. Everything is going to be OK. Just breathe in and try to wriggle through. Don't worry, you won't fall – the nice man, our friend, he will catch you.'

The guard had heard the boy's cries, and Delphine watched, horrified, as the handle turned, then stopped. The angry shouts from the other side of the door were followed by boot and body slamming against it.

Tom yanked hard on Daniel's legs and, with a yelp, the boy finally dropped into his arms.

Delphine lowered herself as quickly as possible into the hole, but the toilet door burst open as the guard kicked it off its lock. He dived forward, grabbed her around the chest, and dragged her out.

As Tom launched himself upwards to help her, she shouted, 'Save the ki—'

Her assailant slammed a fist into the top of her head. She felt the skin on her scalp split and her face hurtled towards the linoleum.

Fighting the pain as she lay sprawled on the toilet floor, she felt rather than heard him spray three suppressed bursts of 9mm into the darkness, then watched him lean as far as he could into the hole to see what he had hit.

60

Tom had thrown himself and the children to one side, shielding them with his body as a flurry of rounds peppered the concrete. Now he dragged them well away from the danger zone and planted them both behind one of the steel wheels.

'Stay there,' he whispered. 'Not a sound!'

They went rigid, but Rose managed a nod.

He moved to the other side of the train, to what was left of the door. He still had to reach Delphine, and then try to get them all out of this shit. That was all he needed to think about. What might happen later wasn't important right now.

He got there just as Delphine's guard cannoned across the threshold. He misjudged the grapple as the man landed, but the fighter was taken by surprise. Both their weapons clattered to the ground. He felt a blinding pain as his opponent's head glanced off his own, then another as the guard recovered enough to butt him full-on and hurl him backwards onto the ground. He lay there for a moment, stunned and winded, as the man landed on top of him.

Tom scrabbled for his weapon but was pinioned in a vice-like bear-hug around his chest and beneath his armpits. He tried to kick and buck, then head butt. The guard was doing exactly the same.

The man's breath was hot against his cheek. It stank of cigarettes and decay. He had a week's bristle on him, rough against Tom's face and neck. He squeezed, his eyes closed, snorting. All Tom could do was keep trying to butt him, keep trying to make contact wherever he could.

Tom somehow managed to get his legs around the Russian's gut and fought to link his feet. The fighter's head jerked back – Tom's opportunity to reach his eyes. Blood and snot glistened on the man's face in the dim glow from the carriage. He fought to breathe through gritted teeth and did everything he could to keep Tom's fingers away from his eyes. He tightened his grip around Tom's chest and shook his head as Tom began to get a grip on his face and dig deeper with his thumbs. He tried to bite Tom's fingers. Tom moved his right hand so he had a flat palm underneath his chin, then switched his left to just below the crown of the man's head and grabbed a fistful of his hair.

He finally managed to interlock his boots. At last he could squeeze and push down with his legs, at the same time twisting up with his arms. His opponent's neck suddenly gave way, with a barely audible crack. His body didn't even jerk. It just went still. Tom rolled over and kicked him off.

He wiped the blood, snot and saliva off his hands on the dead man's coat, and picked up the nearest weapon. He checked that the magazine was on tight, and that he still had a round in the chamber, then started to move back to the carriage door to get what he'd come for.

61

Delphine was still lying on the toilet floor when she heard Tom's voice.

'Delphine . . . *Delphine!*'

It sounded a long way off at first. Perhaps even in a dream. Then a terrible stench assaulted her nostrils. She opened her eyes, saw the bundle of soiled clothing, and started to recover her bearings.

'*Delphine! Come on!*'

Her strength surged back. She started to crawl towards the entrance to the carriage. Tom's face was framed in what was left of the doorway. He raised his hands to help her out.

A smile crossed her face. 'You took your time . . .' She jerked her head sideways before he had a chance to answer. She could hear Laszlo's shouts in the distance.

Tom stretched his arms out towards her. He was only a few feet away.

'Don't stop – *come on.*'

But she couldn't help herself. She glanced once more along the carriage and saw Laszlo approaching, with three of his gunmen behind him.

All Delphine could do was mouth: 'Go . . . the children . . . *go . . .*'

She knew he had to fight every instinct that urged him to stay and protect her. She could see it in his face. Finally he nodded. 'Keep your mobile – I'll come back for you.'

He dropped back into the gloom.

Laszlo strode up to her, ordering his men to jump down from the train. He seized her by the hair, lifted her head and jerked it back. She arched her back, trying to ease the burning pain in her scalp. She looked into his lifeless eyes and, for the first time in her life, felt pure and uncontrollable fear.

'Someone attacked us. They took the kids.' Delphine flinched, expecting him to hit her. But just as quickly, the fear changed to something else. It started to feel liberating. She had no control over the madman standing over her. No matter what she did or said, there was no guarantee he would react as she wanted him to. So what was the point in being scared? All she could do now was cling to any chance she was offered to save herself and the children.

'You lying *bitch*.' Laszlo's expression darkened, and then the blow came. He raised his arm and backhanded her across the face.

Delphine tasted the metallic tang of blood. 'Am I lying about the cuts?' She tried to match his stare. 'Do you think this is makeup?'

Laszlo's fingers tightened in her hair and he dragged and kicked her out of the doorway towards the toilet cubicle. She saw the hole in the floor and the empty 9mm cases scattered around it. He inched forward, his feet making no sound, and peered down through the hole. He was suddenly, dangerously, still. Delphine knew what he'd seen: the guard they'd dispatched to escort her and the children, stone dead, his swollen tongue protruding grotesquely from his mouth.

Laszlo betrayed no emotion. The man had been there to fight and, if necessary, to give his life for their cause. What was he supposed to feel? Compassion? Regret? Those luxuries could be afforded only by the comfortable, complacent middle classes of the West. Laszlo had no doubt that he would rather have died in that way than in the squalor of whatever pig-shit village he had come from.

He turned his ice-cold glare back to the woman. She was defiant, this one. He could see the fear in every fibre of her being, but he could not see compliance. Or understanding. Like every one of her kind, she couldn't comprehend why men chose to fight and die. Maybe these people had spent too long sitting in front of their 44-inch flat-screens, phoning for pizza delivery, knowing the state was always there to feed them if their funds ran dry. Maybe they just had too much to live for.

Laszlo heard Sambor's hurried footsteps and stepped back into the corridor.

'The guy we sent to sort out the radio – he's dead.'

Again, Laszlo's reaction was no more dramatic than it would have been if his brother had announced that a bulb had blown and needed replacing. He shrugged and pointed out into the darkness. 'There is just one man out there. And the children will slow him down.'

He wasn't too fussed if this man had contact with the world outside or not. 'Come, brother – we have more important things to do.'

Laszlo started to head back up the train, then, almost as an afterthought, waved a hand in the direction of the woman. 'Bring her.'

Sambor grabbed the bitch's hair and pulled her to her feet, indifferent to the blood welling from her scalp and starting to dribble down her cheek.

62

Gavin raised his binoculars and stood in front of the hangar, taking in the lie of the land. He scanned the terminal, the rail tracks and the throng of hi-vis jackets that marked the inner police cordon around the tunnel entrance. He checked his mobile, still hoping that Tom was alive and capable of letting them know at some point what the fuck was happening.

Gavin had as much information as he needed on the tunnel's layout, and was pretty sure he knew why they had no radio comms with the train. Laszlo had had no reason to cut them. Why would he, halfway through a conversation? And the design team had assured him the system was fire- and flood-proof . . .

He was suddenly aware of puzzled glances from the nearest of the guys in hi-vis vests, and realized they must have seen his shoulders shake, possibly even heard him laugh.

The design team reckoned they'd thought of everything. But they hadn't met Tom Buckingham.

He gave them a grin and stepped into the building.

As the situation developed, Gavin's boys would be free to roam the hangar, check out the latest content on the boards, ask questions and listen in to the radio traffic between Woolf and Laszlo, and from the call-signs on the ground. Every single member of Blue team would need to know exactly what was happening, when, how and why.

Gavin gave the heli pilot the nod, and he did the sensible thing – got some tea brewing and talked squash with one of the signallers while they waited for the assault group to arrive.

Woolf sat at his rapidly constructed desk, headphones and boom mic already in place, mobile stuck under one of the cans to keep him linked with COBRA. As he listened to the committee going round in an endless series of circles, his bored expression told Gavin all he needed to know about progress in Whitehall.

Woolf had met Clements on a number of occasions under the SAD lighting and hadn't liked him from the get-go. Woolf was a self-made man. He'd left school at sixteen to work in Coventry's MG factory as a trainee upholsterer, but soon learned that he should have thought about university instead of following his parents, who both worked in the same plant. His trainee salary had gone to finance night school, and eventually a University of East Anglia BA in philosophy, politics, economics, Adnam's bitter and one-night stands. It had come as a complete surprise when he was approached by the Security Service. They asked if he would keep an eye on a group of fellow students who were developing unhealthily romantic leanings towards Irish nationalism – which they feared might turn into support for the Provisional IRA. He had turned out to be so good at this task that MI5 had offered him a full-time job before graduation.

Clements trumpeted himself as a champion of social mobility, but only for public consumption. He'd congratulated Woolf on his first COBRA appearance, but privately believed that people like him were made for reasonably effective middle management, that the real power should be left in the hands of those who'd had the upbringing and education to know how to use it. Woolf had read his body language loud and clear within the first minute of that first meeting, which was why he was more than pleased to be in the holding area today, doing the job he was paid to do, rather than pissing around in a Westminster bunker.

'Right.' The signaller tapped on Woolf's can and motioned for him to lift it. 'We'll establish a universal power-line bus and set it to private protocols. You're jacked into the train with either device. All channels are open to you and London.'

Woolf felt his brow furrow as he tried and failed to decipher the geek-speak. He was glad to see Gavin come back over to the briefing area. 'How much longer till the rest of your crew get here?'

Gavin checked the wall screen that displayed the satellite tracking of each of the call-signs driving from Hereford: two clusters of vehicles, Blue just over the Dartford Bridge, and Red hitting the M4 at junction fifteen. 'Another thirty minutes.'

'Let's hope we have some contact with the train – or Buckingham – by then.' Woolf kept his volume low, but he couldn't disguise his growing anxiety. 'If there have been more casualties, London will send you in immediately. There'll be no negotiation.'

Gavin shared his concern. That was the worst option: there would almost certainly be high casualties within the team, and the Yankees would be at the sharp end of it all. Emergency response, almost inevitably, tended to do pretty much what it said on the tin. All he could do right now was issue a set of orders based on what he knew – and that was precious little more than what the train looked like, how it worked and where it was located.

Gavin shook his head. 'Well, if Laszlo does make contact you'd better get your finger out of your arse and persuade him to give himself up. For fuck's sake, you lads are supposed to be able to sell sand to the Arabs, aren't you? Get the fucker to come out of his hole and have a brew with us.'

Woolf sighed, replaced his mobile and headset, and listened again to the Whitehall debate.

The pilot returned with a steaming paper cup. Gavin nursed it as he worked out how the team would respond if they were given control in less than forty-five minutes' time. From time to time, he checked his mobile for a signal and that he hadn't accidentally switched it to silent.

63

Tom's hands were clamped hard over the children's mouths. The slightest sniff or whimper would betray them.

The two men sent to hunt them down had jumped off in different directions, but within a few paces had called out to each other and regrouped no more than five metres from where Tom, Rose and Daniel lay.

Tom heard a muttered exchange. If they got any closer, it would be decision time. Could he hope to be taken prisoner? Not a chance. He'd just killed two of their mates. He could roll out the other side of the train and try to make a run for it, but these guys were unlikely to shoot and miss. He didn't want to leave the kids, and he didn't want to leave Delphine . . .

Tom put his mouth right up against Rose's ear and almost breathed his instruction. 'Don't move. Not a sound.' He repeated the process with Daniel. They both nodded, wide-eyed.

He removed his hands from their mouths and felt around beneath him. His hand closed around a piece of rubble the size of a squash ball. He moved to the far side of the train, eased himself into a semi-crouch, and pulled up his sleeve so the material wouldn't flap. He drew back his arm.

He unleashed the missile and it flew down towards the UK

end of the tunnel. He couldn't see where it landed, but knew it was about thirty metres beyond the gunmen. The moment they heard the noise, they turned and broke into a run.

64

Like the holding area, COBRA was in waiting mode. Someone had suggested that police officers could move into the tunnel and try to establish communications. Alderson had managed to shoot that one down in flames. He'd explained that without tactical support from Hereford to deal with the situation if it went wrong – which was massively likely – it could bring about more civilian deaths.

Sarah Garvey looked at the screen that monitored the progress of the teams to Folkestone, using the same feed as the holding area. 'Mr Alderson, how long now?'

'Ten minutes, Home Secretary.'

Her eyes were still fixed on the two fast-moving clusters of call-signs. 'I want to know what's happening in that bloody tunnel. I want to know if this lunatic has killed any more passengers, and precisely what those explosions were. Can we not get the CCTV back online? Surely there must be *something* we can do . . .'

'If I may, Home Secretary . . . ?' Clements leaned forward and lowered his voice to a confidential murmur in a crude effort to conceal from Brookdale what he was about to say. 'We could simply agree to Antonov's financial demands, and his request for safe passage.'

'You're not serious?' The home secretary's confusion was clear for all to see. One minute he wanted Antonov dead, the next . . . 'You're suggesting we let him go free? Over my dead body. We'd be a global laughing stock. And so would our long-held policy of zero negotiation.'

Clements lifted a hand. 'I don't mean that we actually let him escape. I mean we placate him by apparently giving in to his demands, but only up to the point when the SAS can enter the tunnel or do whatever they need to do to kill him and put this matter to rest.'

Drawn to Clements's lowered voice, like a vulture to road-kill, Brookdale intervened: 'Surely it would be wiser to take our time and negotiate a surrender. Keep this the responsibility of the police and MI5. The military option bothers me, and particularly the possibility of it going wrong. What about casualties? I don't care about the military, of course – that's what they're there for. It's the collateral damage that will impact badly on the government.'

Both Sarah and Clements knew who he really meant.

Brookdale tried to manoeuvre between them. 'Sarah, the net immigration figures should be published tomorrow. If you recall, we thought we'd smuggle them out on a Friday after-noon once everyone had returned to their constituencies, but I recommended we pull publication after yesterday's cock-up.

'I thought it would be best to wait and see where Antonov cropped up next before breaking the news. The numbers do show a most unwelcome increase, and if they were to be announced alongside the revelation that a dangerous foreign terrorist had both entered and left the United Kingdom without being intercepted by our security forces . . .' he paused, enjoying the limelight '. . . well, the opposition wouldn't be slow to link the two things in a way that would be politically very damaging. They're already sniffing around, so we need to keep this situation under what control we can. No heroics, no Men in Black and things that go bang. That will do the government a great deal of harm. Negotiated settlement, lots of saved civilians, does us all a power of good.'

His eyes still fixed on Sarah Garvey, Clements shook his head. 'With respect, Home Secretary, that is not a realistic option. Antonov will never surrender, and you'll have a situation on your hands that is exactly the opposite of what government wants.'

He treated Brookdale to a full measure of his disdain. His message was simple: he should be leaving this to the grown-ups. 'Young man, Antonov – and whoever he has down there with him – is a different breed, a world away from what you have ever dealt with. He doesn't care who won *The X Factor*, or which celebrity is shagging her brother-in-law. He has never tasted sun-dried tomatoes on focaccia. In short, you know nothing, so I suggest you say nothing.'

He turned back to the person who mattered. 'Home Secretary, no matter what we think of Antonov, we must understand him. He will not surrender so, as I keep suggesting, it would be cleaner if he were killed. If he's cornered, he won't hesitate to take as many people with him as he can. And he may well have enough explosives down there to take down the tunnel as well. Just think of the financial implications, quite aside from the PR own goal.

'Let's get him out of that tunnel and kill him at the first available opportunity, and live with whatever collateral damage we have to.'

'That's easy for you to suggest, Mr Clements. Any more collateral damage might include my political future.'

Back on familiar ground, Brookdale waited one beat too long before jumping in: 'And that of this government.'

Clements ignored him – he was just background noise. 'Then with respect, Home Secretary, that's all the more reason to act decisively *now*. As soon as we have regained communications, let us bring him out into the open and settle this quickly.'

She gave him a baleful stare, then glanced at Brookdale. But the head of communications had suddenly developed shoulders like a Coca-Cola bottle. This would have nothing to do with him. Unless, of course, it was a success.

65

The instant the two gunmen had started running, Tom pulled the children out from under the train, dashed about twenty paces in the opposite direction, then dived back beneath the nearest carriage. Rose and Daniel followed him under. For a moment they clung to each other, like survivors of a shipwreck.

Tom waited for their laboured breathing to subside. He strained to hear any hint of their pursuers' return. After two minutes, he motioned to the kids to get into crawling mode and continue up the track on their hands and knees.

As they moved closer to the engine, he turned and signalled for them to keep silent. He pointed into the darkness and mimed gunfire: the PKM (belt-fed Kalashnikov machine-gun) position was out there somewhere and he didn't want to go any further forward. The kids had seen enough dead bodies for one day.

He knew the two guys manning the gun position would be wearing their NVGs to defeat the pitch-darkness of the tunnel ahead of them. He knew they'd be scanning in all directions. And he knew what it would be like behind those masks. All they'd be able to hear was their own breathing, and the gentle whine as the small lithium battery kept the NVGs active.

He guided Rose and Daniel out from under the train and through the mangled green metal door. There were shouts from the other end of the tunnel – no more than weak echoes when they reached them, but Tom still paused momentarily to comfort the kids and keep them as quiet as he could. Soon all other noises were drowned by the sound of something like rainfall, damping down everything but the sickly sweet smell of charred flesh. Tom soon discovered the reason why.

The first thing he saw through the gaping hole that Laszlo's explosives had blown in the fire screen was an incinerated appliance. The back blast from the detonation must have ignited the wagons. The last of the flames had clearly died long since, but only now were the sprinklers beginning to shut down.

The second thing he saw was a steel ladder, bolted to the wall immediately to his right, leading up to an open hatch, through which he could see wavering torchlight. He ducked back out again. They had to keep moving.

'Cover your mouths. The smoke will soon be gone, the further along this tunnel we go.' He hoisted Daniel onto his shoulders and grabbed Rose's hand. 'Come on, kids. Time to go and find you some sunlight.'

66

They dragged the French girl, bruised and bleeding from her scalp, mouth and wrists, along the carriages and threw her to the floor in front of Laszlo.

Sambor nudged her with the toe of his boot, like a curious child with a dead bird. 'Seems their super-hero is still alive after all,' he grunted.

'Are you sure it's the same man?' Laszlo thought for a minute. 'Brother, we have to solve this little problem very quickly indeed, because we'll be facing another much bigger one before long.'

'But the SAS shouldn't even be in Folkestone yet . . .'

'All the more reason to deal with this man while we still can.' He knelt down beside the girl. 'And she is the key that opens the door to him . . .' He took hold of her hair and yanked her head back far enough to stare into her eyes. He switched from Russian to French. 'I think it is now time for you to tell me the truth. I need to know exactly what happened back there.'

'I told you, a man took the children.' Delphine tried not to show her fear.

Laszlo nodded. 'And what was he wearing?'

'A wet suit,' she said, with a spark of defiance. 'He was coming out of the toilet.'

Laszlo's expression didn't change, but he drew back his fist and punched her hard in the face. She slumped to the floor, trying to clear her head. He dragged her up again.

Blood streamed from her nose and tears filled her eyes. 'I don't know . . .' She was having trouble breathing. 'It was too dark. I couldn't see properly.'

Laszlo gave her a contemptuous look. 'Well, let me make it easier for you then. Was he tall or short, fat or fit, dark or light hair?'

'I – I don't know. It all happened so fast. I didn't see his face. I guess he just looked . . . normal . . .'

Laszlo stood up and seemed to translate to his brother. He turned his attention back to the girl. 'Tell me about the man who helped you when you were running to the toilet this morning.'

'What man?'

'The one who was with you when you had to throw up.'

She shrugged. 'I felt terrible. He was just some nice guy who offered to help me.'

Laszlo gave a thin smile. He spoke even more softly, but there was no mistaking the menace in his tone. 'And yet I'm fairly sure I heard you call him Tom . . .'

'Maybe that was his name. I really can't remember.' She gave a hacking cough and spattered blood across the carpet.

'Why would a stranger help you?'

'Normal people do things like that for each other.' She was beginning to regain her composure. 'Not everyone has to be an arsehole.'

Laszlo chose to ignore the comment. The girl had spirit, and he couldn't help admiring that. He glanced at Sambor, who was still standing impassively behind her, and nodded.

Moments later, Sambor held up a battered French passport and a mobile phone. Laszlo took the passport and flicked through it. 'Hmm . . . so, Delphine Prideux . . .' He nodded at his brother and asked him a question.

Sambor reached into his jacket and brought out a sheaf of closely printed sheets. Studying them intently, he ran an index finger the size of a sausage down each page. As he read them out, Delphine recognized the words 'Tom', 'Thomas' and 'Prideux'. Then he repeated the process. 'Tomas Alvarez . . . Thomas George Buckingham . . . Tom Leary . . .'

The alarm began to sound on Laszlo's mobile phone. 'Thirty minutes already.' He switched off the pealing church bells. 'As the English say, doesn't time fly when you're enjoying yourself?' A thought struck him as he put Delphine's passport into his pocket. 'I'm getting careless. I must be losing my edge.' He held out his hand to Sambor. He gave Laszlo Delphine's phone.

Laszlo watched what little colour was left drain from Delphine's cheeks as he began checking through her call register and texts. He didn't have to scroll far. A moment later he turned the phone towards her so that she could see the screen. It displayed the most recent message she had received. It read:

Lock door. Lift toilet seat.

The sender ID simply said 'Tom'.

His hand shot out, grabbed her by the throat and dragged her to her feet. 'Do you know what those church bells tell me? That the British have failed to meet the deadline for accepting my demands.' He didn't wait for a reply. 'It's time to kill another hostage.'

Knuckles whitening as he tightened his grip, he pushed her down the carriage in front of him, towards the driver's cab.

He stopped at the door, among a crowd of terrified passengers still standing upright, hands on their heads, facing the windows. Some of the older and frailer of them were feeling the strain: their arms, legs and, in one case, whole body were shaking from a combination of fear and the sheer effort of holding the stress position.

Laszlo detected a voice cutting through the mush from the speaker beside the driver's controls. 'Ah, they have mastered the technology at last.' He released his grip on Delphine's throat and punched her to the floor. Leaving Sambor to stand watch over her, he walked into the driver's cab, picked up the mic, and kept eye-to-eye with the girl as he spoke.

'So, who am I talking to now?'

'My name is James Woolf.'

'Ah, Mr Woolf . . . We talk at last.'

He had heard about Woolf. Known in the intelligence community as a dogged pursuer, he was the only foreigner who'd actually gone to South Ossetia to find out more about his target. It hadn't taken long for word to reach Laszlo.

'Indeed.'

Laszlo was very happy with the shift up the hierarchy from chief constable. So the British had started to get their act together. Not bad for thirty minutes.

'Well, Mr Woolf, I take it that we have the first element of any negotiation completed. We have a relationship. You know me, and I know you – that is to say, I know *about* you. Whoever else is listening, I don't know you, and I don't care to.'

Laszlo knew that any negotiator needs to build a rapport, a relationship based on a form of trust. He or she needs to show that they are actively listening, to communicate openly so that the hostage-taker feels he isn't being lied to – even when he is. The negotiator needs to connect on a personal level, to show that he or she cares, and to keep the conversation slow. Small-talk first; never straight to business. But that wasn't going to happen today.

'Your thirty minutes are up. What news do you have for me?'

'You must understand that these things take time. What's your intended route, so I can clear it with air-traffic control? Which sun-drenched tax haven is going to have the pleasure of your company?'

'I wasn't born yesterday, Mr Woolf. You sound to me like a man who is stalling.'

'Mr Antonov, I need some more time. I'm trying as hard as I can, but you know how these things work – I have to get permission from COBRA.'

'Mr Woolf, time is one commodity that you do not have. Stop stalling.'

'I am trying to do what you asked – but thirty minutes to organize a helicopter and a substantial amount of gold?'

Laszlo could hear Woolf doing his best to slow the exchange – never antagonizing him, but at the same time not giving him an inch.

'As the saying goes,' Woolf continued, 'the impossible I can do at once, but miracles take a little longer.'

Laszlo gave a sigh, like a teacher presented with some disappointing homework by a star pupil. 'I confess I expected better of you. Can we not dispense with these formalities and speak *really* honestly, one professional to another? Is it absolutely necessary for us to have to go on with this very painful process, killing one passenger here, another one there?'

'But I need detail. You need to help me help you here. I need to know how much fuel the aircraft will require. I need to know the number of passengers so the payload/fuel ratio can be factored in . . .'

The line went silent apart from a gentle electronic hiss.

Woolf's pencil hovered over the sheet of A4 paper in front of him. It was now a mass of doodled caricatures, some charming, some grotesque – his way of attempting to calm himself during the potentially more heated moments of the exchange. He put the pencil to one side and began to build a small barrier of sugar lumps on the desk top.

Finally Laszlo replied: 'May I call you James?'

Woolf took a deep breath. 'No. You may not.'

Laszlo didn't miss a beat. 'Mr Woolf, I am reminded of your prime minister when he told us that we cannot coddle the slowest runners just because they are slow.' He didn't attempt the accent. '"We must inspire speed." Now, please listen carefully.'

Woolf, those at the COBRA table and everyone in the Folkestone holding area listened to the squeak of combat boots followed by a whimper and the sound of a body being dragged closer to the mic.

There was a moment of silence, and then the muffled but unmistakable double report of a suppressed weapon.

67

The sound still seemed to echo in the hangar air, long after Laszlo cut the transmission.

Gavin watched the colour drain from Woolf's face.

'As delaying actions go, that wasn't wholly successful, was it?' The MI5 man was trying to sound his normal, imperturbable, slightly cynical self, but the tremor in his voice betrayed him.

Gavin shrugged. He neither liked nor disliked Woolf, but he had to feel a little sympathy for him in this predicament. 'Mate, I really don't think there was anything you could have done to change that.' He passed his paper cup of brew to Woolf as a comfort offering. 'That cunt had already decided he was going to shoot another Yankee way before he started talking to you.'

Woolf thought about it for a few moments as he took a sip or two of the hot sweet liquid. 'You might be right.' He passed the brew back. They were bonding. 'It certainly fits his profile. But that knowledge doesn't make me feel any better. I bloody hate this part of the job.' He stared into space for a few moments, then made a conscious effort to rally himself. 'What's your best estimate of casualties if the powers-that-be decide to pass control to you as soon as the team is ready to go?'

'Given the linear nature of the Channel Tunnel, and the lack of int . . .' Gavin closed his eyes as if expecting the number to appear magically on the screen inside his head '. . . I reckon up to forty per cent of the hostages will be history in an emergency response. However, if we were given some additional time to work up a deliberate option, we should be able to reduce that number significantly.'

'How long would that take?' Woolf said.

Gavin shrugged. 'At least a couple of hours to allow the snipers to get into position and the assault team to do a close-target recce. But I suspect we won't be allowed anywhere near that amount of time.'

68

Gavin jumped out of his seat as rubber squealed on painted concrete and the first of the Blue team's Range Rovers surged into the hangar. All he had to do was point where he wanted it to go. With another chorus of squeals it pulled a three-point turn, faced back towards the entrance and stopped. Its four occupants had scarcely left the vehicle and begun to unload when the next Range Rover screamed in and pulled up to its left.

When the Transits arrived, they'd line up about fifteen metres behind them. The space between was the Blue team's admin area, where they'd sort themselves out and sleep. The Range Rovers were always in front, in case they needed to rig them up as ops vehicles.

Every item of kit was taken out of each wagon and laid out on grey blankets: sleeping cots; ladders; extra ammo; sledge-hammers; axes; boxes of flash-bangs, and specialist weapons such as Federal riot guns and suppressed 9mm machine-guns.

The moment Gavin had given his orders and the assaulters were tasked, they'd go and pick up whatever was needed. Until then, they'd haul their black party gear out of their ready-bags and put it on, then head over to Gavin's patch to see what he had in mind for the ER.

The first of the Transits arrived. The signal guys tied black bin liners to its back doors as soon as they'd swung open. Otherwise the ocean of white paper cups would become a tsunami.

69

The committee sat on the edges of their seats as Woolf gave it one more try. 'Mr Antonov, please answer.'

Clements broke the silence. 'It's an absolute tragedy, of course, no doubt about that, but we have gained a very valuable piece of information.'

'Do educate us, Mr Clements.' Sarah Garvey didn't turn to look at him, just checked the sea of blank faces around her. 'I'm struggling to see anything but a major disaster in the making.'

'Antonov was obviously planning to kill another hostage right from the start. It's a classic strategy: a demonstration of raw power, a pause for discussions to show that you are open to negotiation and can be reasoned with, and then you go for the jugular with brutal, overwhelming force.'

'So what do you propose we do about it?' she asked icily.

'As I have suggested from the start, we fight fire with fire. Send in the SAS as soon as they're ready.'

Chief Constable Alderson was becoming increasingly exasperated with their sparring but he didn't interrupt.

Sarah shook her head. 'That option is a last resort, to be adopted only when all other avenues have been exhausted.'

'For God's sake,' Clements was making no attempt to hide his irritation, 'do we have to sit here discussing points of procedure while he kills one hostage after another after another, until you finally get the message?'

'You heard the SAS estimate of potential casualties.' She checked her notes. 'It was forty per cent. Even if Antonov kills one hostage every thirty minutes, it would take days to reach that total.'

'Home Secretary, if I may . . .' Alderson received several megawatts of glare from Clements for his interruption, but he had had enough. 'We have no idea what Antonov is up to down there. The demands he has made – to me they seem so basic and naïve. Even the bullion he has stipulated – it comes to just over five million pounds. Hardly worth all this effort. We know he has explosives, and we know he has manpower. This is not an escape attempt gone wrong just because some SAS trooper happened to bump into him on the train.'

Clements was fuming. 'Mr Alderson, you must remember we dictate policy. Your police, and the military for that matter, are simply the instruments of that policy.'

Alderson could hold a stare as long as the next man, but he simply couldn't be bothered. He was actually backing up what Clements had been saying, if only he'd bothered to listen. He sighed inwardly, and tried to console himself with the thought that in two more years he'd retire; he'd no longer have to deal with arseholes like this man.

Brookdale sparked up from his wall seat, tapping on his mobile screen calculator. 'The government would still want to see a negotiated settlement. Even if there have already been more casualties in the explosions, and if we lose one, even two, every thirty minutes during the negotiation, the death to benefit ratio would be acceptable – as long as the number of survivors is still many times greater.

'We could still be seen as saving lives, given that Laszlo had planned to kill many more. The government's gain is well worth a certain amount of hostage pain. But forty per cent? That's a very big number to sell out there on the street, Home Secretary.'

The elephant in the room was the likely scale of their own

casualties: if the SAS attacked, how many of *them* would also be killed? But it wasn't a very scary elephant. The Men in Black had volunteered to do what they did. No one had been press-ganged; no one had been bullshitted. It was their job, and there were thousands only too eager to take their place. The day they didn't like it, they should leave; it was as simple as that. And Brookdale and his people would play the hero card: the nation would be proud of the courageous young men who'd sacrificed their lives in the battle against evil, terror, unspeakable violence . . . or whatever seemed the best way of selling the story that particular day.

The one thing Sarah Garvey was not was indecisive. 'I'm going to need a little more than hunches to convince me. We all share the same distaste at the thought of casualties, but sometimes we have to accept one unpleasantness in order to forestall a much greater tragedy.'

Brookdale was scribbling furiously. She watched him for a moment then continued: 'I will accept additional casualties while we learn more about what Antonov is up to in that tunnel. In the meantime, we continue to try to negotiate.'

She stood and leaned towards them, palms flat on the veneered table top. 'Now I'm going to take five minutes to clear my mind and my bladder.'

70

Tom was in tabbing mode, intent on making as much distance down the service tunnel as he could. His body and hair were soaked with sweat; his jeans clung to his legs as if he'd been in a thunderstorm. He soon hit his rhythm, his breathing constant, his feet kept low, at little more than shuffling height. He gripped the children firmly but not painfully as he moved through the darkness with the gentle echo of his and Rose's footsteps trailing behind him.

Their confined and solitary world suddenly erupted with 7.62 machine-gun fire, each twenty-round burst compressing into one long, loud explosion that rumbled towards them.

Tom dropped flat, Daniel still on his back. Rose followed suit. The children screamed, first in pain and then in fear. Their pursuers' rapid muzzle flash lit up the tunnel six, maybe seven hundred metres away, with the heart-stopping fury of an approaching tube train.

Tom was pretty sure their two pursuers had finally doubled back and picked up the gun team by the green door. They'd screwed up; they knew that. And the only way to try to rectify the situation was to put rounds down the service tunnel and hope for the best.

There was nowhere for Tom and the kids to go but low as

rounds flew overhead, close enough for them to hear the zinging sound before they ricocheted off the walls and ceiling and tumbled onwards at an even higher pitch. The green one-in-five tracer rounds sped towards them in a gentle arc. Some hit the walls ahead and cartwheeled, like demented supersonic fireworks.

All they could do was lie there while the rounds kept coming. Maybe the enemy would come and check the tunnel for bodies later; maybe they wouldn't. He just wanted to protect these two as long as he could, and then make damn sure none of them was here when their pursuers reached this point.

In the glow of the muzzle flash, he saw the shadow of another ladder on the wall to one side of them. There must be another access hatch on the roof.

Tom shouted above the din, keeping an arm across each child so they stayed exactly where they were: he needed their attention.

'D'you have a mobile – you know, a phone?'

Rose shook her head and gave a terrified squeak: 'iPod.'

'Give it to me, quickly.'

He took it, then removed his hands from their shoulders and fished out his own mobile. Slipping it out of its sock, he brought up voice record on the iPod and yelled, 'Gavin Marks. This is for Sergeant Gavin Marks. Get this information to him!'

He carried on at the same volume, telling Gavin what he'd seen, heard and felt. Any int he could think of that might help. 'And the Yankees are lined up against the windows, so you can't make explosive entry on the glass . . .'

He then paired the iPod with his mobile and transferred the X-ray photos he'd taken through the windows.

The firing stopped. The silence was almost deafening.

'Pretty soon – when I say – you two will have to go on without me. I'll stay right here and make sure the bad guys don't follow.' He pointed behind him. 'It isn't that far. You must keep running all the way to the end of the tunnel, and when you get there, some men, some policemen, will be waiting to help you. It's all right,' he said, seeing terror on Daniel's face. 'They'll take care of you. And, Rose, you must take your iPod to a man called Gavin right away. Nobody else. Ask for Gavin Marks, the soldier. Do you understand?'

The firing kicked off again. A new 200-round belt of linked 7.62 had been loaded. Tom had to start shouting once more. 'Both of you say it: *Gavin Marks, the soldier.*'

'Gavin Marks, the soldier,' they chorused.

Tom didn't say he wanted them both to memorize the words in case one of them didn't make it.

The crazy fireworks display stopped again. Tom waited. In his mind's eye, he visualized lifting the top cover of the machine-gun, placing the first four rounds of link into the feed tray, slamming down the top and cocking the weapon. He waited a few seconds more. It was now or never.

Tom handed the iPod back to Rose. 'Go!' he said. 'Run as fast as you can. Go – go – go – *go!*'

As they disappeared into the darkness, Tom felt for the steel ladder and started scrambling up it, one hand held above his head. When it hit the cold metal of the hatch, he felt around the edge of its frame until he found two locking handles.

The gun kicked off once more. He wasn't going to have the luxury of checking the virgin ground before he entered it. He wrenched open the handles and hauled himself up into a warmer and better lit world. He closed the hatch as yet another round ricocheted off its underside.

71

Haunted by images of what was happening to Tom and the children, Delphine choked back tears as she listened to the bullets blasting through the darkness. She fought to erase the horror from her mind. And failed. Her head twitched with every burst.

The old man lay dead beside her, along with his dreams of one more summer of love. His flesh no longer twitched from the shock of the two ceramic rounds that had torn apart the back of his head, but the blood still smeared the window where his face had been pressed against the glass. Giselle would never see her red roses. They would now just wither and die on the table by his seat.

Laszlo had switched off the mic. He wanted to make Woolf and the rest of them sweat. They, too, would be haunted by the memory of the gunfire. He was bored by Woolf's constant attempts to play for time. He caught Delphine's eye as he turned over the old man's body with his boot. 'It was almost a mercy killing,' he said. 'The old fool was shaking so much he nearly made me miss.'

'Why did you not kill the woman too?' Sambor goaded. 'Has living in London made you soft?'

232

Laszlo liked it when his brother was happy. Sambor had become his responsibility now their parents were gone. South Ossetian and Russian troops might finally have won the 2008 war, but victory had come too late for their parents. Along with the rest of the elderly, the women and the children of their village, they had been massacred as the Georgians withdrew. It must have been so easy: their menfolk were all away at the front.

'You're a good man, Sambor.' Laszlo held his brother's massive head in his hands. 'But you need to leave the strategic thinking to me.' Then he smiled gently and hugged him, as he remembered the frenzied search in the burned-out ruin of their parents' home, and their discovery of the two charred bodies.

Both boys had taken the deaths very badly. They had sworn vengeance against their murderous enemy. But while Laszlo could wait and plot his retaliation with infinite care, Sambor had had to lash out immediately. He had led the Black Bears on a one-night killing spree that would remain in Georgian memory for generations.

Laszlo had left Sambor in command as he'd linked up with his Russian allies and guided them to their final attack. He had had no objection to the slaughter. He had spent years killing ethnic Georgians. But now that they were so close to victory, such clumsiness had made the South Ossetians appear the aggressor, not the aggrieved. It had angered him – and saddened him too. Laszlo knew he should have comforted Sambor in his grief. He had let him down. He had let their parents down.

And so it was that Laszlo Antonov had done the honourable thing. He had allowed himself to be blamed for the massacre. He had protected his brother and his men from prosecution after the conflict had come to a swift resolution. At his trial he had been sentenced to death – unless he was prepared to name his accomplices.

Laszlo had held his silence. Despite the beatings, the starvation, the months in solitary confinement, he had never taken the easy road. That was what had made him a true folk hero. If ethnic Russians had idolized him before the war, those in the know had started to think of him as a true hero.

For more than a year he had sat on Death Row, knowing that at any moment the door might be flung open and he'd be marched in front of a firing squad.

The Black Bears had remained fiercely loyal. Under Sambor's leadership, they'd tried their best to hatch a rescue plan. Aside from a suicidal storming of the impenetrable prison fortress, they hadn't come up with one.

In the end, a combination of lies, bribes and promises of future positions of power had left eyes turned and keys hanging where they shouldn't have been. And Laszlo was finally free.

He had defeated the Georgians. But the first promise he had made his brother at their joyous reunion was that, one day, they would have an even more satisfying revenge.

Their faithful followers had also waited for this moment. They had lived too long with their guilt over Laszlo's sacrifice. They had missed the brotherhood of combat and the sense of purpose that battle provided. Better to be a small part of just one mission than to stare at an empty factory and swim around the bottom of a vodka bottle. Better to live just one more day as a Black Bear than to spend a lifetime scampering around the mountains of the Caucasus like a neutered goat.

Laszlo kissed his brother hard on the cheek, then stepped back and held up Delphine's mobile phone. It still displayed Tom's text message. 'Look upon her as an insurance policy.' He winked, and relished the sight of Sambor's slow smile. 'If that 7.62 fire hasn't solved our problem, the lovely Delphine will be much more valuable to us alive than dead.'

72

Sarah Garvey still hadn't returned from the toilet. She was probably fielding 'advice' from No. 10 in the wake of Brookdale's update.

Clements's mobile began to vibrate. He picked it up, checked the caller ID, then frowned and moved hurriedly away from the table and out of the briefing room. He shot a glance at the gathering of Amandas and Gileses, the advisers and junior officials who used politicians as manure. They mushroomed in number year after year, and all seemed to have a godparent at Central Office. Now they congregated in the anteroom like petitioners at a royal court.

He turned his back on them as he took the call.

'We have a serious problem . . .'

Clements paused before replying. 'I'm sorry,' he said. 'I don't know who this is. You have the wrong number.'

'You know exactly who it is. You also understand the nature of the problem, and why you have to solve it quickly.'

Clements's mind was racing. 'I'm sorry,' he said, 'but I really don't have the faintest idea what you're talking about.'

'Then let me spell it out a little more clearly for you – and anyone else who might be listening. I'm talking about Laszlo. Why haven't you persuaded COBRA to attack? Fuck knows what he has going on in that tunnel. We now have a report of medium machine-gun fire down there. This is not a fucked-up escape.'

Clements took a deep breath. He wouldn't be talking like this unless his line was secure.

'If Antonov is killed, all our problems go away. But if he survives . . . ?'

Clements kept his voice low and slow. 'A very good reason to make sure that he doesn't.'

'Correct.' The caller matched the seriousness of his tone. 'It's in your interest to pull COBRA's finger out of its collective arse and shut Laszlo up for ever. Because if I go down, I'll make very sure I take you with me. So you'd better crack on.'

The line went dead.

Clements stared at the Sky News screen but his eyes were suddenly glazed. So he didn't see the presenter walking and talking along a line of parked HGVs as Operation Stack took shape.

73

Clements hovered outside the meeting room as Sarah Garvey came down the corridor. 'A word if I may, Home Secretary . . .' He steered her to one side, checking they were out of earshot. 'We have, shall we say, a delicate matter that needs to be addressed . . .'

'For God's sake.' The home secretary didn't have time for waffle. 'You make the average Whitehall mandarin sound like a model of plain speaking. Enough of this elliptical nonsense. I've seen you at work often enough to know when you're concealing as much as you're revealing. What's really going on? You said more in one hour of that meeting than I've heard from you in all my time in government.'

Clements stared at her in silence for a few moments, debating his reply. 'What do the words "South" and "Ossetia" mean to you?'

Sarah Garvey studied his expression, searching for irony. 'One of those dismal former Soviet republics, mired in corruption, run by thugs and gangsters and so poor that they haven't even got a pot to piss in.' Then it dawned on her. 'And, of course, where Antonov was born and bred.'

Clements nodded. 'That's about the strength of it, yes. But it's slightly more complicated than that. The Georgian government was in control of South Ossetia at the time the BTC pipeline was being built in the nineties. As you may recall, UK plc was a primary stakeholder. And, of course, it still is. We had to make sure that the thing would be up and running within the agreed time.'

Sarah Garvey had read a briefing paper on possible ramifications not long after she'd joined the cabinet. The Baku–Tbilisi–Ceyhan pipeline pushed a million barrels of oil a day a thousand miles from Azerbaijan, one of the countries lucky enough to have a shoreline bordering the oil-rich Caspian Sea, across Georgia, passing just south of its capital, to the Turkish Mediterranean coast.

There was no sign of the metre-high conduit above ground, unlike such structures in the Middle East. They'd buried it, which made it tougher to blow up. And, from the Kurdish separatists to the Islamist militants, there were plenty of people who wanted to.

The Turks were feeling pretty pleased with themselves for owning the business end of the pipeline, from where fleets of supertankers ferried enough of the black stuff to keep the 4x4s of the UK and the east coast of America on the road. The US were keeping a weather eye on things from their huge airbase at Incirlik, right on Ceyhan's doorstep.

The Turks knew they were now such a pivotal part of the process, as far as the US and UK were concerned, that fully fledged membership of the EU was all but guaranteed, however reluctant the French and Dutch might be to have them aboard. The EU-style number-plates some had already fitted to their vehicles were down to much more than mere optimism.

Everyone wanted a piece of the action. Russia had built a pipeline to the Black Sea coast. China was getting stuck in too. Some of the largest untapped energy reserves on the planet – an estimated 200 billion barrels – lay beneath the Caspian. Since the collapse of the Soviet Empire, it had been very much up for grabs – and the UK and US hadn't wasted any grabbing time. They were pumping west as fast as they could.

Sarah Garvey had the kind of itching in her head that often acted as a prelude to the loud ringing of alarm bells. Oil and war criminals made for a volatile mixture.

Clements continued: 'Unfortunately, there was resistance from some of the rural population that fell within the pipeline's footprint. Antonov's job was to help us to make sure the resistance in Georgia was . . . er . . . dispersed.'

The home secretary's face showed her distaste. The alarm bells were initiated. 'And how did he achieve that, exactly?'

Clements gave her a thoughtful look. 'Are you really sure you want to know, Home Secretary? Sometimes it's better to remain in ignorance of certain . . . details. I always feel it adds an air of plausibility and conviction to any denials you might be forced to make. If, that is, Antonov is allowed to live.'

She had had enough of his games these past two days. She raised her hand, her forefinger just inches from Clements's face. 'Stop!' Her eyes bored into his. 'Give me what I need to know. I have hundreds of people who may die at the hands of that madman or those of our own military. Cut the bullshit and get on with it.'

'Home Secretary, if you insist . . .' Clements paused. He was very pleased with himself. He'd thought it would be harder for him to convince this home secretary that she was forcing information out of him. 'Very well. Antonov was recruited and empowered as our advance man, if you like, clearing pockets of resistance – local politicians who were against the pipeline crossing through national parks, villages and towns that opposed it crossing their land or destroying their buildings, resistance to population relocation, that sort of thing. He . . . er . . . cleared the way to allow construction to proceed smoothly, without interruption and to schedule. His engineering knowledge, combined with a deep-rooted ethnic hatred for the Georgians, meant that he was extremely efficient.'

'*Efficient?* At what, exactly?' The home secretary knew she had to ask even though she feared she knew the answer.

'I'm sure you can guess his methods. But that wasn't the

problem. The problem was that he was trained and equipped by us. As you can appreciate, Home Secretary, HMG cannot afford to be too squeamish about the way we ensure that our energy needs are met – and, of course, it's our duty to ensure that our companies always have an edge. Our competitors don't mind getting their hands dirty when it suits them – and many of them are much less likely to be held to account by domestic politicians and the media.'

Clements paused again, making sure she was primed and ready.

'As you know, the Foreign and Commonwealth Office makes greater use of Special Forces in pursuit of UK government aims than any other department. Antonov and his men received arms, explosives, training and mentoring from SAS personnel.' Just in case she hadn't got the picture fully, he added, 'On our behalf.'

Clements always felt he was at his most magnificent when he went in for the kill. The weaker and less-experienced politicians often crashed and burned without his even breaking a sweat. 'Surely the last thing any of us wants is for Antonov to be put on trial. Can you imagine if Hussein, Gaddafi, or bin Laden had gone into the dock and dished the dirt?

'Can you see the situation the government would find itself in should Antonov be given the platform of a trial at The Hague? He would reveal British involvement in rape, murder and ethnic cleansing – the very war crimes of which he himself stands accused. We created Antonov. We, the UK, are just as responsible for the Black Bears massacre as he is. We showed him how. We created him. We created the Black Bears.'

There was more to come, but now that he had stuck the first couple of inches of his knife into her, he waited, letting the initial pain register before she experienced the full thrust. Clements couldn't help but feel a surge of pleasure at finally getting her to do what he wanted. Not just to protect his country but, even more importantly, himself.

The home secretary shuddered at the thought. 'Were you part of this?'

Clements knew he needed to hide his pride. He also knew it was time to inflict more pain. Laszlo wasn't the only one who knew how to achieve compliance through fear. 'Indeed, Home Secretary. I was the London contact for certain interested parties. They needed to know when an area was safe to go into, so they could negotiate the land-rights contracts.'

He allowed himself a moment of reflection. His mind wandered back to the days when people like him were not asked what they were doing for the UK. It was enough for a home secretary to know he was doing what he thought was right.

'In some respects the way Antonov has turned out is quite unfortunate. He cost an incredible amount of money to support. He would still be a rather excellent asset if he hadn't gone off the rails. The SAS did an extremely good job training him and his men.'

She clearly couldn't believe what she was hearing, which was exactly the reaction Clements wanted. The truth always got politicians in a stew.

'Home Secretary, so far the fact that the SAS were involved in this operation has never come to light. However, Antonov is a very thorough and professional operator. Not only could he expose their and, of course, our co-operation with him, he also made it his business to obtain the real names of all those who trained him and his men and, in particular, he knows the real identity of the officer who took part in those illegal operations, even helping to command and control the atrocities on the ground.'

'What? We allowed —'

'Please, Home Secretary ... We didn't allow anything. "Gone native" is the expression that best describes that especially unfortunate and potentially damaging episode. The young man was weak and fell easily under the Antonov spell. It was as simple as that.' Clements knew the pain would be getting unbearable but he needed to twist the knife a bit more. 'Do you now understand why we must clean up this mess? Our creation must die, at any cost. A non-lethal arrest is simply out of the question. I'm sorry that you have been exposed to the uncomfortable truth.'

It was time to stop. Clements had his kill. But he couldn't help himself. 'That is why I strongly advised against his arrest in Hampstead.'

She closed her eyes and took a deep breath. She knew that Clements hadn't told her everything: these people never did. However, she knew he had told her enough. 'Did *you* warn Antonov yesterday, so he could escape?'

Clements was clearly taken aback. 'Home Secretary, I can assure you that I did not. However, I can also confirm that he *was* warned.'

'By whom?'

Clements spread his hands wide. 'Person or persons unknown.'

The home secretary studied his expression for some time, certain that he knew the who, where and when. But Clements remained inscrutable. 'If Antonov is dead, whoever it was will fade into the darkness and never emerge again. I can assure you, Home Secretary, this whole business will simply disappear.'

Sarah Garvey took a moment to assimilate the information. Her reply, when it came, wasn't the one Clements was expecting. 'Why the fuck wait to tell me this now? I should have known it yesterday, and then maybe we wouldn't be facing this dreadful situation.' She had so much more to spit at him, but knew it was a waste of time. She took a step forward and stood just inches from Clements, their faces close enough for them to feel each other's breath. 'You ... fucking ... people ...'

She stared deep into Clements's eyes and could see the lies and deceit that lay there. She no longer cared who Laszlo's warning had come from. That wasn't her problem. She was now consumed by what he might do – now, on the train, and later, if he was given a voice. 'What if he gives himself up during an assault?'

Clements smiled bleakly. 'There are no absolute guarantees in this game, Home Secretary, you know that. He will fight, believe me . . . but I can assure you that we will be every bit as ruthless. I will make sure that he is dealt with in a way that ensures the best possible outcome.'

Without another word, she stormed back down the corridor and re-entered the briefing room as Woolf's voice blared over the table speaker.

'Mr Antonov, there are reports of heavy gunfire. Can you confirm that? Is anyone hurt? If so, can we have access to them for medical treatment?'

Clements turned off the sound. He wanted to make sure there was no doubt in anyone's mind what the home secretary was about to say. He needn't have worried. She had everyone's undivided attention.

'Now that I have been able to pause for reflection . . .' she looked around the table '. . . I will give permission for control to be handed to the military.'

Brookdale went scurrying from the room. One day, Clements thought, he'd have to have his mobile surgically removed from his ear.

74

Tom found himself in a maze of communication cables, power lines and repair conduits. Although the rail tunnel below him had been shut down, up here it was a different story. The cables were still operational. The wires buzzed as thousands of volts of electricity surged through them. Small pinpricks of light pierced the sides of the steel flooring to give a gentle glow. Maybe that was why it felt warmer up here – or maybe it was the incredible amount of energy rushing from one side of the Channel to the other.

This was the strategic core of the tunnel system. The trains might take kids to Disneyland, pinstriped suits to Le Bourse, lovers to the banks of the Seine and HGVs full of washing-machines to Sloane Square, but here was where the real business was done. Fibre-optic cables fed everyone in the UK from money-market traders to porn downloaders. Electricity lines supplied energy from French nuclear power stations. A gas pipeline, two metres in diameter, marked every two metres with a *Danger Highly Flammable Gases* warning sign, fed fuel from Eastern Europe to cookers and central-heating systems in homes across the UK.

Tom bent low, keeping clear of the live wires overhead, as he moved back towards the train. He half ran, half crouched along the duct, measuring the distance he travelled. He knew he took 118 steps per hundred metres, and there was a safety hatch every seventy or so steps. Pacing was one of the boring but vital disciplines that recruits were taught to aid the judgement of distance when moving on a compass bearing. Things like that, no soldier ever forgets.

He passed over the gun position as it fired another twenty-round burst of link. It sounded like an underground train rumbling under his feet. He reckoned he had another two hundred paces until he reached the hatch he was aiming for. Then he'd slip back down into the service tunnel beside the Paris train.

He slowed, keeping his eyes focused on the way ahead, placing his boots as gently as possible so he could get the best use of his ears. Almost immediately he spotted two shafts of stronger light dancing across the conduit walls maybe a hundred metres in front of him. The plethora of pipework and power lines temporarily blocked his view but also gave him cover. He sank down on his hands and knees and made sure his weapon was strapped tightly to his back so it wouldn't fall onto the steel flooring.

He moved closer. There wasn't much sound coming from up ahead. The torch beams were jerking about, still bouncing off the walls and ceiling, but the men themselves were static. He'd known from the start that nothing that had happened today had been the result of him crossing Laszlo's path on the train. He hoped that Gavin would soon get that message as well. So what the fuck was going on?

Tom lay flat beside the next hatch and waited. There was no way he'd risk going down into the service tunnel just yet. Until the PKM crew got tired of their fireworks display, he'd be jumping out of the fire and into the frying pan. And he wanted to check out whatever was going on up here.

Tom's Omega told him he had been on the floor for just over ten minutes. There had been no more gunfire since then and the torches were on the move. Another five and they disappeared completely.

Tom lay completely still, just listening, for three or four minutes more. Then, still keeping low, he inched forwards. The further he went, the more vigorously the reek of linseed assaulted his nostrils. In another life, it would have triggered wistful thoughts of sun-kissed cricket pavilions, cucumber sandwiches and the slap of leather on willow. Not any more. The image of Laszlo's blonde bombshell lying by the rose pergola flashed into his mind.

It meant only one thing.

Trying not to gag, he moved close enough to see a stack of light-green two-kilo slabs wrapped in greasy paper. They looked like small loaves of flat bread. The nitro must have been sweating for years, but snatches of stencilled Cyrillic script could still be read on the stained wrapping – enough for Tom to know that the blow-by date for this ordnance was September 1997.

This sort of PE had become obsolete in the West years ago; it had probably been manufactured when Laszlo was still at school. There must have been thirty or so packages crudely piled under the gas pipeline. With that much PE – 'P for plenty' as it was known in the Regiment – there wasn't much need for finesse.

But as Tom examined the charge more closely he discovered finesse aplenty. There were two initiation devices. The first was a basic anti-handling device. A detonator connected to a 12-volt battery protruded from one of the slabs. One of its thin steel wires had been cut and each bare end soldered onto the opposing jaw of a crocodile clip. A small square of plastic, attached to the pipeline structure by a single thin wire, kept the jaws apart. A sharp tug was all it would take to remove it, and the circuit would be completed.

The second device was more sophisticated: a closed alloy box taped to the rear of the pipeline. Twin antennae extended from it. Tom checked and rechecked the exterior for any hint of an anti-handling device. It had to have one: any dems man worth his salt would have made sure of that. Disturbing just one antenna would probably be enough to initiate it.

Tom was good at many things, but understanding his limitations was what he really excelled at. Gripping the crocodile clip to ensure that the plastic stayed in place, he jerked it from its fixing on the pipe and disconnected one of the det wires from the battery . . . for now.

He picked up the slab with the det still embedded, and another for luck, tucked them down the front of his jacket, and headed for the nearest hatch. The locking handles were still open, so all he had to do was ease the cover upwards. The burned-out fire appliances were immediately below him, the ground around them littered with the bodies of the dead firemen.

75

The last of the black Range Rovers screeched to a halt in the hangar and rocked on its springs as Jockey and Bryce, dwarfed by the hulking figure of Vatu, unloaded their kit. The other members of Blue team were already bombed-up. They checked the whiteboards to see what extra kit they were going to need.

Ashton strode over to Gavin's table. The 3 i/c was at yet another whiteboard, filling in details of which call-sign would do what on-target. It was pretty basic stuff, so he kept writing while he briefed the boss on the ER – which didn't take long because he still had very little to go on. All they could do was smash, bang, and try to control whatever they came up against.

Ashton glanced across at Woolf. 'Looks like he did another fantastic job for us, then.'

Gavin shrugged. 'Boss, to be fair to him, he was on a loser from the word go.'

Ashton looked sceptical. 'Meaning what, exactly?'

'Antonov has no real appetite for negotiation – or not yet, at any rate. He was obviously planning to drop another hostage right from the start. And with the shit that's been going on down there, we might already have a lot more dead Yankees than we think.'

'What about Buckingham? He made an appearance yet?'

Gavin shook his head. He felt-tipped another time on the whiteboard, then started writing up his orders. He'd have to keep a paper record, too. It was a legal requirement – to be kept in the operational folder along with the recorded radio traffic collated by the signallers and archived in the Hereford registry. If charged after the event by some Islington lawyer who wanted to make a name for himself, it was good to have this stuff up your sleeve to prove your innocence – but a nightmare if it showed otherwise.

Ashton leaned closer, though clearly irritated by the squeak of the pen and the chemical waft of the ink fumes. 'You have contact with him? Any comms down there yet?'

Gavin shook his head again.

'What about portable cell sites?'

'We've tried, but still no luck. We need to move them closer, but can't until we have some cover. I'm sending the snipers down as soon as they're ready to CTR [close target recce] because I've got jack shit on the target. The sigs guys can follow behind with re-broadcasters.'

The team needed comms back to the hangar and COBRA. The re-broadcasters were suitcase-sized boxes of tricks with receivers and transmitters that picked up the team's comms, bounced them back to the real world and, of course, brought their own secure comms into the tunnel. They also had a multi-band and network cellular capability.

'All good. I agree. Antonov always planned to kill the Yankees. We have to assume he's killed the French first responders too. We won't know for sure until we're down there – but the French have told us there's not a squeak from them. They're certainly not sending anyone else in until we've done our stuff. We know he won't surrender. He'll fight until he's dead – which means more of our people getting malleted in the process.'

His expression became steelier.

'I tell you what, Gavin, I don't give a shit if he appears before the ICC. What I care about is keeping the team alive. I'm ordering you to make sure they're absolutely clear in their heads that there must be no attempt to arrest this bastard. Kill him and keep safe.' He paused, making sure they had eye-to-eye. He didn't want any misunderstanding. 'We must keep our people alive.'

Gavin didn't need the point to be hammered home. 'Boss, not a problem. I'll brief the lads before they go on the ground. But where has this come from – you? I need to know I'm not going to be nailed to the wall if it gets out.'

'You'll have my backing every inch of the way.' Ashton slowly straightened. 'But we need control first.'

Woolf pulled off his headphones. 'You have it. You have it from now. COBRA wants you to initiate the ER as soon as you can.' He put aside his doodles, selected a fresh page in his A4 pad and started writing.

Gavin wasn't impressed. 'We need more time. There's no CTR yet, no comms, no Red team. I need more guys on the ground.'

He could tell Woolf knew he was right, even though the MI5 man's expression said, 'You don't always get what you want.'

'It's all yours.' Woolf handed the sheet of A4 to Ashton. 'Good luck.'

Ashton held it up for Gavin's benefit: *I hand over control pursuant to the provisions of the Military Aid to the Civil Power Act. J. Woolf*

While Gavin drafted his ER, Ashton got busy with the team. 'OK, Blue team, listen in! We have control. I say again, we have control. Let's get moving!'

At almost the same moment, one of the Slime looked up from his monitor. 'Look at the tunnel,' he shouted. 'We've got runners!'

Gavin grabbed his binoculars and ran to the hangar entrance just as two children emerged from the mouth of the service tunnel. The police ran forward and pulled them to safety, out of line-of-sight of any possible pursuit. They wrapped them in blankets and tried to hustle them away but Gavin could see that the taller of the two, a little girl, kept shaking her head. She pulled away from them, seemed to be repeating something to them, over and over again.

One of the Slime called. 'Gavin, they're holding a couple of kids. The girl keeps saying she's got something for you and she won't speak to anyone else.'

'Get them up here, then.'

Less than a minute later a policeman ushered the two children into the hangar. The little boy, tear-tracks streaking the dirt on his face, clung tightly to his sister's hand and kept his head down, staring at the floor in front of his feet. The girl looked uncertainly from one face to another.

'Hello, I'm Gavin.' He smiled, thinking for a moment of his own kids. 'What's your name?'

'What sort of Gavin are you?' She stared at him warily. 'He told me only to speak to Gavin Marks, no one else.'

Gavin squatted in front of them. 'That's me. I'm Gavin. Who was it who told you?' His voice was gentle, his eyes kind.

'The man in the tunnel.' The girl pointed back towards its entrance as if no one here had the first idea what she was on about.

He gave an encouraging smile as the boy finally raised his head. 'We were on a train to Disneyland.'

The girl still hesitated, worrying her bottom lip between her teeth, then, reassured by Gavin's smile, she took a slim, bright pink sleeve from her pocket. 'My name's Rose. My brother's called Daniel. He told me to give you this.'

'Thank you, Rose. You two have been really, really brave.'

Gavin took the iPod and was about to switch it on when he realized that neither of the kids had moved. Just as he looked up again, the little boy launched himself at the 3i/c, threw his arms around Gavin's neck and burst into tears.

Rose stayed where she was. 'They killed our mummy with a gun.' Finally, the tears started to pour down her cheeks as well.

Gavin caught the look of pain in Ashton's eye, and the look of helpless embarrassment in Woolf's. He gave Daniel a hug, and opened his other arm to Rose. The story spilled out, each sentence punctuated by racking sobs.

After a couple of minutes he gently disengaged himself, explained that he had to upload the iPod, so he could try to help his friend Tom stop the bad men hurting any other mummies. He watched as the kids were led back out of the hangar towards a waiting ambulance. Poor little mites. Their lives had been completely devastated within a couple of hours. They had no mother, their father no wife, and years of coming to terms not only with their loss but also the nightmares and flashbacks of her being killed in front of their eyes.

The iPod screen filled with the first of the photographs. Gavin flicked through to the end of the album, then triggered the voice memo.

As he listened to Tom shouting above the gunfire, he broke into a grin for the first time that day. 'Tom Buckingham . . .' He gave a low whistle. 'You are one magnificent fucking bastard.'

76

The object of that admiration was still crouching in the darkness. Tom watched through the carriage windows, in the dim
glow of the emergency lighting, as one of Laszlo's crew
dragged something heavy along the aisle. The man's shoulders
jerked from side to side as he shuffled backwards with his
load.

Then Laszlo himself came into the picture. By the far end of
the second coach he was just a pace behind whoever was being
dragged. Tom was in no doubt about the purpose of this
performance. Laszlo wanted everyone to see the body, to smell
the blood it smeared along the passageway. *Pour encourager les
autres* ... It was an all-too-visible warning to the surviving
passengers of the fate that might await them.

Tom followed in the shadows, searching constantly for
Delphine. As Laszlo and his shuffling sidekick reached the
third carriage – the last one occupied – he took a deep breath
and tried to cut away from the thought that he might already
have found her.

The body of a white-haired old man tumbled like a rag doll
through the remains of the door at the far end of the carriage,
and hit the concrete with a dull thud no more than three metres

from Tom's hiding place. Ashamed that his first reaction was relief rather than anger, Tom looked up as Laszlo pulled Colin, the head steward, away from his stress position against the first window.

His instructions were clearly audible in the tunnel. 'Give the hostages something to eat and drink from the buffet car. But make it water and sandwiches only, no hot food and no alcohol.' He turned towards the hostages. 'If you co-operate with us, you will be treated with respect and you will survive. If you resist, you will be shot and tossed from the train like that pathetic old man. *Bon appétit.*'

As Laszlo propelled the head steward towards the buffet car, Tom followed once more. And once more he checked each window for a sign of Delphine, desperate to know that she had survived the fuck-up with the kids.

77

Shivering with delayed shock, Delphine still crouched on the floor, next to the spot where the old man had been murdered. He'd begun his journey with such joy and anticipation in his heart, but had now been tossed aside like so much rubbish. Delphine told herself to stay strong. The old man's optimism counted for nothing now, but that didn't mean she should lose hers. Tom had said he would come back for her, and this time she believed him.

Sambor stood guard over her. Laszlo joined him to debrief the two gunmen who had pursued Tom and the children. Although she couldn't understand a word they were saying, she was in no doubt that this performance was at least partly for her benefit. The men now encircled her. A pair of blood-stained boots was planted a few inches from her face.

There was a tremor of fear in the older insurgent's voice as he made his report. 'We think he's dead.'

'You *think*?' Laszlo's voice was low, but dripping with menace. 'Where are the bodies?'

'We couldn't find them. We couldn't go so far towards England . . .'

It wasn't what Laszlo wanted to hear. 'So you do not have bodies?'

'No.'

Laszlo went silent again, still waiting for the answer he wanted. The gunman, even more nervous now, felt he had to fill the gap. 'But the amount of fire we put down, no one would have survived. No one.'

There was another long silence as the fighter waited for Laszlo to reply.

'I would say, almost certainly, that they are *not* dead.'

The unfortunate individuals accepted their error, heads lowered. Neither answered back in their defence as Laszlo continued: 'So, one man and two children are too much for my heroic fighters, and a 7.62mm gun team? Have you forgotten everything the SAS taught you? I suppose I should be grateful that the children weren't armed, or you might all have been killed. You are getting slow and lazy. It's time to step up. We have our unit. We have our history. And, most importantly, we have our pride.' His expression darkened still further. 'We must maintain them at all times.'

'Yes, Laszlo, we must step up. We're sorry.'

Laszlo hugged both men. 'OK. Now go and do your duty.'

Delphine had scarcely been able to breathe during the exchange, but now she released a long, shuddering gasp. She had caught the mention of 'SAS'. Laszlo's tone of disappointment, along with the nervousness of his subordinates, planted a small seed of hope in her heart.

When the two brothers were alone once more, Sambor spoke: 'The pipeline? That is still safe? Escalles?'

Escalles . . . Another word that Delphine understood. She saw Laszlo look down. She instantly dropped her gaze, but could feel his eyes drilling into her.

Sambor stepped away from the girl, and motioned to his brother to follow. 'Whoever this man is, he's no ordinary passenger. He's been very well trained.'

'Perhaps so,' Laszlo said thoughtfully, looking out into the darkness. 'But training is only part of it.' He remained facing the window. 'Brother, do you know the three questions to ask if you want to find a good general?' Laszlo raised an index finger above his shoulder. 'Is he intelligent?' He brandished his middle finger as well. 'Is he ruthless?' And finally his ring finger. 'And is he lucky?'

Laszlo turned back to face his brother, and gave the merest tilt of his head towards Delphine's still prone body. 'This Good Samaritan of theirs seems to be ruthless. And he's certainly been lucky – so far, at least. Let's see if he's intelligent as well, shall we?'

78

The Blue team call-signs were all marked up on the boards. Every operative knew where he had to be and what kit he needed. Not that there was much. Short ladders were the only item on the list.

The snipers had additional instructions. They had to wear party gear. So now they knew they were also going to be used as assaulters today.

Wires, radios and phones were being tested as the signallers got to grips with the comms. The Slime carefully unpacked their geeky stuff from its protective aluminium boxes.

The team stood around Gavin in their black kit, paper cups steaming, Mars Bars in mid-munch. There wasn't a notebook in sight. Anyone who couldn't remember what he had to do and when he had to do it after all these years of training and ops shouldn't be standing where he was now.

Gavin's set of orders confirmed all the details and cleared the legal procedures so that every soldier knew his responsibilities and LOE (limits of exploitation). The elected civil power might have handed control to the unelected military power, but the military was given only enough leeway to do the job required. The baton would then be snatched back at the first available opportunity, and the Men in Black sent home with a pat on the head – until the next time.

Gavin did a quick head count to make sure all forty-two members of the team and their support were present. 'OK, Blue team, listen in!'

At all other times, everyone in the Regiment was encouraged to have a voice. That was how problems were overcome and new ideas created and developed. But when it came to a set of orders for an operation, there was no room for opinions. There would be no Chinese parliament. That time had gone. What the commander said you were going to do, and how you were going to do it, was what was going to happen. Successful operations depended on everyone doing exactly what was required of them, and at the right time. If you disagreed with the plan – tough shit. Trains left Hereford station every few minutes.

Gavin didn't have to wait for the chat to die down. There was instant silence.

'These are the orders for the ER.' He delivered them in an unhurried monotone. Displaying no emotion, fear or excitement was what it was all about. 'The option will go in immediately after these orders.'

A murmur spread around the group. Gavin gave them a couple of seconds. This was the first time for them, and maybe in history, that an ER had gone in so fast and with so little information. The team had already worked out the possible Yankees casualty rate.

'OK, ground. We have three tunnels, two trains and a lot of distance between them and us. The target is the passenger train. The power is cut. It's using its emergency reserve. That means it's immobilized and light is limited.

'Situation.' Gavin checked his Omega. 'Laszlo Antonov, X-ray One, was attempting to escape from the UK via the eight twenty-six Eurostar to Paris. However, Tom pinged him on the train and informed us, and now the whole roadshow is here.

'Antonov's brother Sambor, X-ray Two – check the picture Tom sent us on the kid's iPod – and approximately forty South Ossetian insurgents took control of the HGV Shuttle heading to the UK. They met the Paris-bound Eurostar in the tunnel, fifteen K in from France. That's where the sprinklers went off, and where the French fire-crews were dispatched to. As of now, those crews still haven't reported back.

'They now control the passenger train, with about four hundred Yankees on board – including Tom's girlfriend, Delphine. She was leaving Tom. He tried to get her back. That's why he was a passenger.'

One of the whiteboards behind him had been decorated with a series of crude rectangles, each representing a carriage and identifying the call-sign responsible for hitting it. Gavin pointed with his felt tip. 'The Yankees have been corralled in the first three carriages behind the engine and lined up against the windows, face out.'

He tapped the front rectangle and then the two behind. 'X-ray One has been seen negotiating in the driver's cab, and moving about in those first three carriages.

'The X-rays have suppressed 9mm sub-machine-guns, and two PKMs mounted front and rear of the target train. They also have NVGs and Tom has seen oxygen sets. We will not be using gas, but they might be.'

There was another brief murmur in the crowd. Gas was a good compliance weapon, but in a confined environment, such as the tunnel, quite a few Yankees might comply too vigorously. The oldest among them would simply fall down and die.

'So far, there has been machine-gun fire and explosive entry. They have come prepared – for what, we don't yet know. This situation hasn't come about because X-ray One was pinged by Tom as he tried to escape. This situation was pre-planned. It would have been executed even if Tom hadn't called it in. He is just the source of the int and is still on the ground. On the casualty front, he's also doing his best to even the score.'

Gavin paused. Now was the time to move away from his orders and let them know what he needed to happen once the teams were on the ground.

'You know X-ray One. You know the history of his brother

and their fellow X-rays. Be aware. Be careful. Take no chances with any of them. But especially not X-ray One.'

Gavin deliberately didn't pause for effect. He wanted the last statement simply to be part of the monotone flow. The team didn't need it spelled out. They understood exactly what was implied. This wasn't the first time there had been a 'supplementary' to a set of orders.

'Deadlines. Negotiations – limited negotiations – have been taking place. The first deadline was met, and resulted in the death of a Yankee. So far we have one further possible, and an unknown number who may have died during the explosive entries – plus the French fire response team. X-ray One's demands are for gold and an exit via helicopter.'

Eyebrows were raised in unison.

Gavin couldn't agree more. 'I know, I don't trust it.' He took a breath before moving on to the legals. 'Mission. In two parts. To rescue the hostages and arrest X-ray One. Mission. In two parts. To rescue the hostages and arrest X-ray One.'

The mission statement was always given twice so there was no room for doubt. It was the most important part of the orders set: it was why the operation had to happen. In this particular case, now that the South Ossetian had control of real people, the task was no longer a clear non-lethal arrest.

The main objective was saving innocent people, which meant that Laszlo's killing would be justified and legal – as long as whoever pulled the trigger maintained that, as far as he was concerned, his life, or the lives of others, was immediately endangered by X-ray One's actions. No one else could make that judgement, or decree whether it was justified or not, because no one else could see what he saw or hear what he heard.

Gavin now came to the business end of the orders.

'Execution. Sierra One will take his team forward and get as close as possible to the train, making sure you have a good sight picture on the gun position. Your task is to clear the route-to-target in the service tunnel and train tunnel, and secure your firing point; that will be the team's start-line. You will take out the gun team and any X-rays that could stop the assault group getting on target.

'Assault group . . .' The marker tapped the board again. 'As soon as the Red team rock up, I'll brief them. What you should know is, Red One and Two: window entry on Coach One. All entries will be axes only – no explosives. Red One and Two: their LOE is the cab and their link man with Coach Two. I also want Sierra One to move forward with Red One and Two and take out the forward gun team. Don't wait for the "Go". As soon as you get a sight picture, take the shots.'

Gavin assigned one coach per two assault teams. The idea was to swamp the area with assaulters, to lessen the risk of the X-rays having time to react and start killing the Yankees. A fire-fight would produce even more casualties. This option needed speed, aggression and surprise, if it was to have any level of success.

Gavin turned his attention to the third coach. 'Blue Five and Six, entry on Coach Three. Your LOE is your link man to Coaches Two and Four, which is the buffet car.

'Red Seven, and the remainder of the sniper group, will make entry at the UK end of the train and clear all the way up to Coach Four, the buffet car, and the link man on Coach Three.

'Hostage reception. The reception area will be at the rear of the train. The Yankee handover to police will take place in the tunnel, out of sight and co-ordinated by the Red team.

'ATO [ammunition technical officer] and trauma team. You will move forward with the assault group and be called forward on request from the start-line.

'Signals. They will move with the sniper group and set up the re-broadcasters as you move forward.

'Timings. After these orders I want everyone loaded into the Transits in ten – doors closed, out of sight. The team will move into the service tunnel and debus. The sniper group and re-broadcasters will then use the tunnel transport standing by to get to security gate D11-231. Look at the boards for pictures of the gate markings. This will be deactivated so you can make entry into the Paris-bound tunnel approximately eight hundred metres our side of the target. The team will move five minutes after the sniper group, and support them from the security gate as they move along the Paris-bound tunnel.'

There was a roar of engines and the smell of bubbling rubber as the Red team's Range Rovers screamed into the hangar after their Formula One fast drive. They formed up exactly as the Blue team had done, only closer to the toilet block. The Blue team ignored them. They had more important things to concentrate on.

'The Red team will move into the tunnel as soon as they're bombed-up and will hold in the service tunnel until called forward for hostage reception. Behind them will be police and emergency services. Any questions?'

There weren't.

'Good. Last chance to sort your shit out.'

That was all there was to say. Everybody knew the rest. As the Blue team turned towards their wagons, each assault-team commander was already talking to his guys. The Regiment was good at this. The skills used to make entry and clear an area, while keeping themselves and the Yankees alive, were down to three things: training, training and more training. Hundreds of hours of it enabled the assaulters to carry out often complex tasks without even thinking. It all became second nature – which gave them the luxury of being able to focus fully on any situation as it unfolded. What they saw, what they heard – those were the things that really counted.

'Jockey! Mate, a quick one.'

'Aye?'

Jockey stayed as the rest of the Blue team started to rip the bin liners off their Transits.

Gavin gripped his arm. 'Mate, remember this fucker has something planned down there. Don't take any chances. The sooner he's history the better. Fuck the ICC – keep the good guys alive. Know what I mean?'

'Aye.' Jockey knew exactly what he meant.

Gavin headed back to his table to brief the assembling Red team. Their commander had jumped out of the first of the newly arrived Range Rovers and was already examining the boards.

79

Tom kept parallel with Colin and watched as he passed the shrink-wrapped cases of water along the three occupied carriages. Some passengers made sure the kids and the elderly got a drink first. Others just grabbed the nearest bottle and gulped it down. It made Tom gulp too: he could have done with a couple of those things. The one person he wanted to see drinking was Delphine and he still couldn't find her: neither pushed up against the glass nor anywhere inside, beyond the human shields.

His iPhone vibrated in his pocket. He pulled it out. The sender ID was Delphine, and the text message read:

> where r u?

Tom moved into cover beneath the carriage, hiding the illuminated screen inside his jacket, and tapped a response.

> close

He didn't have to wait long.

> come get me coach 2 i'm scared

He texted back.

sit tight be there soon

The iPhone vibrated again almost at once.

come get me. I can run to the blown up door – meet there –
tell me when you are at door and we can run

Delphine watched, horrified, as her iPhone beeped again.
Laszlo smiled as he read the incoming message.

stand by – may take time

He replied, then signalled his gunmen to position themselves by the door. They crawled quietly and purposefully
along the passageway. Delphine heard a series of faint metallic
clicks as they took their positions and flicked off their safety
catches.

no – now – tell me when at door – only chance want go home

There was no response for a moment, then:

which home?

Laszlo knelt down beside Delphine and yanked her head
back. 'Where is home?'
Delphine muttered through tight lips.
He let go of her hair and let her head fall back.
He tapped in her response.

England

Her heart sank even further as she heard another beep. She
waited, ready to scream a warning. Laszlo looked down and
read the message, then cursed and threw the iPhone to the

floor. It skittered towards her. When it stopped spinning, Delphine could just read the message it contained:

harm her – u die slowly

Laszlo raised his hand and motioned to his men. Then he kicked out at Delphine. She took the force of his boot between her shoulder-blades and curled into a ball of pain.

The gunmen burst out of the carriage and whipped around, shining torches into the darkness, tracking the beams with their weapons. Two of them even climbed up onto the roof of the train.

'Well?' Laszlo called to them.

'Nothing,' came the reply.

He grabbed Delphine by the hair and dragged her violently towards the window. They could see little beyond the pool of light in the immediate area of the window but still he kept looking. She knew Tom was starting to get to him. She also knew Laszlo would not give up easily. And that, from now on, he would make absolutely sure he had control of her all the time. That way, Tom would come to him.

Delphine's scream of pain carried into the dark reaches of the tunnel, where Tom lay in hiding as the torchlight slashed its way wildly across the walls.

As the gunmen got back into the train, empty-handed, he was already moving back towards the three occupied carriages, knowing full well that Laszlo would prepare for his return, and that Delphine was the bait. Knowing that he no longer held his trump card: the element of surprise. And knowing that an even bigger set of problems would be rocking up the tunnel any minute, and they'd all be dressed in black.

80

Laszlo dragged Delphine to the buffet car. It was empty apart from Sambor, who was in the narrow galley area adjoining the counter, rifling through the food drawers. With a look of disgust, he dropped sandwich pack after sandwich pack to the floor.

Laszlo pushed her up against the customer side of the counter and zip-tied her to it. She stared across at him, her eyes blazing with hatred, anger and fear.

At last Sambor found a sandwich filling he approved of and threw it to his brother.

Tom had finally found her. *And she was alive.*

He crouched opposite the buffet car and tried to regain his breath.

He watched, tried to listen to – and even lip-read – what Laszlo was saying to her, while working out how he was going to play this. There were only two of them with her, but they were expecting him.

Sambor had joined Laszlo behind the counter and was using the coffee maker with all the confidence of a black-belt barista.

His brother's fury had abated a little, and his urbane charm was back on display as he turned to Delphine. 'Perhaps you would like some coffee? Sambor is something of an artist with an espresso machine. If we had been born into a different universe, he would have been a most famous chef. Maybe he'd have had his own TV show. They have so many on British TV – have you seen them? I have spent so much time lately watching British TV. They must be a nation of cooks, house-buyers and antique-collectors.'

Delphine stared at him, unmoving.

Sambor glared at her, as if she'd personally insulted every-thing his brother stood for. He poured himself a cup, sniffed its quality, then added four spoonfuls of sugar from a large catering tin.

Laszlo rummaged in the fridge. 'Then perhaps a glass of wine instead? They have a surprisingly decent selection. You French are remarkable that way. You maintain your civilized lifestyle whatever the circumstances.

'Sambor and I read about the banquet that your countrymen served during the siege of Paris in the 1870s. They used the zoo as their farmyard, and cooked whatever else the starving guests could scavenge from the streets. "Cat Flanked by Rats" was one dish, I seem to remember, and "Roast Bear", "Escalope of Elephant with Shallot Sauce" – what elegance you always display, and what a shame you are such weaklings in battle. Do you think the two things go together?' He held up a bottle for her to inspect. 'A little sancerre to soothe your nerves?'

She shook her head.

Laszlo poured himself a glass, then picked up the public-address system handset and stretched the lead to its fullest extent so he could be as close as possible to her.

Laszlo tapped the handset. 'I want to make an announce-ment,' he said. 'But I won't be telling passengers what delights the buffet car has in store. I have something else I want to say. Not to the passengers at all, in fact, but for your very good friend Mr Tom Alvarez-Buckingham-Leary.' He raised his glass. 'Delphine, do take some wine. When our dear mother was pregnant, she drank three bottles of vodka a week. You shouldn't believe everything the doctors tell you about alcohol damaging an unborn child.'

The little remaining colour drained from Delphine's face as she realized where this conversation was heading. Laszlo leaned over the counter, the lead tautening as he moved the handset closer to her. He put down his glass. Delphine could smell the fumes rising from the counter. 'Delphine, my brother and I are perfectly normal.' He picked up the glass again, then took a taster's swig and swill before spitting it onto the floor alongside the contents of the food drawer.

'Neither of us has foetal-alcohol syndrome, and we are certainly not brain-damaged. I was a physics professor before I found a more suitable vocation. And, as I have already said, if it wasn't for all these wars, my brother would have won Russia's *MasterChef*, I am sure of it. So don't believe all the scary stories.'

He raised a toast to the handset, then pointed towards her stomach. 'What are you having? A boy or a girl?'

Delphine hesitated, reluctant to tell him.

Sambor clearly didn't like the idea of his brother being disrespected yet again by this woman. His look was enough for Delphine to answer, and quickly. 'A boy . . . It's a boy.'

Laszlo leaned in so close to her that they could quite easily have touched lips. Delphine tried as hard as she could to control herself, but she couldn't stop her body shaking. It wasn't just fear: she felt physically and emotionally violated.

Laszlo sniffed at her mouth. 'I've always had a very keen sense of smell.' He sniffed again, this time slowly. 'My mother used to say I could have been a *parfumier*, not that there are many openings for *parfumiers* to practise their trade in Russia. I can still smell a little trace of vomit on your breath. There's nothing quite like the smell of morning sickness on a woman's breath. It's unmistakable. You really can't hide it, no matter how many mouthwashes and breath fresheners you use. Though I can well understand why you would want to try. The whole process is really quite unattractive, isn't it? And a harbinger of other, even less pleasant things to come: the swollen belly, the varicose veins, the discharges, the mood swings, all those other delights.'

He stepped back from the counter, took a swig from his glass and smacked his lips appreciatively into the handset. 'So that's what your man Tom has to look forward to, when the time comes. Tell me, Delphine, how did he react when you told him that you were pregnant?'

She stayed silent, head down, gaze fixed on the floor. But out of the corner of her eye, she could see that Sambor had finally found the contents of a baguette worthy of his attention, and was drinking from a carton of soya milk. He held a carving knife by its blade in his spare hand.

'Well, well, Miss Delphine Prideux,' Laszlo continued, a note of even greater triumph in his voice. 'You haven't told him, have you? Perhaps you were wise not to. Some men tend to shy away from commitments, and children can be *very* expensive. That can frighten a lot of them. Especially those trying to exist on a soldier's pay. Even with a Special Forces bonus . . .'

She was determined to remain silent, stone-faced, refusing to rise to the bait.

'He is SAS, isn't he?' Laszlo took another sip of wine. Then he put the glass down and took the knife from Sambor. He ran his thumb along the edge of the blade. 'The calendar on your iPhone contains several appointments at Hereford General. You had a scan only a few days ago.'

Delphine was still trying to hold back her sobs, still trying to contain herself. But silent tears streamed down her face.

'We are soldiers, too, of course.' Laszlo waved the blade in the direction of his brother. 'But before the war we were involved in the property market. In Georgia. We didn't seem to have many long-standing clients, though. By the time we arrived on the scene, most people had already had the good sense to leave. There were always a few who argued, people who said the price was too low, or superstitious peasants who would rather give up their lives than their land.'

He gave her a chilling smile.

'And, of course, we were always happy to oblige them. Others were just stupid as well as stubborn.'

He put down his glass and leaned across the counter.

Delphine flinched as he gently pushed the blade against her stomach.

'Some were invalids. Some were pregnant mothers. Mercy killings and emergency Caesarean sections became a bit of a speciality for us. You'd be amazed at how ... skilled I became ...'

He pressed a little harder. The knife-point pierced the fabric of her top. She felt her skin resist momentarily before a drop of blood glistened on the steel. She finally lost control and broke down, begging for her child's life.

Laszlo didn't have time to react. There was a heavy slap against the safety glass on Delphine's side of the carriage. Their heads spun towards the light green lump the size of a 50p piece that was now stuck to its left-hand corner.

The two brothers knew instantly what it was. But before they could take cover, it detonated like a gunshot.

Tom crashed through, head first, in a shower of glass, and skidded across the window table. In one fluid movement, he landed on the floor and dived for cover towards the luggage compartment by the doorway as Sambor's burst of fire ripped into the softer bodywork of the carriage.

Laszlo cut Delphine's zip-ties and dragged her into the next coach as suppressed ceramic bullets shredded Tom's cover. He tried desperately to locate her. Before he opened up, he needed to know where she was.

During the next lull in the fire, Tom made his move.

He leaped up and ran forward, weapon in the shoulder, both eyes open. His breath was slow, in control, in auto-mode. His legs never crossed, he always kept a stable platform for the weapon – because that was all he was now: a weapon platform. He passed through the staff entrance into the galley area, past the microwave cookers and ovens, his boots crushing the crinkly, plastic-covered shit beneath his feet. He didn't care about the noise. They knew he was here.

He heard shouts from the carriage behind him. A target popped up the other side of the counter in front of him. Sambor had finished loading. Tom took aim, both eyes open. Then Sambor dropped again, but keeping his weapon above him, his hands just visible as he opened up.

Tom ducked for cover. As he did so, he felt a blinding stab of pain in his leg. He ignored it. He kept firing into the counter at ground level, hoping the rounds would penetrate the toughened plastic barrier and whoever was firing at him from the other side.

Almost instantaneously, Sambor stopped firing, Tom ran out of rounds, and more of Laszlo's men burst into the carriage. He had no choice: he sprang up and dropped the weapon. Warm blood ran down his right leg as he looked for an escape route. The other side of the counter was now clear, but gunmen were swarming in from behind him.

He grabbed the safety glass hammer from its clear plastic container next to the kitchen window and flicked on the nearest gas ring. He picked up the large can of sugar and held it there, waiting, waiting . . . His head was clear. He knew what he had to do. He saw everything around him unfold as if it was in slow motion. He wasn't flapping, just waiting. Waiting for the right moment . . .

Three seconds later Tom decided that time had come. As the gunmen passed the galley, weapons in the shoulder, Tom launched the sugar as if it was a bucket of water, creating a fine combustible mist of particles that rained down around him and the men the other side of the counter. It ignited instantly as it made contact with the naked flame.

He slammed the steel-tipped hammer against the corner of the window as the sweet-smelling fireball engulfed them. He could feel his hair singe and the back of his neck blister as the safety glass crazed and he dived against it, ready to accept the landing.

81

Tom tried to protect his head as the right side of his body took the brunt of the fall. All the wind was driven from his lungs. He just wanted to lie there, re-oxgenate and take the pain, but he knew that couldn't happen.

As the adrenalin ebbed, the wound in his thigh began to throb. Shouts and screams of anger and command echoed from the carriages above. He rolled onto his hands and knees and scrambled under the train, out of the line of fire, then started crawling back towards Coach Eight.

He reached the bullet-smashed remains of the toilet bowl and septic tank, and stopped to listen. Hearing nothing, he positioned himself diagonally beneath the hole in the toilet floor, raised his arms and eased himself upwards. Once his head was above the parapet and his elbows were resting on the hard surface, he stopped to listen again.

Still nothing.

He levered his torso and legs into the cubicle, then crawled across to the doorway. A pair of boy's trousers and pants, soiled with shit, packed one hell of a punch, but he left them where they were. No one without a respirator was going to come anywhere near this place unless they absolutely had to.

He craned his neck around the frame and checked that the

carriage was empty. A kid's sweatshirt had been deposited across the arm of a nearby seat. Using the cover of the luggage rack he grabbed the sleeve, took it back into the cubicle and locked the door.

He fished the remaining PE out of his jacket and put it on the floor. It wasn't going to waste. He just had other things to attend to first.

He undid his jeans, sat down, and peeled them past the glistening crimson wound on his thigh. The round had missed the bone, but had gouged a three-inch deep crevasse through the flesh. It had to be sorted, and quickly. The pain wouldn't go away, Tom knew, and infection would soon follow. But until he had a decent cocktail of the right kind of drugs, he just had to accept that and carry on. What mattered right now was stemming the loss of body fluids.

He tore the sweatshirt into strips and began to pack the crevasse. If he didn't, it would just keep bleeding. His head began to swim: he clamped his eyes shut and took a couple of deep breaths to clear it. The sight of his traumatized flesh wasn't helping. And neither was the PE. It was almost as bad for human beings as it was for pipelines. It wouldn't kill you when you handled it, but you were guaranteed the mother of all migraines if it was absorbed into the bloodstream, or if you worked with it in a confined space.

He tried to distract himself by remembering the looks on the gunmen's faces when he'd pulled his stunt with the sugar. Most fine organic substances suspended in air could be ignited. That was why mills and coal mines needed to be well ventilated. And so did outbuildings, if flour bombs were part of your afternoon fun: at Tom's eleventh birthday party he'd accidentally torched his mother's stable block, and burned it to the ground.

Once the cavity was packed, he squashed the edges of the wound together and bound it with the remaining strips of material, like a butcher tying a beef fillet. He needed to keep up the pressure if he was going to stop it leaking.

He checked his handiwork and sat back against the toilet

wall. His thigh was burning now, but he couldn't tell if the pain was making him gag, or the PE, or the stench of the soiled clothes. Jesus, did all little boys' shit smell that bad?

If he and Delphine managed to get through this, he guessed he'd soon find out.

Fuck, he was going to be a dad . . .

Excitement, fear, and then a wave of happiness overcame the pain. He suddenly realized he was grinning like an idiot. He was going to be a father. And if he could persuade Delphine to stick around, he might even be able to make a better fist of it than his own emotionally retarded, gin-soaked parents had.

But first he had to sort this shit out. The pain surged back as he thought about what might be happening to her now.

He was pretty sure Laszlo would keep her alive, at least for the time being. Since discovering their connection, X-ray One had known Tom would be coming back for her. And coming back for her was top of his list of priorities.

A plan was beginning to form in his fevered mind.

After his exploding window trick he still had two slabs of PE, but no detonator. He'd bitten a small lump of PE off one of the slabs and, wincing at the taste, chewed it until it was sticky and pliable, then folded it around the detonator and reconnected the battery.

After slapping it on the glass, he'd flattened himself against the side of the carriage and pulled the square of plastic from the crocodile clip. The det alone would have shattered it; the PE gum stuck it to the target and made an even bigger bang.

Budget-quality PE had plenty of drawbacks, but some distinct advantages. The high nitroglycerine content made it extremely sensitive to shock and heat.

Tom hauled himself to his feet, unscrewed one of the light-bulbs in the ceiling of the cubicle and ripped away the wiring behind it. He stripped off the plastic sheathing with his teeth and got busy with the fuse.

PE combusts like paper – but with much greater intensity. Its chemicals burn at such a rapid rate that a vast amount of energy escapes immediately. The detonator is the match. And this stuff was so inferior that all it would take to get it burning was the heat of the bulb.

He took the two slabs of PE and inserted the fuse between them like the filling in a sandwich. He moulded the material to make a device the size of a small loaf of bread, then twisted the two leads from his makeshift detonator together to avoid them acting as an antenna. Finally, he zipped up his jacket and shoved the device inside to keep it secure.

82

Keenan could hear nothing but the sound of his own breathing as he led his four snipers in single file down the right-hand side of the tunnel. If his NVGs made him look like an overgrown wasp, his Arctic Warfare Super Magnum was the sting. Keeping the weapon tight into the shoulder, he leaned into it so it became an extension of his body.

He could see the target eight hundred metres ahead. His NVG magnified the train's low lighting hundreds of times until it appeared floodlit. The glow of the enemy gun team's own NVGs gave away their position almost as quickly. They appeared unaware: their heads moved easily; their jaws weren't jutting forward or jerking around. Keenan knew that he could get closer. He'd get a better shot, and the assaulters would have less distance to travel to their part of the task.

Keenan exaggerated every step, as if he was walking through long grass. He was losing some perspective through the NVGs so he took his time, hugging the wall. It wasn't long before the concrete floor of the tunnel became wet underfoot. He carried on, placing his boots even more carefully. Silence was everything right now.

The signallers were behind him, putting the last of the

re-broadcasters into position, antennae raised, on the other side of the open security gate, so that the team's comms could be sent and received from both tunnels.

The Blue team assault group were close by, safety catches on, ready to go. Some knelt; others sat or leaned. Their foam-tipped, seven-rung black aluminium ladders lay securely on the floor. Nothing was left to chance: anything propped against a wall could fall and clatter.

Each had his NVGs on, respirator hanging off his free, non-weapon-firing arm by the head-straps. No one talked. There was no need.

Keenan kept advancing towards the target, Gavin's voice – a cool, measured monotone – in his earpiece.

'Sierra One, Alpha check.'

Keenan stopped and gently pushed his chest pressel twice.

'Alpha, roger that.'

The net went dead once more.

Click-click, click-click.

Gavin's response was immediate. 'Is that Sierra One in position?'

Click-click.

'Alpha, roger that. How close?'

Click-click, click-click-click.

'Roger that, five hundred. The gun team still in position?'

Click-click.

'Roger that. Any changes?'

Gavin waited for five seconds.

'Alpha, roger that, no changes. Blue One, acknowledge.'

Jockey was number one on the door. Like the rest of the Blue team, he got slowly to his feet, picked up the ladders so they didn't bang into each other, kept control of the weapons so they didn't either. Slow and deliberate was the key to tactical speed.

Jockey checked that each line had formed up, either side of the security gate.

'Blue team, moving now. Out.'
He led his ghost force into the Paris-bound tunnel.

83

Laszlo stared ruefully at his broken watch. The case hadn't survived his dive for cover, but it was still capable of telling him that the minutes were ticking by.

As Sambor dragged Delphine back towards the buffet car, she gave a sudden cry. Laszlo barged past the hostages. Two of his men stopped tending their burns and jumped out of their seats to follow him. Laszlo burst into the buffet car. The British soldier was standing on the other side of the glass door at the far end.

He was unarmed. His arms were raised. He was delivering himself to Laszlo. The door opened.

'Tom – *no!*'

Laszlo wasn't going to allow himself to be distracted by the woman's pitiful plea. Neither was his adversary. The man's eyes were locked on his.

The battery in his hand, and the two leads connected to it, told their own story. The plastic square was still in place, keeping apart the jaws of the crocodile clip that would complete the circuit. He took a step closer, his other hand tightening the wire that would wrench away the plastic insulator. Laszlo saw the greasy, light-green substance bulging from the top of his jacket.

He sensed rather than saw the gunman immediately behind him thumbing down the safety catch of his weapon and lifting it, ready to fire. He raised a warning hand. 'Don't.' He kept his voice slow and calm. 'Can't you see what he's wearing?' He switched to English. 'I see that you have found my PE.'

The man smiled bleakly. 'I'm afraid you're now a couple of slabs short of a picnic.'

'I don't think we'll miss them.' Laszlo spent some moments studying Tom. He was wounded, beaten and bruised, totally swamped by the strength of his opposition, yet still he kept coming back. Just like Laszlo did. 'There's still more than enough left to do what I need it to do. I've bet my brother that the blast will be powerful enough to fracture the rock over-head. The English Channel will suddenly develop a plug hole.'

Laszlo turned to his brother and translated.

Sambor didn't find it as funny as he did. 'We kill the country!'

Laszlo patted his brother's shoulder, then said to Tom, 'I imagine you're as intrigued as I am to find out if I'm right . . .'

The Brit shook his head. 'I'm much more interested in whether you've thought *this* through.' He nodded at the explosives strapped to his chest. 'Are you feeling suicidal?'

'Of course I'm not. I am a professional soldier, not some cheap street terrorist.' Laszlo took a couple of steps, grabbed Delphine by the hair and pulled her towards him. 'But I think your delightful companion might be.'

'If so, she'll take you with her. You won't get out of this tunnel alive – not now. You know that.'

Laszlo tightened his grip on the woman's hair and gave it a twist. She gasped with pain, but his adversary didn't even blink. 'There will be an assault, Laszlo. You will fight, and you will die. Whatever you have planned, you will not live to see it. None of you will.'

Laszlo shrugged. 'If it were up to certain members of your government, I'd already be dead.'

'That's not true. We were sent to arrest you. It was a non-lethal arrest.'

Laszlo paused, intrigued. 'So you *were* there, were you?'

'Only a couple of minutes or so behind you. Your coffee was still warm.'

Laszlo was impressed.

'But that's history. You've now taken the non-lethal option off the table. Unless you help me. Come with me now. We disarm the device, then we walk out of the tunnel and live.'

Laszlo couldn't help laughing. He shouted a translation to Sambor, who still didn't share his amusement. Neither did the men behind him, who looked like they ached to take a shot.

'If you choose to fight and die, that's up to you. But these people, the real people, the innocent people, they don't deserve to go down with you, do they?'

'You disappoint me, Tom. I didn't think you'd be so naïve. No one is truly innocent. And nobody cares about real people. Each corpse only costs your government . . . what? A little over a hundred thousand pounds in compensation. I'm sure that would be a very small price for them to pay for my death. Tom, you are a young man so you do not understand the subtlety of this situation. Some of your people have a strong vested interest in seeing me permanently silenced.'

Tom held his gaze. 'So what? Set the real people free and we can walk out together. Then I'll be able to protect you.'

Laszlo gave a mirthless smile. 'You can't really believe that. And I certainly don't.'

'At least free some of these people. Why do you need so many? You have the tunnel gift-wrapped, after all.'

'Precisely my point. The tunnel is more precious to them than a million hostages. I will release these people when I am ready. So stop playing at suicide bombers and start being more productive. Go back to Folkestone and tell your lords and masters what you know and what you have seen, and why they must accede to my demands.'

'Let me take her.'

Laszlo shook his head. 'If you wish to keep Delphine and your child alive, you should go now, and do what I say.'

Sambor and the two Bears had inched towards the

Englishman while Laszlo was speaking, their weapons up. He could probably feel their hot breath on the back of his neck. They'd be itching for a head-shot; they knew as well as he did that a high-velocity round could detonate the PE as easily as the crocodile clip snapping shut. But as their target moved back behind the glass once more, Laszlo lifted his hand and signed to them to back off.

Laszlo watched Tom fix his eyes on Delphine. What message was he trying to convey? That he would be back? That he would try to get her out? Whatever it was, her reply was a small, rather touching smile.

Laszlo gave a smile of his own. How foolish women could be. To side with the underdog; to see hope where there should be only despair. Did they never understand the true dynamics of power?

A moment later, her lover jumped from the train and disappeared into the darkness.

84

The team stood in two single files against each of the tunnel walls. Three of Keenan's four snipers lay over the tracks ahead of them. The fourth was confident he could take the 500-metre shot from a sitting position.

Keenan hit his pressel.

Click-click.

'Is that Sierra One ready?'

Click-click.

Keenan took hold of an ankle of each of the two snipers in front of him. If either lost his sight picture now, he'd just move his foot. Keenan needed to know that at least half his team could get a shot on target on the 'go'.

'Alpha, roger that. Hello, all stations, I have control. Stand by.'

The snipers took first pressure on their triggers, maintaining the sight picture.

'Stand by.'

They emptied their lungs of oxygen, then stopped breathing altogether.

'Go.'

There were four dull thuds. Less than a second later,

Laszlo's PKM team toppled like bowling pins.

Jockey was straight on the net. 'Blue team moving.'

85

'You really think he is going to do as you say?'

'Sambor, my brother, we have a plan to execute, and I have a call to make. The last thing I need now is an Englishman with a rather badly fitted explosive waistcoat getting in my way.'

Once back in the engineer's compartment, he picked up the radio mic, switched on the speaker and settled back into the seat, resting his boots on the oxygen sets bungeed to skateboards that Sambor and the fighters had lugged from their vans. 'Mr Woolf?'

'Yes, Mr Antonov. What can I do for you?'

'It is time I allowed you to turn the power back on. Some people are sick, the elderly are suffering, women and children are crying. I'm sure their welfare is dear to your heart.'

'And what are you willing to offer us in return? Let me have the ill and the old. They need—'

Laszlo laughed. 'Oh dear, Mr Woolf, is that what they teach you in hostage-negotiation classes? You would have been better off in Las Vegas, learning some of the basic rules of gambling – for example, that it's dangerous to bluff when you don't hold any cards. But I'm a generous man. I'll tell you what I *won't* give you if you turn the power back on: five more dead bodies.'

'Wait one moment, please. I have to seek permission, you understand.'

'Of course, but hurry. I will give you two minutes. Then I start the killing. I know that your government does not care for these people, but you all have families. Think of your loved ones. What would you feel if *they* were on this train? You will all be *directly* responsible for their deaths. Will you be able to live with that? Will any of you be able to live with that?'

There was a click as Laszlo cut the comms and glanced down at the driver. His eyes were threatening to pop out of their sockets. Whatever Woolf thought, this man was in no doubt that he might only have two minutes left to live.

86

Aided by their NVGs, the Blue team moved painstakingly slowly through the darkness. Only when they got to the train would the goggles come off and the SF-100 respirators go on. And then the ladders would go up and all hell would break loose.

Jockey was up front of the single file. Mentally, he rehearsed the sequence for the attack, from the moment the axe man in each four-man call-sign crazed the glass, to punching through the flash-bangs, to the entry itself, when they'd push, hit, elbow their way through the human shield with their 9mm Sig pistols raised.

To double the number of men dominating the battle space, a call-sign would blast in at each end of a carriage.

Gavin's voice came through on the net. 'All call-signs – stop, stop, stop. Blue One – confirm.'

Jockey halted and hit his pressel.

Click-click.

The men behind him came to a standstill too.

'All call-signs, this is Alpha. Power will be turned back on in the train in less than five. I repeat, power back on in less than five. Blue One, acknowledge.'

Click-click.

'Roger that. Blue Two?'

Click-click.

'Roger that.' Gavin went through the other call-signs before he pushed on with the rest of the information Woolf had relayed from COBRA. 'The option is still a go. You will continue with the option. I say again, you will continue with the option. Blue One, acknowledge.'

Click-click.

'Roger that. Can you talk, Blue One?'

Click-click.

'What have you got for me?'

Jockey clicked his pressel once and spoke quietly. 'Wait out.' Whispering could carry further, and it was hard to understand over the net. Radios were good enough to pick up slow, gentle speech.

Jockey knew that as soon as they heard his instruction to wait, the team, the hangar and COBRA would all do exactly that. They could tell him to go and do the job, but not *how* to do it. They couldn't see what he could see, or hear what he could hear.

Jockey raced through the options in his head. The route to target would be floodlit in less than five minutes. If they were still in the open, it would take a miracle for them to reach the carriages without being spotted. The op would go noisy. It would be a long, hard fight to get as far as the front three carriages. By then, all the Yankees and call-signs might be dead. To make matters worse, there was a gun position at the French end. If this kicked off, the gun would simply swing round and start hosing them down.

The decision took Jockey a matter of seconds. Realistically, there was only one option. He came back on the net, his voice quiet and calm.

'Blue team, listen in. We will move to target in a new order of march. Blue Seven will take the lead. At the train, Blue Seven will make entry into the first carriage. It can then move forwards along the train, clearing the route towards the first three carriages.

'All other call-signs will follow behind Blue Seven in the same order of march as now. Blue Seven will go static when it reaches Coach Four, the buffet car, which will be Blue team's start-line.

'On my "go", Blue One to Six will exit on the right-hand side of the train and move to our entry point in double time – and make entry immediately.

'Sierra call-signs: you will give cover forwards towards the gun position, and back onto the front three coaches. If at any time it goes noisy, Blue Seven will take on the threat while Blue One to Six bypass the contact and move to their target any way they can, in double time, and get on with the emergency response. Sierra call-signs will cover. Wait.'

Jockey gave the call-signs time to let it all sink in. He had more to say, and no one was allowed to come on the net before he spoke again. He gave it a couple more seconds. 'Blue Two, acknowledge.'

Click-click.

Jockey ran through all the ground call-signs before addressing the hangar. 'Alpha, acknowledge.'

'Alpha, roger that.'

Blue Seven, with Vatu in the lead, were already on the way past him. Jockey and his assault group fell in silently behind.

87

Laszlo watched the driver close his eyes and pray. It was a curious sight, because he looked like a man who hadn't done anything of the kind since he was a child. Except, perhaps, when his football team was two-nil down with ten minutes to go before the final whistle.

He switched the mic back on. 'Mr Woolf, I still do not have power.'

'Mr Antonov, as a gesture of good faith, we're willing to restore the power to the train, *and* food and drink, as well as any medical care that may be needed.'

'How kind you are, Mr Woolf.' Laszlo bared his teeth in a smile. 'And how stupid you must think I am. We have no need or desire for food, or care of any kind. If you were thinking of dressing your SAS as pizza-delivery boys, you can tell them to stand down. And I know that the power can be turned on remotely. Make sure that it is done that way. If I see *any* Special Forces soldiers masquerading as electrical repairmen . . .'

For a moment Laszlo considered telling Woolf to call off Tom as well. But he decided against it. He admired Tom's determination. He admired his sheer guts. And, more than anything, he enjoyed the fact that he didn't have the slightest idea what was really happening here.

'Mr Woolf, no more games. Just do it.'

He switched off the mic again and smiled at Sambor. 'And the Lord said, let there be light and, lo, there was light.'

A moment later, right on cue, the fluorescent strips flickered and the air-conditioning unit began to emit a low hum.

The driver began to sob.

Ignoring the pathetic gratitude of the man on the floor, Laszlo stood. 'You won't have long now before they send in their dogs. Work quickly.'

Sambor nodded. But before he could move away, Laszlo gripped his arm. 'And, brother, I think it's time to put Delphine on the menu. If it's the SAS team who were in Hampstead yesterday, they will know Tom. And very probably they will know her.'

88

Laszlo put down his weapon and produced a roll of silver duct tape, which he proceeded to wind around Delphine's neck. He dragged her across the buffet car, manhandled her up onto the far end of counter, and wound the tape around the stainless-steel shelving pillars behind her. Sambor did the same with her arms, waist and thighs. By the time they had finished, she looked like a badly wrapped present.

Laszlo and two of his men then set to work on the junction boxes that were set into the bulkhead at the end of the carriage.

Delphine stared up at him. She knew it was pointless resisting, but she could still show the defiance that Tom had mustered in her. The hatred in her eyes was all her own. 'I will *not* be bait for your trap,' she hissed.

Laszlo gave her a look of contempt. 'You almost make it sound as if you have a choice in the matter.' He reached for his weapon and pressed the muzzle against her head. 'Would you prefer me to pull the trigger and end it now for you and your child?'

'Yes.' She pushed against the cold, hard steel. 'And don't forget to say goodbye to Tom for me when he cuts off your balls and stuffs them into your mouth.'

Laszlo merely smiled. 'I can see why he was attracted to you.

You have more than a child in your belly. There is fire, too. *Spirit*.'

An expression appeared on his face that she hadn't seen before. She wondered for a moment if he was a little jealous. She suspected that Laszlo had been fighting and hating for so long that he had never had the time to find a woman, let alone worked out how to keep one.

He nodded slowly. 'You are extremely lucky to have each other.'

She worked her jaws for a second and spat at him.

He paused to wipe his cheek. 'Hmm . . . Perhaps too much spirit.'

Pinpricks of light danced on her retina as he punched her just above the temple.

'I think it may be time for some silence.'

He tore another length from the duct tape and wrapped it around her mouth and the back of her head.

'You seem very confident that Prince Charming is going to ride to your rescue. It may surprise you to hear that I hope he does, too. And I hope he brings his black-suited friends with him.' He forced her head back against the shelving to duct tape her neck even closer to the unit. She wasn't going anywhere: she was the prize perched high on the counter for all to see.

She soon heard the splash of water behind her in the galley. Sambor appeared in the customer area, pushing a drinks trolley in front of him, laden with beer, wine and mineral water. Delphine stared at them, baffled, as the two brothers smashed the neck of one bottle after another against the edge of a table and poured their contents onto the floor.

She saw Laszlo select a Châteauneuf du Pape and pause for a second. He invited her to admire the label. 'A good wine like this should be savoured, don't you think?' Then he smashed that one too and thrust its jagged spout closer and closer to her cheek.

Time came to a standstill as she watched a globule of crimson liquid glisten on the razor-sharp edge of the glass.

His face once more devoid of emotion, Laszlo inched it

towards her eye, but at the last moment he tipped it, too, onto the floor.

When they had finished, a pool of froth-slicked liquid covered the middle of the buffet car. Laszlo was pleased with their work. He beamed at Delphine. 'I imagine that you share my excitement about what will happen next,' he said. 'You won't be disappointed. It promises to be quite a spectacular performance, a veritable *son et lumière.*' He turned and ushered Sambor down the carriage, towards the front of the train. A moment later the glass door slid shut behind them.

Delphine summoned up as much of her dwindling reserve of energy and defiance as she could muster, and began straining and heaving herself against the duct tape that bound her. It held her fast. She breathed in as deeply as the constraint would allow, trying to ease the tension from her shoulder muscles and the feeling of dread that rose inside her.

89

Vatu had made entry through the first blown-in door he came to, four coaches from the rear of the train. His assault group pulled on their respirators and eased themselves into the carriage. Sig 9mm semi-automatic pistol up, both eyes open, both hands on the weapon, he kept as far to the left of the passageway as he could. His number two, immediately behind him, stayed as far to the right. That way, their two weapons could fire at once, and cover the whole arc of the space in front of them.

They moved quickly and deliberately, jerking their heads left and right to check no one was hiding behind the seats. Their forward and peripheral vision from inside the respirators was good. All they could hear was the gentle rasp of the diaphragms as they breathed.

Jockey and the rest of Blue team stood poised to follow.

Vatu hunched his shoulders forward to create a firm support for his weapon as he entered every new carriage. His number two was so close behind him that his barrel almost brushed Vatu's right shoulder. Numbers three and four of the call-sign carried Heckler & Koch 9mm sub-machine-guns, and stayed static immediately after moving left and right into each seated area.

They kept as close to the sides of the train as they could. Their job was to cover Vatu's advance down what was in effect a well-upholstered gallery range and put down suppressive fire if any X-rays bounced into view. Vatu and his sidekick could keep pumping forward without ever crossing the arcs of fire of the weapons behind them.

The further Vatu and his number two moved down each carriage, the narrower the arcs became for the static three and four, but that was where trust kicked in. It was why the team always trained with live ammo. You needed total conviction to sit in a close-combat room feeling the blast from 9mm rounds against your cheek. Vatu was so confident in the others that he'd stand between two wooden targets in the dark while they burst in with pistols and torches and fired either side of him.

Each team member literally put his life in the hands of the others. One mistake and you could kill your best mate. There had been casualties over the years, but given the high number of rounds that were fired – more than by the rest of the British Army put together – they were very low.

90

Tom worked his way towards the rear of the train as rapidly as his wound allowed. The team option would kick off any minute. It had to. COBRA wouldn't let this go on any longer. He had to intercept them. It was the only way he had left to save Delphine. And – if Laszlo's plan was to detonate the pipeline – the life of everyone else aboard.

The power had come back on. Lights blazed through every pane of glass, splashing across the sides of the tunnel. He'd had to move deeper under the train, right into the middle of the track, and it slowed him down.

He was now on his hands and knees. His thigh burned with every movement, but he kept driving himself on. He had to link up with the assault team. He had to tell them about the device on the gas pipe. Was he going to kick it off as soon as the team turned up? All Tom knew was what he'd seen and what he'd heard. He didn't even know if Laszlo was still sticking with the negotiation pantomime, issuing a string of demands and deadlines. All he knew was that if an option went in it could result in disaster. And Laszlo could be right: the explosion might be enough to fracture the tunnel.

But how to intercept the team? He had two options. He could go to the end of the final coach and wait; Keenan and his mates would take out the PKM position before moving on. Or he could try and get beyond the gun, and intercept the team on their way in.

With four carriages to go, he heard movement above his head, four sets of boots thumping across the linking steel-plate walkway. The sound receded and he carried on.

Tom finally reached the rear of the train. The lighting was good: too good for him to try and get past the PKM. He could see the silhouettes of the two-man team about a hundred metres ahead. But they weren't sitting or standing, one ready to fire, the other feeding in the link: they were lying prone on the tracks. Unless they were asleep, they were dead. And from what he'd seen of these guys – and their commander – he knew they wouldn't be sleeping.

Alarm bells started ringing in his head. The four sets of boots . . . The team was already aboard.

91

Vatu neared Coach Four and peered through the glass door into the buffet car.

Delphine was gagged and duct-taped on the counter. As soon as she saw him, she made frantic attempts to free herself, moaning and twisting, bucking and shaking her head, but the tape was so tight she barely moved.

Vatu had a job to do – to keep moving and take down whoever and whatever was in his way. Once he'd sorted that, once the attack was going in, he'd come back and sort Tom's girl. She looked like shit, but she was breathing. She wasn't bleeding. She was alive.

If it was a trap, he'd soon find out. And then the South Ossetians really would have the mother of all battles on their hands.

Delphine watched in desperation as Vatu piled through the door and the liquid on the floor splashed across the tops of his boots. There was a blinding flash. Sparks flew from the barrel of his Sig and the weapon fell from his hand as if a lightning bolt had erupted from inside his body. He crashed to the ground, collapsing into Laszlo's supercharged cocktail. His huge, friendly body convulsed and twitched.

Smoke streamed from the wiry hair beneath his hood.

Insulated by the counter, Delphine was numb with shock. Stock still, she stared in horror. This was the first time she'd seen a human die. And he'd died horrifically, in excruciating pain. This wonderful, generous, invincible giant of a man had been transformed in the space of a few seconds into a smouldering corpse.

The rest of Blue team were close behind. Jockey got straight on the net. 'All call-signs, go! Go! Go! All call-signs, go! Go! Go!'

Blue Seven made a lunge for the nylon-webbing grab-handle on the back of Vatu's body armour and tried to pull him back. The call-signs in the middle of the carriage dived to the right and slammed their axes into the windows, pushed their way through the large frosted panes and spilled down onto the track. The rest of the call-signs joined them, covered with glass sequins, pistols pointing forwards as they ran towards their entry points.

Keenan sprinted along the tunnel, ignoring the carriages on his left, not caring if there was fire or movement coming from the human shields within. His job now was to get forward and take out the PKM position.

He heard a couple of double taps from one of the team's Sigs. They must be taking incoming. He'd heard no shots. Laszlo's crew must have suppressed weapons. He heard more glass smashing as the assault groups started to swarm into their target carriages. He stopped short of the engine as a long burst of heavy-calibre fire streamed towards him.

The first rounds ricocheted off the front of the train. Green tracer tumbled and bounced from about a hundred and fifty metres further down the tunnel. The whole area filled with the sound of gunfire and the screech of brass on steel.

Keenan hit the floor, trying to use the PKM's muzzle-flash to get a sight picture onto the gunner.

92

Tom limped fast along the side of the train, loaded with the PKM and as much link as he'd been able to hang around his neck. His leg was agony. 'Bin it!' he screamed. '*Jockey, fucking bin it!*'

A couple of hundred metres away, Jockey couldn't hear a thing. He was up his ladder, with numbers two and three so close behind that their respirators impacted on the body armour of the man in front.

Number four, the axe man, punched a flash-bang through the freshly crazed glass. Jockey threw his weight against it and tried to push through. A blinding flash lit each end of the carriage, followed immediately by two deafening bangs.

The detonation of the metal-oxidant mix of magnesium and aluminium created the equivalent of 300,000 candlepower, momentarily activating all light-sensitive cells in the eye, making vision impossible for five seconds. The 160-decibel blast seriously fucked up the fluid in the eardrum. It shocked and stunned, and disrupted the balance function of anyone within range who wasn't wearing protective gear.

To Jockey's amazement, the Yankees didn't budge. Almost immediately he saw why. They couldn't. He tried punching and elbowing his way through from the top of his ladder, but there were too many of them, and they were being forced up against the windows by their guards.

A flash-bang bounced off the impenetrable human wall and back down into the tunnel. The detonation kicked off and the Yankees screamed, unable to move and take cover. Two teenagers screamed to each other in French. Their arms reached out to Jockey, thrust from behind like lemmings at a cliff edge.

He checked left. The other team was having the same problem. Some had taken hits below him. Yankees tumbled out of the windows and onto the track. It was like a siege on a medieval castle, men swarming up ladders to scale the parapets. But instead of battlements and boiling oil, there were so many bodies it was never going to happen.

Jockey jumped down onto the concrete and hit his pressel. 'All call-signs – bin it! Bin it! I say again, move back, move back, *move back*!'

Keenan heard him loud and clear, but he was going to stay until the team was on the move. Unable to see the gunner, he aimed just above the muzzle-flash and took a shot. The PKM stopped for about five seconds, then kicked off again. He sucked in big lungfuls of air to stop his body moving and affecting his aim. The noise and chaos around him was just moving wallpaper in his head as he took aim once more.

Jockey brought him back into the real world with a boot in the thigh. 'Get moving, you mad Cornish hippie!'

Tom saw the team start to withdraw to the rear of the train. He swung the gun down and behind one of the wheels and stood with his hands up, not wanting to become a casualty. He waited for the first of the team to approach.

The man in black grabbed him before he recognized Tom's face.

'Mate,' Bryce yelled, 'where the fuck have you been hiding?'

Tom spun him against the train, shouting over the din of the flash-bangs covering their withdrawal. It echoed and resonated tenfold when the pressure had nowhere to go but up and down the tunnel. 'Jockey? Where's Jockey?'

More members of the team streamed past as Bryce got on the net. Jockey was the last man back, making sure every casualty was picked up, and every flash-bang was used to keep the chaos going. When he appeared, Bryce threw out an arm and Tom gripped his sleeve, pulling him close. 'There's a device on the gas pipeline!' He pointed upwards. 'Up there, above the service tunnel. Laszlo has a grab bag – it has to be the initiation device, it's the only thing he never lets go. I don't know what the fuck he's planning, but his brother keeps saying, "Kill the country." So go, mate – go! Give Gav the message.'

Jockey ripped off his respirator. 'You've got to come with us.'

Tom's eyes locked on his. 'No, I'm staying. Delphine's still in there. End of.'

The rattle of machine-gun fire filled the air. Rounds drilled into the concrete further along the train.

Tom ducked and grabbed the PKM as Jockey and Bryce legged it towards the UK. Tom positioned the bipod to the right of the wheel. He needed every bit of protection on offer.

He lay down and cocked the weapon. The working parts were already to the rear, but old habits died hard. He had to ensure the gun was made ready. He started to fire: short, sharp, five-round bursts, making sure that every round hugged the side of the train en route to its twin.

93

Battered and bloodied, the Blue team regrouped and re-organized at the mouth of the service tunnel. The trauma team had their work cut out trying to stabilize the military casualties, who were still being brought in. Electric carts then ferried them back to the Transits for a covert exit to hospital through the massed ranks of media and rubbernecking onlookers.

Jockey stopped his sit-rep to Gavin mid-flow when he saw Ashton storm over, his face red with fury. 'Blue One, wait out . . .'

'What the fuck did you do in there?'

Jockey wasn't in the mood for Ashton – or any other fucker – getting on his back right now. He took a pace towards him. 'I'll tell you what the fuck I did down there. We walked straight into a fucking ambush, and I tried to get everyone out alive. That cunt knew exactly when and where we were coming. And if it hadn't been for Tom we'd all be fucking toast. Not just poor bloody Vatu, the whole fucking lot of us.'

'Buckingham? He's still alive?'

'He was ten minutes ago. The gun was still firing – but he could have run out of ammo by now. And he won't be leaving that train unless he's taking Delphine with him.'

Ashton shrugged. 'Which means they're both coming out of there in a box.'

Jockey's fists clenched this time. He stared at Ashton with absolute contempt. 'You'd better order some more, then, because they're not the only ones.' He pointed across the tunnel to where the big Fijian's body was being carried onto the back of one of the carts. Another three wounded soldiers were straggling alongside. 'So, if you've finished, Boss, I've got a sit-rep to send.'

Keenan, his face flushed with anger, broke up the stand-off. 'Boss, when are we going back in to settle things with those fuckers?'

'Right now,' Ashton said. 'Get rehydrated, get bombed-up. I'm going to move up the Red team. Fuck sorting the hostages – the police will have to take care of that.' Ashton jabbed a finger into the front plate of Jockey's body armour. 'You have fifteen minutes to brief them before you go back in. I want everyone up-front-and-bags-of-smoke. Make Laszlo history – now!'

Jockey knew the infantry saying. It meant simply: get all your men up front, no reserves; get the smoke down to cover them during the attack. No finesse, no sophisticated tactical manoeuvres: just get into the battle space and win the fight.

He kept his eyes fixed on the OC.

Ashton glared back. 'Well, what the fuck are you waiting for? Get on with it!'

Jockey was tempted to give him a smack there and then, but jerked his head at Keenan instead, motioning him out of earshot. His eyes drilled into Ashton's, but he managed to keep his voice as low and reasonable as a Jock with size issues could. 'Boss, like I was trying to tell Gav when you charged in, Tom has seen a device on a gas pipeline somewhere up above here.' He pointed to where the sky would have been. 'If we go back in immediately, that fuck Laszlo might just kick the thing off. Then we'd all be in the shit. So right now I need to get the int back to the hangar, get COBRA to fuck about with it, then we'll see. I trust Tom more than you, COBRA, even my own fucking mother. We need to regroup and rethink how the fuck we're going to stop that cunt.'

Jockey turned away and got on the net. 'Alpha, this is Blue One . . .'

94

Tom's PKM took a round into the front of its feed tray. The force of the impact punched him back. A split second later the round splintered, peppering the side of his face with brass and lead fragments. The combined momentum hurled his head against one of the solid steel wheels.

The next thing he saw was a shitload of boots tap-dancing all around the track. Three of Laszlo's sidekicks yelled at him, and motioned for him to get out. They wanted to see his hands. Tom had ended up lying on his back, starfish-style. He felt his boots being grabbed and hauled out into the open.

As he emerged, they gave him a couple of kicks for good measure, and gestured for him to get to his feet. He heaved himself up, hands in the air. He stared straight ahead, no scowl of defiance, no eye contact. His training had taken over. There was no way he'd show them that he was scared in a situation like this; he just stood there, took a deep breath, closed his eyes and let them get on with it.

One of his new best mates jabbed him with a machine-gun and signalled for him to get down on his knees. Tom did exactly what he was told. When he looked up, the kick to his jaw knocked him backwards against the train. Blotches of intense white light filled his head. He opened his eyes. Through the starbursts, he saw the world closing in.

He took another boot to the side of his head. He wasn't going to come up from that one in a hurry, even if he'd wanted to. His brain felt like it had been shaken loose and everything was spinning.

Even though he was winded, Tom's instinct for self-preservation programmed his body to roll itself over. Face down on the concrete, he curled into a tight ball. He knew he had to accept what came his way; there was nothing he could do to stop it.

He tasted blood in his mouth. One half of his mind was telling him to close his eyes and take a deep breath, and maybe it would all go away. But at the back of the other lurked a small but insistent voice that said, *Let's wait and see, maybe they won't, there's always a chance . . .*

It was trampoline time. They leaped in the air and landed on his back and legs. He felt each impact, but no longer the pain that went with it. His system was pumping too much adrenalin. He wasn't blacking out – Tom had never been totally out of it from a blow of any kind – but he was sinking into a world of mush. He tightened his stomach, clenched his teeth, tensed his body as much as he could, and hoped they weren't going to start to give him a really serious filling in.

The whole performance couldn't have lasted for more than a minute or two, but it was long enough. When they backed off, he kept himself in a tight ball, but trying now to slide his arms underneath his body. His mind was numb. The kicks to his head had been punctuated by well-aimed toecaps to the kidneys.

When they finally wrenched him into a standing position, he fell down almost immediately onto his hands and knees, coughing up blood.

He felt them search his clothes – and find his mobile, passport and wallet – then push his face down into the concrete. His hands were pulled behind his back and zip-tied. He tried to raise his head so he could breathe, but someone seemed to be standing on it. He gasped and inhaled blood. He felt as if he was going to suffocate. Every sound was magnified, distorted, then diminished. He heard distant voices debate whether or not to kill him. And, for an agonizing second or two, he thought it would be quite nice if they did.

95

Tom was dumped on the buffet-car floor, the side of his face thumping hard onto its unyielding surface. A couple of small shards of broken glass pierced his cheek. His hands were still zip-tied behind him, but he'd have been incapable of breaking the fall even if they'd been free. He lay in a pool of liquid and it trickled into his open mouth. The alcohol burned his cuts.

Tom could hear Laszlo barking out orders nearby.

'Be quick!'

But he couldn't really work out where he was, let alone try and turn what was left of his head to look for the speaker.

'Brother, I want this train fully operational in ten minutes. You need to organize the equipment. I will meet you at the engine.'

Another kick helped him get his bearings.

He opened one eye to see Laszlo squatting beside him. He felt the South Ossetian grip his wrists, then slice through the zip-ties. With the speed and elegance of a magician, Laszlo liberated his Omega.

As he stood up once more, Laszlo dropped his own broken wristwatch next to Tom's head and left the buffet car.

96

Her hands and thighs still duct-taped together after she'd been cut loose from the shelving pillars, Delphine was now being dragged towards the engine by a fighter. The deafening explosions, machine-gun fire and men in black trying to force their way onto the train might have stopped, but the cries, sobs and prayers of the hostages had not.

The floor was strewn with broken glass. So were many of the hostages. The reek of cordite hung in the air, mingling with the haze of smoke from the devices that had made her ears ring. One was still smouldering – it had ignited the fabric and foam innards of a chair. The stink of burning plastic was acrid and frightening.

Old men gripped their wives protectively as Delphine was pulled past them. Some just cowered and looked away. Parents comforted their children.

She saw Laszlo enter the carriage.

He paused every couple of steps and pointed at selected passengers. 'You are now free to go.'

Nobody moved. They just looked puzzled. Some didn't understand him; those who did couldn't bring themselves to believe him.

Laszlo walked slowly along the carriage, pointing as he

did so. 'You . . . you . . . you four . . . you two . . . and you.'

Delphine was fearful. There seemed no particular logic in the choices he was making. She couldn't help thinking that it was yet another of his tricks.

'You . . . and you . . .'

He stopped and turned back to a group of four at a table he had freed, and pointed at a thin man with short grey hair, dressed in a black Puffa jacket and jeans. 'You will stay.'

The woman next to him burst into tears. He tried to comfort her, while almost hyperventilating about his own potential fate.

The air was thick with suspicion. After all they had been through that day, Delphine shared their disbelief. By the time Laszlo got to the end of the carriage, he'd selected a total of twenty males to remain in the tunnel. Some looked resigned; some couldn't conceal their envy of those whose nightmare might – just might – have been about to end.

He turned, smiling benevolently, like an Old Testament prophet preparing to lead the chosen ones from the desert. 'Go. Walk back along the tunnel. You will find yourself in England, in sunlight and open air, and all this will start to seem like a bad dream.'

One of a four-man group finally raised a hand, braver, Delphine thought, or perhaps more foolhardy than the rest. 'How do we know you aren't just fucking us about? You know, we get off the train, and then you kill us.'

Laszlo spread his open palms in a theatrical shrug. 'I just may do that.' Then his face changed. The smile became chilling. 'But if you're still in this carriage in one minute, I'll kill you anyway. So what have you got to lose?'

There was a moment's hesitation and then a mad scramble of the chosen ones towards the exit. The sound of Laszlo's laughter pursued them as they clambered down onto the track.

Delphine could no longer see them, but she heard no shots. She heard murmurs. She imagined them looking around them, perhaps expecting guns to go off, then finally turning and starting to run breathlessly along the tunnel. The murmurs receded.

Laszlo looked at Delphine and laughed. 'Some of them must be your fellow countrymen. They're heading the wrong way, towards France.'

He moved into the next carriage. Delphine was dragged along with him. He barked at the hostages that they were all to be released. The same happened in Coach One too. She almost dared to hope that it would be her turn next.

She was pushed into the driver's compartment and dumped on the floor. She watched, bemused, as Sambor detached what looked like oversized skateboards from the sort of oxygen sets she'd seen fire-fighters wear.

Laszlo appeared pleased. He reached down and cut through the duct tape with his knife, and pulled her to her feet.

'It's perfectly safe now.' He peeled the last of the tape from her skin and thrust her against the wall. 'The fireworks are over. For the moment at least.'

Delphine looked down at the limited edition Omega gleaming on his wrist, dreading what it implied.

97

The tightness of Delphine's bonds had cut off some of the circulation to her legs, and she gasped as her capillaries started to refill with oxygenated blood. The driver remained curled up on the floor, having tried his best to get his body as far under the control panel as he could, as if he was pulling a duvet over his head and hoping this was all just a nightmare he'd wake up from.

Her eyes were still glued to the Omega on Laszlo's wrist.

'Yes,' he said. 'It was Tom's. He was responsible for my own being damaged, so it seemed only fair . . .'

He slipped the watch off his wrist and showed her the engraving on the back of its case. 'BU . . . And a lovely winged dagger.' He smiled. 'Vanity is a terrible burden, isn't it, Delphine? Really, I thought your Mr Buckingham would have been beyond this sort of thing.'

He turned back to the radio mic and switched on the speaker. 'Mr Woolf, it is time for you and me to converse once more.'

A voice crackled back over the speaker. 'What do you want, Antonov?'

Woolf clearly thought the time for diplomacy was over, that

the situation was far too advanced now for anything but an exchange of cold, hard facts.

But Laszlo didn't see it entirely that way. He still wanted to play a little. Why not, when he so obviously had the upper hand? 'Well, for a start, I think it would be a nice gesture if those fools at COBRA stopped sending their people in to try and kill me. It's really not helping.'

Woolf didn't bite. Laszlo thought he heard the sound of a pencil on paper. So that was how the MI5 man kept himself under control.

'You left them with no other choice, right from the moment you started killing hostages.'

'Believe me, I do see your point, Mr Woolf.' Laszlo was enjoying himself immensely. 'But if you had not been so impatient, you could have congratulated me on releasing so many hostages. They should be with you quite soon, hundreds of them, though I think some ran towards France. Maybe they're still hoping to make their appointments. I will give you thirty seconds to make sure a reception is organized for them.'

While Laszlo waited, he produced a taped and modified handheld VHF radio from the desert-tan grab bag that had never left his shoulder.

Woolf took no more than twenty seconds. 'Thank you for their release. But I know it's because you don't need them any more. They must just have been getting in the way. You have a device on the pipeline now. You have traded up. What do you plan to do with it? Is it just leverage? Or are you really going to try and destroy the tunnel?'

'Mr Woolf, I feel the tone of our conversation has deteriorated somewhat. You were once so . . . congenial. Perhaps we would both benefit from the services of a suitable mediator. I think I have found the perfect woman for the job. Introducing a real person into the mixture will serve to remind you *all* that there is a matter of common humanity to consider. Sometimes these people become little more than statistics as we each move forward with our own game plans.'

Laszlo turned to Delphine. He held the radio mic up close to her mouth. 'Say hello.'

'Fuck off.'

'I do hope our conversation isn't being broadcast to the nation.' Laszlo wiped her saliva once more from his face. 'It would be a shocking example to set. I'm afraid this young lady's vocabulary leaves a lot to be desired. But she has had a very exhausting day.'

Laszlo held the device inches from Delphine's face. 'What would you say I was holding in my hand?'

She didn't answer. Perhaps she didn't know.

'Mr Woolf, the item she is refusing to describe to you is the initiator for the pipeline charge. I built it myself. It has no need for re-broadcasters in the tunnel, and of course will defeat your electronic countermeasures. I am extremely proud of it.'

'Get to the point, Antonov.'

Laszlo nodded to himself, with some satisfaction. 'Well, simply put, if you attempt to launch another attack, I will detonate the device. If you do not meet my revised demands, I will detonate the device.' He paused. 'In fact, to distil the situation completely, Mr Woolf, if you disobey me or deviate from my instructions in any way at all, I will . . . well, I'm sure you can complete the sentence.'

'And what are these revised demands?' Woolf was still trying to sound calm, but Laszlo could hear his vocal cords tightening with stress. His voice had risen half an octave. Laszlo liked that.

'My price has now doubled, to three hundred kilos of gold.' He pulled a folded sheet of paper from the grab bag and moved closer to Delphine. She moved away an inch. There was nowhere to go.

Laszlo cut the comms to the hangar. 'Perhaps you'd like to read Mr Woolf the detailed list of my requirements. If you do, I'll have Tom brought to you. He's alive.'

Laszlo didn't get the reaction he was expecting. Instead, she launched an even angrier mouthful of spit onto his face.

Laszlo merely wiped it away again, with the back of his

hand. 'Now, Delphine, just read what's written on the paper to Mr Woolf, and you will be reunited with the father of your child.' He handed her the sheet. 'Nothing more – but nothing less, either.'

He held Delphine's stare. 'Young woman, put aside your hatred and pride. In our world, these wild emotions only get people killed. This is not about *you*. It's about all those people who are still with us, wanting so desperately to survive.'

Delphine's eyes broadcast her feelings for a moment or two longer, then she dropped her gaze. Laszlo turned on the comms and she started to read.

'The Eurostar, along with the remaining hostages, will be driven back to Folkestone. No barricades or other obstructions are to be placed on the tracks. The Chinook will be positioned twenty metres from the track, at the mouth of the tunnel. Air space is to be cleared of all air traffic in a twenty-kilometre radius from that point, in all directions.'

Laszlo glanced at the Omega and retrieved the mic from Delphine. 'Thank you. Mr Woolf. You now have ninety minutes.' He switched off the comms system.

The train driver still lay face down on the floor, but he was no longer a picture of defeat. He knew at last why he had been held for so long on his own. Laszlo turned him over with the toe of his boot. 'Very soon you will be resuming your normal duties. But, as you may have gathered, there has been a slight change of plan. We will be returning to Folkestone. So now you must make your way to the other engine and carry out whatever preparations you need to.

'One of my men will be with you at all times. If you do exactly as you are told, you will live to tell your grandchildren the story of what happened to you today. If not, there will be one more body lying at the side of the track.'

Laszlo kicked open the compartment door. One of his men responded to the signal and escorted the driver away. The next moment, Tom's semi-conscious body was dumped at Delphine's feet. She gave a small cry and dropped on her knees to comfort him. His clothes were covered with dirt and oil; his face was cross-hatched with cuts and bruises and bullet fragments. One eye was half closed by a livid red swelling, and his lips were swollen and split. The makeshift sweatshirt dressing around his left thigh was stained with blood. It had dried to a dull brown at the edges, but was still a dark, liquid crimson at the centre.

Delphine didn't know how to help, what to soothe. All she could do was gaze down at him, horrified. 'Tom . . . *Tom* . . .'

He looked like a drowning man, fighting his way to the surface. He managed, finally, to open one bloodshot eye and give her the ghost of a wink. His lips moved. He seemed to be trying to say something to her, in the faintest of whispers.

She leaned closer, her ear inches away from his mouth. She felt his breath on her cheek.

'You . . . OK . . . ?'

'She's fine.' Laszlo squatted beside them. 'Though, as you can see, she's a little tongue-tied at the moment. Still, no permanent harm done and, by the way, I'm sure she'll make a very good mother to your child when the time comes. I have an instinct for these things.'

'Why are we still alive?' Tom mumbled. His words were still barely audible. A thread of saliva fell from the corner of his hideously damaged mouth.

Laszlo tutted. 'All those blows to the head must be affecting your brain, Tom. I'd have thought the answer was blindingly obvious. It's because I like you both. I admire you for the way you have conducted yourselves during our time together and maybe, just maybe, I am a little envious. Your commitment to each other is quite inspiring, in its touchingly bourgeois way.'

He stood and headed for the door. 'And, of course, because you are going to help me escape.'

98

A guard had been positioned the other side of the open door. He shouted down the passageway towards the first carriage. Another group of Laszlo's gunmen shouted back. Some of the hostages started shouting too, and Delphine thought she could hear more of them outside on the track.

She cradled Tom's head in her lap, gently smoothing his blood-caked hair away from his forehead. It was the only thing she could think to do; it was the only thing that didn't appear to hurt him.

Tom had his good eye focused on her. A smile gradually took shape around his bruised and battered lips. He peeled them back, painfully slowly, displaying chipped and blood-stained teeth. 'Delphine . . . we're going to have a son!'

She felt tears well in her eyes and begin to fall. They splashed down onto Tom's face. 'You told me you didn't want children while you were in the SAS,' she blurted. 'You said that it wasn't the right time . . .' She wiped some of her tears from his forehead, making a smear in the encrusted dirt. 'I should have told you, my darling. I *tried* to tell you – but you didn't make it easy for me, you stupid, stupid man. The mistress . . . Yemen . . . the team . . . your work life always seemed so much more important—'

Tom wrenched himself upright and brushed his fingers against her trembling lips, but she carried on, wanting to explain: 'I was scared, Tom. *So* scared. I was afraid you wouldn't want our child. I panicked. I thought . . . I thought I had to leave . . .'

With infinite care, Tom caressed her cheek, then held her against his chest. Delphine tilted her head so she could gaze into his eyes. There were tears there too.

'It's not your fault, Delphine. I'm so sorry. You're right. You're right. But not about everything. I *want* to be a father. I'm *ready* to be a father. We're going to have a son!' He kissed her gently on the temple and whispered in her ear, 'You kept asking what I wanted from you.' He didn't wait for her answer. 'I finally worked it out. I want you to be my wife.'

'I've fantasized for so long about this moment.' Delphine's smile felt as if it filled her whole face. 'Somehow I imagined it would be a little more romantic . . .'

'I'll make it up to you, Delphine. I promise.'

She nodded slowly. 'And I will make sure you do. But right now I need you to do something. I need you to get me and your child off this horrible train.'

99

COBRA was not a happy place to be right now. Each department affected by the emergency had its own communications set up on the desk. The lines were hot.

The military were receiving rolling sit-reps about their casualties and what options could be laid on the table. Alderson listened intently to his ground commander as he broke the latest on the hostage reception he was organizing. It wasn't just about the number of escapees they might have to cater for: they had to try to find out if they'd seen anyone fall and get left behind on the track, and how many might still be running around in the tunnel.

The Foreign Office staff liaised with the French to let them know there might be runners heading their way.

Sarah Garvey watched the clock on the wall facing her. She'd given everyone an extra five minutes to talk to their departments before she'd have their full attention. When those five minutes were up, they were going to have to move on with whatever they knew. She made a mental note: she needed to reshuffle COBRA. Each department needed leadership in place on the ground, capable of concentrating on the unfolding situation, instead of sitting in the committee room, trying to command from a distance. The people in this room had to be big-picture, but not necessarily the biggest hitters.

She looked at the clock again and started to fume. She wasn't happy with Clements. Where was that slippery snake?

Brookdale paced up and down the corridor outside the briefing room, a mobile phone stuck to his ear, briefing his boss. Clements was out there too, but well out of earshot of anyone else as he listened to his mobile ring. Whoever was at the other end didn't sound remotely impressed when they finally answered. 'What the fuck do you want?'

Clements never gave anyone the satisfaction of replying in kind. Power came with control. 'The same as you, I presume. Antonov's head on a stick. So I suggest you put a little more effort into making that happen. All the indications here are that she plans to submit to his demands.'

The voice exploded: '*What?*'

Clements always liked listening to other people losing control. He'd never experienced the feeling himself, and it fed his conviction of his own superiority.

'*He should have been fucking dead by now!*'

Clements shrugged. 'Well, you need to make every effort to ensure he doesn't come out of the tunnel alive. Is that soldier still on the train?'

Sarah Garvey watched the second hand count down. The committee had three minutes left to sort out their different chains of command. And she had three minutes to sort out Clements. She looked around. He still wasn't back. Was he deliberately avoiding her?

She got up and walked out into the corridor. There seemed to be more people out here than in the committee room, all of them busy in their own little worlds, protecting their minister or department boss and blaming everybody else – especially, no doubt, the home secretary – for the cock-up so far.

She saw Clements in the distance, and ploughed her way through the Amandas and Gileses to get to him. Clements quickly closed down his mobile when he saw her coming.

She squared up to the civil servant as if she was trying to provoke a pub brawl. 'I've had enough of your bullshit, Clements. I want to know what this kill-the-country thing is all about. Is it revenge, or is it about ransom? I saw your face when Woolf told us. I want to know.' She poked her finger into his chest. 'Why is Laszlo trying to destroy us?'

Clements looked as shocked as if he'd just been mugged in the parliamentary lobby. 'How dare— Home Secretary!'

She wasn't having any of it. She kept on jabbing. 'Tell me what you know. I want anything you have that will help me. I've got a negotiator down in Folkestone who has nothing, absolutely nothing, to work with. *I* have nothing to work with. I don't know if this is some kind of suicide mission, or if he just wants to take the gold and disappear. I want to know all that you know.'

Clements was still on the back foot. But he had regained his composure. 'Home Secretary, I should think that whatever I may or may not—'

She leaned into his face and shouted, 'I don't give a shit what you may or may not! Tell me what you *know*.'

The corridor fell silent. The Amandas and Gileses swapped glances. It would make a fantastic diary piece in one of the Sundays. Juicy gossip endeared them to the news corps, and they constantly had to hedge their bets in case they were thrown out at the next election.

The fact that this display was so public would be even more brutal for Clements than the chest poking. His face reddened. He guided Sarah Garvey into one of the side rooms. 'Home Secretary, do not ever address me in that manner again. I have a position to maintain.'

She didn't even bother to look up. She checked her watch. 'Listen to me.' She pointed her index finger at him. 'I have no more time for this. If I don't get answers, I'll be going direct to the PM and telling him that you've been a complete liability throughout, and have personally endangered the lives of those passengers. I'll also tell him about the shoddy history with this Antonov.'

At a stroke, Clements felt he was back in the driver's seat. He knew that the PM wouldn't want to hear about anything that might embarrass the government, especially as his party had been in power at the time. If that was her best shot, then Clements was bulletproof. The smile returned to his face. 'Sarah, don't be so naïve. We're dealing with important matters of state here, not wheelchair access to libraries.'

'Exactly.'

Clements knew at once that he had seriously under-estimated her. She'd sensed she had him at his smuggest, and therefore most vulnerable.

'So therefore I will resign on principle if you do not tell me – the principle being that I cannot work alongside a civil service that condones rape and murder. Yours will be the first name I use as an example.' She gave him no more than three seconds to register what she had said. 'So tell me what I need to know. Is this revenge? Is he going to blow himself up inside the tunnel? Or is he going to come out, escape, and still blow the tunnel up? Or is he just going to fly away? For God's sake, man, can't you see the danger this country is in? Tell me what I need to know!'

Clements grimaced. A cabinet minister resigning on principle was a nightmare for any government. He was a smart man. He had taken less than one of those three seconds to understand. 'I agree, Home Secretary. There is a lot at stake.' For himself as much as for the country, but he chose not to mention that. 'What I know is that the Antonov parents were killed by Georgian military units that we financed and trained. The Antonovs are aware of the facts, Home Secretary. I should imagine he will detonate at some stage.'

Sarah Garvey's arms dropped to her sides. Her eyes rolled like those of a two-year-old in a strop; she stared up at the false ceiling and the air-conditioning ducts and lighting. She took a deep breath, composing herself. 'You people and your fucking games. We're facing a national disaster now because you thought it would be a "jolly good idea" if we backed both sides in some grubby little bygone war.' She finally looked at him. 'Is that what you're telling me, Clements? Have I got it right?'

Clements shrugged. 'We – UK plc – will of course give support to anyone who can further our national interest. The BTC pipeline . . . that oil was, and still is, our total focus in the region.'

She was now so close that her nose almost touched his. 'Well, you have not been fucking focused enough. Your un-professional work has got us into this position. Even I would have had him dealt with somehow after we finished laying that pipeline. Shoddy work, Clements. Shoddy.'

The door burst open. Brookdale dashed over the threshold, BlackBerry and notebook in hand. He'd been rushing about trying to find them after he'd got word the pair were fighting in the corridor.

Sarah Garvey reacted before Clements did. She raised a palm. 'You – shut up.' She started towards the door. She didn't bother to wait for Brookdale to move out of the way for her. She looked as if she was going to walk through him.

Clements watched her storm down the corridor and into the committee room.

Alderson was still talking to Folkestone. Everybody else was just waiting.

Sarah sat down, not waiting for Clements or the others to resume their places. 'Right – the tunnel. If Antonov does blow the pipeline, what's the damage?'

The junior minister from the Department of Energy checked his notes. 'Home Secretary . . .' He flicked through the pages. 'The economic consequences would be absolutely catastrophic. Aside from the gas pipeline, electricity comes into this country down that conduit, as well as communications – both Internet and landline.' The junior minister coughed, more from em-barrassment than anything else. 'Much of London's electricity, including Number Ten's, comes from French power stations via these cables.'

She watched Brookdale scribble furiously as the junior

minister continued: 'The cost to the British economy would be measured in the hundreds of billions.' He checked through another couple of pages of his notebook. He didn't look up this time. 'The fact is, Home Secretary, the Channel Tunnel is pretty much a one-way street. Most of the traffic in that conduit comes *into* the UK. We have very little going out, apart from the Eurostar passengers. If we lose the conduit, it really does go a way to severing the umbilical cord . . .'

She didn't acknowledge what had been said. There wasn't enough time. She turned to the Department of Transport under-secretary. 'Could the pipeline exploding cause the tunnel to fracture?'

The guy nearly jumped out of his seat, as if this had been suddenly sprung on him. When he had turned up at COBRA this morning, he had probably thought he'd be home within a couple of hours. Wasn't the train going to become a French responsibility? Weren't they just going to arrest Antonov? 'Ah, no, Home Secretary. However, we know nothing of the dev—'

'Yes, yes, enough of your insurance cover note from the Department of Transport. Chief Constable Alderson, give me an update.'

Alderson checked his notes, then left them where they were. She was pleased that he at least focused on the senior person in the room. 'Home Secretary, as of two minutes ago, we still do not have any contact with the hostages. If they are in the tunnel and on foot, it will take a while longer for them to reach the military in the service tunnel. Once we do make contact, the hostages will be taken out of the tunnel. They will receive medical aid and be debriefed immediately. Anything we learn of value will be with us as soon as possible.'

'And how's the media story standing up?'

Alderson shrugged. 'So far, so good. But that will only last until the hostages get access to their mobiles. We'll confiscate them as soon as they're within reach, of course, but as soon as the injured start going through the medical care system, we'll lose control.'

Sarah Garvey nodded. 'Thank you, Chief Constable. The hostages will not be released from the service tunnel until I give you the express order to do so. Give medical care, whatever they need, but not one of those hostages must have access to the world until I am ready to let them.'

She prodded a finger in the direction of Brookdale. 'Do something useful and get the PM to make some calls to the French. We need their co-operation on this.'

Brookdale looked conflicted. He was probably happy for the excuse to talk to his boss, but he didn't want to miss anything in the meeting room.

'Go on. Tell him it's all right. The helicopter will never take off with Antonov on board. The PM can appear on this evening's news with a smile. Go.'

The spin-doctor got up and left, doing his best to look as if it had been his own decision. Sarah Garvey allowed herself a smile.

She placed her palms on the dark oak table and inspected her nails as she waited for the door to close. 'Let me explain my perspective on the situation.' She looked up sharply. 'And then let me tell you what is going to happen. I will stop between the first and second parts and you may tell me if I've got it wrong. But until then, please, be silent.' She swung round to make sure Clements was within reach, and that he acknowledged what she'd just said.

She continued. 'We must assume that Antonov has a device and the means to detonate it. We must assume that there will be no negotiations. That is clear. Even if he gets what he wants, and flies away to buy some small African country with his gold, there is no guarantee he won't detonate the device. And I believe he will detonate. So, to put it bluntly, we are in the shit. Have I summed things up correctly so far?' She knew she had, but wanted no one to be in any doubt. Minutes might not be taken at COBRA meetings, but that didn't mean a record wasn't kept in people's heads.

Alderson sounded as if he still didn't understand Antonov. 'Home Secretary, his demands, the gold, the helicopter – they don't fit with this chap's profile. He's far more intelligent than this, surely. We know nothing of his men, either. We don't know whether he really does plan to take off in the Chinook. There's something missing.'

She agreed. 'But, fortunately for us, we don't need to know. We don't need to waste time second-guessing. Because we are going to stop him.

'First we need to get Antonov out of that tunnel. I will submit to the demands and get that train out into the open.' She turned back to Clements. 'Have you organized the bullion?'

Clements nodded. 'Yes, Home Secretary. But if he's still alive he may—'

She turned to face the MoD man. 'The Chinook?'

He nodded. 'Nearly there, Home Secretary.'

She inspected her nails again and took a deep breath. 'So, I will get the train out into the open. The bullion and the helicopter will be waiting. Everything will be as he wants it.' She pointed to the director of Special Forces: 'From the moment that train is exposed, in the open, until Antonov takes the first step to board that helicopter – that is your window of opportunity. I do not expect him to be able to detonate that device.'

The DSF answered immediately: 'Yes, Home Secretary.' But he hadn't expressly told her he could do it.

'Can you kill Antonov and minimize the risk to any hostages while you do it?'

'Yes, Home Secretary, we can, but—'

She lifted both hands from the table. 'I know, I know. What if he hasn't got the initiation device? What if hostages get in the way? What if this, what if that . . . what if, what if, what if . . . Give me the percentage chance of Antonov not being able to detonate that device when you attack.'

The DSF didn't need to think about it. 'I'm looking at fifty per cent.'

She nodded. 'I'll accept those odds. Even if more casualties are taken, it's going to be worth it. We all understand that the security of the tunnel is of paramount importance. Antonov must be stopped from detonating that device by all means necessary. That, gentlemen, is what we're going to do. And the military are now going to tell us how they're going to do it.'

Clements sat back. He didn't have to listen to a word of the DSF's plan. It wasn't going to be needed. Laszlo was going to be killed by that SAS trooper, or whatever they called themselves, while he was still in the tunnel. And a dead man didn't have even a twenty per cent chance of living.

100

Gavin was still making arrangements for the Yankees' reception. At some stage the hostages were going to be coming down that tunnel and they were going to meet Jockey, with the Blue and Red teams, at the entrance to the service tunnel. They'd be the initial link in the escape chain – if Laszlo was telling the truth.

He glanced up as Ashton strode across to his desk. He pointed at Gavin's mobile. 'Is Tom's phone on that?'

Gavin shook his head. 'Boss, I want to call him as much as you do. But we can't. We need to know what the fuck is happening down there, but we can't risk compromising him. We haven't a clue where he is. We haven't a clue what he's doing. If his iPhone rings, he could be fucked. We have to wait for him to call us. He knows the re-broadcasters are up. In the meantime, I'm not going to be the one to take that risk. We just have to wait.'

Jockey's voice kicked off over the speakers. 'Alpha, Blue One, we have the first Yankees coming into the service tunnel. The first lot are coming out now.'

Gavin grabbed the radio handset. 'Roger that, Blue One. How many?'

'A dozen so far – maybe more. Wait . . .'

Jockey kept his pressel down for a few more seconds. Gavin could hear screams, shouts and a few sobs as the team dragged the Yankees into the service tunnel; the trick was to calm them and grip them at the same time. Jockey shouted, 'It's going to be all right. You're safe now – just wait there.'

The net went dead. He'd have taken his hand off the pressel. He came back on a few seconds later. 'It's got to be a hundred plus, so far.'

'Alpha, roger that. Out.'

Gavin went straight over to the Slime's desk. 'Tell the police ops room they're coming out. Tell them to get them out of the tunnel ASAP in case we have to go in again.'

Ashton leaned forward and opened Gavin's mobile. He hit B on his contacts list, found the number he wanted and keyed it into his own phone.

The major moved away from the desk and out of the hangar. He turned immediately right through the shutters and kept walking until he was out of sight. Emergency vehicles and personnel buzzed around the front of the tunnel ahead of him.

The mobile rang five times before it was answered. 'Yes?'

He'd have known that voice anywhere. 'What the fuck are you playing at? I warned you so you could get away, not hang around and start the Third World War.'

The silence echoed in Ashton's head.

'Calm down, my very English friend. I'm eternally grateful for what you did. But I think it's true to say that you still owe me enormously.'

Ashton wasn't having any of this cool, calm and collected bullshit. 'Fuck the friend bit, you psychopath. What the hell are you playing at?'

Laszlo responded with a theatrical sigh. 'Marcus, we've helped each other very much indeed over the years. I scratched your back in Georgia, and you scratched mine in Hampstead. Things have gone very well for both of us. It would be a shame for this to end in tears. So I need you to do whatever you can out there to make sure my brother and I escape from this hole in the ground. If you do not, I need hardly remind you of the embarrassment I could cause you and your less than blameless fellow countrymen. What it boils down to is this: are you with me or are you against me?'

Ashton turned to face the hangar wall. The wind gusted, raising the short hairs on the back of his neck. Finally he muttered, 'With you, of course.'

'Excellent. We must get together, after this is all over.' He gave a chuckle. 'For old times' sake.'

The line went dead.

Ashton stared at the screen with the kind of intensity he would have employed had Laszlo been there in the flesh. The South Ossetian held the key to unlocking his complex past, and the past was an ever-present danger to Ashton's future.

The Antonov balancing act had taken care and skill. But his two most recent texted warnings, to Hampstead and the train, had had only one objective. Laszlo must not, under any circumstances, be taken alive.

101

Where the fuck was Ashton?

Gavin charged out of the holding area and scanned the outside of the building in both directions before deciding to head right, towards the tunnel entrance.

'Boss! We're back on. The train's coming out, and we've got a sniper option . . .'

Ashton spun round, pocketing his mobile.

Gavin exploded – the major bending his ear was the last thing Tom needed right now. 'I said not to call him, for fuck's sake. He's got enough on his plate!'

Ashton stood his ground. 'When I want your advice, Warrant Officer Marks, I'll ask for it.' He turned and stormed back towards the entrance to the hangar.

Gavin followed, close on his heels. Something wasn't right. If Ashton hadn't made the call, why was he being so defensive? And if he had, why didn't he have the kind of up-to-date int that Tom would know was vital to the formation of a plan of attack?

Gavin made himself a promise. One way or another, he'd find out what Ashton was up to. And if the boss had put Tom's life in danger, he'd be in severe shit. Gavin would make sure of that.

They went through the shutters together. Gavin got straight on the net. 'Hello, all call-signs, this is Alpha. Sit-rep. A Chinook will be landing in plus ten. And soon after that the train will exit the tunnel. The X-rays will exchange from the train to the heli.

'This is a warning order for a sniper option. All Blue and Red Sierra call-signs, return to the holding area now. All other Blue and Red call-signs to remain in the service tunnel for orders over the net. You are to detain all of the Yankees in the service tunnel. I say again, all Yankees to remain in the service tunnel until after the option. Blue One, acknowledge.'

'One, roger that,' Jockey said.

Gavin could still hear screams in the background. He glanced through the window. Emergency vehicles were being hurriedly moved away from the killing area. He saw Ashton striding towards the Transit van. He kept one eye on him as he started to write a quick set of orders for the sniper option. Something definitely wasn't right . . .

The sniper option was a co-ordinated shoot, all weapons firing simultaneously at multiple targets. Blue and Red marksmen would both be on the ground, as close to the killing area as they could be without compromise. The normal distance was about three hundred metres. They'd position themselves at as many different heights and angles as possible. Each X-ray would be allocated at least two snipers, to increase the odds of at least one hit.

Keenan would place both teams' snipers as soon as he'd done a quick recce and been shown the killing area – the twenty metres that the X-rays would have to cross between the train and the Chinook. Keenan would then go and tie bits of tape to fences unless there were enough wind markers already – a flag maybe, fluttering on a flagpole. There usually were some in places of strategic importance for exactly that reason. He'd put a series of indicators at different heights, so the snipers could judge and compensate for the varying strengths of wind. They had to get it right first time. The objective was one round, one kill.

Since X-ray One was carrying the initiation device, Gavin wanted Keenan and two other snipers on him. He'd normally have commanded and co-ordinated, and not taken a shot. But Gavin wasn't sure how many X-rays were going to be coming out, and it was all hands to the pump.

The objective – to drop every X-ray a split second after Gavin had given the 'go' – involved a major feat of co-ordination. The Yankees would take a second or two to assimilate what had happened, like deer caught in oncoming headlights. Bodies would have tumbled to the ground, blood spurting and splattering all over the place. Some would go into shock and stand frozen to the spot; others would scream, shout, run around, drop to the ground. There would be absolute chaos.

Also on the 'go', at the moment the snipers fired, the assaulters would pour out of the service tunnel and swamp the killing area. They'd aim to control the Yankees and take on any X-rays who hadn't been dropped or were just wounded. The theory was simple, but Gavin knew these options rarely went according to plan. The X-rays didn't always do what you wanted them to do. Sometimes they were too well covered by the Yankees for a sniper to get a clear sight picture on them. Which meant the assault team had to deal with them. And fast.

The Sentinel SCS (sniper co-ordinated shoot) device helped Gavin give the 'go' at exactly the right moment. It looked like a fat laptop. A series of green and red lights – three rows of eight – sat side by side beneath the lid. The call-sign it represented could be written alongside each pair. Gavin could therefore have twenty-four snipers on one co-ordinated shoot. He wished he had more than half that number today.

When each marksman had a clear sight picture on his allocated X-ray, he'd take first pressure on his trigger. A transmitter in the weapon's butt would signal the Sentinel's console to switch the light from green to red, telling Gavin that he could take the shot.

If the sight picture was lost, first pressure would be released, and the light would return to green. No individual sniper had any idea of anyone else's readiness. It didn't matter. They weren't co-ordinating the shoot. All they had to do was concentrate on their own perspective and wait for the 'go'.

Gavin's eyes would be glued to the screen as the X-rays exited the train and crossed the killing area. In a perfect world, he'd be looking at ten red lights. In the real world, they blinked from red to green and back to red. If he waited too long for a complete set, he could screw up and lose the shoot. If he went too early, they might leave too many X-rays alive. The result hardly bore thinking about: more dead hostages as the team came out of the service tunnel; more dead team members; and a South Ossetian madman with an initiation device they had to assume would detonate the pipeline charge.

As far as Gavin was concerned, as soon as he had two red lights on X-ray One, he was going to give the 'go'.

102

The twenty remaining hostages were still in Coach Three. Laszlo's men had herded them together into the centre of the carriage, where the windows were still intact. They sat, as ordered, in the aircraft brace position, guarded by half a dozen seated gunmen.

The Black Bears rose as one to their feet when he and Sambor appeared. Laszlo was moved to see the expression on their faces. He knew this was an emotional moment for them too; a moment they had planned and prepared for as long as any of them could remember.

'All passengers, stand!' Laszlo barked. As they complied, exchanging nervous looks, his men walked up and down the line, scrutinizing them closely. Laszlo stopped opposite the man in the black Puffa jacket ,whose freedom he'd suddenly denied. 'You – take your clothes off.'

'What? *Why?*'

Laszlo slapped his hand so hard across the man's aquiline face that the sound echoed through the space. 'Do it now!'

Unable to hide his fear and humiliation, the man unbuttoned his jacket and began to undo his belt.

Laszlo pulled a day-sack off the shelf above the seats and

emptied it onto the floor. He pulled the initiation device from the grab bag and placed it in the day-sack, then unwrapped a chocolate-covered PowerBar and chewed it while he, too, stripped off.

When the man was down to his underwear, Laszlo threw him the Eurostar uniform and grab bag. 'Put these on.' He raised his hand, as if to strike him again.

The man flinched and swiftly complied.

Laszlo pulled on his clothes. The jeans were a little big around the waist but the brown leather belt soon rectified that problem.

Sambor followed suit, exchanging his clothes with the tallest of the hostages. The six gunmen exchanged jackets and put other items aside for their brothers at each end of the train. They then concealed their sub-machine-guns under their fresh clothing.

The previous owner of the Puffa jacket was shaking so badly Laszlo thought he might pass out. He straightened the grab bag over his shoulder then took the man's face gently in his hands. 'Just be calm, and do as you are told. Take a deep breath – go on, deep breaths – try to control yourself. It may just save your life.'

Sambor embraced the six, exchanging a nod and a few words with each in turn. Laszlo, too, hugged and kissed them all, knowing that, whatever the outcome of the next few hours, they would never meet again.

The fighters, for their part, were just proud to have repaid their debt. Their guilt was expunged. They thanked him for giving them back their dignity.

If they survived, he told them, the gold was theirs. They had been unwavering in their loyalty over so many years; it was the least he could do for them. Whatever happened now, it was better to die like a Black Bear, if it enabled Laszlo and Sambor to escape and continue the fight. They all promised that they would do so with smiles on their faces, knowing that the brothers would take their revenge. Knowing they would kill the country.

The embraces and valedictions were over; the last hand-shakes were done. Laszlo and Sambor left their weapons and headed back towards the front of the train, Laszlo with the day-sack on his back and a new jacket under his arm, for the man guarding Tom and Delphine.

When they reached the bomb-damaged door to Coach Two, Sambor jumped from the train and Laszlo continued forward.

103

Tom watched Laszlo wipe the dust off the Perspex lenses of two oxygen masks.

'Prior preparation prevents piss-poor performance.' Laszlo grinned. 'You British, you taught me that.'

'The same people who now want you dead?'

'The very same people.' Laszlo smiled ironically. 'You also may not find them as ... reliable as you might hope.' He reached into his jacket and tossed Tom's mobile towards the front of the carriage. Tom followed its flight, then his eyes jerked back to the door as Sambor lugged a third set of breathing apparatus into the compartment.

He felt Delphine's grip tighten on his arm.

Sambor opened up the valve and listened to a two-second hiss of pressurized oxygen.

Laszlo squatted beside Tom and Delphine while his brother retested all three sets. 'Tom, you will not be joining us on the next part of our mission. But we will be looking after your girl – and your unborn son – as long as you don't do something to make me change my mind.

'Most people, they disgust me. Their self-pity is so un-attractive. But you two, you have something that needs to be preserved. There have been moments in the last few hours when I found myself wondering whether your ancestors might have come from South Ossetia . . . '

Laszlo shouldered a small day-sack and one of the oxygen sets. Sambor followed his example. 'But that is precisely why I have to control you both. Delphine, you will come with us. And you, Tom, are staying on the train.

'Once our work is done – and without interruption – we will release Delphine. The question you need to ask yourselves is quite simple: live or die? The choice is yours.' He opened the cabin door and stepped out.

Sambor grabbed Delphine's arm. She leaned across and kissed Tom before she was wrenched to her feet. As her lips brushed his cheek she whispered, 'I love you . . .'

Sambor left him in no doubt that following Delphine out into the tunnel was not an option. He raised his hand and a gunman appeared, wearing a long brown corduroy coat and an expression which told Tom that pulling the trigger would give him nothing but pleasure.

The two Black Bears embraced. Sambor picked up the two oversized skateboards leaning against the wall and thrust Delphine in the wake of his brother.

Mr Corduroy yanked Tom back through to Coach One.

104

Tom eased back a little from the carriage window, where he'd been planted alongside the other hostages, and slowly turned his head.

A thin man in a Eurostar uniform stood five bodies along to his left, with the strap of Laszlo's precious grab bag firmly across his shoulder. He was too busy trying not to shit himself to be a totally convincing double, but a quick look at him through the sniper optics and you still might pull the trigger.

Tom had given up trying to second-guess Laszlo, but had started to build up a picture of how the South Ossetian was hoping the next hour or so might pan out. He was intrigued by their performance with the oxygen sets, and that none of the Yankees had been zip-tied; they were hands-free, just like the X-rays.

He risked swivelling his head further.

One of the guards spotted the movement, yelled, and forced Tom's face back against the glass.

The background hum of the electric power suddenly changed in tone, and there was a loud hiss. It sounded to Tom as if the brakes had been released. The train lurched, and began to move back up the track towards Folkestone. The hostage immediately next to him gave a small whimper of anxiety.

Tom leaned his face against the window, trying to see outside, but the reflection from the internal lights made it impossible. He pressed his cheek against the cool of the glass to try to distract himself from the throbbing pain in his thigh. Then, swaying back with the movement of the train, he shot another glance along the aisle. He managed to get eyes on Mr Corduroy, the nearer of the two gunmen guarding him.

'Where's Laszlo?'

No response.

Tom moistened his swollen lips and tried again. 'Laszlo is my very good friend. I worry about him—'

The man swung his sub-machine-gun towards Tom's head, then made the mistake of leaning over to confer with his companion.

Tom shot out his left hand and grabbed the barrel of the weapon, pushing it upwards as he launched himself into both men. Still gripping the weapon with his left hand, he extended the right, propelling them backwards. As they lost their footing and toppled over the armrest of the seat on the other side of the aisle, the weapon fired a burst. There was no sound, just the judder of its recoil and a cascade of glass fragments as the ceramic rounds pulverized the window behind him.

Tom had already jinked to his right. Now he swivelled back towards the empty frame and launched himself through it. A rush of air hit him as he met the slipstream from the accelerating train. Tucking his head into his chest, he tried to roll for the landing. The next thing he knew, he hit the wall, ripping his clothes and grating the skin from his knees and elbows. He bounced off and plummeted onto the equally unforgiving concrete track bed.

He lay there for several seconds, dazed and winded.

Another burst of suppressed fire followed him out of the window, but the Eurostar had already moved too far up the track for Mr Corduroy to get a clear shot. A couple of rounds rattled harmlessly above Tom's head as the sound of the train faded into the distance. Apart from a line of low-level red LEDs at twenty-metre intervals, the tunnel was now almost completely dark.

Tom stumbled to his feet and swayed for a moment before hobbling on as quickly as he could. If Laszlo, Sambor and Delphine needed breathing apparatus, then so did he.

105

Delphine felt like Laszlo's mule. She was pushed and hustled along the tunnel, fifteen kilos of oxygen tank loaded on her back.

She dragged her feet, partly through pain, partly because she was still hoping against hope that Tom would find a way of escaping from the train and catching up with them.

Not for the first time, Laszlo read her mind. 'He is not coming back for you, Delphine. So keep moving.'

They passed the body of the old man she had so briefly befriended. She hardly had time to look down at him. It was almost a mercy that Laszlo kept pushing her on.

The stench hanging in the air – of charred equipment and something else, something sickly sweet that she couldn't quite identify – caught in the back of her throat. Then they tumbled into a segment of the service tunnel that seemed to be filled with burned-out vehicles.

Sambor hauled himself swiftly up a steel ladder set into the wall. Light streamed through a hatch above his head. She watched him push through the two skateboards and dis-appear. Laszlo hustled Delphine after him. She tried stalling again, but only managed to antagonize her captor.

'Move!'

Laszlo drew a knife from his belt and jabbed it into her calf, drawing blood. She cried out and tried to jerk her foot away from him, but only succeeded in dislodging her shoe. As it tumbled to the ground, he simply dug the tip a little further into her flesh. 'If you continue with this foolishness,' he breathed, 'I will be forced to remove this from your leg, and insert it into your stomach instead. Your child's life is entirely in your hands.'

She clambered up the ladder.

Once inside the conduit, she kept her head low to avoid the power lines buzzing overhead. Sambor was standing maybe twenty metres ahead of them, next to a large steel pipe. Something seemed to be strapped onto it, and twenty or thirty slabs of some revolting green substance were piled on the floor beneath it. The reek of linseed made her gag. She guessed it was some kind of bomb.

106

Tom shook his head, trying to clear the ringing in his ears. Waves of pain pulsed through his body and fresh blood oozed through the makeshift bandage. But he had to keep moving.

He limped past the shattered remnants of the two South Ossetians from the gun team. Their bodies had been mangled by hundreds of tons of train as it rolled towards Folkestone. Body parts were strewn along the track. Tom checked the torsos for mobile phones in the dull red glow. He found none. He wiped his freshly bloodied hands on his jeans and carried on down the tunnel.

Another body lay sprawled to one side of the track, a shock of white hair, matted with blood, plastered across a terrible wound in the head. Tom patted him down in the dull red glow. He found what he was looking for in his jacket pocket, and felt like the worst kind of thief as he dragged it out. He steadied himself against the wall, switched on the mobile and dialled.

It rang just twice.

'Yeah?'

'Gav? It's me.'

'Fucking hell, mate, thank fuck for that. I've been flapping here big-time. You all right?'

Behind the almost jocular tone, Tom knew Gavin was fighting to hide his emotions. There was work to do.

'What you got for me?'

Tom, too, had to cut away and get on with business. 'Gav, listen in. The train's heading your way. Antonov is not on board – repeat, not on board. He has a decoy, a Yankee, in a Eurostar uniform. He had the grab bag over his shoulder the last time I saw him. The X-rays are hiding their weapons. They're going to try and blend in. Antonov is still in the tunnel, and still has the initiator. The device must still be active. Gav, do you understand what I'm saying?'

'Mate, got it. We know about the train. We've got an option on it at the exit. It's all we've got left. If I fuck it up we have another major drama on our hands. You stay right where you are – I'll come in and get you straight after the option.'

'I can't.' Tom slid his back down the wall until he was sitting on the concrete. 'Gav, the fucker's got Delphine . . .'

'Oh, shit. Be careful. Find her, but be careful.'

'I don't have a choice.' Tom hesitated for a moment. 'She's pregnant . . .'

'You dirty bugger. You've only been on that train a few hours.'

'Very funny.'

'Mate, seriously . . .' Gavin went silent for a moment. 'Something fucking strange is going on this end. Did Ashton call you? I don't know what the fuck he's up to.'

'No. Antonov took my mobile. Last time I saw it, he dumped it in the driver's cab. I didn't have time to get it back.'

'All right. We'd better sort that shit out later. Please be careful. And one more thing . . .'

'What's that?'

'Can I be godfather?'

Tom somehow managed to raise a laugh. 'You couldn't even spell "godfather". But, hey, why not? As long as we don't have to call the poor little bastard Gavin.'

He cut the call, got himself back on his feet and staggered through the green security gate. He stumbled across a pile of rubble and through the hole that Laszlo and his mates had blown in the steel fire screen. The air was still heavy with the stench of burning and death.

Light streamed down from the hatch above as he headed for what was left of the appliances. He saw at once that his mission was hopeless. The fire-fighters were little more than charred carcasses. None of their oxygen sets had survived.

He turned back to the steel ladder leading up to the pipeline conduit. And at the bottom he found one of Delphine's shoes.

107

Sambor moved ten paces further down the conduit to a red access door into the airlock chamber welded onto the gas pipe. He reached for the locking handle, but Laszlo held him back. He turned to Delphine. 'Do you smoke? Do you have matches, a lighter, anything electrical on you that we didn't take? The pipe is full of heavily concentrated gas. It can ignite instantly.'

Delphine checked her pockets, slowly and methodically, for the lighter and matches she knew she did not have. Finally, she shook her head.

Laszlo pulled his full-face oxygen mask over his head and handed Delphine hers. His voice was instantly muffled. 'Make sure your hair is pushed back, so you don't break the seal with your skin. When you breathe it will give you oxygen on demand.'

Laszlo switched on her set as Sambor pulled open the access door.

'But remember, do not breathe too heavily – or you may run out before it is time.'

Through her mask, Delphine saw Laszlo reach out to help his brother with his breathing apparatus. She turned and ran back towards the hatch.

She didn't manage to get far. The oxygen set was heavy, and

she had only one shoe. She heard the scuffle of boots on the floor and muffled shouts behind her. A hand grabbed her hair and yanked her backwards, off her feet. The weight of her oxygen tank brought her crashing down. The clash of metal on metal as it cannoned against the side of the pipeline echoed along the conduit.

The air was punched from her lungs. As she struggled for breath, Laszlo dragged her backwards. The escape attempt had been futile. She had known it would be. But it had slowed them down.

108

Tom was halfway through the hatch before Sambor realized what was happening.

Laszlo's hand grabbed for his carving knife but Sambor was quicker. He whipped out his own double-sided fighting blade. 'Brother, I will take care of this. I, too, have a debt to repay. Go. I will meet you at the other end. If I don't, promise me to fulfil your pledge. For both of us.'

Laszlo nodded. 'Be quick, brother. I will take her, just in case.'

Sambor ripped off his mask, dumped the oxygen tank and ran towards Tom, who was now through the hatch. Sambor knew he wasn't invulnerable: he could just as easily lose this fight as win, but even losing would buy Laszlo time and distance.

As soon as Laszlo was on French soil the device would be detonated. Sambor wanted to be with him when that happened. If that wasn't possible, he had to die some time, and this would be the best way. His debt to his brother had been a heavy weight to carry; now was his chance to repay him. He would make sure Laszlo was free to carry out the pledge of revenge.

Sambor advanced to within a pace of his adversary, no hesitation, no fear, eyes glazed as he aimed for a quick kill.

Sambor angled his blade, ready for the fight. Tom glanced beyond him to see Laszlo and Delphine disappear into the airlock, then ripped off his jacket and wrapped it as fast as he could around his left hand and forearm.

He stood his ground and waited.

Tom felt the rush of the knife against his cheek as his left arm deflected the stab at his head. Then he heard a rending sound as the blade, keen as a razor's edge, sliced through the jacket's leather. Sambor struck again and again, shredding the fabric as Tom parried the strikes. He felt a searing pain as the blade sliced through the material bunched around his fist and pierced his knuckles. But, finally, he managed to get inside the giant's reach.

The fight was now more even – or, at least, it felt that way to Tom. He pushed his weight into Sambor, forcing him backwards against the pipe, knowing that if he could not finish him quickly, they were all fucked. He couldn't take much more punishment. Keeping his head hard against his opponent's chest, he threw a flurry of punches into his body. He heard Sambor grunt, and the knife clatter to the concrete.

But it wasn't over.

A flash of light exploded in his head as Sambor's fist smashed into his temple like a jackhammer.

Tom forced himself to rally. Sheer willpower made his body respond. He launched another attack, unleashing the same combination of punches that he had used to knock out Ashton during Fight Night. But Sambor didn't go down: he just seemed to soak up the punishment as Tom got weaker. Tom threw everything he had, every ounce of his being, into one last blow, a savage, twisting uppercut to Sambor's chin.

Sambor still didn't go down, but he stumbled. He lunged at Tom, his fingers clawing at his face, searching for his eyes.

Tom seized his chance. He piled a vicious right to the other man's kidneys and as Sambor reeled, dived across the concrete, scrabbling wildly for the knife. He felt the air being driven out of his lungs as Sambor toppled onto his back – but at that instant his left hand closed around the knife handle.

Stabbing backwards, he felt the blade tear into the soft flesh beneath Sambor's ribs. He stabbed again, not caring where, and worked the blade into whatever part of the big man's body the weapon penetrated. He twisted the blade into Sambor's soft tissue and heard him grunt and moan. He churned his hand up and down and round, any way that he could to maximize the damage.

At last the Russian started to shift his weight, now desperate to remove himself from Tom's immediate killing area. It was enough for Tom to extract the blade from his side, turn, and ram it into Sambor's chest. He felt the steel jam momentarily, as it wedged itself between the man's ribs.

Managing to get both hands on the handle, he pushed it home. Then he held Sambor close, so he couldn't do any more damage to him as his life ebbed away.

109

Gavin's eyes never left his monitor. The emergency vehicles had been pulled back from the killing area. So had all personnel. The only movement near the tunnel mouth came from the ramp of the Chinook and one of the team's Transits parked beside it.

Gavin watched as Ashton and the heli's two pilots and load-master trans-shipped the last of the crates. He knew the same pictures were being beamed to COBRA's screens, too. They also had access to the Sentinel display. They'd soon be listening in to the Sierra call-signs as they took up their fire positions.

The Chinook's engines had been cut, and they were going to stay that way. Keenan didn't want the rotor-wash deflecting his snipers' rounds. And there was something about the roar of a helicopter's engines and the sight of whirling blades that got people sparked up. They rushed towards the aircraft like they expected it to lift off any second. Those in command of the killing area didn't want that happening today. They wanted the X-rays to hang around in the marksmen's sights for as long as possible.

The three air crew looked as if they were struggling with the weight of their body armour as much as the weight of the gold. Up to their chins in Kevlar, their orders were to position themselves in the cockpit and make sure the X-rays spotted them at the controls. As soon as things kicked off, they were to make a run for it to a carriage inspection ditch sixty metres away – and not come out again until they were told to.

Gavin's eyes flicked to Sentinel. All the lights were green. Keenan would still be making sure he covered all angles and heights. The higher the sniper, the better the sight picture, and the better the arc of fire. The ideal was looking down at about forty-five degrees. Wherever they were, they'd be using unsuppressed weapons. Once this option kicked off, it didn't matter who heard what.

He peered at the aerial view, fed in from a camera on the hangar roof. Some of the snipers were in buildings, set back from the windows, in shadow. Others were out in the open, using whatever cover was available. They didn't just have to conceal themselves from the X-rays and Yankees. Operation Stack was still in force. Trucks were parked up only 600 metres away. They couldn't risk a driver inadvertently raising the alarm.

Gavin had eight snipers ticked off on the marker board so far, but it wasn't good enough. He got on the net. 'Sierra call-signs, this is Alpha. You need to get a move on. We haven't got long. Out.'

The two remaining marksmen must still be trying to find a good fire position that supported their weapons. The train might stop in the tunnel. It was no good contorting yourself into some weird and wonderful position for hours: your body had to be naturally aligned into the point you were aiming at.

And you had to have muzzle clearance. The optic sight could be as much as four to six inches above the barrel, depending on where you set it for your individual eye relief. It didn't make much sense having a really good sight picture of the killing area 300–500 metres away if your barrel was pointing directly at the mound of earth in front of it.

Gavin had had better days. ID-ing the X-rays was going to be next to impossible unless they openly carried weapons. He wasn't even sure how many of the bastards there were.

The executive decisions had been made much higher up the food-chain. COBRA had told Gavin the way they wanted this to play out. The home secretary's instruction had been clear and concise. The decoy with the Eurostar uniform must be treated precisely as if he were X-ray One. The grab bag was the last known location of the initiation device. It was all about the grab bag, not who was carrying it. It was a tough call but, hey, it was a tough world. The only certainty was that there were going to be more dead Yankees today. It was inevitable.

Gavin watched Ashton sling his ready-bag over one shoulder. He picked up one of the half-metre-square aluminium crates by its handles and lugged it to the ramp, then disappeared into the bowels of the Chinook.

Gavin accepted that the powers-that-be couldn't take Tom's information and assessment as gospel. It was a big decision, and the home secretary was the one being paid the big bucks to make it. Regret, fear, worry: they were all equally un-productive, before, during and after any job. The best they could do was work with the information they had – or thought they had – and what it might mean. There was no such thing as a perfect solution.

Ashton emerged from the heli and made his way back to the Transit. He no longer had his ready-bag. Gavin knew nothing about a bag going on board. Was this connected with Ashton going to the MOE wagon? Why had he insisted on supervising the loading when he should have been joining the Red and Blue teams in the service tunnel, ready to lead the assault? Was there another agenda Gavin hadn't been told about? It wouldn't be the first time.

Decisions were made. Depending on your pay grade, you were either let in on them or you weren't. Maybe COBRA or the DSF had another little option tucked away in case the job went tits up. But if that was the case, he should definitely be in the loop. Gavin felt the first stirrings of anger. They could be putting the whole team at risk here. Ashton should be protecting them. He was supposed to be one of them – he was their gatekeeper, not some Whitehall lackey.

He took a deep breath. Now wasn't the time. The train was going to emerge any minute and he had a job to do. If he did it right, there would be no need for any secret option. And he'd find out soon enough if Ashton had tried to call Tom and risked compromising him. Gavin would make fucking sure of that, but only after the job was completed. Then, if there was shit on, he'd be leading the charge.

A speaker burst into life: 'Sierra Four, ready.'

'Alpha, roger that. Test.'

Sierra Four took first pressure on his trigger and red replaced green on the tablet screen.

'Alpha, that's a red.'

They'd tested the comms before they left the hangar, but they had to test them again. The best fire position in the world is no bloody good if you can't tell the commander you have your target.

Gavin felt a hand on his arm. He looked up as Woolf placed a paper cup of tea on the trestle table.

The speaker barked again: 'Sierra Eight, in position.'

'Roger that. Sierra Eight, test.'

His red lit up.

'Alpha, roger that. All call-signs, the Sierras are in position. We now wait out.'

Gavin picked up his brew and nodded his thanks. His eyes flicked back to the monitor. The one-metre lengths of mine tape were fluttering on top of the Chinook. The wind must be getting up.

Woolf patted his shoulder. 'Everything that can be done has been done. Good luck.'

Each took a sip of his brew.

The Slime came on the net for all to hear. 'The ETA of the train is one minute. Repeat, ETA, one minute. One minute from the tunnel mouth.'

Gavin lobbed his empty cup onto the floor to clear the decks. Woolf took a step back. They both stared at the monitors. Headphones clamped to their ears, the signallers and the Slime monitored their transmitters and receivers, continuously reaching forward to make endless microscopic adjustments.

Gavin got to work. 'All stations, Alpha radio check. Blue One.'

Click-click.

'Red One.'

Click-click.

'Sierra One.'

Gavin watched Keenan's red light spark up. And then he radio-checked every single sniper one final time.

110

A small flock of gulls that had been disputing possession of a stolen sandwich crust suddenly took flight, soaring skywards, then settling once more above the tunnel's entrance.

Moments later, the long, sleek nose of a Eurostar locomotive glinted in the sunlight beneath them. At no more than walking pace, the rest of the engine slowly unsheathed itself from the tunnel. Through the tinted-glass windscreen, Gavin spotted the pale, frightened face of the driver. His head was half turned. His lips were moving. He was speaking to the man directly behind him. Gavin guessed there was a machine-gun rammed into his back. A hand gestured at the Chinook, as if the driver couldn't see it, or had suddenly developed the magic power to steer straight off the tracks towards it.

'Alpha has an X-ray in engine – brown bomber jacket, short dark hair and beard. He is carrying.'

The snipers would have eyes-on, but not the Blue and Red teams down the service tunnel. And they didn't have monitors.

Carriage by carriage, the Eurostar inched out of the tunnel. The gentle rumble of its engine carried as far as the hangar.

Gavin dominated the net. 'Coach One clear . . . Two . . . clear.

Coach Three – bodies in carriage . . . wait . . . wait . . . twenty to thirty . . .'

The snipers would be locked on Coach Three. They didn't need to be on the net: their job was behind their weapons. Gavin was the only one who had to talk.

'Four, clear . . . Five, clear . . .'

Gavin felt a knot of tension in his stomach, but kept his voice flat and even. 'Slowing . . .'

The seventh coach emerged from the tunnel.

'Slowing . . . slowing . . . Stop, stop, stop. That's Eurostar static. Coach Three, closest to the Chinook.'

A figure appeared at the open doorway and clambered down.

Gavin scrutinized the man. He didn't look like any of the X-rays Tom had photographed, but it was hard to be sure.

Another figure emerged, then a succession of them. They huddled next to the train. Someone was controlling them. Another couple jumped down. The driver's legs almost gave way beneath him as he touched the ground.

Next out was the one who'd been standing behind the driver.

'Alpha has the driver's-cab X-ray now in the killing area. Sierra Nine and Ten confirm.'

Two reds.

'Roger that.'

One of the Slime ticked the board beside their names. They had a target.

Another figure emerged.

'Alpha has X-ray One now in the killing area.'

Sierras One and Three red lit.

'Confirm, Eurostar uniform and grab bag. He is in the middle of the pack.'

Sierra One's light suddenly went back to green as the grab bag was lost in a sea of bodies.

The Slime held up a number count for Gavin on a whiteboard.

'Alpha has twenty-eight in the killing area, still static by the train. No more movement in Coach Three.'

The strips of mine tape were flapping. The sky had darkened. A gust of wind blew rain across the Folkestone compound. The hostage group squinted into it. Someone near the centre of it said something. All of them began to shuffle slowly towards the Chinook.

'Stand by, stand by . . . the group is mobile.'

Gavin checked Sentinel. He wasn't concerned about Sierra Nine and Ten's target as their lights flickered between red and green. It was Sierras One, Two and Three he had to worry about.

One red . . . then two . . .

Gavin pushed the radio pressel, ready to send.

Back to just one light.

Then none.

He looked at the monitor. The group was halfway to the Chinook. If he got one red, then that Sierra would have to take the shot.

Sierra Three flashed red.

He pushed the pressel. 'All stations, I have control. Stand by, stand by . . .'

Sierra One went red.

'Go.'

He heard two high-velocity cracks from the other side of the hangar. The snipers' weapons recoiled and their rounds ripped through the air, each carving its track through the huddle and severing its target's brain stems at the same instant. The two bodies crumpled.

There were a few beats of silence, broken only by the squawk of seagulls as they took to the sky once more. Then the hostages realized what had just happened in their midst. A woman screamed.

Simultaneously, two call-signs made entry into the train and the Blue and Red teams poured out of the service tunnel. The air crew, too, were out and running.

The single scream soon became a chorus as Laszlo's men

drew down their weapons. They stood their ground, knowing they were about to die, but determined not to go without a fight. The snipers dropped the ones they saw.

Jockey, Bryce and the rest of the team raced forward, throwing flash-bangs as they went. A bunch of Yankees broke ranks and ran towards them in blind panic, grabbing the assaulters, like drowning swimmers clinging to the closest available life-raft.

The Blue and Red teams pushed, punched and knocked them out of the way as they surged towards the main passenger group. The snipers continued to drop any threat they detected. Some Yankees took rounds in the chaos. Flash-bangs exploded with deafening, blinding force.

The assaulters reached the middle of the killing area. Any Yankee left standing was forced to lie face down on the ground by a combination of boots, fists and weapons. Everyone had to be gripped as if they were an X-ray, because some of them would be.

Gavin watched Ashton take a long, hard look at the body with the Eurostar uniform and the grab bag. He lifted what was left of the man's head, checking the face against a printout of the picture Tom had taken. From the way he let it fall back to the ground and stood up before he got onto his radio, Gavin knew it wasn't good news.

'We do not have the initiation device and we do not have X-ray One. I say again, we do not have the initiation device.'

Gavin acknowledged.

Now that all the train group were zip-tied or dead, Jockey checked the casualties.

'Alpha, roger that. Blue One, what you got for me?'

Jockey checked one last corpse before turning to face the camera. Gavin felt his eyes drill through the monitor.

'We have eleven dead, seventeen breathing. We need to go back in the tunnel and find X-ray One.'

He didn't have to spell it out. It wasn't just Antonov and the device they wanted. Tom and Delphine were still in there somewhere. If they could stop Antonov, they might be able to save their friends.

Jockey remained staring into the camera as police vans raced into view.

'Alpha, roger that. Wait out.'

Gavin spun round to Woolf. 'Get on to COBRA. Get permission. We need hot pursuit. We need to stop this fucker.'

111

Gavin leaped into a Range Rover and screamed down towards the tunnel entrance. The moment COBRA green-lit a follow-up, he wanted to be the one leading the team.

The military option was complete; the police had begun mopping up. Hands on heads, the Yankees lay face down in the rain as blue flashing lights swamped the area. They were taken into the back of a van one at a time. It wouldn't be long before the whole world knew this hadn't been an electrical fault.

The team was reassembling inside the service tunnel as Gavin screeched to a halt. He ran straight over to Jockey. 'Mate, any luck with the mobile?'

Jockey tossed it to him. 'They just retrieved it from the cab. Tom, Delphine . . . We've got to get fuckin' moving.'

'Mate, I know. Make sure the boys are ready. We're waiting on the "go" from COBRA.'

Gavin hit the keypad and scrolled down the call log. He saw it at once. Ashton had been on the line when he was outside the hangar. He turned to Jockey. 'Where's the Boss?'

'Gone back to the heli.'

Gavin broke into a run. He sprinted the thirty metres past the line of soaked hostages and straight onto the Chinook's ramp. Rain drummed noisily on the aircraft's aluminium skin.

Ashton was just behind the pilot's bulkhead, next to the stack of gold. He had his back to Gavin and was holding a mobile to his ear. Tom's phone vibrated in Gavin's hand. He closed in on Ashton, passing the full bladder of extra fuel rigged up to supplement the main tank. Strapped to the deck, it looked like the floor of a bouncy castle.

Ashton spun round at the noise of footsteps.

'What the fuck were you doing?' Gavin yelled. 'You told me you didn't call him. But you did, didn't you? And Antonov had this fucking thing, not Tom. What the fuck were you talking about? You were on this fucking thing for more than two minutes.'

Gavin closed on Ashton, thrusting the mobile's screen at him. 'And what the fuck is all that about?' He pointed at the ready-bag the other side of the gold.

Gavin felt angrier with each stride he took. 'It was you that warned him yesterday. It was, wasn't it?'

Ashton stood his ground. He let the mobile drop an inch or two in his palm so half of the phone was sticking out, like the blade of a dagger. He tightened his grip.

The NCO ranted at him: 'Tom and Delphine are still in there, with that fucking nutter . . . If I find out it was because of you, I'm going to fucking destroy you. What the fuck do you—'

Ashton's fist tightened around the phone. Before Gavin could gather himself, he swung it round and down, making brutal contact with Gavin's right temple. Gavin staggered under the blow. Ashton moved closer, pounding the mobile into his head with all the force he could muster, once, twice, three times.

Gavin sank onto the ridged floor of the Chinook. Ashton grabbed him under the armpits and shuffled backwards, dragging him behind the stack of crates. He got down onto his knees and stabbed the hard plastic case repeatedly into the side of Gavin's head.

Whimpers and groans filled the air. It took Gavin a moment to realize they were his own. He felt the power ebb from his hands as he tried to stop the onslaught. The skin split under the pressure and blood streamed from the wound.

Another thirty seconds and Gavin struggled one last time, with all the frenzied strength a man draws on when he knows he is dying. His hands stopped grasping. The movement in his legs subsided to no more than a spasmodic twitching. Seconds later he lay still.

112

Ashton clambered to his feet and admired his handiwork for a moment. He retrieved Tom's phone from where it had fallen and tossed it down beside the warrant officer's body. Then he headed down the ramp and out into the rain.

He tapped the dialling pad on his mobile as he made his way back towards the mouth of the tunnel, where the Red and Blue teams were busy sorting their gear.

He ran through the story in his head. Planting the device on board the Chinook had been Gavin's idea. If the sniper option failed, they'd have to stop Laszlo some other way.

But there had been a terrible accident. Gavin must have tried to disarm the thing, and it had detonated.

It wasn't perfect, but it would have to do.

Ashton highlighted Tom's number.

And then he pressed *Send*.

A blinding flash filled the sky as two kilograms of PE4 kicked off the fuel bladder. Within the tight confines of the aircraft, the combustion pressure turned it into an instant fireball, which, in turn, ignited the main tanks.

The Chinook's rotors broke off and spun drunkenly into the cloud of fire and smoke.

Ashton was knocked to the ground by the blast. He landed

only metres from the tunnel entrance. As he picked himself up, chunks of fuselage and fragments of unidentifiable metal rained down on the surrounding area.

Jockey powered towards him, distress vibrating from every fibre of his taut Glaswegian frame. '*Gav!*'

113

Delphine braced herself as Laszlo reached past her once again and scooped down to propel their skateboard along the smooth interior of the pipe. He sat behind her on the board, his legs either side of her, as if they were kayaking. They were deep under the English Channel, and for many miles each breath she had taken from her compressed-air tank had echoed down the cylinder like the air bubbles of a diver in the ocean depths.

The skateboard slewed from side to side, rolling up the curve until gravity took over. She could feel the rush of gas as she lay there, and see wisps of it streaming over her mask. Her breathing accelerated with her rising fear of Sambor's imminent return.

Sucking hard from Sambor's oxygen mask, Tom wasn't sure how far Delphine and Laszlo were ahead of him. There was hardly any light, just a dim white glow every five hundred metres or so, through the glass panels on the airlock doors. Tom had no idea what he was going to do when he caught up with them. His head was empty of all thought; his body was using up every reserve of energy to make best speed on Sambor's board. For now thinking was pointless. The work he needed to do was physical, not mental.

Tom paddled his hands along the floor of the pipeline and felt the skateboard pick up speed. It swooped up to the right. Tom instantly knew it was going too high. He tried to compensate, leaning hard left, but was too late. He came off like a bobsleigh rider on a fast bend.

His oxygen tank slammed into the metal superstructure and the clank of steel-on-steel echoed along the cylinder. Tom skidded fifteen feet, eyes closed, expecting the friction to ignite the gas at any moment.

He finally managed to bring himself to a halt and listened to the skateboard doing the same somewhere ahead of him. There was no time for him to take a breath or thank the pipeline designers. He rolled over onto his chest and started crawling forward.

Laszlo seemed to be moving more cautiously as they approached the next circle of light. He must have been concentrating hard: he didn't seem to hear the loud metallic echo that washed over them.

Delphine did, and it immediately filled her with dread. It meant Sambor was alive. But then she realized that Tom wouldn't have come to that conclusion if their positions had been reversed. Until he knew otherwise, Tom would have thought it was Delphine coming for him. She needed to think the same. She needed to believe it was him.

They came to a stop next to another steel door. She saw numbers stencilled on the glass panel. Laszlo crawled off the skateboard, allowing Delphine to take deep breaths to re-oxygenate her numb body. The respite lasted no more than two seconds before he grabbed her and made her kneel alongside him as he worked the handles.

She needed to slow him down. She needed to stop him blowing the pipeline. She eyed his recently acquired day-sack.

She lay there asking herself one question, over and over. *What would Tom do?* Until he caught up with them, she would have to take matters into her own hands. Whatever it was going to be, she had to do *something*.

*

The sequence of airlocks was designed to allow safe passage of maintenance engineers and emergency crews between the pressurized interior of the gas pipe and its exterior. Laszlo had done his homework.

An LED glowed and he heard the suction of gas as the air pressure in the chamber equalized with that of the environment beyond the outside door.

He glanced at Delphine. Laszlo knew exactly what was going through her mind. He'd heard the crash behind them, but decided it was pointless to react. There was no reason to believe it wasn't Sambor. And sooner or later he would know for sure. The most important objective for now was getting himself and his brother out of the pipeline and into a safe position from which he could trigger the detonation.

Another LED illuminated and he swung open the outside door. He turned and grabbed the tube that led from Delphine's oxygen tank to the mask. As the mask started to lift from her face she soon followed. Laszlo pushed her into the chamber, slammed the steel door shut behind them, and pushed a yellow button. The floor vent inside the airlock sucked out the gas and another above them replaced it with oxygen. The noise was deafening.

The sudden slam on the other side of the door they'd just come through made Delphine give an involuntary cry.

Tom's masked face appeared at the window.

114

Delphine heard Tom throw himself against the other side of the door; she could almost feel his grunt of pain and frustration as he failed to open it. She threw herself across the airlock and grabbed the handle. Laszlo didn't move a muscle, just watched her pitiful attempts to wrench it free. It took her six or seven frenzied and fruitless heaves to realize that it wouldn't unlock until the gas exchange was complete.

As the green LED started to blink, Laszlo shoved her ahead of him through the outer door. She felt his grip harden once more on her arm. He manhandled her up a steel ladder towards a hatch. She tried again to slow him down, but didn't have the strength to put up much of a fight.

He forced the lever open with his free hand and climbed out, pulling her with him. She ripped off her mask and breathed in until she thought her lungs would burst. After what seemed like hours of tainted oxygen, it was the sweetest air she had ever breathed. She just wished she wasn't sharing it with Laszlo.

She shuffled away from the hatch, along the mound that covered the outer skin of the conduit, and looked around. The stark geometry of the pipeline had been landscaped to blend in with the hillside. It was camouflaged by squares of grass interspersed with gravel drainage beds filled with lumps of flint, the size of Stone Age tools, that glistened wetly in the sunlight.

She was on high ground, above the tunnel system. The breeze ruffled her hair, carrying the smell of gas towards the maze of rail tracks, sidings, platforms and gantries that surrounded the French end of the tunnel.

Police and military vehicles and fire appliances crowded around its mouth. She was standing beneath a cluster of power lines that sloped down towards an electrical sub-station a few hundred metres below them. Ahead and to either side of her lay a patchwork of fields and copses, and in the distance, just inland from the cliffs flanking the Channel coast, she could see the grey stone spire of a church and a handful of red pantiled roofs of a tiny village. Escalles ... Of course. She heard Sambor's voice in her head: 'That is still safe? Escalles?'

Laszlo turned his back to her as he closed the hatch. His day-sack was looped across his oxygen set, the straps as loose as they could go. She knew that it contained whatever he needed to detonate the pile of rancid explosive beneath the gas pipe. She had a sudden dreadful premonition of the fireball that would surge along the pipeline, destroying everything in its path. And engulfing Tom ...

She stooped low, scooped up a handful of flints, and hurled herself towards him. When she was still a metre away, Laszlo began to turn. She focused on the shape of his head as she leaped at him, swinging her body to the left, her right arm crooked, the flints protruding from between her fingers like Stone Age arrow-heads.

She didn't care where they connected, so long as they did. Laszlo gave a loud groan and a sigh, like air leaving a balloon. She didn't feel the stones tearing the flesh above his eye, just the pressure of her arm being stopped dead as the rest of her body carried on swivelling.

He spun round, propelled by the momentum of her onslaught. She swept her left hand, also bunched and loaded, towards its target. This time she could feel the hardness of his skull beneath the blow, felt it scrape across the contour of his head as he sank to his knees. He moaned again, more loudly and with even greater anguish.

She brought her right hand down hard on the top of his head. The flint edges, sharp as blades, cut deep, hitting bone and stripping back the skin. She gouged a thick furrow from his scalp; the flint held its line for a couple more inches and then veered free.

Laszlo slumped to the ground. His hands scrabbled to protect his head, then fell away and he lay still. He was still breathing, but he must have gone into shock.

Delphine didn't have time to draw breath. He wouldn't stay like that for long. Dropping the flints, she rolled him over onto his stomach, loosened the straps of the day-sack and pulled it from his shoulders.

Laszlo groaned.

She fumbled for the zip. She could see the loop of nylon cord attached to it, but her fingers didn't seem able to follow her brain's instructions. Finally she managed to hook a finger into it and peel it back.

Her mind was filled with the image of Tom on the train, confronting Laszlo and Sambor, the battery in his hand, the two leads connecting it to the detonator on his chest. The plastic square separating the jaws of the crocodile clip that would complete the circuit . . . His other hand tightening the wire that would wrench the insulator away . . .

Somehow she'd expected to find something similar inside Laszlo's precious bag: wires, clips, batteries. A box with a plunger, maybe, or a tangle of different, brightly coloured wires attached to a ticking clock, like in a Hollywood movie.

All she unearthed was some kind of walkie-talkie, a military olive green, with a stubby aerial, a numerical keypad and a red dial, graduated from zero to twelve. At the moment it was set to zero. Alongside the dial was a flick switch, and beside it a small graphic of a lightning bolt that told its own story.

She stared at it, puzzled.

But of course . . . The device she'd seen strapped to the

pipeline would hardly be connected to the day-sack by a long wire. It must be activated by a radio signal.

Laszlo stirred.

She remembered his chilling words: '*I've bet my brother that the blast will be powerful enough to fracture the rock overhead . . .*'

She stared at the radio. What could she do? What would Tom do?

She thought of him again, the battery in his hand, the two leads connected to it . . .

The battery . . .

Without a battery, a radio couldn't function.

She flipped it over, pressed down on the cover and slid it open. Inside sat a square power pack. She lifted it out with trembling hands and disconnected it.

Laszlo's fist smashed into the side of her head. She went down hard. Another blow glanced off her cheek and flipped her over. Laszlo pulled the knife from his belt. Blood bubbled from his almost-closed right eye.

'Give it to me.'

'I don't have it.'

'*Give it to me!*'

She opened her hand. 'Here.' She sat up, appeared to be about to hand it to him. Then she hurled the battery as far as she could, down the hill and into the long grass, and smashed the radio casing on a nearby rock.

She watched, fixated, as the sun glinted off the blade of the knife arcing, in slow motion, towards her throat.

'Killing me and my baby won't stop him,' she rasped. She kept her voice taut, determined not to give him the satisfaction of hearing her fear. 'He will not rest until he finds you. Then he will kill you. I'd want that. I'd want it to happen slowly . . .'

She felt the cold metal on her throat and a warm trickle of blood ooze down her neck. Her breathing was fast and shallow. As she stared at him, unable to move, everything seemed to freeze. She could feel the breeze in her hair, the sun warm on her skin. She could hear the song of a blackbird in the nearby wood.

It seemed so cruel to be murdered in bright sunlight, with birdsong in her ears and a child in her belly that had never experienced those joys; a boy child who didn't even have a name.

There was a sound from the hatch, almost like the beating of a gong. She felt the pressure ease on her throat. Laszlo withdrew the knife, but held it for a moment in front of her face. She saw the reflection of her darkly terrified eyes in its blade.

'You're right, of course. He comes for you. And if you are not here, he will come for me.'

He drew back the knife and ran its blade down her body, towards her stomach. His good eye stared deeply into hers.

The blade stopped. She could feel its tip starting to pierce her skin. Then he seemed to change his mind. He lifted it away once more and plunged it deep into her right thigh.

'I really do hope that Tom manages to keep you alive.' He nodded down at her stomach. 'And to lose a child is never easy . . .'

Delphine felt no pain at first, just saw the crimson fountain spurting from the gash in her jeans.

She pressed her fingers against the wound, but was unable to staunch the blood gushing from her severed femoral artery. Faintness swept through her in waves. She felt her hand slide helplessly away, and fail somehow to break her fall.

Her head smacked against the still wet grass, and the light inside it seemed to dim, as if a cloud had drifted across the sun. She could no longer feel its warmth. She heard ringing in her ears. All other sounds now seemed to be coming from a very great distance away.

Laszlo moved swiftly to the two zip-wire harnesses – with a loop of rope at each end and a plastic wheel at its centre – that Sambor had secreted beside the hatch.

He shoved one into his pocket and hooked the other over the nearest power line, slid his hands into the loops and accelerated down towards the sub-station.

115

Tom dragged himself out of the hatch in time to see Laszlo release his hold on his makeshift zip-wire and drop like a paratrooper onto the lower ground. He rolled, sprang to his feet and began to move away.

Delphine's crumpled body was lying beneath the power cables, the shattered shell of a VHF transmitter beside her. Blood spurted onto the grass with every pump of her heart.

Her eyelids fluttered and her chest heaved as he knelt and cradled her head. 'Stay with me, sweetheart,' he said. '*Stay with me . . .*'

He undid his belt and looped it around her thigh, above the wound, then yanked it tight and twisted it tighter still. The leather squeaked as it bit into her flesh.

'Speak to me, Delphine . . . *Speak to me!*'

This time, she registered his voice. Her eyelids flickered.

'Come on, sweetheart. You're still breathing. You're still winning!' He gave her cheek a stinging slap and her eyes fluttered open. 'Keep still. The more you move, the more you'll bleed.'

With the belt, twisted as tightly as possible, in his left hand, he tore at the blood-soaked cut in her jeans with his right. There was no point in trying to be gentle with casualties in the field. You just had to grip them and get on with the job of keeping them alive.

'This is going to hurt, but I want you to stay as still as you can.'

He took a deep breath and pushed his fingers into the wound, probing for the artery. Delphine lurched upright, howling with pain. He ignored it. If she was screaming, she was breathing.

'Lie down. Get back down!'

With her cries echoing in his ears, he kept groping inside the wound, probing with his fingertips among the torn flesh and gushing blood for the severed end of the artery. At last he found it, like a slippery rubber tube, and tried to pinch off the blood flow. But the wound was too narrow. The muscle around it had tightened. Delphine's body's natural defences were doing their best to apply the necessary pressure to stop the life cascading out of her. But Nature wasn't working.

'Stand by for more screams,' he yelled. 'Keep them coming!'

He saw her eyes widen as he pulled Sambor's knife from his jeans. Her screams redoubled as he inserted the blade into her wound and cut the flesh longer and deeper. The gash opened like freshly sliced meat on a butcher's slab. He went back to work with his fingers until he felt the twitching mouth of the severed artery. He seized it and held it firm, clamped between his thumb and forefinger.

He saw her chin sink towards her chest. 'Don't fucking flake out on me now, Delphine. We're nearly there. Keep screaming!'

Weak and trembling, her face white and shiny with sweat, she gave an exhausted nod. Tom released his grip on the belt, stooped to cut a six-inch length off his bootlace and used it to tie off the artery.

'Lovely job.' He touched her cheek lightly with his blood-slicked fingers and gave her an encouraging smile. 'But keep still. The show's not over yet . . .'

He fished out the old man's mobile, dialled Gavin and held it to his ear.

Where the fuck was he?

The flat, continuous 'unobtainable' tone drilled its way into his head.

Next, he dialled 112, the EU emergency number, and spoke rapidly into the mouthpiece.

'They're on their way, Delphine. They won't be long. They're just down the hill.'

Tom checked her wound. It still glistened in the sunlight, but the haemorrhaging had stopped. He cut the cleanest strip of material he could find from his shirt and used his belt to bind it over the gaping hole in her flesh.

Delphine fought for breath. 'Laszlo . . . ? Tom . . . Laszlo . . . ?'

He shook his head. 'Laszlo's gone.' He nodded at the remains of the initiation device and its empty battery compartment. 'It's over.'

She put a hand on his arm, gripping it tight. Her eyes burned into his. 'No . . . Until he's dead, it'll never be over . . . Go . . . Go and get him . . .'

Tom gestured towards the now deserted sub-station and the empty fields around it. 'I don't even know which way he went.'

'But—'

'Just lie still.' He rested his hand on her arm, calming her. 'You've lost a lot of blood.'

'But I know . . . I know where . . .'

'Delphine—'

She pushed his hand away. 'Listen . . .'

Tom closed his mouth.

'Escalles . . . that village . . . over there . . .' With the last remnants of her strength she lifted an arm and pointed towards the cluster of rooftops just visible among the trees.

'How do you know?'

'I do . . . Now go . . . Go and kill him.'

Tom paused long enough to take a bearing on the village and check behind him that the approaching trauma team were on their way.

Then he checked he still had Sambor's fighting knife and jumped off the mound.

116

He watched the ground rush up to meet him, waited for the agony to return as he rolled to take the landing, trying to protect his injured leg as he did so, but without much success. He got to his feet, wincing with pain, and began to hobble towards the electricity sub-station.

From his landing point, Laszlo had left a trail in the wet grass. Tom took one last look back over his shoulder. Three or four figures in hi-vis vests were lifting Delphine onto a collapsible stretcher.

In heavy limping mode, with his half-laced boot flapping at every step, he began moving across the field and through the small wood where drifts of beechnut covered the ground.

He clambered over a barbed-wire fence and vaulted across a stream. Dairy cows, grazing on the browning grassland or chewing the cud in the shade beneath the trees, watched him impassively as he broke into a halting run across the open pasture.

He heaved himself over another barbed-wire fence and cut a swathe through a field of crops, trampling the stalks under-foot. He was about halfway across when he heard a furious shout. Face puce with rage, a farmer was running along the track at the furthest edge, intent on cutting him off. Tom neither changed his course nor slackened his pace, stumbling on with the same relentless, ground-devouring stride.

'*Vandale! Voleur!*'

The farmer's torrent of abuse died on his lips as his gaze took in the blood-soaked bandages around Tom's leg, his battered and bloodied face, the knife in his hand and the murderous look in his eye. Muttering apologies, he began to back rapidly away.

Tom didn't spare him another glance, kept ploughing on in the same straight line, indifferent to crops, contours or obstacles. The rolling fields dropped away into a shallow valley to his left, but he kept to the ridge leading towards the village. The roofs now seemed tantalizingly close.

He crossed another muddy track and found himself slipping and sliding through the turned earth, wet mud and churned-up tractor tracks of a recently harvested field. He managed to maintain much of his pace as he crossed it, but he felt the gruelling conditions underfoot sapping his last reserves of strength.

He speeded up again, crashing through a field of sunflowers, their stalks brown, heads blackened and drooping. Dust, pollen and leaf fragments stuck to his skin as he forced his way past them, and clouds of flies buzzed around his head, attracted by the blood and salt sweat on his skin. He paid them no attention, his every sense straining to catch the least sight or sound that might lead him to his quarry.

117

Sambor had rented the farmhouse on the edge of the village for the Black Bears to gather and prepare themselves after their individual journeys across Europe. The narrow, winding road outside was deserted; the only sign of life was the barking of a dog chained in a neighbouring yard.

The windows of the farmhouse were cracked, cobwebbed and dusty. The yellowing, tattered curtains, the weed-choked garden and the general air of dereliction suggested that it had been some time since anyone had lived and worked there. A perfect base from which to launch an attack.

The cobbles in the yard were almost invisible beneath a blanket of moss and leaf mould. Laszlo ran across them, making for a barn set apart from the main farm building. Its timbers were blackened and ancient. The roof sagged where a beam had given way. There was a clatter of wings as he approached. Two pigeons flew out of a gaping hole where the tiles had cracked and slipped off their battens.

The barn doors were not locked, merely held shut by a stout plank suspended between two wrought-iron brackets. Laszlo lifted it clear and threw it to one side. The hinges creaked and protested as he swung the doors wide open, allowing light to stream into the dark interior.

Motes of dust and pollen danced in the shafts of light as he hurried inside. Bales of mouldering straw and hay were stacked at the far end of the building and rusted farm tools were propped against the walls. A selection of smaller hand tools lay on a bench among a jumble of jars, tins and packets, with cracked and faded labels.

Laszlo kicked and dragged seven or eight heavy straw bales off the edges of a dirty green tarpaulin in the middle of the floor. Beneath it was a blue Peugeot Tepee MPV. Nothing about this vehicle invited a second glance: the French roads were full of them, either crammed with families and loaded to the gunwales, or stacked with agricultural produce on the way to market.

Laszlo crouched down beside the wheel arch by the driver's door and felt along the top of the tyre until his fingers closed around a key-fob. He pulled it out and pressed the button. An answering beep and flash of lights was followed by the click of releasing locks.

He walked round to the back and opened the hatch. Two small Samsonite suitcases stood inside, each containing a neatly folded set of clothes – the sort of middle-of-the-road, department-store casual shirts, trousers, pullovers and shoes that would pass without notice almost anywhere.

His jaw clenched as he ran his hand along the second suit-case and thought of his brother. Laszlo had made a promise to Sambor, a promise he still intended to fulfil. The havoc wreaked by the SAS man and the girl was just a setback: Laszlo would return to kill the country.

He filled a bucket with water from an ancient pump in the yard, stripped off and washed as much of the caked blood and muck from his head and body as he could. He glanced quickly in the MPV's wing-mirror. There wasn't much he could do to disguise his damaged eye, but a beret, pulled low, covered most of the damage Delphine had done to his scalp.

Neatly wrapped bundles of euros, all used and of differing denominations, were stashed beneath the clothing. He extracted a few notes and slipped them into his pocket, shoved in his borrowed Puffa jacket and jeans, then closed and locked the case.

Marginally refreshed by the cold water and clean outfit, Laszlo slammed down the hatch and climbed into the driver's seat. The engine fired first time. The thick hay on the barn floor rustled against the underside of the MPV as he put it into gear and drove outside.

He crossed the yard, stopped, got out and closed the gates behind him. Avoiding the village, he followed the narrow track past a field of sunflowers. He drove slowly, easing the vehicle across a succession of pits and potholes. Deep, muddy puddles from the recent rains had gathered at either side of the long, grass-topped spine between the wheel tracks.

Screened by the stalks of the dying sunflowers, the Peugeot was almost invisible, only the sound of its engine revealing its presence. The impact of a flying body against his windscreen and the crash as Tom started pounding a rock against the glass almost paralysed Laszlo with shock.

118

Laszlo stared, slack-jawed, at the scarred, bruised and blood-soaked apparition. But only for a moment.

Tom grabbed one of the roof rails with his left hand and pounded the windscreen with his right. Three spider webs had already formed on the glass, and a fourth was on its way. Laszlo accelerated and began to swerve from side to side, bouncing the MPV in and out of the potholes. Legs flailing across the bonnet, left arm stretched to breaking point, Tom still managed somehow to keep pounding with the rock.

Laszlo fish-tailed and lurched, stamping on the brakes, then accelerating again, but Tom kept his hold. As Laszlo spun the wheel in yet another desperate attempt to dislodge him, the Peugeot skidded off the track, into the field, mowing down ranks of sunflowers as it went.

Finally, Tom was thrown into the air and smashed against a wall of vegetation. He collapsed onto the ground as the Peugeot bottomed its suspension. Laszlo spun the wheel wildly from side to side and gunned the engine. The Peugeot's tyres chewed into the earth and tossed a barrage of crushed sunflower stalks behind them.

Laszlo flung the vehicle into a spin, throwing up more stalks and earth, then lost control completely. The MPV slewed and eventually stalled in the midst of a circle of the flattened crop.

He quickly sparked up the ignition, turned the wheel towards the still prone body of the SAS man and pressed the accelerator pedal to the metal. The tyres spun furiously in the chewed-up soil and the car didn't move. He tried again in a higher gear, barely touching the accelerator, but the wheels just buried themselves deeper and deeper in the soft ground.

Laszlo threw open the door, leaped out and began running towards his attacker.

At first Tom didn't see Laszlo coming. But he could hear the desiccated crackle of the sunflower stalks as the South Ossetian forced his way across them.

His wounded leg was now so sore and swollen that he could barely put his weight on it, but he had to stand his ground.

A boot smashed into Tom's thigh; the searing pain almost made him throw up as he fell back into the damp earth. Targeting the wound, Laszlo kicked Tom's bandaged leg again and again, relentlessly. Then he moved to the rest of his body. Tom saw the other man's eyes become totally lifeless. The body at his feet no longer belonged to a human being; it was nothing more than a target to beat into submission.

All Tom could do was fold himself into a tight ball, try to protect himself against the offensive.

When Tom opened his eyes again, he realized that – for the first time – he must have blacked out completely. The kicking had stopped. Laszlo stood above him, breathing heavily, spitting out the excess saliva his efforts had generated. His expression had changed. If Tom hadn't known better, he might have mistaken it for something like humanity.

'Tom . . .' Laszlo's chest heaved. 'Tom, go home. Go home to your new family. You have killed my brother. You have killed many of my men. But this is not your fight . . .' Laszlo spat another globule of mucus-tinged saliva onto the dark earth beside him. He took deeper and deeper breaths, trying to calm himself. 'Go. Just go . . .'

Tom wasn't going anywhere. He wasn't sure he could, even if he wanted to. His knees were curled into his chest. 'So you can still try to kill my country?'

'Just as you would.' Beads of sweat fell from Laszlo's face as he leaned forward. He rested his hands on his thighs and inspected the damaged body below him. 'People like us, we never give up. You know nothing of my past dealings with your countrymen. You see, Tom, they lie, they cheat and they kill. They kill with great brutality, to protect their interests. They feel superior now, of course. They tell the world that *I* am the evil one. But you will soon discover that these people are out of our league. So, just this one time, give up your fight with me and go home. Please go home.'

'What people? Who are you talking about?'

Laszlo straightened his back. Tom could read the frustration on his ravaged face. 'I am trying to save you from yourself. If you knew, they – not I – would kill you. Now go. If you do not take this opportunity to live, you will make me regret a kill for the very first time.'

Tom wasn't giving anything up. His hands clutched his stomach, but his fingers felt their way to the handle of Sambor's knife in the front pocket of his jeans.

Laszlo sighed. He scanned the ground nearby, caught sight of a fist-sized rock.

Tom aimed for Laszlo's leg, the nearest part of his body, hoping to get him down onto the ground any way he could. He moved as fast as he could, but not fast enough. Laszlo blocked the knife thrust and pounded the rock down onto his shoulder. More out of desperation than anything else, Tom wrapped his arms around Laszlo's ankles in a feeble rugby tackle, then pushed against his shins.

Laszlo lost his balance and went down, arms flailing but failing to break his fall. Tom drew back his right hand, launched himself forward and slammed the knife into Laszlo's chest. He withdrew the blade and plunged it down again, this time into his stomach.

Laszlo screamed, but there was no fear or anger in his face.

He just seemed to accept his fate. He watched, as if from a distance, as Tom used up his last dregs of strength to slam home the blade once more, burying it to the hilt between Laszlo's third and fourth ribs, then collapsing on top of his suddenly still body.

As Laszlo's blood began to pool among the sunflower stalks beneath them, Tom rolled over and wrenched himself into a sitting position. He dragged out the old man's mobile and tapped in a number with numb, blood-soaked, slippery fingers. The unobtainable tone continued to mock him.

The setting sun glinted for a moment on something beneath the dead man's sleeve. Keeping the phone clamped to his ear, willing Gavin to answer, he reclaimed his Omega from Laszlo's wrist.

Epilogue

The sergeants' mess at the Lines was packed for the joint memorial service, almost six months to the day since Gavin and Vatu had died. These things always seemed to be late. The challenge was to find a date when most of the squadron were in the UK, not spread across the planet.

It was a cold March night. The warm, beer-laden fumes inside the mess had misted the windows with condensation. The tables were already overflowing with empty glasses, bottles and cans, and more were being added all the time.

The SAS troopers were all smartly dressed in their number-two parade uniforms. Boots and medals gleamed. Wives and girlfriends were there as well, and children slalomed between everyone's legs. Bryce's kids had found a jar of cam cream and were busy daubing it over their faces and everything else they touched.

There were a number of other honoured guests, including Chief Constable Alderson and a couple of his police colleagues. A group of Eurostar personnel, led by the train driver and the head steward, had been given a trip to the Lines as a reward for their bravery. They rubbed shoulders uneasily with a sprinkling of spooks and ministry officials.

The civil servant called Clements looked like a fish out of water.

Tom watched the man who was huddled in a corner with Ashton. He was taking frequent surreptitious looks at his watch, as if he couldn't wait for the ordeal to be over.

The bouncy castle had been deflated, folded and stashed behind a stack of chairs. The walls were hung with photographs of Vatu and Gavin from every phase of their service with the Regiment: with their families, in training, preparing for ops, off duty with their mates in various far-flung parts of the world. The more embarrassing the circumstances, the more likely they were to be included.

All their personal possessions – bits of kit, spare uniforms, no matter how old and threadbare – had been taken from their lockers and laid out on a row of tables set at right angles to the bar. Tom presided over the Dead Man's Auction – an SAS tradition following the death of comrades that was as old as the Regiment itself.

As was the custom, each item was sold to the highest bidder, and the proceeds given to the next of kin or squadron funds. The two dead men had already footed the bill for the evening. Every trooper left five hundred pounds in his will to be put behind the bar. The practice wasn't macabre: it was part of the culture. If you worried about your mates on the squadron getting hurt and killed, you'd spend your life on anti-depressants.

Fuelled in part by the drink, but much more by the respect and affection they felt for Vatu and Gavin, they had been bidding well above market value for every lot on offer, and each exuberant bid seemed to trigger another rush for the bar and another round of drinks. As the two men's clothes, even down to their underwear, were auctioned off, the successful bidders draped them over the top of their own uniforms.

The auction was now almost over. Tom was down to the last item. He picked up a cardboard box filled with CDs. 'Right,' he said. 'All we have left is his music collection.'

'Fifty quid!' Jockey shouted.

'Get off the grass.' Tom laughed. 'Fifty quid, you tight Scots git? Each CD's worth more than that!'

'Bollocks,' Jockey yelled, from the midst of a backwards moon dance. 'He wouldn't know good music if it gave him a slap on the head.' He looked around. 'I don't see anyone else bidding. So hand them over.'

'No, I want more.' Tom started fishing random CDs out of the box. 'There's some real quality here: Razorlight, Kaiser Chiefs, The Killers, Keane, and a bit of real quality, Lang Lang. I bought that for him myself.'

'Lang Lang?' Jockey raised his belligerent Glaswegian eyebrows. 'You're right, Tom, now I know that Lang Lang's in there, I withdraw my earlier fifty-quid bid.' He paused, timing his punchline to perfection. 'Make that ten quid instead.'

'Very droll.' Tom waved the CD at him. 'But for a tight-wad like you, you're missing a trick. If you don't like it, you can even sell it. It's still in its wrapper.'

'Why don't you buy it yourself, then? You might as well – no one else is going to listen to that shite.'

Delphine got to her feet and waved a hand. The other rested lightly on her bump. 'One hundred pounds.'

There was a stunned silence from around the room. Jockey picked up the CD and stared suspiciously through the shrink-wrap, as if it might conceal a winning lottery ticket. 'Do women really go for this ying-yang shit?'

'Well, it certainly worked on me,' Delphine said. 'Do you remember that first night, Tom, when we were . . . ?' She paused, leaving a roomful of people to wait for what would come next. 'Well, you don't want to hear about that, do you?' She gave them the ghost of a smile. 'But anyway, thanks to Lang Lang, here I am, two years later, still coming back for more.'

Jockey gave her a sceptical look. 'It sounds like bullshit to me,' he said. 'But go on, just in case it's true, I'll bid one twenty-five.'

Bryce waited until Jockey started reaching for the box, then said, 'Make that one fifty.'

Jockey wasn't impressed. 'Why the hell are you bidding for it? From the number of your ankle-biters running around this room, I'd say your seduction technique was working just fine.'

He paused. 'All right, one seventy-five, then, and that's my final offer.'

Keenan gave Delphine an appraising look. 'In that case, I'll bid two hundred.'

'OK then, two fifty.' Jockey was well in the mood.

'I thought one seventy-five was going to be your last bid?' Bryce said. He was taking a breath when a voice boomed from the back,

'Five hundred!'

Before whoever it was could change his mind, Tom slammed his fist on the table. 'Sold!'

As Tom scanned the crowd to identify the bidder, he saw that Ashton and Clements were still in their corner. They were arguing. The seed Gavin had planted in his head was growing. Something told him all wasn't right about those two. Ashton's story about Gavin planting a device in the Chinook didn't ring true. If Gavin had planned to do that, why hadn't he told Tom during their call? Gavin had said the sniper option was all he had. If he fucked up, they had a drama. No mention of a Plan B.

The auction over, the crowd hovered in small groups with their families, lining up for the curry buffet.

Tom watched Clements slip quietly out of the mess. If Ashton and Clements had been involved with Antonov and was responsible for Gavin's death, Tom would find out.

Ashton walked over to Tom and Delphine as they congratulated Woolf on his purchase. Ashton raised his glass. 'To Vatu and Gavin,' he said. 'We've lost two good men there.' He was studying Tom's expression. 'You'll miss Gavin, won't you? You two were best mates.'

Sensing trouble, Bryce and Jockey joined the group.

Delphine laid a placatory hand on Tom's arm. 'We'll never forget him, will we?'

Jockey took the CD from Woolf to inspect what might have been. 'The poor little bugger will be well hacked off with you two when he's old enough to realize what a crap name you've given him.'

Bryce smiled. 'Gavin Buckingham, eh?'

Tom looked around the room. 'God, I'm going to miss this.'

Delphine shot him a glance. 'What do you mean you'll miss this? You're not really thinking—'

'I'm not thinking about it,' Tom said. 'I've already decided.'

Delphine stared at him in disbelief.

'Yeah, I'll be giving it all up in, let's see . . .' he checked his Omega '. . . in exactly ten . . . years from now.'

He ducked as Delphine threw a mock punch at his head. Jockey started singing 'The Eton Boating Song', pretending to row a scull as he cracked on with his backwards moon dance, and one by one they all joined in. Only Ashton remained stone-faced. Tom had eye-to-eye with him and there was a connection, but it wasn't anything to do with the joke, with the Regiment – with anything, except each man knowing that the other man knew.

Delphine suddenly gave a startled cry. There was a puzzled look on her face and then she broke into a dazzling smile. She took Tom's hand and placed it against her bump. 'Tom? I think it is time . . .'

ABOUT THE AUTHOR

Andy McNab joined the infantry as a boy soldier. In 1984 he was 'badged' as a member of 22 SAS Regiment and was involved in both covert and overt special operations worldwide. During the Gulf War he commanded Bravo Two Zero, a patrol that, in the words of his commanding officer, 'will remain in regimental history for ever'. Awarded both the Distinguished Conduct Medal (DCM) and Military Medal (MM) during his military career, McNab was the British Army's most highly decorated serving soldier when he finally left the SAS in February 1993. He wrote about his experiences in three books: the phenomenal bestseller *Bravo Two Zero*, *Immediate Action* and *Seven Troop*.

He is the author of the bestselling Nick Stone thrillers. Besides his writing work, he lectures to security and intelligence agencies in both the USA and UK. He is a patron of the Help for Heroes campaign.

www.andymcnab.co.uk

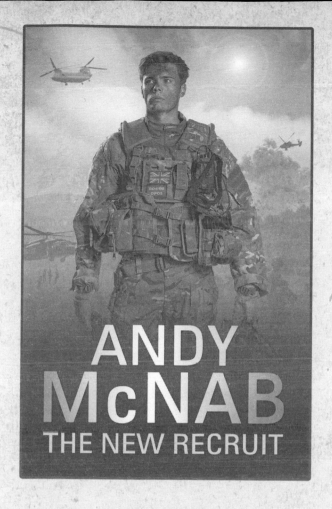

ANDY
McNAB
THE NEW RECRUIT

YOU THINK ARMY TRAINING IS TOUGH?
WAIT TILL YOU REACH AFGHANISTAN.

THE NEW RECRUIT
COMING SOON